FIDALI'S WAY

A Novel

GEORGE MASTRAS

Scribner

NEW YORK   LONDON   TORONTO   SYDNEY

SCRIBNER
A Division of Simon & Schuster, Inc.
1230 Avenue of the Americas
New York, NY 10020

First Scribner hardcover edition January 2009

SCRIBNER and design are trademarks of
The Gale Group, Inc., used under license
by Simon & Schuster, Inc., the publisher of this work.

For information about special discounts for bulk purchases,
please contact Simon & Schuster Special Sales at
1-800-456-6798 or business@simonandschuster.com.

Designed by Kyoko Watanabe
Text set in Minion

Map by Guenter Vollath

Manufactured in the United States of America

10   9   8   7   6   5   4   3   2   1

Library of Congress Control Number: 2008007471

ISBN-13: 978-1-4165-5618-3
ISBN-10: 1-4165-5618-4

For Hope, Sophia, and Alexandra

Birds make great sky-circles
of their freedom.
How do they learn it?
They fall, and falling,
They are given wings.

—RUMI

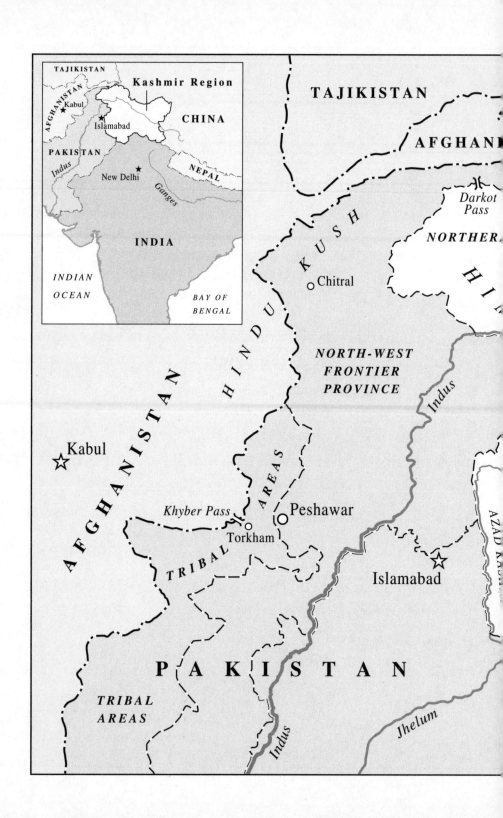

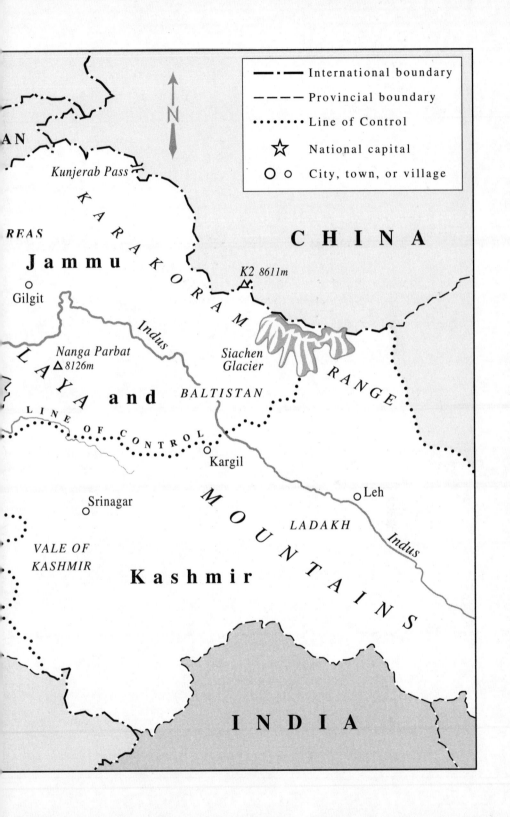

PART I

PROLOGUE

Tribal Areas, Pak-Afghan Border

Everywhere was sun.

Hours ago, he had prayed for it to rise. The stabbing cold of night had nearly killed him. Only adrenaline and fear had kept the blood moving through his veins. But now even the durable creatures of the desert had scrambled for cover from the sun's death rays, burrowing under sand and crawling into holes, slithering into fissures of combusted rock.

For him there was no shelter anywhere. He was alone in a wasteland that stretched as far as he could see, to the scorched foothills of the Hindu Kush, obscured by rising heat on the horizon. His legs lumbered, his throat felt as parched as the earth under his feet, and his flesh, long deprived of its ability to sweat, ached painfully under his tattered *shalwar kamiz*. His mind, however, had never before felt so acute, more profoundly aware—but of one thing only: His search for refuge had become a quest for a suitable place to die.

Finally, he came to a large boulder. Not much, but the best place he could hope to find in the barren landscape. Surrendering to the heat, and to a fate that he felt he deserved, he dropped to the kilnlike sand. Leaning his head against the rock, he turned his face into the torment of the sun. He could almost feel the hot earth grill the life from his body. Until he felt no more.

CHAPTER 1

Peshawar, North-West Frontier Province, Pakistan

Nicholas Sunder should not have been surprised when he heard the knock on his hotel room door. For Nick was not a man blessed with great luck. He had no choice but to open it, for whoever was in the hallway would have been told by Shahid, the receptionist, that he was in. He glanced at his watch, envisioning himself sitting anonymously on an eastbound minibus packed with raucous Pakistanis, and cursed himself for not leaving half an hour earlier. Shutting his eyes, he inhaled deeply to garner his wits. Then he opened the door.

Standing in the doorframe was a barrel of a man with a flat head perched atop a trunklike neck. His face, dark and pitted, was bisected by flaring mustaches, and punctuated with obsidian eyes. He wore the distinctive sky blue uniform of the Peshawar police.

"Yes?" Trying his best to comes across as confident, Nick overcompensated, and his voice sounded forced and irascible. This did not go unnoticed by the officer, who scrutinized Nick briefly before stepping aside to reveal a partner. Bespectacled, lithe, with sensitive eyes, this second man was at least ten years younger than the larger one—perhaps in his midthirties—not much older than Nick. But his dark skin and jet-black hair contrasted starkly with the pastel blue of his uniform, making him appear even younger.

"Mr. Sunder?" said the corpulent officer in Punjabi-accented English. "I am Inspector Rasool Muhammad Akhtar with the Investigation Wing of the Peshawar Police." His voice was gruff from excessive smoking, devoid of the soothing lilt so often characteristic of subcontinentals. "And this is Sub-Inspector Abdul Shiraz." He gestured openhandedly to his younger partner, who greeted Nick with a smile too congenial to be genuine.

There was a long silence—too long, it seemed to Nick—as he waited

5

for the inspector to speak. "Well?" Nick said finally. "You speak English, don't you?"

"We would like a word with you, sir," said Akhtar in a tone that implied he was not asking.

Nick hesitated. "Okay," he replied, "but I'm busy at the moment. If you could come back later . . . in a couple of hours or so, I'd be happy to—"

"It is urgent," chimed in Shiraz from behind his boss, Akhtar.

Nick paused, wiping the sweat from his forehead. He nodded, then stepped out into the hallway to avoid letting them into his room. But Akhtar shuttled toward Nick like a bulldozer, forcing him to backpedal awkwardly. As Akhtar passed through the door, he propped it open, permitting Shiraz to follow.

The inspectors scanned the room, their eyes settling on Nick's packed rucksack. "Where are you going, sir?" said Akhtar. "Home to America?"

"No. To India. Amritsar."

"When?"

"My bus leaves in forty minutes, actually."

Akhtar raised his brow. "Yet you ask us to return in a couple of hours? Either you are being very rude, or are you hoping to leave Pakistan without speaking to us."

Realizing his error, Nick became aware of the hot blood rushing into his face. "I apologize. My mistake. It's this heat—it's driving me mad," he demurred, forcing a cordial smile to no effect.

Akhtar studied Nick, then pointed to a wooden luggage rack bestrewn with clothes—a woman's clothes: underwear, smallish socks, cutoff T-shirt. "To whom do these belong?"

"A friend of mine," Nick replied.

Akhtar plucked a pair of T-back panties from the pile. Dangling the lingerie between his thumb and forefinger, he extended his arm stiffly in front of him.

"A *female* friend," Nick clarified.

"Friend," Akhtar muttered. "We do not have female *friends* in Pakistan. We have wives. And we have daughters who will soon be wives. All the others are trouble."

Nick nodded halfheartedly, unsure whether the comment was intended as a joke. Then he shrugged his shoulders. "I've prepaid for my ticket. I'd appreciate it if you'd tell me what this is about, so I don't miss my bus."

Inspector Akhtar stepped toward the American with a swagger that indicated his girth was an advantage—not an impediment. "This *is*, in fact, about your girlfriend."

"She's not my girlfriend."

The inspector weighed Nick's remark with doubtful eyes. To Akhtar, the handful of intrepid backpackers who still came to Peshawar each year despite the volatile political climate, with their long hair or modish shaved heads, tight clothing, and appetite for hashish, epitomized the depravity of the West. Nick and the girl were sharing a room; ergo, they were carnal.

"Very well," he said. "Her name is . . . Yvette Dee . . ."

"DePomeroy," Nick responded.

"Thank you. English I can speak. But French? So many letters that have no meaning. So, where is the girl now?" inquired Akhtar in a manner that suggested he already knew the answer.

"Last time I saw her was yesterday morning. Why, is something wrong?"

"You are the one who has not seen her since yesterday. *You* tell us."

Nick felt weak. He sat down on the bed, staring blankly at the wall. When Shiraz finally saved him from his trance, he had no idea how long he had been suspended in dumbfounded silence. "Why, sir, did you not call the police when she failed to come back to the room?" Shiraz asked.

"I, um . . . I don't know. . . . I just figured she was staying with a friend—another traveler maybe," Nick said. "I wasn't her only friend."

"You see?—*trouble*," Akhtar said, snorting in self-validation. "Come with us—there will be no bus for you today."

The pungent stench of decaying bodies burned Nick's nostrils as Akhtar swung open the double doors. The morgue was nothing more than a large, cement-walled room with bodies laid at odd angles upon the floor. The corpses were wrapped in white sheets knotted over the faces, some stained with dried blood. Others, the ones that buzzed with the most flies, were moist from large slabs of melting ice wedged underneath them.

"Follow me," Akhtar said, casually stepping over the corpses. Nick did not want to follow, not only because he felt it to be somehow disrespectful and unlucky to step over the dead. At his very core, he feared what they had brought him there to do. But when he turned back and saw Shiraz behind him, urging him onward with a stern nod, Nick knew he had to show them he could go through with it, if had he any hope of getting out of Pakistan soon.

Nick wiped the cold sweat from his brow, covered his nose and mouth in a futile attempt to ward off the stench, and then stepped across the bodies to where Akhtar was standing. At Akhtar's feet lay a sheeted bundle labeled with a piece of masking tape with red Urdu script written on it. Akhtar squatted to untie the sheet.

Nick felt the room spin. He began to topple. "Sir . . ." said Shiraz behind him, reaching for Nick's arm.

Nick grabbed Shiraz's elbow, barely avoiding a fall. Vomit welled at the back of his throat. He forced it back down, nearly gagging. He breathed deeply for several moments, until he was sure he had regained his legs. "Is this . . . really necessary?"

"I am afraid so," Akhtar replied. "We tried to locate her parents through the French embassy in Islamabad, but the authorities are very slow to find them. We are concerned that by the time they are located, the body will not look like . . . anyone. We are transferring the body to the central morgue in Islamabad, but . . . well, it will take time to process. So . . . unless you happen to know where her parents live?"

Nick rubbed his temples, trying to focus his thoughts. He spoke through his hand, cupped over his mouth and nose. "She'd lived in Paris, she told me. But I don't know about her parents. Small town, maybe. I don't think she was close to them . . . just the impression I got."

Akhtar eyed Nick. "Then we have no choice but to proceed." With a sort of unseemly gusto, he tugged sharply at the ends of the sheet, peeling them open to reveal its contents.

Nick clenched his eyes shut. He had seen more than a few dead bodies in his life, and not just the well-manicured corpse of his father at his open-casket funeral, all signs of his slow death by cancer concealed under a thick mantle of cosmetics. In the East, the presence of death was ubiquitous, so much so that it seemed to Nick very much a part of life, not merely the end of it. For some reason, be it morbid curiosity or a deeper yearning to comprehend this strange, fatalistic world, Nick had found himself during his travels gravitating toward places where the worlds of the living and the dead collided. He had gone out of his way to view bodies burned on wood-fueled funeral pyres in Katmandu, bloated corpses of the snake-bitten ritually dumped into the Holy Ganges, and Tibetan "sky burials" in which leathery-skinned nomads chopped their ancestors into fist-sized chunks for the vultures to devour. But this was different. This was life he had coveted, a body he had known intimately, over which he had run his fingers until every freckle, curve, and recess of skin had been impressed in his memory. He struggled to numb his emotions, to force his mind to perceive what he was about to see as a mere phenomenon, another stop along on his journey to understand.

Nonetheless, when he finally forced his eyes on the body, he could do nothing but stare, speechless, feeling as though the small hole of emptiness in his chest that had always been there had opened to swallow the entirety of his being. He felt like *nothing*. He felt like *he* was dead.

"Well?" said Akhtar, eyeing Nick closely. "Is this your lady friend?"

Nick did not register the inspector's words. Yvette looked just the way he remembered her. Her torso, exposed through the tears of her dirt-stained shirt, was unbloated; her breasts, though waxen, were still smooth and flawless. A blond tousle of her hair splayed across her cheek. Her feet, striped with the tan lines of sandal straps, were still embellished with the lavender toenail polish Nick had painted on for her days ago. And her eyes, like limpid pools of trapped sky, were placid and beautiful as they had been in life. One might have thought she had died in peace, were it not for the deep black trench slicing across her throat.

"Sir . . . is this her—Ms. DePomeroy?"

"Yes," said Nick finally, nearly choking on his words, his eyes blurring with tears. "Yes, it is."

"Such a beautiful girl," Shiraz interjected with melancholy. "Some goatherders found her in the Tribal Areas, near a jeep trail off the road from Landi Kotal—in an area where Westerners are forbidden. Do you know how she might have gotten there?"

Nick shook his head no. Wiping his eyes, he turned from the body. "Please . . . I've seen enough."

"As you wish," said Shiraz.

But as Nick headed for the door, Akhtar called out brusquely—"One more thing"—stopping Nick in his tracks.

"What do you make of this?" Akhtar motioned to Shiraz, who rolled the body onto its side. The smooth, narrow back was pocked with deep contusions of bluish flesh, as though someone had jabbed her repeatedly with a metal prod.

Nick could glance only briefly before shielding his eyes. "I wouldn't know," he said. He stood there a moment, distracted by a loud pounding behind his ears, as if someone were thrashing the back of his head. Until he realized it was his own blood surging to his brain.

Sub-Inspector Shiraz followed Nick out of the morgue. "Please, sir—just a few more questions," he said, as they waited for Akhtar to wrap up the body and rejoin them. Because of his younger age, Shiraz—unlike his superior, Akhtar, who had been robbed of all compassion by his years of exposure to drug smugglers, terrorists, and corrupt bureaucrats—had not yet lost his ability to empathize. This was evident in the way he stared at Nick with rueful eyes, as if beseeching him to confess for the sake of his salvation.

"Questions . . ." repeated Nick. He felt as though Shiraz's words were filtering down to him at the bottom of a deep well, where he was struggling to keep his head from sinking into icy blackness.

"Sir, a young woman has been murdered. We need a little more information . . . to guide our investigation. Her family will wonder, when we find them. It is their right to know."

"Yes . . . yes, of course," Nick replied. "I'll help any way I can. But . . . I'm afraid I didn't know her that well. We were rooming together just for convenience. Budget travelers do that—join up on the road, share accommodations to split costs. I think I pretty much told you everything I know about her already . . .

"I do need to get to Delhi by Friday to catch my flight home—people are expecting me," he added. This was a lie. Nick had no intention of going back home to America, at least not right away. His father had died when he was a teenager and his mother had followed not long before he decided to travel. He had no siblings or other close living relatives who might raise a fuss through political channels; nor, for that matter, any loved ones who might even notice him missing. He was an expatriate in the profoundest sense—a man alone in the world. And now, for the first time, his total independence made him feel more vulnerable than free. His instinct told him it would be better to make the inspectors think he knew people who would press the authorities if he were held up for too long.

"It is required procedure. Just a brief statement. Then you may go."

Statement. The legalistic nature of the word did not sit well with Nick. "Just so I'm clear, you mean . . . if I tried to walk out the door right now, you would detain me?"

Sub-Inspector Shiraz gave a sigh of frustration. "Come, sir. It is better for everyone that you cooperate. Surely I need not remind you how simple it would be for us to deny you an exit visa."

They led Nick into a so-called conference room—a bleak chamber with a cement floor and walls of cinder block partially covered with crumbling plaster. In one corner stood a wooden table flanked by roughly hewn chairs. The only other furnishing was a steel toilet bowl fixed to the wall. It was swarming with flies, and so besmirched with mold and excrement it appeared not to have been cleaned since the days of the British Raj. A thick steel slab of a door contained the only window, and the interior of the chamber reeked of urine.

Shiraz urged Nick to sit and demanded his passport. During his more than two years backpacking through the remote, sometimes dangerous parts of Asia, Nick had stuck to a policy of never letting his passport out of his control. Like a soldier terrified of losing his talisman, he felt he could defy great odds so long as it was in his possession—in his money belt, around his neck, or buried in his underwear. Without it, however, he felt naked. But these were the police—he had no choice but to provide proof of his identity. Nick opened his passport to the photo page and slid it across the table, pinning it there with his fingers for the inspectors to review. But Akhtar snatched it up, before signaling toward the open door for a third policeman, who entered and left with it.

"Wait!" Nick protested. "Where's he going with that?"

"It will be safe, sir," said Shiraz. "I assure you."

Shiraz sat down opposite Nick. Akhtar propped himself, arms folded, on the table to Nick's left. Even though Shiraz was doing the talking, it was clear by the way Shiraz kept petitioning Akhtar with his eyes that the elder was in control.

"When was the last time you saw the deceased?" asked Shiraz.

"Around ten o'clock yesterday morning. We had breakfast at the hotel. After that, we went separate ways. I didn't see her again until . . . well, now."

"What did you and the girl discuss over breakfast?"

Nick shrugged his shoulders. "Small talk—our impressions of Peshawar, stuff like that. We mentioned our travel plans. I told her I was going to leave for Lahore, then head into India. She said she was going to stay in Peshawar."

"And you argued about this?"

"No. It wasn't like that."

"But you must have been upset she did not want to come with you?"

Nick looked into Shiraz's eyes. "I'm not sure what you're trying to imply . . . but I don't appreciate it."

"No one is pointing any fingers, sir," Shiraz replied without flinching. "We are only trying to get to the bottom of a vicious crime. It is important for us to know the victim's state of mind. Whether she was upset, excitable, panicked."

Nick took a deliberate breath. "I'm sorry. It's just, this whole thing— her murder, having to identify her body—it's a total shock to me. And now to feel like I'm being interrogated or something. . . . It's not the treatment one expects as a visitor," said Nick, hoping to tap into the Pakistani sense of hospitality, which he had come to learn was a matter of creed. The inspectors' expressions, however, did not change.

"As I was saying before," Nick continued, his nerves forcing his words to come out in clipped phrases. "Our relationship was casual. We met in Kashgar. We were both planning to head down the Karakoram Highway to Islamabad, and then go to Peshawar. It made sense to join up for a while. Friendship is cheap on the road. You meet someone, travel together for a week or two. And never see them again. There's no hard feelings. It happens all the time."

"Yet, when you viewed her body you seemed very . . . emotional," Shiraz said. "Like you knew her much better than you are suggesting."

Nick lowered his chin. "No," he said in a faltering voice. He pinched the bridge of his nose between his eyes, gathering his composure. "It's just . . . it's a horrible thing, what happened to her. Even if I didn't know her that well."

Shiraz and Akhtar glanced at each other, their own silent language. "Did the girl say what she was going to do after breakfast?" Shiraz continued.

"She said she was going back to the hotel."

"And after breakfast, what did *you* do then?"

"Toured the cantonment, wandered the bazaars. I didn't return until evening. When I got back, she wasn't there."

"When she did not come back for the night, you said she was with a friend?"

Nick hesitated. "Well, that's what I assumed. The other day she mentioned she had come across some people in the bazaar—some other backpackers she'd met a few months ago on the circuit—Goa, Katmandu, I'm not sure exactly. At breakfast she said something about meeting someone for tea that evening. When it got late, I figured she must have decided to stay over with whomever she'd met, instead of walking back alone after dark. They say it's not a good idea for a Western woman to be alone in the bazaar at night."

"Do you have a name or nationality?" said Shiraz.

Nick shook his head. "I'm a little older than most backpackers. I had no interest in meeting any more university dropouts with wanderlust. I didn't ask."

Shiraz considered Nick's words, tapping his ballpoint pen on the table. "May we ask what are you doing in Peshawar, sir? Your country has been dropping bombs just across the border in Afghanistan for years now. Sometimes, on this side, too. In Bajaur, for example, not more than two hundred kilometers from here, your air force shot a missile at a madrassa and killed eighteen children. They said they were after senior al Qaeda. In a *school* for young boys? There wasn't even a pilot in the plane to see what he was shooting at. It was one of your . . . what do you call them . . . *drones*. Like some kind of computer game."

Nick remembered seeing the bloody news clips on Pakistani television of the crushed, blue-lipped children, their wailing, veiled mothers kneeling over the bodies, pounding their chests and pulling their hair. The U.S. government had denied the strike in Pakistani territory. Yvette had been with him. She was brought to tears by the images of the dead and dying children, and cursed Nick in anger, as if he were somehow responsible for his government's actions. "The French are fighting in Afghanistan, too—how do you know it wasn't the French?" Nick had blurted out defensively. She kicked Nick out of the bed that night. A few weeks later, the U.S. government's official denial was recalled. The incident had been placed "under investigation," which more often than not was the prelude to an eventual admission of responsibility forced under the pressure of incontrovertible evidence.

Nick lowered his eyes. "I didn't know that," he lied.

Shiraz frowned. "You must not read the newspapers," he said, his tone sardonic. "Many people here have fled from the fighting. They still have relatives across the border. They are angry at being bombed by your country for the actions of a few. They do not like America for this. Not at all. And I cannot remember the last time we saw an American tourist in Peshawar. A few Europeans, Japanese, Australians—but *very* few of even them. The only Americans in Peshawar are spies."

"I don't know what to say," said Nick after a pause. "I mean . . . I was curious, that's all. I wanted to see Peshawar. And there wasn't any rule against me coming. Maybe some people here are opposed to America and the war. I understand that. But I figured Pakistan and America are allies, right? Look, all I really want to do at this point is leave. Please."

Shiraz smiled ironically. He gathered his notes.

"Are we through?" Nick asked. Ignoring the question, the inspectors made for the door, slamming it shut behind them. Nick heard the bolt slide.

"Hey!" he cried. Nick ran to the door. He pounded on the thick steel with the heel of his fist. Peering out the small window at the door's center, a Plexiglas porthole wide enough for a single face, he sought to make eye contact with someone—*anyone*—watching from the other side. But the only figure staring back at him was a reflection of himself.

He studied the image of his face. Mirrors had been a rare luxury in the low-budget hostels and guesthouses at which he had been staying, and he was shocked at how much he had changed since crossing into Pakistan months ago. He was only thirty-three years old, but the thorny beard he had grown made him look nearly forty. His dark hair hung down to his shoulders. Creases stretched like spokes from the corners of his eyes. Once well muscled, he had lost nearly twenty pounds over the past year, and his veins swelled under the taut hide of his hands. He ran his fingertips over the lines of sinew etched into his neck. Though his beard grew thickly across his sunburned face, it did nothing to disguise the fear in his eyes.

He turned away from the window. His back sliding against the door, he let gravity pull him down to a crouch. A roach scampered across the floor. Sweat rolled down from his scalp, stinging his eyes. He clutched his head in his palms and waited.

As he sat alone in the cell, Nick was haunted by the vision of Yvette's corpse. Her body had appeared fresh, mercilessly intact, despite the stench of the morgue. Were it not for the hideous wound across her neck, he might have imagined her waking from a long slumber. The fact that he could not drive the image from his mind, even after such a horrible death, struck Nick as a proof that Yvette's beauty had been her curse.

He remembered the first time he saw her. He had been wandering the ghats along the holy lake in Pushkar, India, when he spotted her surrounded by a troop of frenetic monkeys wielding garlands of flowers. With her light blond hair, short-trimmed to an epicene bob, she could have been mistaken for a boy at first glance were it not for her tapered waist and girlish hips. A flash of her profile revealed high cheekbones and a thin nose, slightly too long for her almond face and full lips. She wore a red tank top that clung to compact breasts, and khaki pants halfway down the shin, exposing ankle bracelets, and stretched tightly around thighs as thin and smooth as her calves.

"They are clawing me—get them off!" she had cried to the young Rajasthani, one of the many hustlers who trained their monkeys to harass tourists with *puja* flowers until they would agree to buy them at extortionate prices. Her boyfriend, Simon, a lanky Englishman in his midtwenties with shoulder-length hair and a downy Vandyke, rolled in laughter nearby as Yvette cursed in French and swiped at the screeching primates leaping onto her shoulders. To Nick, however, her panic was too real to be humorous. He ran toward her, pelting the animals with rocks. The Rajasthani, angry at the assault on his livelihood, stepped toward Nick with a club, only to retreat when Nick, a larger man, cocked his fist. Afterward, perhaps to make a point of Simon's less chivalrous response, Yvette thanked Nick by buying him a Kingfisher at one of the lakeside bars.

Nick had been instantly drawn by the couple's joie de vivre cloaked beneath a thin veil of cigarette smoke and anti-American sarcasm. By the time he arrived in India, he had already traipsed through Australia and Southeast Asia. Australia had been unremarkable, America with marsupials and more desert. But Southeast Asia, especially Cambodia and Vietnam, with its overgrown temples, lantern-laden alleyways, and stunning brown-skinned girls, had hooked him. At times he felt he could travel forever, staying in one country or another until he desired someplace new. However, after some six months, he started to become road-weary, alienated, tired of communicating in phrasebook terminology and improvised sign language. And worst of all, he lived in fear that the indefinable emptiness from which he had fled, which he had hoped somehow to leave behind in America, was still there inside him, a sore that would bleed again as soon as the scab of diversion was torn off.

When Nick met Yvette and Simon in Pushkar, he found their energy to be infectious, reinvigorating, filling the vacuum caused by his loneliness. It did not matter to Nick that they were a couple who had been traveling alone together for over a year. After having no one with whom to share his experiences for so long, he craved their company, despite his being more than ten years their senior. So, when they invited him to join them, he gladly accepted, and the three of them traveled together through India, Nepal, and Tibet.

Yvette and Simon had made friends everywhere, frequently running into people they had met on the road—Katmandu, Varanasi, Yangshao, Hanoi, Bangkok, everyone passed through Bangkok. Over beer and hashish, they would talk all night, swapping adventures and theories of life, always looking forward to the next journey, be it one of pleasure or travail. Because Simon and Yvette were perpetually running out of money, they traveled by the cheapest means possible—hitching rides on cargo trucks, perched atop buses, or packed in sweaty train cars with the masses. Nick, for his part, had enough money that he could have traveled with less hardship. His companions assumed as much, based on his occasional trips to banks and American Express offices to stock up on cash whenever they were in larger cities. His savings, however, left over from his years of gainful employment as a lawyer in America, were not as much as he would have liked, and constantly dwindling. Nonetheless, he never felt exploited when, tired of budget accommodations, he covered their costs for a splurge—a good meal, a comfortable train, or a hotel with hot water. When Simon and Yvette slept together at night, Nick would hide his jealousy as best he could—and sex came easily enough with other freethinking backpackers, which, to Nick's satisfaction, would sometimes make Yvette suffer a little jealousy of her own.

Despite all the time he spent with them, Nick learned little about their pasts, other than where they hailed from and where they had traveled. As with most long-term Western travelers, what one did back home was irrelevant and rarely came up. Indeed, he found that many travelers, especially the younger ones, had done virtually nothing in their home countries before traveling—no jobs, no children, no university training—and their lives were cut wholly from the fabric of their journeys as they went. This might have been the case with Yvette and Simon. But then, what had Nick actually done that had any genuine meaning?

Nick, who had always felt himself too guarded by nature, envied Simon for his dauntless sense of adventure and his seemingly effortless ability to bridge cultures with little more than a good-natured slap on the back and the offer of a cigarette. And Yvette was unlike the girlfriends he had known in America, who might have fancied themselves as "independent" but were nothing of the sort. She was a maverick, bent on forging her own path, her ultimate goal being nothing more than the journey itself. Always on the move, never succumbing to pressure or guilt, she seemed disappointed only by the lost opportunity to try something new, to see a new place, to touch something of the vitality of life. One day in Lhasa, for reasons unexplained, Simon ran off to Southeast Asia with an Israeli girl. Notwithstanding all of Yvette's Buddhism-inspired proclamations about not becoming "attached" to anything in life, she brooded for days. Until a few weeks later, on their first night in Kashgar, she slipped into Nick's room.

Nick and Yvette continued to travel alone together, sharing the same bed for three months, before they received a telegram from Simon at Chinar Bagh Hotel in Kashgar. It was from Rangoon, and it said to meet him in Peshawar.

The steel door swung open, startling Nick back to the present. He scrambled to his feet as Akhtar and Shiraz marched into the cell. "I want to call my embassy," Nick insisted.

"That is not possible," Akhtar replied. "Now, sit."

Nick's eyes moved from Akhtar to Shiraz. "There's got to be *some* rules in this country," he rejoined. "You can't just lock me up in here."

"Sit . . . *down!*" Akhtar bellowed, his words riding on a gust of foul breath.

Nick slowly slid back into his chair. He fixed his eyes on the table and waited for Akhtar's anger to ebb. Then, out of pure desperation and fear, he did the only thing he could think of at that moment. He gambled.

"I'm sorry," Nick said, his voice trembling. "*Please* believe me. I'm trying to help. I just don't understand what more you want from me." Nick glanced up at Akhtar. He was staring back at him, his eyes black and impatient.

"Please don't take this the wrong way," Nick continued with caution, "but . . . well, I feel I should tell you something. Something you might want to know. I know a lot of people—some important people—in America. If I don't leave Peshawar today and I miss my flight, someone is bound to make a fuss. If that happens, well, it might not look so good for you . . . for your careers."

Akhtar hit him. His huge hand swooped across the table, crashing hard against Nick's temple. Nick's vision whirled in a flash of lights, and when it settled he was on the floor, his chair lying over his legs. Akhtar's face hovered above, bloated with rage, his open mouth daubed with spittle.

"You think we treat you special because you are American!"

"*Fuck you,*" Nick heard himself say, his own words barely audible above the buzzing in his ears. He had no cognizance of his execution of the words, only that they were said. It was as if some other person had momentarily possessed him, acted on impulse, and then vanished, leaving him to suffer the outcome alone.

There was a blur of confusion. Nick felt himself being dragged, then thrust downward, a viselike grip clutching the back of his head. Darkness enveloped him. His eyes burned as he pushed against the floor, the muscles of his neck straining in effort to crane his head from the rank void of the toilet. But the force and weight pressing down were too much.

He felt the dull snap of his septum. Blood welled at the back of his throat. Feculent sludge seeped into his mouth. His arms grew heavy. He felt himself slipping into blackness, drowning in piss and shit and his own blood.

Nick was nearly unconscious when Akhtar dropped his head onto the cement. Dripping with foul water, he vomited until nothing came up but blood and sputum.

The inspectors watched Nick gasp on the floor. Akhtar kicked him in the ribs. He cried in pain. He tried to crawl away, but Akhtar grabbed the back of his shirt, hauling him to his knees.

Akhtar took a handkerchief from his pocket and wrapped it around his knuckles. When he was done, he clutched Nick's chin in his thick palm, forcing Nick's head up, while he cocked his fist.

Shutting his eyes, Nick braced for the blow. He would be killed right here, he thought, and nobody would ever know. The anonymity of dying alone in that cell terrified him as much as the prospect of death itself.

Just then Shiraz placed his hand on Akhtar's shoulder. "Inspector . . . please," he said. Akhtar glanced at Shiraz, then spat on the floor at Nick's knees. "Let me talk to him." Shiraz's voice was almost pleading.

Akhtar's eyes shifted between Shiraz and Nick, as he held Nick fast. After a long moment, he wrenched Nick's head by the hair. "Last time," he sneered. He shoved Nick back onto the floor. Then turned to Shiraz. "If you want to coddle him like a baby, you do it alone."

CHAPTER 2

"The inspector does not take kindly to threats," said Shiraz as Nick wiped the blood from his face with a towel Shiraz had given him. "It only serves to irk him. But I suppose one should expect no less—from a *barrister*."

Nick registered Shiraz's comment with dread. He had not told them he had been a lawyer years ago in America. The inspectors must have checked into his past, which meant the U.S. embassy was probably already aware of his detainment. Had the embassy washed its hands of his case? Yvette's body, after all, had been found in the Tribal Areas—the lawless area along the Afghan border infamous for drug smuggling, an area forbidden to foreigners. Nick knew from his days as a defense attorney that the U.S. embassy, in the interest of reciprocity, will do little to intervene with local authorities when American citizens are suspected to have violated the drug laws of a foreign country, unless, of course, they are sons or daughters of people of influence. Despite his failed effort to convince the inspectors otherwise, Nick was not among them.

"As a former barrister, you must agree. When you tell us one untruth, we can only assume you have been untruthful about everything. It makes us very suspicious." Shiraz clicked his tongue against his teeth reproachfully. "Did you not think we would be able to track down the Englishman?"

Nick shook his head, causing a fresh stream of blood to dribble from his nose. "I told you. I thought she went to meet someone the night before she disappeared."

"You *knew* the man, yet you failed to identify him," Shiraz retorted. "The inspector . . . he is a good Muslim," he whispered. "But sometimes I think he has a demon inside. I cannot protect you unless you choose to help me.

"We know you and the girl were more than acquaintances. Moreover, we have information that a vehicle carrying a beautiful girl and a Western man bribed its way across the checkpoint into the Tribal Areas yesterday. The way we see it, that man was her killer. And he was either the Englishman . . . or *you*."

"No," said Nick. "I don't believe you. You're just trying to pin it on a Westerner instead of a local because you don't want to scare away the few tourists who are still foolish enough to come here. You know as well as I do, the men around here practically turn into rabid dogs at the sight of a Western girl—especially one so attractive and blond. She was probably abducted by one of those scam artists pretending to be 'guides.'"

Shiraz frowned at the insult. "It is true, it is not recommended for a Western woman to go about alone—especially in the Tribal Areas where foreigners are mostly forbidden. But most of the time the Westerners—who come here to take drugs and play with guns—bring trouble upon themselves. But your comment, sir, is very telling. It indicates to me that you—a man so suspicious and cynical of Pakistani people—would never let a woman go to the Tribal Areas unescorted."

Shiraz stood. He placed a hand on Nick's shoulder. "Unfortunately for you, we have found no verification that you were wandering the bazaars at the time of her murder. . . . Still, there is one thing I don't quite understand," he said, shaking his head solemnly. "The *bruises*. Whatever caused them, the girl died a very painful death. How could you, even as a dishonored lover, do such a thing?"

Nick opened his mouth, but then, afraid of what he might say, clamped it shut.

"Do you know the *hadd* punishment for murder, Mr. Sunder?"

Nick shook his head no, although he knew quite well the severity of punishment under Islamic law, its appetite for the death penalty as voracious as that in Nick's own country.

"You are *hanged*," said Shiraz. "A woman's infidelity, however, is often viewed as a mitigating circumstance to the death penalty. So long as you confess. You think about your predicament. But not for long. The inspector's patience will run thin."

Shiraz escorted Nick down a smoky hallway and ushered him into a holding cell. The cell was barred and open to view from the main floor, where several jailers wearing *shalwar kamiz* and berets stood behind their desks, cigarettes dangling from their mouths, staring in amused curiosity at the foreigner entering their custody. Wood benches lined the walls of the cell. On the eastern wall, a single, barred slit of a window situated above eye level opened to the outside. Shiraz salaamed the jailers, locked Nick inside, and left.

Nick sat on the bench and surveyed the dim surroundings. Huddled on the floor to his left was a figure propped against the cinder-block wall. The prisoner wore a torn T-shirt and dirt-stained jeans. His arms were clasped around his knees, his legs crossed at the shins. As Nick's eyes grew accustomed to the darkness, the man turned his head so that the wan beam of sunlight coming through the window fell upon his face, revealing sandy hair and a familiar profile. His eyes, half-open, glared at Nick from the shadows.

"Simon?" said Nick, shocked to be looking at the same man he had seen only a few days ago. His eyes were opaque. His hair, once long and natty, now drooped to his shoulders like a greasy dishrag. Simon's raw and unflappable energy seemed to have vacated his body. As Nick approached him, he shifted on his haunches, exposing the soles of his feet, bloodied and raw.

"My God . . . Simon, are you all right?"

Simon snickered. "Paki pedicure. All good until the meds wear off." As he uncrossed his legs and touched the bottoms of his feet to the floor, his sarcastic sneer turned into a painful grimace.

Nick stepped closer. "Here, let me help you . . ."

"Stay away from me!" Simon snarled.

"What . . . ?" Nick said. He glanced over his shoulder. "Keep it down, man." A few of the jailers looked up from their desks before returning to their paperwork.

"Listen to me," Nick continued in a whisper. "We've got to stick together. They're going to try to play us off against each other, to catch us in a lie."

"*I* haven't lied about anything," Simon retorted, again too loudly.

Nick wiped his brow in frustration. "Look, Simon, what happened to Yvette, it's . . . I can't even believe it happened, it's so horrible. But it did. And as fucked up as it is—as angry as we both are at whoever did that to her—nothing we can do is going to bring her back. Right now, we've got to focus on us."

"Us? You're an asshole, Nick. Who the hell do you think—"

"Simon, *don't*," Nick interjected, raising his finger to his lips. "We can't afford to argue over who should have done what to prevent what happened. . . . Just tell me what you told the police. That's the only thing that's important right now."

Simon stood up despite the pain. "What do you think, you sonofabitch? I'm not going to lie for you! I told them the truth. That it was *you* who went with her."

"What are you talking about?" Nick said. "It was your idea to go out there. *You* arranged the driver."

"They said they've got a witness," replied Simon. "Someone who saw her cross through the checkpoint into the Tribal Areas with a white guy hours before she was murdered. I know that guy wasn't me. And she didn't have any other friends here."

Nick stepped toward him. "If they had a witness—a *real* witness who could swear to the identity of the guy who was with her that day—then someone would be charged with her murder by now. Don't believe anything they say, Simon," Nick said, his voice simmering. "You *know* me. You know I wouldn't do something like that. Not to Yvette. Not to anyone."

"I don't know anything about you. We traveled together for—what?—a few months at the most? We weren't that close. What I *do* know is what Yvette told me: that you were—"

"Keep it down!" Nick snapped, his temper flaring. "They could be listening . . ." He glanced over his shoulder again. This time Akhtar was among the jailers.

"Look," Simon continued, ignoring Nick's plea. "I don't give a shit what you say to them. But if you want me to play it dumb for you, you've got to level with me. I want to hear you say it—admit to me what you did, or so help me I'll tell them anything they want to hear . . ."

"I said *shut up!*"

"You killed her, Nick. I know you did!"

Nick grabbed Simon by the shirt, shoving him back on his heels. Simon slammed into the wall. Nick heard something fall onto the floor. He glanced down and saw the casing of a miniature recorder. "*What the . . . ?*"

Blinded by rage, Nick swung, driving his fist into Simon's wizened body, buckling him like a bag of rice. Simon tried to cover up, but Nick hit him again and again in the face and the back of Simon's turned head. Until suddenly something bit hard into Nick's neck, pulling him back off his feet. Writhing desperately, Nick struggled to free himself from the baton digging into his windpipe. But it was hopeless. He felt a sharp thrust to his gut, and then was on the floor, doubled in pain.

Gasping to capture his breath, Nick saw a bare arm jut out of nowhere and snatch the recorder lying on the floor. Instinctively, Nick grabbed for it, hoping to wrestle the device away—not even thinking about the futility of such an act. Tugging at the man's bony wrist, his eyes fell upon a series of bruised striations in the crook of the man's elbow.

His eyes scaled the arm to find Simon, looking down at him, tears and blood streaming off his chin. It was then that Nick remembered his words—*when the meds wear off*—which he had dismissed as one of Simon's typical sarcasms.

Nick winced as he felt handcuffs clamp tight around his wrists. "They're feeding your fucking head?" he said to Simon in disbelief. "Is that all it takes for you to turn?"

"No, Nick—it's on *you*," said Simon, his voice choked. "You didn't give me any choice."

As Nick peered into Simon's eyes, two Pakistani jailers grabbed Nick by the legs, hauling him backward.

"Don't believe him!" Nick cried as his face slid across the grime of the floor. "He's a goddamned junkie! He'll say anything!"

CHAPTER 3

Nick stayed locked in the tiny interrogation cell for five days. Each morning, a toothless, scoliotic old man brought him a tin bowl of stale chapati, *dhal,* and water—the last probably fetid, since he suffered acute dysentery throughout the ordeal. With no private facilities, he was forced to empty his bowels in front of his interrogators.

And then there were the beatings, rudimentary at first—a kick to the ribs, more blows to the head and, most painfully, to his broken nose—they graduated to the pummeling of his thighs and calves with a board. Akhtar inflicted the blows with the rote professionalism of a man who had learned torture as a tool of his craft. Though Shiraz did not partake in them, he watched with a mournful expression that, however sympathetic, Nick learned to detest almost as much as Akhtar's cool violence. At times he feared that he had been beaten past the breaking point and might sign, without reading, whatever confession they stuck in front of his face. But, somehow, perhaps more out of seething hatred and spite than from principle, Nick refused to tell them what they wanted.

Then, when Nick had lost all track of time, the beatings suddenly ceased. Two officers ushered him back into the holding cell where he had confronted Simon. The fishy stench of unwashed bodies penetrated Nick's blood-clogged nostrils, but the cell appeared devoid of occupants.

After his eyes grew used to the dim surroundings, however, a trace of movement drew his attention toward the far end of the cell, where he barely made out two figures hunched over in the cone of light penetrating the window. Kneeling on woolen mats and draped in loose-fitting *shalwar kamiz,* their billowy forms were obscured in the mote-filled half light. With unshod feet, they prostrated, chanting with closed eyes, palms held open before them. What Nick had in his exhaustion almost mistaken as some ghostly ritual was in fact Muslim prayer.

Judging from their flat, Chitrali-style *pakol* caps and feral appearance, Nick guessed they were mountain people. Faces smeared with poverty, their clothes dirt-stained, they had the look of men who had been sleeping outdoors. One was quite short, the other massive, and they were of different races. The more compact of the two had a round Asiatic face and eyes, wide nostrils, and a wispy beard tapering to a spear-point, while the big man had the elongated nose of a Caucasian and a thick black tangle of a beard that encroached high on his cheekbones. Their movements—kneeling, prostrating, standing—appeared mechanical and unthinking. Nick had witnessed *salat* many times since traveling in Pakistan, but never before had he realized how *foreign* the ritual struck him as being—how absurd it seemed to him. He longed for a familiar face—a *Western* face.

Then, inexplicably, Nick was wracked with contempt. He burst into a barrage of vitriolic laughter. The worshippers must have heard it. Nonetheless, they ignored him. This only heaped frustration atop Nick's antipathy, until he wallowed in the bitterness of a man aware that he could not even succeed in insulting another. Stooping, he buried his face in his hands, struggling to prevent his grief from erupting in sobs.

Hours later Nick was roused from sleep. Startled, he searched the darkness. Did someone touch him? Or had he been dreaming? There was a salty taste on his tongue. Black blood mottled his shirt and—to his surprise—he found himself wrapped in a *blanket*. Curious, he rubbed the back of his hand over the material. The itchy texture was more like that of a carpet, he concluded.

Nick heard a sudden shuffling behind him. Alarmed, he swung around to find a large, indistinct silhouette looming over him. He slinked back from the bench, straining to free his arms. But they were snagged under the carpet wound tightly around him as if he were a mummy. He panicked. Kicking his feet against the cement floor, he tried to propel himself away from the hovering intruder.

"No problem, mister . . ." The words, thickly accented in a smooth, lilted voice, reminded Nick of a man trying to soothe a horse. "No problem."

The voice, however, did not come from the figure above him, but rather from across the cell. Nick squinted into the darkness. It was night-time, the only means of illumination a fluorescent bulb hanging from the hallway ceiling. The floor outside the cell was silent.

The silhouette near Nick shifted. He perceived it was the larger of the two Muslims who had been praying before he had drifted off to sleep. Fearing the man was bent on exacting retribution for his scornful outburst, Nick shook himself free from the carpet.

"Please, sir . . . Fidali means you no harm." This time Nick was able to follow the sound to its source, barely making out the hunched figure of the smaller man squatting against the wall. The man nimbly scuttled across the floor in a crouched position like a crab. Nick froze, minding the shadow of the larger man in front of him.

"You were shaking from cold, sir. So we cover you in our prayer rug. You see?" The crouching figure pointed to the carpet now lying on the floor. He still saw no reason why the larger man had been hovering over him while he was sleeping, unless he was bent on crushing Nick's skull.

"Back off!" Nick snapped. The squatting man motioned with his hand, signaling his larger companion to recede.

"You dream bad things, sir," said the one on the floor. "You cry out, strike at the air. You fall off bench and your nose start to bleed. You see?"

Nick considered the blood, the blanket, and the man's words. Finally, he concluded that if they really had meant to harm him, they would have attacked without waking him first. "We think maybe you see a djinn," the man added.

Nick touched his tender nose and winced. "A what?" he asked, pinching his nostrils to stop the hemorrhaging.

The speaker rose from the floor and moved toward Nick. When he stepped under the light, his spherical face was awash with a fluorescent glow. He had an elfish grin, his wide eyes sparkling under his cap. His straggly beard extended from ear to ear. In comparison, his reticent companion, with massive hands and a black beard, seemed like some mythical behemoth.

"It is like angel. But sometimes they are evil and will visit men in dreams," the elfin one rejoined.

Still clutching his nose, Nick shook his head. "Thanks for the warning, but I don't believe in angels, or whatever you call them."

"Djinns, sir," he said in a tone indicating he was incredulous anyone might *not* believe in such a thing. "In the mountains near our village there are many," he replied with sincerity. "Angels and fairies, too."

"You've got lots of fairies, do you?" Nick muttered, unable to hold his sarcasm.

"Oh, yes," the man responded matter-of-factly. "There is the fairy Bajdan, who lives in the clouds and throws ice and snow on the foreigners who try to climb to the top of the big mountains. And there are the fairies that live in the *nallah*s, and others who groan in their ice castles deep under the glaciers. And there are many angels, of course—like the archangel Jibreel, who you English call Gabriel; and Israfil, the trumpeter; and Isra'il, the angel of death . . . and there is an angel of healing. She could mend your nose for you, inshallah."

"Typical god—never around when you need 'em," said Nick.

"There is no god but God, sir," he corrected, wagging his finger at Nick like a schoolteacher. "I said she is angel."

"And you've seen this angel, have you?"

"No," the man replied without pause. "But she lives. We hear many stories from traders who pass through our *nallah*. She takes sick people to her secret healing house. It does not matter whether they are Muslim, Hindu, Buddhist—she heals everyone 'same same.' You see, sir, Allah is sad for the people because they are ignorant and always fighting, so He send down a beautiful angel to help the wounded. He is the Merciful One—*Allah-o-Akbar*."

Nick nodded in deference to the strange man's words, hoping to put an end to his chatter. Just then Nick noticed the man's giant partner working something in his cupped palm with the fingers of his other hand. When he finished he approached Nick, holding two tightly rolled wads of cloth.

"Fidali has something to put in nose, sir," the sitting man advised Nick. "If it pleases you. It will stop the blood. Too much bleeding no good."

The man called Fidali motioned with thumb and forefinger toward his own thickly mustachioed nostrils. Wary of his intentions, Nick held up his hand. But before Nick could wave him away, the prodigious figure had firmly clutched the back of Nick's head and, with surprising precision, inserted the two plugs of cloth, one in each bloody nostril. Almost immediately, after an initial jolt of pain, the fillings braced Nick's loose septum, halting the blood.

"Now nose shall heal, inshallah."

The whole thing happened so quickly, Nick was flabbergasted. But the plugs seemed to be serving their purpose, and he could barely feel the intrusion. He thanked the men in a nasal voice, feeling somewhat ashamed of the way he had mocked them hours before. Just as he began to wonder whether he might apologize—

"No more speaking—sleep now," said the talkative one. "'Allah does not forsake you by the darkness of night'—so it is written."

Nick lay back on the bench and drifted off to sleep, too exhausted to think any more of the odd tribesmen and their superstitions. This time, however, his djinn stayed away.

CHAPTER 4

Sub-Inspector Shiraz stepped into the cell the following morning. He held Nick's confiscated backpack. "It is time," he said, dropping it at Nick's feet. "Come."

Bewildered, Nick picked up his pack and slung it over his shoulder. As he followed Shiraz out of the cell, he glanced around for the strange tribesmen who had helped him during the night. They were gone.

Shiraz led Nick down a hallway to an open door. He ushered Nick inside, where Inspector Akhtar was waiting for them. Akhtar pointed to a table and chairs. Nick sat.

"We have come to a decision," said Akhtar. "You are to be released."

Nick did not believe him. He said nothing, convinced his interrogation had entered a new stage of psychological torture. Akhtar thrust out his lower lip, amused.

"There is a condition. You will testify against the Englishman. In his trial for the murder of the French girl."

Nick stared at Akhtar, and it dawned on him that Akhtar's words were sincere. "But I didn't *see* him murder anyone."

"You need only to testify that you were present when the Englishman arranged the necessary bribes and transport into the Tribal Areas. And that the last time you saw the deceased, she told you she was going to meet with him. You will also explain he was jealous of the French girl's affections for you. He did track her down all the way from Myanmar, did he not? Along with his narcotics habit—which establishes his weakness of character—the prosecutor is quite sure he shall secure a conviction."

Nick shook his head in indignation. "You'll *execute* him."

"Why is that your concern?" Akhtar said. "He did murder your lady friend, did he not? Or is there now suddenly something more you would like to confess?"

Nick closed his eyes, exhaling deeply. "No."

"Very well," said Akhtar. "Then this is your choice. Commit to testifying against your friend and be released today. Or else, since you are still considered a viable suspect, we will keep you in jail indefinitely until we have obtained a conviction—which may be a very long time indeed."

Akhtar leaned in closer. "Then again, with time and baksheesh, witnesses tend to come around—even in the Tribal Areas, where we Pakistani police are not very much liked. Memories have a way of eventually returning. Someone could step forward. Perhaps someone who suddenly remembers getting a good, close look at the Westerner who was reportedly with the victim when she bribed her way through the checkpoint shortly before she was murdered. Or, who knows, maybe someone who even witnessed the violent act itself. Then the issue of your testimony could be moot."

Nick paused. He shut his eyes, breathed deeply, and then moved his lips. Though his mind had blocked the words from his ears, he knew from the repugnant taste on his tongue that he had spoken his assent.

Shiraz pointed to Nick's backpack leaning against the wall. "Everything is where you left it. Including your money."

Nick walked over and started to rummage. "What about my passport?"

"*That* we will keep, in case you are thinking about trying to leave Pakistan, which would be a very stupid thing to do. You will get it back in a few weeks' time, after you have testified at the Englishman's trial as agreed. Come, we will take you to your hotel."

For pure, unadulterated misery, the Khyber Hotel took first place among the long line of squalid hotels that had been Nick's homes during his two and a half years of wandering off-beaten corners of Asia. Roaches the size of mice crawled the floors, rats scampered up the banisters, and the bedsheets were torn and blood-spotted where bedbugs had bitten off chunks of flesh from unfortunate bunkers.

The only things the place had going in its favor were the paltry sixty-rupees-a-night rate and the no-questions-asked policy of Shahid, the receptionist. Shahid, a fuzzy-chinned Pashtun in his early twenties who relished Van Damme karate movies and hashish, turned a blind eye toward his guests' penchant for narcotics and illicit sex. This was a clear advantage to young Westerners traveling in a region inundated with the world's finest opiates yet at the same time reeling on the verge of fundamentalist revolution.

Shiraz swerved the police car to a double-parked halt in front of the hotel, transforming the monotonous stop-and-go congestion into virtual gridlock. Akhtar ordered Nick out of the car. Though he obeyed, Nick had no intention of taking a room there. He could not bear to stay at the place where he and Yvette had spent her final days. Instead of leaving him curbside as he had hoped, however, Akhtar and Shiraz took him inside.

Shahid sat behind the reception desk, his eyes glued to the undulating gyrations of buxom Indian starlets cavorting on the television—a pastime from which he seldom deviated. He did not notice they had approached until Akhtar slammed the tinny reception bell. Startled, Shahid leaped upright, quickly switching channels with the remote, like a boy caught watching porn. He was stoned.

"Watching that Hindu filth again?" Akhtar scolded him.

"I am sorry, sahib, I didn't . . ."

"Shut up and give me the key, before I decide to report you to the morality police. They would be glad to tear this brothel of yours to the ground."

Shahid bowed his head in obedience. Without acknowledging Nick, he plucked a key from the cabinet behind the reception desk and handed it to Akhtar. As it passed hands, Nick saw *4-E* on the wooden block that served as the key chain. He cringed.

"No, thanks," said Nick. "I'm going to wander down the street and find another hotel. One with a working air conditioner," he added for pretext.

"You are staying here," Akhtar interjected. "Where we can keep an eye on you. We reserved your old room—so that you will feel at home."

"No," Nick shuddered. "You can't make me stay here. Not in *that* room . . ."

"Back to jail then," Akhtar said, grabbing Nick's elbow.

Nick's eyes shifted to Shiraz, who subtly nodded—an indication there was no use debating. Nick wondered if it was some kind of psychological tactic—an assertion of control, perhaps, to establish that the police would be dictating his every move from here on in. He stewed a moment, debating whether to protest. Finally, thinking better of it, he snatched the key from Akhtar and trudged with his backpack toward the staircase.

"Sir," Shiraz called out as Nick climbed the first stair. Nick turned. "For your own sake, remember the bargain."

*   *   *

Nick entered the room and locked the door behind him. He strode across to the single wood-framed window, forcing it open as wide as possible. Hazy light splayed across the grimy floor, casting a soft glow upon the bed he had shared with Yvette.

He dropped down onto the wooden chair below the window and stared at the bed. His body was bruised and ragged, his exhausted mind addled with grief and lament. There was so much he could have foreseen. That he *did* foresee. So many opportunities to escape the path that had led to Yvette's death. But still, he went along knowingly. Willingly.

As his mind teetered toward sleep, his thoughts drifted to a time several months prior, shortly before he and Yvette had crossed into Pakistan from China. He had hired a young Kyrgyz herdsman named Izzat to guide them to the Karakul Lake, a pristine alpine lake high in the Pamir Mountains along the China-Tajikistan border. "Your lady friend—she is good rider of camel—very fast," Izzat had said, his words punctuated by the wet, slurping sound of his sucking on a piece of grass.

Nick had privately referred to Izzat as "Smiley," due to the solicitous, often lecherous grin permanently emblazoned under his conical fur-lined cap. Izzat spread his index and middle fingers and pointed them down like an inverted peace sign. "Like boy," he added, tossing his eyebrows suggestively, referring to her style of riding astride like a man in lieu of the more modest sidesaddle.

Nick had begun to regret retaining the young Kyrgyz soon after hiring him in Kashgar, the dusty trading town in the far western reaches of China, situated on the ancient Silk Trail. In fact, Nick had felt a creeping suspicion that Izzat had purposely given Yvette the most fleet-footed beast just so he could ogle her bobbing backside. At one point, under the pretext of controlling the animal, Izzat had jumped on behind her, smugly clutching her hips until Nick barked at him to get off. Since that incident there had been an awkward tension among them—Izzat stewing in disgrace over Nick's reprimand, and Yvette irritated at Nick by what she viewed as his overreaction. Nick, for his part, feared Izzat might abandon them in the desert, and he desperately surveyed the landscape in an effort to get some kind of bearing.

"She's French, from Paris," Nick replied, as if that explained a penchant for speed.

"Ah, I see," Izzat said. "Bad drivers, like Chinese."

Izzat's eyes had opened a diameter wider when Yvette began unbuttoning her blouse, leaving her tanned torso clad only in a tight tube top she had picked up in the hippie quarter of Rishakesh. Cursing, Nick kicked, compelling a meager burst of energy from his camel's flanks. Since entering Muslim Western China, Yvette's continental preference for scant clothing had become a source of anxiety for Nick. Though she was not incapable of naïveté, her disapproval of Nick's reaction to what he had considered Izzat's transparent effort to grope her on the camel left Nick feeling that she was trying to prove something to him—exactly *what*, he did not know.

"Whoa," Nick said when his camel caught up. "Normally I wouldn't be one to complain. But last I checked, we weren't exactly on the Riviera."

"What do you care, Nicholas? I am still covered. It is too hot to wear sleeves."

"That may be. But you're not making it any cooler for Smiley over there."

Yvette peered across her shoulder to find Izzat leering at the outline of her pert breasts under the taut material of her top. She huffed with frustration. "Always telling me what to do? Simon never did that."

"Simon ran off with the Israeli, remember? What was her name—Talya?"

"Talya, Talya, Talya . . .why do you always have to mention that big-titted *salope*? He left you, too. I think you miss him more than I do."

Nick had come to expect such statements from Yvette, calculated to cover the fact that Simon's abandoning her months ago had sent her into a bout of peevish gloom. Perhaps only because she denied her jealousy so adamantly, Nick did not feel it too cruel to remind her of Simon's betrayal on occasion.

"I doubt it," Nick replied. "I'm not the one who slept with him."

"You should have, Nicholas. He was very good."

She said this without expression, and with just a tinge of sarcasm. Her humor had often been delivered in this manner: straight-faced and difficult to read, one of many idiosyncrasies Nick had grown fond of, but also had found perplexing. In this instance, Nick was particularly hard-pressed to detect whether she had meant it as a joke. Yvette was a sensual being, open with her sexuality, not at all wedded to convention in any aspect of her character. Nick guessed she would not think it taboo to have sex with a woman, provided the circumstances made it seem "natural," an adjective she used liberally to describe things that made her happy, including her indulgences. (For example, the flocks of curious children that seemed to follow her everywhere they went were "natural," as was hashish and afternoon sex.) Why should she not suspect the same nondiscriminating sexuality from others?

"I'm *kidding* you," she said finally. "I know you are not the type." She pursed her full lips in a pout, a girlish expression he had found endearing, but which Nick, who had become wary of such things, knew could also come off as erotic.

"You say that like you're disappointed," Nick replied. "Like I'm not adventurous enough for you. You're telling me Simon *was* the type?"

"Of course. You mean you don't know how badly he wanted to have sex with you?"

Nick glanced at Yvette curiously. She stared back at Nick, perfectly composed, letting him stew a long moment, before finally giggling. "That's two times in a row. You are so easy to fool, Nicholas, it is ridiculous," she said, clicking her tongue against her teeth. "You and Simon *are* very different. For one thing, Simon knew me well enough to know when I was making a joke."

"I knew," Nick lied, shrugging is shoulders. "I was just playing along." Truthfully, Simon *had* known Yvette better than he knew her. Their year of travel together before Nick had joined them had made certain of that. In fact, it had seemed to Nick that nothing he could do with Yvette would ever be novel to her. And although Nick would not have traded his time alone with her for anything, he could not deny that Simon had an energy, a charisma, that had lifted them both.

"All right, I miss him a little," Nick had admitted to Yvette as their camels spat and grunted, struggling to ascend a steep rise. "But my point is, we're in the middle of nowhere. And our guide—whom we met only hours ago—is carrying a rifle and a machete. The last thing we need is to get him riled up. He already copped a few feels off you when he jumped on your camel."

Yvette shook her head petulantly. "Typical American. Always thinking the worst of people. I will put it back on. Only because I do not want to argue."

As she buttoned up her overshirt, they reached the crest. They came upon a vast basin surrounded on all sides by the snowcapped peaks of the Pamir. In the middle were two crystal lakes the color of sapphire. The oval shoreline was dotted with conical yurts, where clusters of camels and yak grazed on lush fields of marsh grass. "Here, Karakul," said Izzat, driving his camel up and over the ridge.

At dusk the sun seemed impossibly large as it dipped behind the mountains of Tajikistan. They watched the humped silhouettes of camels wading along the lake's shoreline. Yvette sat, hips flush against Nick's, on a wood-carved bench in front of a yurt they had rented for the night. They took turns pulling on a joint, holding the cool, thick smoke in their lungs, the sweet smell of hashish teasing their nostrils.

They kissed. When he pulled away, Nick's reflection stared back from the mirrors of her pupils. He had an odd sense of release, viewing himself in her eyes. He was not sure why. Perhaps it was the awareness that a new version of himself existed in her mind. It held a promise of change.

Later, when she sat straddling him, he was drunk on her scent, the salty taste of her skin, her warm breath tickling the hairs of his arms. With her face pressed against his chest, they gazed out through the goatskin doorway of the yurt. Morning was descending over the glaciated peaks.

"I don't know about Pakistan," Nick said. "The travel warning is pretty grim."

"America has a warning for everywhere," she said petulantly.

"I suppose that's true. Nobody likes us."

"You're arrogant. Of course nobody likes you."

Yvette possessed the honesty of youth. This made Nick sensitive to her every criticism, even the obtuse ones.

"How modest of you to say." He locked her wrists with one hand, tickling her with the other. Yelping, she struggled to free herself, but her skinny arms were no match for his grip. As Nick held her fast, he maintained a veneer of playfulness. But his inner desire was to assert physical dominance—as he did, much to her satisfaction, during sex.

"I am tired of China," she said when he finally let go. "Too many tourists. Pakistan is untouched. And there's lots of good hashish," she added.

"I think you just want me around for company until Simon gets there."

She waved him off. "There you go again. 'I think, I think.' You live in your head. Stop it. It is the boring lawyer in you. I want to go to Pakistan because it is someplace new. Yes, it will be nice to see Simon. But I am with you now. Can't you please just accept that and come along with me? Don't make me beg."

Nick clutched her firmly by the chin and pulled her into a deep kiss. Staring into her eyes, he paused in thought. She had a point.

"I am leaving tomorrow, with or without you," she said. "What are you going to do?"

Nick sighed, running his fingers down the smooth of her back. "You think I have a choice?" he said, not intending it to be a question.

She pressed her lips to his ear. "I think you are not done fucking me yet," she whispered. Reaching behind his knees, she shifted her weight, easing herself onto him. Nick clasped her torso greedily, as though if he were to grasp her tightly enough, somehow that part of her he coveted most would surge into him, where he could finally claim it as his own.

When Nick awoke the following morning, a piercing pain bore into his skull. It was all he could do to sit up, rub his temples, and wait for his mind to clear.

The hotel room was just the way he remembered: spartan, filthy, airless. It appeared as though it had not been used since his arrest nearly a week ago—a possibility, given the dearth of tourists. Yvette's presence was everywhere—the smell of her hair on the sheets, her scented soap in the dish above the moldy basin, even the ashes from her cigarettes scattered in the tray on the tea table. He remembered the last time Yvette had sat before the room's only window, three stories up from the cobbled alleyway too narrow for traffic other than pedestrians, *tuk tuks*, and high-pitched motorbikes. She had rolled her tobacco and smoked, cradled in the chair after lovemaking, with her knees drawn to her chest, watching children fly kites from the rooftops. "I think I love you," he had told her then.

She drew on her cigarette, spouting a long plume that curled from her mouth like a snake. "*Oui*, Nicholas," she sighed without looking at him. "I know."

Nick shook his head until his thoughts fell in place. He stood and went to the same window where Yvette had been perched. A cluster of street urchins were boiling their morning *dhal* over a kerosene stove in the alley below, their poverty like a smelling salt thrusting Nick back to reality. He was startled by his reflection in the windowpane—the swollen bridge of his nose, his nostrils scabbed over with dried blood, pockets of fatigue drooping from his eyes. But his wounds were nothing compared to the weight of circumstance.

Even after Simon had cooperated with the inspectors in trying to lay the blame on him, Nick knew he could not testify to send his former friend to the gallows. Nor was he so selfless as to risk his own freedom by defending Simon. In Nick's mind, he had but one choice. And it required finding Masood—the only man Nick knew of who could possibly help him.

CHAPTER 5

Nick dressed in a *shalwar kamiz* so that he would not be easy to spot as a *firenghi* from a distance. He put on the flat *pakol* cap Yvette had bought him in Hunza, and then he descended the stairs.

He had expected to find a police officer waiting in the lobby, and was surprised to find only Shahid. "Mr. Nick, I am so sorry, sir," Shahid said sadly. "For Ms. Yvette, and for you . . ." Then, with a surreptitious toss of his bushy brow, Shahid motioned outside the bay window in the direction of the street corner across the way. There, haggling with a street vendor, stood a lean, mustachioed man in a tan *shalwar kamiz* and conspicuous boots instead of the cheap sandals worn by most men in Peshawar. Nick gave Shahid a subtle nod of appreciation.

"All night this police spends in my lobby," Shahid said in a hushed voice. "He smoke all my cigarette, drink all my tea. Now he go out to buy more. You think he offer to buy any for Shahid? These police, they are like bad case of worms—they would steal your food right from your stomach. You going, Mr. Nick?" asked Shahid anxiously. "Where should I say you are off to? I must tell them something."

It was clear to Nick that the police had Shahid bent over a barrel. There was much they could do to exact his cooperation—not the least of which would be to revoke his hotelier license. "Whatever you want, Shahid. Tell them I was hungry."

Shahid's expression congealed. Nick wondered what he made of Yvette's murder. Did he suspect Simon? Or Nick? Or some local? During his stay at the Khyber, they had become friends, smoking and talking until late at night, sharing the insights and grievances of two outliers from very different worlds. The flip side of Shahid's infatuation with Western pop culture was his constant fear of fundamentalist, pro-Taliban parties taking control. Already, bands of vigilante "morality police," unofficially sanctioned by the conventional police, had been leading gangs around the city for some time, incinerating videotapes and CDs, defacing bill-

37

boards depicting women, and vandalizing schools for girls. Whenever the national government tried to rein in the fundamentalists, they answered with bombs, assassination attempts, and outright insurrection, so that even President Musharraf—a former general and once all-powerful military dictator until widespread political revolt and mass rioting compelled him to relinquish authority—had at one time capitulated to a truce in North Waziristan, one of the more rebellious regions of the Tribal Areas. It was common knowledge that many in the national government and military were allied with the radical Islamists. Indeed, the majority of Pakistanis had presumed elements of Pakistan's military had conspired with Islamists in the assassination of Benazir Bhutto, the female opposition leader and former prime minister beloved by the poor, who had vowed to do better than Musharraf in cracking down on pro-Taliban radicals. Certainly, the local authorities in conservative Peshawar, where the fundamentalists enjoyed much support, had neither the will nor the means to resist them. "*Shit people,*" Shahid would say. "They kill my business, my spirit. Next thing, they try to take away the hashish."

Nick exited the hotel and walked east toward the *Andar Sehr*—or "old city"—comprising the chaotic bazaars and wood-façaded merchants' quarters, the crumbling Bala Hisar fortress, and at its western end, the old cantonment built when Peshawar was a remote outpost of the British Raj. He stopped at an intersection packed with people and quickly glanced behind him. He expected the man in the tan outfit to be on his heels. Instead, the man had stayed put, watching Nick through the choking traffic as he spoke into his cell phone. Certain that another policeman would soon be tailing him, Nick hailed a motor rickshaw. Seconds later, one stopped, briefly blocking the policeman's view. In that moment, instead of climbing into the rickshaw, Nick slipped down a narrow alleyway. The driver cursed and drove off.

Instantly, Nick had vanished into the bustling arteries of the medina. As he threaded his way through the winding passageways, he concentrated on imprinting the intricate twists and turns into his head. For finding his way in the darkness, where there were no streetlights or signs for guidance, would be crucial. The task was complicated by the mind-boggling clutter of men and animals—green-turbaned Baluchistanis, long-bearded Hazaras in flowing white clothes, herdsmen from Chitral and Swat driving flocks of goats and humped zebu cattle. He stepped over limbless beggars crawling on their stumps like crippled crustaceans, and child beggars from

Afghanistan—refugees with striking green eyes and reddish-blond hair—groping under cloaks and trousers for something to steal.

It had taken Nick weeks to learn to navigate the serpentine walkways, and still he often got lost. He knew to turn south at the butcher shops, stacked with the disembodied heads of goat and sheep, then east at the spice vendors, with their rows of burlap bags filled with bright yellow and green curries, red peppers, and coriander. After some twenty minutes of sinuous turnabouts, he stepped into a carpet shop. There he sat for a time, drinking tea while a young Uighur boy unrolled carpets at Nick's feet. Nick pretended to study them, while keeping an eye on the human traffic crossing outside the open storefront. When satisfied that he had lost anyone who might have been trailing him, he left the shop, wending his way further into the bowels of the old city, until he came to a tiny side street near the cantonment.

Barely wide enough for two men abreast, the cobbled walkway wound through a series of shops open to the street, lined with burnished brass pots, teakettles, hardware, and stacked sheet metal. Bearded metalworkers sat cross-legged on the shop floors, loudly pounding out wares with wood-handled hammers. Nick rushed by one of the shops, his eye catching a flash of bright colors. He stopped, and upon closer inspection saw the red, white, and blue star and bars of an American military roundel painted onto an olive-drab sheet of steel. Nick realized he was staring at the stabilizer of a U.S. Army helicopter. The metal was dented and scraped from shrapnel or rocks kicked up from a crash. He also spotted a gray-painted piece of wing or fuselage with German writing on it, a Humvee door riddled with bullet holes, stacks of spent artillery shells, and even some unexploded ones with holes drilled down the middle where they had been defused—all scavenged from the war in Afghanistan and carried over the passes for sale as valuable scrap metal.

"Hey, Engleesh," said the shop owner, startling Nick, who had not seen him approach from behind a hanging blanket at the back of the shop. The owner was a black-bearded Pashtun with a deep scar slicing across his face, and a white lump of scar tissue in lieu of a right eyeball. "You want souvenir?" He pointed his open hand toward the mangled helicopter stabilizer with the U.S. insignia. "American Chinook." He closed his fists and mimed aiming a shoulder-fired missile, then made the sound of an explosion. "Taliban shoot. For you, twenty American dollar."

"No, thank you," Nick replied, wondering what the shopkeeper expected him to do with something so large, even if he were inclined to make such a purchase. He salaamed the man and continued walking.

After another ten minutes, the walkway funneled into a small plaza, where clusters of Pashtuns sat at wooden tables, smoking and drinking tea. More than a week earlier, in this hidden corner of the bazaar, Nick had asked Masood to arrange transport to the Darra bazaar to explore one of the most infamous gun factories of the Tribal Areas.

An Afghan refugee, Masood ran a black market business arranging transportation for journalists and occasional drug tourists wanting to travel to regions of the Tribal Areas, where the government had forbidden foreigners to go. However, his main source of income, he had openly admitted to Nick, was the smuggling of humans.

Nick knew that with the police watching him so closely, he could not make it out of Peshawar undetected if he used a conventional bus or train. And even if he somehow did manage to sneak out of the city, and got as far as one of the borders of Pakistan, he would be unable to pass through any official checkpoint without his passport. The Tribal Areas offered him the only real chance of escape. Teeming with war refugees, and governed by tribal *jirgas* more interested in breaking away from Pakistan than enforcing its laws, the Tribal Areas were a hub of human trafficking. The Pakistani army units posted there were stretched way past their limit fighting al Qaeda and the Taliban. They had no ability to interdict the perpetual flow of refugees camped in the vast region from passing to and from Afghanistan, into Iran, or northeast into the scarcely populated Northern Areas of Pakistan where they could cross into India, hoping to find further transport to Europe, Australia, or someplace else where they might scrounge a living.

For Nick, India was the only plausible destination. A white face would not get far in Afghanistan, in the throes of perpetual war against America and its allies, where he would be captured and killed in the rugged Taliban-controlled areas straddling the Pak-Afghan border; nor in authoritarian Iran, also on the verge of war with America, where a Westerner would quickly be apprehended and, in Nick's case, sent back to Pakistan or imprisoned as an American spy. In India he could blend in with other Westerners—tourists, expats, and the like—until he figured out how to get back home, or somewhere else safe, without his passport.

It was not hard to spot Masood. He had lost an arm in an airstrike on his village, although his inestimable age made it impossible to tell whether it was a Soviet or American bomb that had done him the violence, despite the fifteen years between the invaders. His head was severely dented—a skull fracture caused by the explosion that took his arm—but the wound had not diminished his sharp wit.

The Afghan instantly recognized Nick and offered him a cigarette, which Nick knew better than to reject. "Where is the lovely lady today?" he asked, catching Nick off guard. Masood had learned some English as a boy in a school built with Swedish aid money in one of the refugee encampments, before it was burned down by Taliban. He was soft-spoken, albeit intense, and when he inquired about Yvette, he gave the impression of being sincere, not probing or lecherous.

"I sent her back—to take care of the children," Nick replied, wondering whether Masood knew Nick had lied about their marriage. It was a lie that he and Yvette had frequently propagated during their time in Peshawar, not least because it stopped all kinds of prying questions.

"That is wise, my friend. So, how can I be of help to you?"

"I need transport again . . . this time to Torkham."

Nick turned toward a sudden ruckus. Two men were arguing loudly across the street, each backed by a few of his clansmen. Masood noted Nick's jumpiness. "Torkham is very risky for you," he said. "Many Taliban. No need to go all the way there. This time of year the hashish is just as good in Peshawar."

"I'm not concerned about that," Nick replied.

The Afghan frowned. He had expected more openness. Nick, however, was reluctant to tell anyone his final destination. This was not to say he mistrusted Masood. On the contrary, Masood was an Afridi Pashtun. As such, his name, word, and honor were everything, and he had no love for the police. Still, Nick figured that the fewer people who knew where he was headed, the better his chances. Once he got to Torkham, a smuggling center on the Afghan border, he planned to arrange further transport on his own.

Masood nodded, despite the affront. "A wise man does not write his intentions on his cap. When would you like to go?"

"Tonight. After midnight."

"That is a good time." The Pashtun frontier guards posted at the checkpoints into the Tribal Areas commonly extorted bribes from transporters to permit the flow of refugees, many of whom were officially "wanted" by the Pakistani authorities on suspicion of militancy. Traveling late at night was advantageous because there were fewer guards, and they were too tired and lazy to haggle much over the price. "It can be arranged."

"Where do they pick up?"

"Please—have patience, sir," replied Masood. "You are a guest in my country, so I must tell you first. If you plan to cross into Afghanistan at Torkham, it is too dangerous. Do not do it. The border is closed to all foreigners. And even if you get through, paying a big enough bribe—or dressed as a woman in burqa, perhaps—the road to Jalalabad is controlled by Taliban. They will stop you. These Taliban dogs, they search even the women. Any Americans they will kill. Even journalists they are shooting."

"Thanks for the warning," Nick said. "I don't plan to cross."

Intrigued, Masood cocked his chin. "The only other road that could interest you, sir, goes north to Chitral. From there, one can go west—crossing the Hindu Kush on foot into the north of Afghanistan—the way of the opium smugglers. Or else, one can go east: the route of the mujahideen on their way to Kashmir to fight India. But . . . if you are going to India, why not just take bus on the highway from Peshawar to Lahore? The border crossing at Amritsar is open."

Masood peered into Nick's eyes, drawing inferences from Nick's silence.

"But of course, you know this. And must have a good reason for not going through the official border check. Otherwise . . . why would you be coming to me?"

Nick shifted in his seat. Masood placed his hand firmly on Nick's shoulder.

"Do not worry, sir," Masood said, looking squarely into Nick's eyes. "You can trust me to tell no one. It is my duty to protect you."

"I appreciate that," said Nick.

"India is very far. The way you choose to go is difficult. The places you will pass through have many dangerous people. And the borders are patrolled by many army and police. If the transport is not arranged by me in advance—with proper baksheesh paid to the right people—you will surely not make it. Let me help you, inshallah. It is the only way."

They settled on the price of two thousand dollars cash, which included all the necessary bribes, transports, and a guide to lead Nick across the Line of Control, the heavily militarized, de facto border separating Pakistani- and Indian-occupied Kashmir. Half of the money he paid to Masood up front, with the rest to be paid when Nick arrived in Gilgit, the dusty trading town in the center of Northern Areas, the Pakistani-occupied regions of disputed Kashmir.

Masood said the truck would pick him up at a hidden lot near the cantonment at one o'clock in the morning and carry him through the Tribal Areas checkpoint, where tribal police would be bribed in advance by Masood to look the other way. Then, at a village near the foot of the Khyber Pass, Nick would change trucks and continue to Torkham. Instead of crossing into Afghanistan, a jeep would carry him north to the village of Chitral, and then east over the Hindu Kush to Gilgit. There, Nick was to board a cargo truck and travel on the road southeast to the region the Pakistanis called Azad ("Free") Kashmir, where a guide would take him on foot into Indian-occupied Kashmir. It was a long, indirect route, but remote and unpoliced compared to the southerly, more direct alternatives, which all went through populous areas. If things went according to plan, he would be in India in about ten days.

Not the least of Nick's difficulties would be slipping out of the hotel at night. Escaping through the lobby would be impossible. The policeman who had been spending nights there, even if dozing, would be roused by the creaking stairs as Nick descended. Aside from the lobby door, the window presented the only other way out. However, it was on the third story above the cobbled alleyway—too high to jump. A fire ladder led from the adjacent room's balcony, but reaching it would be difficult. Once down, Nick would have to move swiftly, the lack of street lamps at once a blessing and a curse.

After paying Masood the one thousand dollars up front for the first half of the transport fee, Nick had only nine hundred U.S. dollars left on his person and less than one hundred dollars' worth of Pakistani rupees—not enough to cover the second half of the transport fee, let alone afford him any reserve at all to pay for food, shelter, and unexpected expenses along the journey. He needed to obtain as much cash as possible from his U.S. bank account immediately, preferably in dollars, which were considered by locals to be more desirable than the rupee, and which he could use once he got into India as well. Based on experience Nick knew that he could not cash traveler's checks or get a wire transfer at a bank in Pakistan as a foreigner without presenting his passport, which the detectives had confiscated. This left ATMs, not an ideal option given their withdrawal limits.

Before heading back to the Khyber Hotel, Nick walked to three different international banks in the financial quarter and withdrew from their ATMs as much cash as the machines permitted (two hundred dollars' worth of rupees per machine, a large sum in Pakistan). At the fourth bank, his ATM card was rejected, indicating that the electronic security mechanism had finally kicked in, shutting him off from more withdrawals for at least a full forty-eight hours, if not longer. He then headed back into the bazaar with his pocket stuffed with an inch-thick fold of rupees worth six hundred dollars, and with them bought American dollars from an Iranian carpet dealer, mindful that carpet salesmen, who frequently sold to foreign buyers in bulk, often did their business in foreign currencies for the favorable exchange rates. After paying a hefty 16 percent commission, he had netted a little over five hundred U.S. dollars. It was not nearly as much cash as he would have liked before embarking on a long journey through remote areas where there would be no banks at all, but it was the best he could do without a passport in such a short time.

Nick finally returned to the hotel in the late afternoon. He made a point of smiling courteously to the policeman in the lobby. Then, after eating dinner in broad view at the kabob stand across the street, he retired to his room to set aside his belongings. He had to travel light, so he stuffed his small daypack with only the essentials—enough dried fruit, crackers, and canned sardines to sustain him for a few days, a wool sweater, extra socks, a hat and gloves, a pocketknife, iodine to purify water, sunglasses, matches, and cigarettes. He concealed all his money on his person. In his money belt, along with his ATM card and Massachusetts driver's license, his only remaining ID, he stored the one thousand dollars he intended to pay to the truck driver in Gilgit, and in his boot, his reserve of five hundred dollars and change—altogether a veritable fortune in Pakistan, well more than what most Pakistanis earn in a year. Finally, he strapped a water bottle to his pack and waited out the final hours of the day in the hotel room, thinking about all the things that could go wrong.

The dark alleyway beckoned through the night. Nick fought the temptation to leave early. The prolonged time on the street would increase the chance of his being caught. For this reason, he had allotted no more than ten minutes on top of the half hour he had calculated it would take to reach the liaison point, in case he took a wrong turn in the darkness or was forced to take a detour to avoid a suspicious follower.

With shaking fingers, Nick tied a dark T-shirt over his head as a makeshift turban and then slipped on his rucksack. He waited for his watch to tick off the last few minutes until the ordained time—a quarter past midnight. Finally, he unlatched the window and poked his head out into the night.

He peered into the alleyway below, until he was sure that no one was there. Then, not knowing whether the hours ahead would bring him freedom or perdition, Nick clambered through the window into the obscurity of darkness.

CHAPTER 6

Village lore has it that Aysha was born to heal. But most of the villagers who actually remember her as a child know that her passion for healing did not emerge until much later—when she was seven years old.

The vast mountainous regions straddling northern Pakistan, India, and western China—where a mere traverse from one valley to another can bring about a complete change of language, religion, and race—attest to the hermetic possibilities of extreme geography. The village of Gilkamosh lay hidden like a lost jewel in the midst of this impenetrable landscape of rock and ice.

Until recently the area had never been properly mapped. When cartographers finally discovered the village, some said it lay in southern Baltistan. Others claimed it should be considered part of Kashmir proper, and still others marked it as a parcel of Ladakh. Most who opined, however, had never been there. If they had, they would have known—Gilkamosh was a world unto itself.

The village was cradled at the bottom of a deep valley carved by the Gilkamosh River, its mighty waters fueled by ice melt from the massive glaciers of the Karakoram to the north. Walled in by sheer mountains too precipitous to hold snow, Gilkamosh Valley exuded a monastic spirit; not just because of the black schist and basalt spires that struck one as a natural altar to the heavens, but for the valley's cloistered feeling of isolation, which was not oppressive but inspired meditative reflection. The valley was a verdant place. Each May apple and apricot trees burst with white and red blossoms, while the hillsides brightened with wildflowers. In October the aroma of harvested apples, mulberries, and barley sweetened the air.

The people who lived there were the descendants of diverse ethnic groups who, driven from their lands of origin over the centuries by war or famine, had somehow survived the treacherous passes and stumbled upon it. By the time Aysha was born, as in many villages in the northern reaches of Indian-controlled Greater Kashmir, the majority was Muslim—an almost equal mix of Sunni and Shia, and a few Ishmaelis—while about a third was Hindu of various castes and stocks, with a smattering of Sikhs and Buddhists. Despite such differences, each group practiced its customs as it saw fit—the tranquility of the valley seeming to dilute any aggressiveness in those who professed to monopolize the "Truth."

As is common in long-isolated villages of the Himalaya, the people of Gilkamosh, especially the elders, were slow to give up their belief in mysterious things. Occasionally, mysterious things sometimes still seemed to happen in Gilkamosh.

Aysha Fahad was the seventh of twelve siblings—four sisters and eight brothers—a large family even by Muslim standards. Her father, Naseem, was a wool merchant as proud of his virility and thick peasant hands as he was of his ability to feed his progeny, a feat he had accomplished by his self-motivated transformation from subsistence goatherder to tradesman. Naseem could have sustained a second wife, financially and libidinously, but he had neither the heart nor the patience to invite rivalry into his home, being far too fond of his wife to risk disappointing her. Fatima was attractive enough and certainly fertile, and was a stickler for tending home and hearth. He was hard-pressed to complain.

Aysha was Naseem's fifth daughter. She was a pretty girl, blessed with the high cheekbones, light complexion, and silky hair that hinted at Mogul, Tajik, or even Persian extraction. Despite her beauty she was shy, though unusually sharp-witted. Like many clever children, she had an ability to entertain herself for hours—playing with her pet goats, picking wildflowers in the high meadows, or dallying along the riverbank, contemplating the effervescent designs formed by the reflection of sunlight on the running water. Because of her self-sufficiency, she was ignored by her parents, who preoccupied themselves with her more demanding siblings. Aysha did not care, for she was content with what she would later come to realize was her oddity and uniqueness. The knowledge that she was different from the other girls inclined her, much to her parents' worry, toward becoming a child recluse.

*   *   *

The arrival of her brother Sahib drew Aysha out of her solitude. Sahib was born coincidentally on Aysha's seventh birthday. Perhaps the mystique of their shared birthday contributed to their bond. Whatever the reason, it soon became clear their relationship was destined to be closer and more profound than that of most siblings.

Sahib had been born sickly. Indeed, the child's pallid complexion was the very thing that had inspired his parents to give him the name "Sahib," a word of colonial origin sometimes still used on the subcontinent to designate whites. As a newborn, he was listless, and his condition only worsened. When he turned seven months old, his parents made the long journey to a doctor in Srinagar, who confirmed their fear. Sahib was afflicted with the "lazy blood."

Sahib's case was acute, the oxygen-carrying capacity of his blood so thwarted by disease that he would die, the doctor said, before his first birthday. Some expensive medicine might prolong Sahib's life another few months, but the drugs would only delay the inevitable. At that time Naseem was by no means a wealthy man. With his nest already brimming with eleven strapping children, he made the difficult decision to count the family's blessings and save his money for the healthy ones, fully expecting Allah to exercise His will in accordance with the doctor's prognosis.

Fatima could not bear to look into her infant son's sallow face without her matriarchal sense of justice rioting against her previously unquestioned religious faith. "Why has Allah cursed me so? If He is so merciful like the Book says, why did He not take the child at birth and spare me the pain of loving him?" Unable to bear the sound of Sahib's crying, she plugged her ears with cloth and abstained from feeding him, praying for the quick and painless demise Allah seemed unwilling to bestow.

Aysha was incensed. How could her parents simply give up on her baby brother? Did not miracles happen in the world, especially in Gilkamosh? Perhaps out of childish faith and not a little rebellion, she refused to stand by idly. After all, she and Sahib shared the same birthday—did not the Archangel Mikail, the provider, send Sahib to her as a gift, as much as a test of her will?

When Fatima was not looking, Aysha began to slip quietly beside Sahib's hammock and feed him fresh goat's milk from a nippled vesicle made out of a goat's bladder. Fatima eventually found out and admonished Aysha that it was all for naught—that it would only protract the infant's suffering. But Sahib nonetheless grew stronger, surviving beyond the maximum lifespan the doctor had given him.

"You are a miracle worker, Aysha," Fatima said. "Allah has granted you a gift." Fatima, of course, resumed caring for Sahib as soon as he showed some signs of improvement, and she felt more than a little guilt for her resignation. But it was Aysha who had mothered Sahib back to strength when everyone else had written him off, and who thereafter would take care of him as if she herself had somehow carried the baby in her immature womb.

Although he remained feeble, never able to lumber more than a few yards before falling to his knees, Sahib grew into a happy, intelligent boy. At the age of four, he could recite whole suras from the Qur'an by heart and had memorized a name for each of the some two score goats in his father's herd. For hours on end, he and Aysha would play, floating bark boats in the pools of the irrigation channels, laughing together until Sahib tired and could take no more. "Allah made you this way so that your big sister can love you more," Aysha would tell him when his thin limbs gave way to exhaustion. And Sahib believed her, for Aysha had a sincerity about her that lent verity to her every word.

Then, on a morning after Sahib's fourth birthday, a day filled with boisterous celebration and perhaps too much excitement for his overburdened heart, Aysha was unable to rouse Sahib from slumber. Her face contorted with grief. She cradled his lifeless form, still wrapped in blankets, and carried it to the banks of the river. She waded chest-deep into the treacherous waters. Cringing from the cold, she held the little body up to the sky and, crying at the top of her lungs, demanded Allah take her instead of her brother.

The villagers differ in their accounts of what happened next. The more mystically inclined, most of them octogenarians or older, say that Aysha, still clutching the corpse, threw herself into the icy depths, only to be regurgitated onto a riverbank far downstream by a mysterious belch of water, possibly emanating from a colossal fish conjured by the Archangel Jibreel himself. Others purportedly saw Aysha, frozen in awe as she stood in the river, imbued with Holy Spirit, reciting in Arabic like the Prophet himself, and at that moment, through divine intervention, the nature of Aysha's gift was revealed to her. In the rendition espoused by village pragmatists, including Naseem, it was Naseem himself who pulled Aysha to shore, saving her from certain peril.

The divergent versions, however, share one essential aspect, which by its commonality can perhaps be said to contain a kernel of truth: It was on that morning when Sahib was taken from her that Aysha vowed forever to devote her life to healing her people. From then on, to the villagers of Gilkamosh, Aysha became their very own angel, gifted to them by Allah, endowed with the power to cure. After all, the expensive doctor in Srinigar, for all his extravagant medicines and modern learning, proclaimed it was impossible for Sahib to survive beyond a year; yet Aysha had kept him alive four times as long. A miracle, in a place where miracles required no proof beyond living.

CHAPTER 7

When Aysha was a child, Gilkamosh was accessible only by a single, unpaved jeep road. When the road was clear, the drive to Kargil or Drass, the closest towns where one could obtain supplies and basic services, would take at least two days. Gilkamosh, however, was completely cut off from the world from November until late June, when the winter snows melted and boulders deposited by avalanches could be cleared from the road with dynamite, pick, and shovel.

By the time Aysha approached her teens, Gilkamosh was in the midst of a boom that would change it forever. Tourism in the neighboring Vale of Kashmir had already been surging for some time. The focus had been Srinagar and the villages around it. But some of the more intrepid travelers—young backpackers from Europe with a thirst for the less-beaten track—had somehow found their way to Gilkamosh by hiking or hitching rides on the backs of Indian army jeeps. Predictably, they fell in love with the place. Most were keen to keep the remote village an unspoiled secret. But word leaked out. Within a few years of the first Westerners' stumbling upon it, an exclusive club of seekers was making Gilkamosh their perennial mecca. The trickle of visitors rapidly gave rise to new businesses. Outfitters opened shops catering to foreign trekkers. Several hotels were built, as well as restaurants and shops selling crafts, all cluttered on the main dirt road bisecting the town.

The titillating scent of rupees for the picking wafted southward across the subcontinent, wetting palates like the aroma of fresh-baked naan permeating a New Delhi shanty. Migrants, mostly Hindus from the south, followed the path of the tourists, lured by opportunity. It did not matter that they had never heard of Gilkamosh, or even whether they knew it was in Indian territory. Indeed, the government itself had not known, until it claimed the region when its rivalry with Pakistan forced the issue.

The villagers benefited from the migrants, many of whom had become

51

experts at gleaning profits from unsavvy Westerners in the heavily touristed cities of the south, such as Manali, Pushkar, and Mumbai. The Fahad family was no exception. Naseem's business thrived, supplying pashmina wool to the new crop of craftsmen and entrepreneurs. One of these newcomers was Advani Sharma.

Advani and his wife moved to Gilkamosh from the Indian province of Jammu, setting up several factory-sized looms for the manufacture of handmade scarves, sweaters, and shawls. Unlike most of the other Hindu migrants, Advani was not indigent. His ancestors were pandits, members of the ministerial caste who had moved to Kashmir more than half a century earlier to take government positions when it was an independent princely state under Hindu leadership. True to his bloodline, he looked and acted the part of an Indian bureaucrat: portly around the midriff, balding, mustachioed, convivial in demeanor but remarkably astute.

Advani employed local girls on his looms. Although the wages were by no means lavish, the income they earned made ends meet for many Gilkamosh families. More important for the Fahad family, Advani bought large quantities of wool from Naseem, boosting his business at least fourfold. Advani did not need to buy through a middleman like Naseem. He could have purchased directly from the goatherds at a cheaper price. But Advani was not a greedy man, and he was as ambitious at politics as he was at commerce. He chose to patronize Naseem because his large clan included many of the well-to-do Muslims in the village. A symbiosis developed between the Sharmas and the Fahads—Naseem and his clan profited lucratively from Advani's business (as did other families, but none so much as Naseem's), while Advani rose to a stature of prominence in the eyes of Hindus and Muslims alike.

Newcomers like Advani quickly learned Aysha Fahad was not a typical village girl. Ever since she had miraculously protracted Sahib's life span, Aysha's healing abilities had become ingrained in the village ethos. Whenever someone in the village became sick, Aysha was called upon to nurse him, and she accepted this function out of a sense of duty as much as compassion.

Aysha was sufficiently aware of her own limitations to insist patients with serious ailments be transported to Srinagar or Leh to be treated by a "real" doctor. Or, if the patient were immobile, she would insist a doctor be imported, in which case she was always present as an adjunct. Aysha learned much from these visits, as well as from her own self-study, impressive but nonetheless limited by the inaccessibility of medical texts. Whenever villagers visited a city in Kashmir or beyond, they would make a point of procuring medical books or supplies for her.

Aysha eventually expanded beyond treating purely physical ailments—colds, fevers, cuts, simple broken bones, and minor congenital illnesses—to problems of the more psychological sort. She became something of a therapist for the village women. As a result, she was far more mature than other village girls her age, and knew enough juicy scuttlebutt to make the most seasoned village gossips envious. She came to know such delectable tidbits as which husbands were not sleeping with which of their wives, and which wives wanted nothing to do with their husbands, and which of her classmates still wet their beds. She was even privy to such salacious rumors as which boys were feared by their mothers to be inclined toward Sodom, and which men partook excessively in the "Gilkamosh water," a mulberry-based moonshine forbidden by Islamic mandate. Aysha safeguarded the women's confidences with keen vigilance. She never leaked a secret, as tempting as it was, or exploited one to her advantage, though she easily could have.

By the time Aysha turned fifteen, she had blossomed from a modest, cerebral girl into a stunning beauty. With straight, raven black hair; wide, piercing green eyes; a sleek nose; and a slender body, she was fondly referred to as "our emerald" by the villagers. But the veneration did not make her conceited. On the contrary, she was oblivious to it, perhaps because of the chilling effect her beauty, coupled with her heralded position, had on the confidence of potential suitors. The village boys rarely mustered the mettle to speak to her. Not surprisingly, therefore, it would take an outsider, a student at the new madrassa, to win her affections.

CHAPTER 8

The new madrassa was built adjacent to the town's largest mosque and across the street from the Temple to Shiva. All the villagers welcomed it, both Muslim and Hindu. Advani Sharma was, as the town leader, the master of the dedication ceremony, attended by the new mullah of the mosque, Mullah Yusuf, the madrassa's principal teacher and headmaster. Advani made a speech lauding Yusuf and his madrassa as harbingers of much-needed literacy for the rural youth and as a symbol of the village's longstanding tradition of religious tolerance.

It was an unremarkable structure, modest in size, with a small office for the mullahs adjacent to an elongated classroom where students would sit on the floor for their daily drills. No one bothered to inquire how or why the madrassa had appeared so suddenly, as if by divine intervention, nor did they ask any questions about the source of its funding. And why should they? Who would think to question a school run by a religious charity?

Had the villagers had more than an idle curiosity about its sudden appearance, they might have found it odd that the funding for the school came from Islamic charities based in Pakistan and Saudi Arabia—not from the usual groups in Kashmir or India proper—and might have been surprised by the strident rhetoric of the new mullah. They might also have questioned the timing of the school's appearance. For instance, why did the madrassa and others like it start cropping up in Gilkamosh and neighboring villages exactly at a time when trouble in Srinagar seemed to be brewing again?

Perhaps the villagers would have been more vigilant if the problems that had plagued the Vale of Kashmir over the decades been more than mere rumors of only passing interest filtering through the mountains. Since the partition of the subcontinent in 1947, after which the Hindu Maharaja Hari Singh of the Princely State of Jammu and Kashmir made the fateful decision to join his mostly Muslim subjects to Hindu India in lieu of Muslim Pakistan, Pakistan had tried more than once to wrestle

Kashmir away from India by force of arms. But Gilkamosh had always been far removed from the reach of either nation and completely isolated from any of the fighting. In the villagers' minds, they were neither Indians nor Pakistanis, which suited them just fine.

But the flow of migrants brought with it all the issues of the world, including news of rising tensions in the Vale. Politics became, for the first time, the topic of dinner conversations. Villagers watched—adults with mild trepidation and the children with awe—as convoys of Indian troops perched atop intimidating vehicles of war began to pass through Gilkamosh, forging trails to remote outposts at the Line of Control to the north. The villagers became versed in the discourse of the Kashmir "question," and the Muslim United Front, an Islamic party led by theocrats and youth leaders preaching independence from Delhi, even started sending some representatives to Gilkamosh to shore up support.

"Why do those troublemakers have to come to *our* village and spread their propaganda?" a worried Advani asked Naseem one evening over *pokhoras* and tea. "We should send them back to Srinagar. Along with that new mullah."

"Do not worry, Advani," said Naseem. "Gilkamosh is not like the rest of India. People here have never cared about politics. There is no reason for them to start now. And the mullah—I agree he is a firebrand. But he is well liked, especially by the boys from the countryside. He is doing a lot of good, teaching those boys to read and write. That is a lot more than the Indian government is doing for them."

"True," Advani agreed. "The government school is too costly for the poor."

Naseem nodded. "*Everything* is too damned expensive, thanks to those crooks in New Delhi. It does not matter as much to you and me—we are successful merchants. So long as the tourists keep coming, times are good. But the goatherds and sharecroppers are not getting a big enough piece of the action. I can see the envy in their eyes, as our bellies grow thicker. That, Advani, is far more likely to fuel resentment toward India than any hot-headed mullah preaching about morality and the return of the caliphate."

Advani gently patted his bald pate as if probing for hair, a habit of his when he worried. "Yes," he conceded, "inequity can be serious fodder for unrest. But there have always been rich and poor in India—that alone does not incite people to madness. You are underestimating the power of a few well-placed fanatics, my friend. Up here, you were isolated from the horrors of Partition. I had two uncles in Gujarat hacked to death by their neighbors. My aunt was gang-raped, her breasts cut off, left in a field to die. I came here, to this paradise, to escape those ghosts. I love this valley, these mountains, these people whom I serve as if Gilkamosh were the place of my birth. I am all for tolerance, Naseem. But when people start using religion and freedom in the same sentence, man is easily transformed into a beast."

"You worry too much, Advani. We are neither Indians nor Pakistanis. If rabble-rousers and politicians want to quarrel over labels, let them. We know who and what we are, and none of us is about to spill blood over it."

Naseem reached across and slapped Advani's back with his thick, strong hand. "What can we do about it anyway, my friend?" he said. "India is a democracy, is it not? The mullahs can say what they want."

Advani sighed fretfully, again patting the shiny skin on his crown. "Oh, Advani, and one more point," Naseem added, as he fixed his cap. Advani looked up at him.

"Your hair, it is still gone." Naseem smirked, winked at his friend, and then walked out the door.

As time passed, it appeared Naseem was right not to worry. The politicians preached at the mosque, demanding the overthrow of the Indian yoke and the installation of the fundamentalist variety of Islamic rule. No one seemed to take them seriously, save a few youngsters who were of that age when *any* voice of rebellion rings true. And so what if Mullah Yusuf was teaching his students that jihad was the Sixth Pillar of Islam? Or that their poverty had been caused by the Hindu migrants' stealing jobs and land from Muslims? That was not how the people of Gilkamosh thought.

There was no reason to believe one mullah could change a whole mindset built on a centuries-old culture of tolerance. In Gilkamosh, life went on, idyllic and peaceful as it always had been.

The same could not be said for the Vale of Kashmir. Ever since questionable results during state elections had raised the specter of vote-rigging in the late 1980s, Muslim youth in the Vale had been convinced they would never get a fair shake under the Indian yoke. When Indian democracy had failed to empower them, the AK-47 did. On July 31, 1988, a bomb blast obliterated the office of the Srinagar *Telegraph*, a pro-Delhi newspaper, killing dozens. In the Vale, the Kashmiri uprising had already begun.

CHAPTER 9

Her hair. The blackness of it highlighted her eyes, sometimes turquoise, other times pure emerald. She was too beautiful to be of this world, Kazim thought, she was supernatural, like the djinn he had read about in the Qur'an.

At fifteen Kazim Ullah Baig was tall and lean, his body banded with muscle. His dark beard, though still sparse, sprouted with promise. Despite his striking presence, he was shy yet determined, the kind of boy who would climb the stairs to the mosque two steps at a time.

Kazim's father, Raza, was a goatherd from Passtu, one of the many tiny hamlets surrounding Gilkamosh connected only by an ancient network of rugged foot trails. Raza, his wife, Kazim, and three daughters subsisted on goat milk and yogurt they churned themselves, and the few vegetables they could grow in the small plot behind their mud-brick dwelling. From snowmelt until late fall, Raza and Kazim would drive the herd to the high pastures, where they would live in stone huts with the other men from their village, while the women, spoiled as Raza permitted them to be, stayed back to tend home and hearth, happy to have their men out of the way.

Necessity demanded that Kazim drop out of the government school when he was eight years old. Raza could not afford Kazim's education and needed him to assist full-time with the herd. If Raza had a few more sons, then perhaps he could have spared Kazim for a while; indeed, he might have retired. Regrettably, it was Raza's lot to work until he dropped dead among his goats or was nagged to death first by his virago wife, whom he had not the heart to beat despite the advice of his neighbors. For these reasons, when the strange, Urdu-speaking mullah named Yusuf visited Raza one day, offering to teach Kazim free of charge at the new madrassa in Gilkamosh, Raza was far from enthusiastic.

"Why should my son not work all day with his father? That's what I did, ever since I learned to walk," said Raza, berating the foreign mullah with disdain.

But Mullah Yusuf was tenacious—he returned time and again to inveigle Raza with his arguments and homilies. "Kazim is a bright boy," the mullah cajoled. "And he wants to learn to read more than anything. You should be proud of this."

Raza rolled his eyes, but he knew the mullah was right. Kazim did have an unusual curiosity about the world, constantly peppering his father with questions about the nature of things. Raza knew all the answers were in the Qur'an, but he did not have the capacity to read it himself, let alone convey its wisdom to his son.

Mullah Yusuf reminded Raza he had three daughters, who could handle the hard work in Kazim's absence. "Allah put women on earth for childbearing and labor. Why spoil them by letting them sit around the house with nothing but cleaning and cooking to do? Send those girls out to the fields, and up here to the pastures to help with the goats! Drag them by the hair if necessary!"

In the end only the spiritual angle convinced Raza to relent. "Every man has a duty to learn to read, so that he can study the Qur'an," the mullah told Raza on his fifth visit to his home. "For you, Raza, it is too late—for the mind, like water, freezes in the winter of life. Though you have lost the capacity to learn, you will do Allah the greatest service possible by allowing your son to do so in your stead. If you do this," the mullah explained, "He will surely look upon you with favor in granting access to Paradise come the Day of Judgment."

Raza pulled on his graying beard. "Paradise?" he thought. The mullah looked as if he should know all about that. He seemed the epitome of righteousness, learned and beneficent, with his long noble beard, intimidating scars slicing from his chin to his eye, and his authoritative manner of speaking, which infused his words with moral clarity. "He is persuasive, that Mullah Yusuf," Raza admitted silently. The prospect of a better life beyond looming large in Raza's tired mind, he eventually gave in to the will of the mullah to recruit his son, and that of his son to learn.

Soon thereafter Kazim began walking to school each morning down the long, steep foot trail from Passtu to Gilkamosh. To the surprise of Yusuf, who had really picked Kazim more for his broad shoulders and rugged mountaineer's upbringing than any expectation of cultivating a thinker, Kazim's education was an immediate success. His facile mind absorbed lessons as the parched plateaus of Baltistan drank September rain. He was quickly discovered to be the brightest student in the school.

Moreover, because Kazim was the largest boy in his class, he was singled out as a natural leader, as much for his physical superiority as for his intellect. While the other students struggled over the difficult passages of the Qur'an and Hadith, memorizing the sublime lyrics came easy to Kazim. He was enraptured by the classical Arabic, his impassioned recitations so inspired that even the mullahs were envious. Before long, the mullahs bestowed upon him the honor of leading the other boys in the tediously long morning prayer sessions.

Along with the standard Qur'anic drills, Mullah Yusuf started to assign Kazim extra readings, which they would discuss after class. Kazim learned all about the sacred duty of jihad and the honor of martyrdom. For the first time, he learned of the oppression of Muslims by infidel Indians in Kashmir. These teachings filled Kazim with great pain, for he had never even known a genocide of Muslims was being perpetrated right under his nose in his own homeland. How could he have been so blind? Kazim's heart found something to latch on to—not just to Allah, to which Yusuf had promised Kazim's father he would be devoting his time, but to freedom.

Mullah Yusuf was ecstatic with his protégé's ability to absorb his teachings. "Here is one fish we could use," he thought, "not like the other dim-witted, indolent Kashmiris." For Yusuf was of the opinion that Kashmiris, especially mountain folk like the people of Gilkamosh, had evolved to acquire the sheeplike qualities of their ubiquitous livestock. What the mullah did not foresee, however, was that a powerful competitor would soon be vying against him in the struggle for Kazim's future.

Kazim was playing cricket with some boys from his class the first time he saw her. He had run off to fetch a ball that red-haired Abdul, his best friend, had batted some length down the street when Aysha strolled out of the gate leading from Advani's home near the village center. She walked right through the cricket grounds, not at all intimidated by the crowd of boys, who froze at the sight of her. When Kazim returned to the pitch to find his friends oddly entranced, he turned curiously toward the object of their gaze.

He, too, could do nothing but stare. She was dressed in the blue pastel skirt of her public school uniform and a light green sweater. There was a poise about her that made her seem unapproachable. Her jet-black hair appeared to carry the shimmer of wetness, and her walking stride had an effortless grace.

As Kazim stood enraptured, he was unaware that Abdul had snapped out of his own paralysis. Trying to impress Aysha, Abdul swung fiercely at a ball bowled by another boy, driving it toward the makeshift wicket of piled rocks where Kazim stood stupefied. At the very moment Kazim's eyes locked with Aysha's, the ball slammed into the bridge of his nose.

The next thing he knew, Kazim was on his back. Aysha's face, wide with concern, was so close he could feel the heat of her breath. He could have done the unthinkable and brushed her cheek with his hand had he been born brash enough to do it. He marveled at her scent, the flawlessness of her skin, the emerald pools of her eyes. She blotted his nose gently with a kerchief, and though Kazim could taste the saltiness of his blood, he was numb to all pain.

"Pinch the nostrils to pressure the ruptured tissue. It will reduce the blood flow. Tilt your head back. . . . Are you dizzy? How many fingers do you see?"

Kazim was hearing her words, enjoying their warmth and the subtle movement of lips that formed them, but he was not comprehending them.

"Oh, dear!" she said, her voice urgent but composed. "Can you see *anything*? . . . Speak to me."

Just then, Mullah Yusuf made his way through the crowd of boys. He was at once surprised and dismayed to find a girl over Kazim, his prize student and class leader. "What is this?" he barked.

Aysha was used to viewing adult displays of anxiety as psychological conditions to be analyzed or treated, not to be feared. She responded aloofly. "He's been severely bludgeoned. His nose is hemorrhaging, and there is a possibility of concussion. If you help me take him inside, I will begin treatment immediately."

Mullah Yusuf was quick to judge the girl's intelligence as insolence— *female* insolence, the worst kind. An example needed to be made.

"Back away from him, you unveiled slut!" he snapped at her with palpable disgust. "How dare you pollute one of my boys with your touch!"

Shocked, Aysha looked up at the mullah. No one had ever spoken to her in such a manner. She noted the ashy gray of his beard, his yellowed teeth visible through his scowl, and the deep scars from his eyebrow across his cheek. He appeared to her as a hideous, hateful demon of a man. Though she was not scared, she nonetheless felt an irrepressible impulse to get away from him. She turned her back and, parting the circle of boys, calmly walked across town, straight to her home.

There, she shut herself in her room, and after ensuring there was no one around to witness it, she cried. Her tears were not those of anger or fear—for she thought little of that turbaned tyrant—but rather of pain. She had failed in her one chance to impress the new boy with the light skin and sad eyes that reminded her so much of her little brother, Sahib. She had spotted him in the village days ago. Even from afar, she had seen that he was a boy—the only one other than her Sahib—whose face stirred in her the melancholy and suffering of all men. When she saw in him this essence, she had smiled, not understanding quite why.

For Kazim, there was no point in resisting his punishment. "Get up!" yelled Mullah Yusuf in front of the other boys, their envy of Kazim now turned to ridicule. "You should be ashamed of yourself. Being touched by a female in public is disgraceful enough . . . but you just lie there, letting yourself be nursed like a sissy! Have you no honor? You have humiliated not just yourself but all of us!"

Still clutching Aysha's bloody kerchief, Kazim picked himself off the ground. Mullah Yusuf slapped him hard across the face and, twisting him by the ear, pulled him back to the madrassa. Inside, he made Kazim sit blindfolded facing the wall, while the others were instructed to beat him.

CHAPTER 10

"I washed it in the river," Kazim said, "rubbing it with stones like I have seen my mother do. I must have rubbed too hard."

Aysha held open the kerchief that she had used a week ago to wipe the blood from Kazim's nose. There was a large, ragged hole worn through the middle. "It's okay. My father sells cloth. We have plenty."

"Oh," said Kazim. Aysha waited as Kazim stared blankly, unsure what more to say. Finally, she turned to leave.

"Are you sure?" said Kazim. "Can I make it up to you somehow?"

Aysha stopped. "Don't be silly. It's just a kerchief. I go through them all the time in my work."

"Work?" said Kazim, without thinking.

Aysha gave him a surprised look. "You mean you don't know?"

Of course, Kazim knew about Aysha's unique function, but his normally nimble mind was distracted and not registering her words.

"Oh, well, I suppose you are not from our village," Aysha said. "I am—how should I say it . . . I help the sick. I am not a doctor or anything. It is just what I do."

There was a long pause as Kazim considered her response. He frowned. "So that's why you did it."

"Did what? You mean, stopped to help you when that foolish boy batted the ball into your face? Of course that is why. What did you think?"

Kazim averted his eyes. He had been raised on the notion that a man must never show emotion. In front of Aysha, however, he nonetheless felt vulnerable and skittish.

"Oh, I see," she said. "You thought I stopped because I fancy you?"

"Of course not," he denied, feeling himself blush.

"Good, because it would take more than a handsome face to make me fall in love. I need to get to know a boy first, before I could conclude whether he is suitable," she continued, at the risk of being brazen.

"School will finish in an hour. Perhaps you might like to walk me home? If you want."

"Do *what*?"

"Walk. You *are* hard of hearing, I think."

"Together? But what will people think?" Kazim said.

Aysha shrugged. "Maybe they will think you are my patient. Who cares?"

"Mullah Yusuf, for one," Kazim replied worriedly.

Aysha considered this for no more than a second. "Yes, he is probably the one person who *would* care. But he does not set the rules."

One walk home turned into many walks home, and then into longer walks, through the communal rose gardens and along the river valley, up to the meadows blanketed with wildflowers and the high pastures overlooking the village. The landscape could not begin to dwarf the enormity of what they felt in each other's presence. Nor could the disapproving eyes of Mullah Yusuf keep them apart.

The void each filled in the other made them forget that they had been strangers for most of their lives. In Kazim, Aysha found the boy for whom she had longed since the death of Sahib, a handsome boy in a rugged man's body, but who seemed to need someone to cling to. He smelled of mountains and toil.

As much as Kazim was drawn by Aysha's beauty, her unbridled spirit mystified him. In the insular microcosm of his mountain hamlet, there was a clear dichotomy of the male and female affecting all aspects of life, from the types of labor each sex could perform, to the rooms of the house and the parts of the village where men and women could venture, to manners of dress and speaking. Each sex knew its place, and they mingled only in unspoken, nocturnal interludes within the sanction of marriage, sweaty moments of passion that frequently had awoken young Kazim from the deep, exhausted slumber of an overworked child, frightening him in his infancy, arousing him in his youth. This way of life had always served his people well, and he grew up without questioning it.

But Aysha seemed unhindered by the fetters that Kazim had associated with all the other women in his life—his mother, sisters, and cousins. It was evident in the brash manner in which she had confronted Mullah Yusuf the day she had tended to Kazim's nose, and in the great deference afforded to her by the villagers by virtue of her role as a healer. Perhaps it was not surprising, therefore, that they soon became oblivious to aspects of their own behavior that would be considered scandalous without the sanction of marriage.

One summer afternoon several months after they had first met, Kazim and Aysha sat on the rocks of the riverbank under a shady arbor of drooping poplars, near the exact spot where Aysha had once waded into the treacherous waters and cursed Allah the day Sahib had passed away.

The farmers had succumbed to the heat, vacating the fields and affording them solitude. The water flickered with silver light. For a long while they said nothing, tossing dandelions into the river, trapping midges in their palms as they floated through the air. Kazim stole glimpses at Aysha and marveled at the glistening mass of hair splayed across her nape like an Oriental fan and the small delicacy of her feet as she wriggled her toes in the cold river.

"There is so much water coming down from the mountains this year," Kazim said wistfully. He spoke solely for the sake of breaking the silence, not sure why such a trivial thought crossed his mind. "What do you think happens to it all?"

"What do you mean?" replied Aysha, thinking Kazim, whom she rightly detected was a bright boy, surely must know the answer. She smiled warmly. Kazim's curiosity reminded her of Sahib. He too used to ask her all kinds of questions about the nature of things, simply to garner her attention.

"It flows into the River Jhelum, which in turn flows into the Indus, which runs into the sea, where it mingles with all waters of the world. So you see, our water is no different from any other—it all becomes part of the same."

Kazim pondered this for a moment. "That does not seem right," he said, frowning. "Just because it drifts away from us, does not mean it is no longer ours. Everything in Gilkamosh is different from everywhere else. I think if you could trace it on its journey, you would know—it stays Gilkamosh water forever."

"Nothing is forever, Kazim. The water becomes part of something else—another river, the oceans, the clouds, the rain and the glaciers and the snow—always changing. The only permanent thing in this world *is* change."

Kazim ruminated on her words. He did not want to hear about

change. "I do not believe that. The things that matter do not change. The *truth* does not change. It never does."

Aysha peered at him obliquely, as if noticing something about him for the first time. "Perhaps you are right," she conceded. "Truth, like love, must be absolute. Or else it is false, and therefore untrue."

Her words incited a throbbing in his chest that he had been feeling lately in her presence. It seemed only to grow worse the more time he spent with her. Just last night he had come to the conclusion that it would never go away unless he told her it was there and that she was the cause of it. "Aysha . . . ?"

She turned. "What is it?" Aysha goaded him. "Please, tell me."

Kazim could not bear to look at her, instead staring at her reflection in the smooth eddy at his feet. He could see the outline of her torso, craned daringly close to him. He felt her radiance draw the words from his throat.

"I am not like you, Aysha. I do not know anything about how people are supposed to feel . . . but if love is like pain . . . a pain you feel inside that just won't go away . . . I have that feeling. . . . I have it for you."

Fearing he had done something unmanly, Kazim lowered his eyes. He kicked nervously at the water, churning clouds of sand that quickly vanished in the current. He felt that the sand was his soul and now that he had revealed his feelings to Aysha, it would be swept away and lost in some far-off ocean, where someone else would call it his own. The silence seemed interminable, and for a moment, he considered leaving, running away from that place, never talking to her again. How could he be so stupid as to lay his heart bare?

And then, without looking up at her, he felt her warmth against his face, the sound of her breath above the din of his own heartbeat. She was just inches from him, but still, he could not look into her eyes.

Then she did something unbelievable. She touched his cheek. Tenderly, she guided his head toward hers. Though his eyes were still clamped shut, Kazim felt her hot breath tickle his chin, smelled the sweet fragrance of her hair. When her moist lips pressed against his, he felt a fearful impulse to pull away. But gradually the heat of their bodies mingled, drawing them closer until their kiss became deeper, open. They mashed teeth clumsily but did not care; for that single moment melted away all thoughts of their selves, so that they each tasted the other's breath and knew the other's desire, as their own.

When they separated there was a depressed silence as they trained their eyes on the horizon, grappling with the knowledge they had done something forbidden, and that their lives would never again be so simple.

The wooded dell by the river became their own secret haven, where they could be free together from the restrictions of a world that required love to be an arrangement before it became a passion. No one but the two of them knew they had deigned to kiss, and it would be madness to tell. They savored their transgression with an unspoken fervor, each knowing, without saying, that they would take it to their graves.

Not even the tirades of Mullah Yusuf were a match for the passion that filled Kazim when he was with Aysha. But the mullah was a patient man. He knew that if he intervened now, he might lose the boy forever. And he also knew that time inevitably sours the innocent. If he played his hand at the right moment, he would prevail in the end. He had done his job well and had already planted the seed of rancor deep enough in his young pupil that it surely would germinate in time.

CHAPTER 11

The whole village treated Aysha as a daughter. As with any parent, it followed that the villagers felt they had a collective right to approve of Aysha's suitor and, effectively, they did.

The villagers were a protective lot and were hesitant to accept Kazim, despite the children's desire for each other. Though they were tolerant, they were not without parochialism. Being from an outlying hamlet, Kazim was an outsider. The few who knew his father vouched Raza was a good Muslim, but reported he was rather reclusive, if not a rustic. The villagers whispered that their Aysha could do better by marrying a Gilkamosh boy. Most were probably just jealous, loath to renounce their hope she might choose one of their own sons someday.

It took a voracious specimen of *Uncia uncia,* the Himalayan snow leopard, to change this. During the hot summer of Aysha's seventeenth birthday, one of the cats felt the urge to stray from its normal diet of ibex, markhor, and wild Marco Polo sheep. Though snow leopards had always taken their share of domesticated sheep, goats, and young yaks, this cat was gluttonous, tormenting the goatherds no end. Little was done about the feline goat snatcher, however, until it extended its gastronomical forays to a new, human level.

At dusk Nabir Beg's son, Ganu, a boy not much taller than a full-grown goat himself, was prodding his father's herd down from the pastures to a stone-walled pen nestled in the river basin. As he drove the animals along a narrow berm at the edge of a cascading glacier, the cat pounced from the boulders above him.

Though no one witnessed the incident (the boy did have a paw mark on his back to prove the attack), Ganu claimed he narrowly escaped death when the roar of a conveniently timed avalanche frightened the leopard just as its teeth were about to sink into the boy's jugular. More likely, however, the animal was startled by Ganu's high-pitched shrieking, which could be heard all the way to the outskirts of town.

Days later a hunting party of five of the most able-bodied trackers set out for the craggy peaks. When they finally returned, they had nothing to show but some silvery tufts, scat in a bag, and a large fang extracted from the breastbone of a half-eaten goat.

Hopelessly outwitted by the beast, the villagers were at a loss. Goatherds burned bonfires at night around their pens, and old-timers trained in the skills of their shaman forefathers were dragged out of retirement. They whirled in circles to the beat of goat-hide drums, pouring libations of mulberry wine and chanting incantations to aggrieved mountain fairies, much to the disdain of Mullah Yusuf, who berated them as infidel pagans. Still, the leopard continued to snatch its quarry with ease, littering the mountains with mutilated carcasses. To the superstitiously inclined, the Summer of the Leopard, as it came to be called, was an ominous omen, portending that the years of fortune and tranquility enjoyed by Gilkamosh were coming to an end.

Then, one crisp autumn morning, Kazim strolled into town with a silvery pelt over his shoulder and sold it at Ashfaq Muhammad's souvenir shop. The town rejoiced.

"How did you kill the devil?" Ashfaq asked.

"Lucky, I guess." Kazim smiled, a trace of mystery in his eyes.

The townsfolk would have none of that. Kazim was said to have snapped its neck with his bare hands after it jumped him. In another version he tracked the beast for five weeks, into Baltistan and then back, until he finally spotted the cat on a mountainside. It was too far for an accurate shot, so he cleverly shot above his target, causing a rock fall that crushed it to death. Yet another story had Kazim outsmarting the wily cat with a goat sprinkled with marmot poison, which had the effect of slowing the beast just enough so that Kazim could squeeze off a heart-piercing shot.

In the end it did not matter how he had killed it. Though it was far from clear that the pelt belonged to the beast in question, the next summer the carnage did not repeat. Kazim was a savior, his deed forever ingrained in village lore.

Ashfaq stuffed the pelt and displayed it in his shop with the hope of drawing in tourists. Under the trophy he placed a plaque that read, dramatically, EATER OF MAN AND BEAST—SLAIN BY KAZIM "THE LEOPARD SLAYER" OF VILLAGE PASSTU.

Sometime thereafter, in the wake of Kazim's increased esteem, Naseem began seriously to consider Kazim's courtship of his daughter, though the decision was probably based more on Naseem's desire to finagle a cheap source of wool from Kazim's father than on the boy's reputed heroism. Naseem sent one of his sons up the passes to Passtu to invite Raza over for tea. He also invited Advani, Naseem's best friend and confidant. Advani was the village leader and spokesperson, and since Aysha was the concern of the entire village, it made sense to include him.

The meeting was not without awkward moments. Raza seemed surprised that Naseem would keep company with a Hindu, and kept looking at Advani, unsure what to say to him. But after his initial discomfiture, Raza settled down to himself—a dismal conversationalist with a noxious habit of chain-smoking whole packets of unfiltered Pakistani cigarettes. Still, there was an endearing quality in his simplicity, and things ended on a high note when Raza agreed to sell his wool to Naseem at less than market price. Raza did so not out of poor business judgment, but rather a desire to win such a fine wife for his boy.

As soon as Raza left, however, Advani voiced his concerns. "There will be other boys, Naseem. Why not wait and see what comes around the bend? Perhaps it will be someone more suitable to your daughter's wit, from a family more commensurate with your status."

Though Naseem valued his friend's judgment, he felt an affinity toward Raza's humble origins, which were much like his own. He took Advani's comment as caste-based snobbery, something, though palatable to Hindus, wholly unbecoming a good Muslim. "We are all of the same caste before Allah, Advani. Raza is of simple people. But good people," Naseem said politely.

Advani diplomatically held his tongue, for he was always the politician.

From that point on, the boy and girl had the blessing of the village. They spent a year in each other's company, much of it in the privacy of their cloistered arbor along the riverbank where they had first kissed. It was on one of these occasions, at a time when Aysha thought she knew every aspect of Kazim, that a small spark of concern ignited in her.

"Why does your father associate with that Indian, Advani?" Kazim asked in a vexed tone, a few months before his eighteenth birthday.

Aysha looked probingly into Kazim's eyes. His moods had been shifting of late, especially when he met her right after his lessons. Aysha had tried to get him to explain the root of his frequent disconsolation, but he refused to discuss it. Today, it seemed he was fraught with anxiety beyond the normal peevishness.

"What do you mean? He is my father's friend."

"He doesn't belong here," Kazim said.

Aysha paused, perplexed. "How can you say that? He does nothing but good for this village. He employs people. Puts food on their tables."

"He is a parasite," Kazim scoffed. "He takes business that should be ours. And he struts around here like he owns the place, while he pays homage to those fat pigs in Delhi, who tell us what we can and cannot do."

Aysha stared at Kazim in utter disbelief, unable to fathom how *anyone* could harbor ill feelings toward Advani. It must be jealousy, she concluded. Aysha had been spending a lot of time lately caring for Advani's wife, Shanti, who had fallen ill with whooping cough. The poor woman was in a bad way, too sick to move, and Aysha had been at her side daily, preparing vapors to help her breathe made from herbs she had gathered from the hills. Still, it was the first time she had heard enmity in Kazim's words, and she found them deplorable. "You're wrong about him, Kazim," she said, perhaps too assertively.

Kazim's face flushed with anger. "You think you are so smart," he replied. "You score high marks in their schools. You nurse them when they are ill, run around like their little pet chicken. But you cannot see it, can you? So smart, yet you are so blind. It makes me sick sometimes. Embarrassed even."

"See what? This is my village. These are my people."

"*I* am your people. Your parents, *they* are your people. Not Advani."

Aysha saw where he was going, and it filled her with sadness.

"No, Kazim. He is not Muslim. But he does a lot more for Muslims than most Muslims I know. Probably more than your mentor, Mullah Yusuf."

"What do you know about Mullah Yusuf!" he erupted.

"Not a lot," she said. "But what I do know does not make me desire to get to know him any better."

Kazim's emotion mounted, until he had to rein in his nerves just to manage to speak. "Mullah Yusuf is a great man! He is a *hafiz*—he knows the whole Qur'an, as if inscribed in his heart. He fought jihad against the Soviets—killed so many of the infidels that he lost count. The godless communists tortured him, that is why he has that scar on his face. It is a scar of honor. . . . Don't you *ever* disrespect him again!"

Kazim's words shocked Aysha. She had never seen him snap like that before. It was as if he had suddenly changed into a completely different person, a younger version of the maniacal Yusuf himself.

Kazim noted the sudden control his anger had over her. Though he often felt disarmed by her beauty, it empowered him now to see the way he had silenced her with his rage. Mullah Yusuf was right, he thought. No matter how smart and haughty a girl might be, or how bewitching her charm, Allah granted Man dominion over Woman. If He had wanted it otherwise, He would have created Woman the physical equal of Man. But He did not.

"Things will change around here," said Kazim. "Someday soon. You will see."

"I don't want anything to change." Aysha cast her eyes upon the milky river, noting its cloudiness, unusual for that time of year. "I like it the way it is."

CHAPTER 12

Her entire life Aysha had dreamed of becoming a real doctor. But as the third youngest in a line of twelve children, and a girl to boot, she had never imagined attending a university. Thus, Aysha was caught wholly off guard when Advani, Naseem, and a few of the village elders paid her a surprise visit shortly before her eighteenth birthday.

Advani explained that he had quietly called together the council of elders, and they had come to a collective decision affecting Aysha's future. In a show of gratitude for all that Aysha had done to help the villagers over the years, each family had agreed to pitch in whatever rupees it could spare, scraping together enough tuition for her to attend medical college for at least the first two years. In due time Aysha would learn that Advani had himself promised to pay the lion's share in consideration for the compassion Aysha had shown his wife, Shanti, when she had whooping cough. But the majority of families had pledged something, even some who were foolish to do so.

"Medical college?" Tears of gratitude welled in Aysha's eyes. She hugged her father, who could never dream of paying for her schooling himself. Advani announced a village feast in Aysha's honor. "Slaughter a goat! Slaughter twenty goats! Gilkamosh is going to have its first certified doctor!"

"But wait," Aysha protested. "I have to be accepted first. Practically every straight-A student in all of India sits for the entrance exam each year."

"True," said Advani, "it is very competitive, and you will have to rank high on the exam. But I have every confidence in you, Aysha. I have spoken to a friend on the faculty at the Institute of Medical Sciences in Delhi. He said that they reserve one or two spots for girls from rural villages, and that he would put in a good word for you based on my recommendation."

The possibility of pursuing her dream made Aysha shudder with excitement, and the villagers' gracious decision to pay her tuition touched her deeply. But scoring well enough on the exam seemed far too much of a long shot to allow her to start making plans to move to Delhi. Her tiny school in remote Gilkamosh was no match for the elite prepatory schools of the subcontinent, where well-to-do Indians groomed their children for such entrance exams practically from birth. What chance did she really stand among this kind of competition?

And what about Kazim? In the unlikely event she were accepted to the institute, surely she could not expect him to move to Delhi, a filthy sprawl of concrete swarming with homeless poor, where there were no mountains or livestock for him to tend, and the air was sweltering and brown with smog. What kind of work could he find in an overpopulated city where Muslims were a minority treated with suspicion?

She felt compelled by her sense of honesty to tell Kazim the villagers' plan. But the question of whether she would go to Delhi, with or without him, was purely hypothetical in the absence of her acceptance, and it would probably hurt his feelings to think that she would even consider leaving him. Why raise the issue prematurely and invite tension into their lives while there was no real decision to be made? It seemed smarter and much easier to wait and first see what happened. So, she traveled to Jammu with her father, took the state-administered entrance exam, and sent her application to Delhi without saying a word to Kazim about it.

Advani's friend on the faculty of the Institute of Medical Sciences had told Advani to expect a decision on Aysha's application within five months of submission. After six had passed, and Aysha had still heard nothing, she was sure that she had been rejected. The exam, after all, had been difficult, and many of the topics on it had not even been covered by her lessons at her school in Gilkamosh.

After the seventh month, Advani finally received a status report. "I am so, so sorry, Aysha," he said, deflated. "Given the passage of time, my friend says it does not look good. He says the class has already been filled. Official rejection notices will be going out in a week or two." Advani fretted, rubbing his hairless head. "Maybe you could sit for the exam again next year, try to score a little higher?"

Crestfallen, Aysha frowned. "I don't know, Advani. I gave it my best shot already. There's so much more I still need to learn."

"Think about it. You know you can do it. I'll see to it that the village's offer remains open."

Though her parents and Advani were terribly upset with the news, Aysha, after her initial wave of disappointment, felt relieved. In the months during which her application had been pending, she and Kazim had only grown closer. The prospect of life without him had been causing her nerves to knot up with anxiety. Her nights had been sleepless, and often she had been unable to eat. Had she been accepted, she would have faced tremendous pressure from her parents, Advani, indeed the whole village to go to Delhi. Her failure to achieve her dream had lifted a dreadful burden from her shoulders.

The morning after Advani relayed the negative news about her candidacy, Aysha awoke feeling strangely giddy, as if drunk with the knowledge that her love for Kazim would never again be threatened by the weight of responsibility. Her whole youth, ever since she had taken care of her sickly brother when she was seven years old, she had always been a healer—a confidante of adults with a window into their world—but never really a child. On that day, for the first time ever, she felt imbued with the carefree lightness of being a girl.

Later that afternoon they met by the river after school. A black thundercloud suddenly floated over the spires to the north, catching them by surprise. As the storm approached, sheets of rain fell in streaking lines of gray, sweeping swiftly across the valley floor. The torrent headed straight for them as they sat idly at their secret spot on the riverbank, but they cared not a bit. Since their first kiss, they had come to the view that the whole world was theirs to reject. And now nothing, not even the jagged bolts of lightning lashing the craggy peaks, could scatter their resolve to challenge everything.

A wall of rainfall advanced across the swollen river, the sound of the pelting drops building to a furious crescendo. They felt as though they were standing before a rushing train, but the fear of collision only augmented their excitement. Armed with the arrogance of youth, they laughed in the face of the storm. And then, just as the wall of rain and wind slammed into them, they kissed, giggling through the play of their lips. In the chaos of rain and thunder and their own wild delirium, Kazim's hand brushed Aysha's breast; inadvertently at first, the back of his hand pressing against the flesh under the thin, soaked fabric of her shirt as he struggled to hold his mouth against hers in the midst of their uncontrollable laughter.

Aysha felt a tingling sensation, like a small dose of electricity applied to her skin. She shied away, her mouth slightly agape. Sensing her skittishness, Kazim backed off. Unexpectedly, however, she twisted back toward him, her breasts nestling against his chest, her thigh pressed against the swelling between his legs. Their laughter subsided as their mouths locked again, turning, twisting, tasting the rainwater streaming off each other's lips, while the deep roar of the river and pattering rain drowned out all but the sound of their breathing. Then, when it seemed they had no choice but to turn the corner to the unthinkable—to cast their lives down forever on forbidden rocks—the rain suddenly stopped.

Startled by this instantaneous whim of nature, they pulled away. Aysha's black hair dripped rainwater, her face flushed pink. When she spoke, her voice was hoarse and quivering. "We had better go. Before it comes again."

They hesitated a moment, as if each hoped for the other to object. Then they stood, pausing before they started to jog to a stand of poplars at the far side of the floodplain. Inexplicably, their trot accelerated, until they were madly sprinting for some reason neither understood, as if being chased by something more powerful than just the storm or anything that the natural world could hurl at them. And as they ran, side by side, Kazim could not resist glancing at Aysha's breasts undulating under the clinging fabric of her wet *kamiz*. He marveled at each stride of her long, tapered legs, and at the dark circles of her small areolas visible under the wet cotton.

When they reached the shelter of the trees, the rain was falling again but now more gently, it seemed. They sat down under the shelter of apricot trees, their lungs heaving from their run. The trees had long lost their fruit, but the canopy of the leaves was ample shelter from the rain, creating the impression that whatever they did under the arbor, wherever they ventured, would be their own secret. The humidity trapped under the branches kneaded the perspiration from their pores, the sweet smell of their sweating bodies melding with the scent of wet loam. The light was dim and glaucous. It was burning season, and the turbulent air wafted through the branches carrying the musty, charred scent of scorched hay stubble squelched by the rain.

Though they had escaped the storm outside, soon they were confronted with another, even more relentless. Kazim, a shade of disquietude now cast upon his face, struggled to restrain the unfamiliar sensation within him—a physical pain that shook his very roots, which he had for so long disguised under the veneer of decorum. He reached for the back of her wet hair and pulled her face into his chest. She pushed him back with her palms, but at the same time, she could not keep her lips from opening to taste the salt on his chest and neck. Kazim was surprised to find that his own free arm slipped under her *kamiz,* finding again the supple curvature of her breast, now damp with warm rainwater, until the tips of his fingers touched her hardened nipple.

"We mustn't," she said, resisting, yet at the same time inadvertently guiding his hand as it traced a line down the center of her belly and over her navel, where it fumbled to untie the string of her belt. He lifted her onto the ground and, kneeling over her, slid the wet cloth of her pants down over her hips. It was all new to Kazim, for no one had taught him any clues to unlocking the mystery that was suddenly, unexpectedly, unfurling before him.

But Aysha, who had been privy to so many of the intimacies of the village women, understood well enough, even if all the gossip and tawdry confessions could never prepare her for the madness that was now spiraling through their bodies. She also knew that she could not permit him to continue, as much as she wanted him to, for the ramifications of the act were such that they would taint her forever. But even while she pounded her balled fists against his back, her tears melding with the rain dripping through the branches, she found herself drawing him in, marveling at the relief she felt beneath the pain. Ever since she had been a child, when she had cried over the pale body of her little brother Sahib as he hung lifeless in his hammock, pain was something she had vowed to fight. At that moment, with Kazim's passion forging a new path inside her, she had invited it into her life.

Naseem and Fatima had been sitting cross-legged on the floor for hours, barely able to contain themselves, when Aysha finally tiptoed into the house. Her cheeks appeared flushed under the kerosene glow of the lantern, her black hair disheveled and slick with rainwater. Naseem studied her from afar as she quietly shuffled toward the women's quarters before he stood, a tower of a man, and moved to intercept her.

Aysha saw her father's large frame bolt from the shadows and she froze. They locked eyes. As Naseem stared at her intently, he turned his head sidelong. Slowly, his brow furrowed with disapproval. Then anger.

Aysha began to tremble. Feeling as if she might faint, she dropped to her knees. *Allah have mercy on me,* she prayed to herself. *He knows!*

Stunned, she pressed her palm over her mouth. A farmer must have spotted them under the trees and reported back to Naseem. Or a classmate of Kazim's, probably that redheaded Abdul, had followed them and spied their naked bodies entangled in sin. Abdul, no doubt, would have told the whole village just to spite her, if not to assuage what she had always suspected was jealousy.

Regardless, her life was now *over.* Having been proven unchaste in the eyes of the village, she had destroyed not only herself but also the honor of the entire Fahad clan. Her family's name could never be restored, except, according to a ruthless tribal tradition that few in Gilkamosh wanted to admit still existed in some circles, by her death—at her own hands or those of a family member. Aysha began to weep.

As Naseem watched his daughter cry, he sighed deeply. "Damn, that Advani," he grumbled. "*I'm* your father—not him! I made it very clear that *I* wanted to be the first to tell you!"

Aysha was confused by her father's words, but her tears continued unabated as Fatima stepped toward her and ran her fingers through Aysha's damp hair. "Oh, Naseem," she said. "Advani probably felt so awful, he could not wait to correct his mistake. Remember, this could have never happened were it not for him."

Fatima reached for Aysha's hands and urged her to her feet. "Stand up proudly, my daughter. Like the Prophet's favorite wife after whom you are named."

Aysha did as she was told. As she stood, she saw that her mother was also crying.

"Well . . . I see that tears of joy are contagious all around," said Naseem.

Aysha turned to her father. Naseem smiled as he rubbed an eye with his index finger. "I knew Advani's friend would not have the last word on it," he said.

Fatima squeezed Aysha's hands. Aysha looked back at her blankly.

"I am going to miss you so *very* much, Aysha," Fatima said, the tears now streaming freely down her cheeks. "But I am so proud of you. A real live *doctor.*" Fatima shook her head in disbelief. "Who could have thought such a thing possible for a girl from Gilkamosh? I *knew* you would be accepted. I said to you when you were just as tall as my navel, it is Allah's will . . . it *always* has been."

CHAPTER 13

Kazim first caught wind of the town's plan to send Aysha away to medical college several days after she had learned of her acceptance, when Mullah Yusuf brought it up during a lesson. Had anyone else denigrated with such vitriol the girl he loved, Kazim would have been enraged. But the mullah was a principled man. He could not help speaking out against blasphemy wherever he saw it. Kazim had to respect him for that, even while the mullah's words cut him deeply.

As for Mullah Yusuf, the event gave him just the stake he needed to drive into young Kazim's soul and claim it.

"Do you see how ignorant our people have become? This is what happens when Muslims permit themselves to be subjugated to the leadership of an infidel. Once again the Kashmiri Muslim has been robbed blind by the Hindu. But this time, the result is far worse than just theft. The Muslims of our village have not only been defrauded of their wealth—Allah forgive them for their stupidity—they have been stripped of their Islamic principles . . . the very fabric of their souls!"

Mullah Yusuf paused a moment, nodding silently, while the students murmured and shifted with agitation. "How has the Hindu infidel done this, you are wondering?" he continued. "Not by forcible larceny, as is usually the case. Nor by usurping our businesses, squatting on our land, levying extortionate taxes, or paying slave wages to our farmers and laborers. No. This Hindu Advani has done it with his silver tongue—the deceitful, forked serpent's tongue of a Hindu pandit. With this weapon he has persuaded these feeble-minded fools to piss away their hard-earned life savings—money they should be using to support their families, to grow their flocks, or to pay *zakat* for the benefit of the poor. And for what reason do they so freely give away their cherished nest eggs at the beckon of the infidel? To send a Muslim *girl*, with whom he no doubt wishes to fornicate, to a school run by infidels in order to become, of all things, a doctor.

"A *doctor* . . . ? Where has their morality gone!" the mullah shouted, shuddering with rage as he began to work himself into a frenzy. "Do not any of them have any scruples left in their indolent sheep brains! How can any self-respecting Muslim sanction such a thing—permitting a woman's eyes to wander over the bare bodies of thousands of men, to touch them, even to fondle their genitals! The pious have a name for this: *prostitution!*"

Mullah Yusuf stopped to catch his breath and wipe the droplets of foamy spittle from his long, straggly beard. He surveyed his students as they sat cross-legged on the floor in silent exhilaration. All were wide-eyed and thirsting for more, save one—Kazim. Yusuf was pleased to see the expression of his prized pupil change from shock to something darker, more profound.

"A woman's place is with the family," he continued, calming himself so that he could build again to a crescendo. "Her obligations are to serve her father until married, and thereafter, to serve her husband and his sons. These are a woman's sacred duties, bestowed upon her by Allah. She *cannot* dishonor them by venturing out into the world to work among men. And certainly *not* to examine and molest their bare flesh! A woman doctor is an affront to Allah. She is as degenerate and impure as a whore!"

Mullah Yusuf locked his eyes on Kazim, slicing the air with his finger as he bellowed: "Any man who permits his wife to pursue such an odious path repudiates the will of the Almighty! He shall die the agonizing death of a traitor and burn for all eternity in the hottest chambers of hell with the putrid, worm-eaten corpses of Islam's most accursed enemies!"

The mullah's voice resounded off the walls, until it gave way to a stunned silence. Then, after a suspended moment, the classroom erupted with thunderous applause.

As Kazim forced himself to clap with the others, he looked down to evade Mullah Yusuf's gaze, which he could feel boring into him. He admired his teacher more than anyone, and like the other students, he could not help feeling inspired, sometimes immobilized, by the intensity and passion of the mullah's diatribes, even this one.

But he had read the Qur'an countless times, and remembered nothing about women being forbidden from working. The Holy Book says that women must be modest and obedient to their husbands and should not commit adultery or otherwise compromise the trust of their marriage. But it says many of the same things of men. Would Mullah Yusuf deny men the opportunity to be doctors, too? Were not issues like secession from India, equal rights for Muslims, and union with fellow Kashmiris across the Line of Control more crucial than keeping women locked up in their homes? But with Mullah Yusuf, the larger issues that impassioned Kazim were always packaged with the window dressing of morality and sin.

"Kazim! Are you listening?"

"Yes, Mullah," Kazim replied, his eyes glazed in his own thoughts.

"What did I say? Go on, tell me!" he insisted, prepared to punish the boy.

"It is a sin for a woman to become a doctor. . . . It is a sin for a woman to work. . . . It is a sin for a woman to be out on the street without a burqa. . . ." Kazim's voice grew louder, more fervent as he spat back the mullah's rantings. "It is a sin for a woman to talk to a man who is not her husband! It is a sin for a man to touch a woman when she is menstruating! These are all sins! All sins!" Kazim slammed his fists on the floor, leaping to his feet. His eyes were wild with rage.

A dead silence fell over the madrassa. Taken aback, the mullah stared silently at Kazim. Then, after several long moments, a smug smile broke across his face. It was a smile of victory.

"Good . . . very good, my boy. . . . You show much promise."

As much as Kazim disagreed with Mullah Yusuf's invective, Aysha's betrayal had rendered him but a hollow shuck of the self-assured young man he had been only days ago. He was certain there had been a clear understanding between them that they would be married. He was only waiting for the opportune time, when he had attained a position of undeniable promise in his own mind, before asking Naseem for her hand. Now he had learned, from someone other than her, that she had planned to leave him all along, even while she had offered herself to him so convincingly. Clearly, his love was not good enough for her, not even to deserve her simple respect. She had made him her fool. And in so doing, she had gutted his pride, which at the painful transition from boyhood to manhood was something he held more precious than life itself.

Kazim avoided Aysha for three whole days while she desperately scoured Gilkamosh and the surrounding pastures, before she finally tracked him down.

* * *

October. The crisp air possessed utter stillness. They strode along the trail that cut into the mountainside above the village, affording a vista of the whole valley spread out on either side of the meandering river. The orchards were mantled with a dusting of newly fallen snow; the branches of the fruit trees, heavy and frozen, drooped toward the earth. Aysha and Kazim had spent many evenings strolling together through those groves, talking of their future. But this day they suffered from the deadlocked silence of two people who each know the other one has something consequential to say.

Finally, Kazim could bear it no longer. "I cannot believe you, Aysha," he scolded. "You are such a hypocrite! How could you not tell me? Do I mean nothing to you?"

Aysha frowned at the proof of what she had suspected—that he had found out about her acceptance to the institute. Her eyes begged him forgiveness. But perhaps because she felt she did not deserve it, her words lodged in her throat.

Kazim grabbed her firmly by the elbow. "I want an answer, damnit! Look me in the eye. Tell me why you never said you were leaving me to go to Delhi!"

Aysha raised her eyes. "Because I am not."

Confused, Kazim stared at her. "What do you mean you're not going? You have always wanted to be a doctor. And it's what *they* want . . . what they expect."

"I know. That is why I let it go as far as it did. What a mess I made. I'm sorry, Kazim, *please*. I didn't tell you, well . . . because I didn't think I'd get in." Aysha pressed her palm to Kazim's chest. "I love you, Kazim. And if I go, and lose you, I would want to die."

Kazim's eyes softened. During the last three days while Aysha had been trying to find him, he had prepared himself for a parting of ways. Aysha's alternative choice—to stay with him in Gilkamosh—had never even entered his mind as a possibility. In his self-pity he had miscalculated her feelings and underestimated himself. He turned his back to her, afraid an embarrassing tear might cut loose from his eye.

"Kazim . . . ?" She reached above his elbow, cupping the firm muscle of his arm. He merely glanced at her hand, afraid that by holding it, she would disarm his inner resolve. Tears began to stream down Aysha's face. "Speak to me, Kazim, please! Tell me you're happy that I am staying."

Kazim gazed out at the snow-laden valley. Goats were foraging the hill-sides, nosing under the snow for vestiges of greenery. A shepherd boy, clutching a lamb, ran to catch up to his flock. Kazim saw in the boy a glimpse of himself ten years ago, and it filled him with melancholy. Things were so much more complicated now. Life was not just a matter of tending his father's herds, falling in love, and having children. There were principles and ideals, things for which to fight. The struggle had already inflamed the Vale of Kashmir. Real mujahideen—Islamic freedom fighters—were engaging the Indian troops. At times just the thought of it made him delirious with pride.

Over and again, he had rehearsed in his mind what was going to happen. She would tell him that she was leaving for Delhi, and he would feign unconcern. But now that Aysha had chosen the unexpected, nothing was going as he had anticipated. Still, he had made up his mind to choose a higher calling. The arrangements had already been made. It was too late to change it now.

"I love you, too, Aysha. I wanted to marry you since the first time I saw you."

"Oh, Kazim, *please* . . . let's do it right now!"

"No," he cut her off. "That's not what I am saying."

"Then, what is it?"

"You should go to Delhi, Aysha."

"Go . . . ? You are coming with me?" Her eyes sparked with hope.

"Please, just listen to me. We can be together later. When you are done."

"That could be over five *years* from now. You would wait that long?"

Kazim nodded.

"But . . . I don't want to wait, Kazim," she said, her voice growing desperate.

"You must. Even if you were to stay in Gilkamosh, you must."

"What do you mean?"

"I am leaving, too," said Kazim. "I cannot say where. But I will be gone for a long time."

"You can't say? Well . . . why not?"

"You would not understand it," Kazim replied.

"Look, I know I'm in no position to complain. But if I am going to wait for years to be your wife, you at least have to tell me what you will be doing until then."

Kazim considered this. She was right, there was no hiding it. Not from his love. "You must swear to me that you will never tell anyone. I mean it."

Aysha paused, perplexed. "But I keep everyone's secrets. Surely, I can keep my future husband's."

"It is more than just a secret. If you tell, it will risk my life."

Aysha's eyes widened in fear. He stared back unflinchingly.

"I would never," she said. "I swear. By my love."

Kazim hesitated. "I am going across the Line of Control into Pakistan. I will be training to become a mujahideen."

Aysha looked at him in disbelief. What she had read in the newspapers about the insurgency sweeping the Vale had appalled her. How *anyone*, let alone her Kazim, would want to be part of it was beyond her comprehension.

"Whose idea was it? Mullah Yusuf's?" Her voice was filled with hostility.

"What kind of a question is that!" Kazim snapped. "You think I am too ignorant to have my own ideas?"

"People don't decide to kill themselves on their own! It's like . . . deciding to get a cancer!" Aysha shouted, pressing her palms to her temples.

"I told you, Aysha!" Kazim fumed. "I told you, you would not understand. But you . . . you begged me. So now that I have done as you asked, do not go and belittle me like you always do!"

His words stung her. It was the "other" Kazim speaking to her now— the one she had seen a year ago, when he said all those hateful things about Advani. She wiped the tears now flowing freely from her eyes.

"So then you will go and fight for these . . . guerrillas. And if the police or the army do not kill you first, then whenever it all ends—two years or five or ten years from now—we will get married. Is that your plan?"

"It will not be that long . . . but, to be fair, Aysha, I am telling you to go to Delhi. Become a doctor. Do what you have always wanted to do."

"*Fair?*" Aysha pounded his chest with her fist. "What's fair about being in love with a man who wants to go off and kill himself!"

Aysha fell to her knees, her face buried in her arms. A moment earlier Kazim could have slapped her for her arrogance. Now he was riven with his own sadness, and resentment for having misread her love. He just wanted it to end.

"I'll be back, Aysha. I promise," he said gently, stroking her silken hair, as she kneeled at his feet like a child.

Kazim lifted her chin with his fingers. For the first time, he saw that she was suffering the same pain of uncertainty he had always known in her presence, and he could not help feeling an odd sense of bittersweet satisfaction that by making her suffer, he had the ability to perfect her beauty.

"Who knows," Kazim said at last, "maybe by the time you are done with your training, the war will be over. When you come home, you will open the first new hospital in free Kashmir."

"Stop it, Kazim! All I want is *you*. Not your damned freedom."

He shook his head. "I am sorry, Aysha. I must do this. I must go."

CHAPTER 14

Nicholas Sunder lifted his knees, one at a time, onto the windowsill of his hotel room. Slowly, he spun himself around so that his head and shoulders faced the interior. The bulk of his rucksack, something he had overlooked, forced him to hunch his back and lean forward in order to avoid snagging it. This caused his knees to slide out from under him. His legs plummeted.

Nick lunged for the lower lip of the window frame, his kneecaps slamming against the outside wall. Digging in with his fingers, he struggled against the pull of his weight. He was slipping.

Nick twisted and writhed like a hooked worm, swinging his legs in a wide arc. His boots scraped against the outer wall, dislodging a chunk of stucco that smashed loudly on the cobblestones below. At the top of its swing, the toe of his right boot barely caught a hold on the fire escape. Thrusting his hips sideways, Nick shifted his weight onto his toehold and lunged with both arms, just managing to snatch the metal railing with his fingers before gravity could suck him down.

Nick pulled himself onto the escape ladder. Certain that someone must have heard the shattering stucco, he froze in panic, expecting floodlights to blind him. But the moment passed. He climbed down the ladder and vanished into the dark alley.

Nick scurried alongside the hotel, hugging the walls as he moved. Wan starlight provided the only illumination. He walked swiftly but with measured steps, searching the darkness for pitfalls—fetid gutters, gaping potholes, loose bricks fallen from moldering walls, the lumps of sleeping homeless. One misstep could cause a tumble onto the head-splitting cobblestones or send him plunging into an open sewer.

When he reached the inner recesses of the old city, the humid air was thick with the odor of stinking bodies. Whole families slept in the street, huddled together under shawls or beneath the narrow alcoves formed by shop fronts, now cordoned off from would-be thieves by sheets of corrugated steel fastened shut by huge medieval-looking padlocks. But for the occasional staccato of a sickly cough, the street people were sepulchral in their muted stillness.

He veered right, down the sinuous footpath leading into the produce sector of the bazaar. He stopped briefly to check if anyone had trailed him before following the pungent odor of rot through the closed vegetable and bread stalls. The signs of Darwinian struggle between man and vermin were everywhere. Clans of homeless children—Afghan war refugees—rummaged in the darkness, through gutters and heaps of garbage piled outside the bakeries, using sticks to beat the rats away from stale scraps of bread discarded the day before.

When he saw the parapetted silhouette of Bala Hisar Fortress suffused with moonlight, Nick knew he was close. He scuttled down the walkway behind the Mosque of Mahabat Khan toward the crumbling caravanserai, which served as an atrium to the fortress's western entrance. He halted in front of the dark parabola of the stone archway leading into the courtyard where the truck was to be parked.

He scanned the dark for signs of police—*nothing*—then checked his watch. It was a minute before one o'clock. He could hardly restrain himself from sprinting.

Passing under the archway, he walked the inner berm of the ancient fortress, reaching the far side of the ruin where the remains of the old colonial fire station stood. The large-spoked wheels of the antique horse-drawn fire wagon—a tribute to posterity aimed at the handful of tourists who visited Peshawar during safer times—cast an eerie, striated shadow over the ground. He crept around the back of the crumbling walls of the fire station, where several donkeys stood humped over and asleep in the walkway, and came upon a stand of shrubby junipers.

He saw an open space of packed dirt across the trees, partially concealed by the walls of the compound—the lot where the truck was supposed to be. *But there was no truck.*

Feeling exposed, Nick moved among the trees, stumbling over a figure sitting cross-legged in the shadows. "Allah!" the shrouded man whispered hoarsely.

"Sorry," Nick replied in a hushed tone—foolishly in English.

The seated figure shuffled, his shawl concealing his face. "No problem," he replied, also in English, before returning his gaze to the lot. As Nick scanned the darkness, he noticed that lumpy shadows he had previously dismissed as bushes were the hunched forms of other men covered with shawls.

As crucial minutes slipped away without any sign of the truck, Nick grew increasingly nervous. Could it have left already? Crouching amid the mingled scent of juniper, tobacco, and unwashed bodies, he prayed for the truck to arrive.

A half hour later, a truck finally approached, one of the old British-built Bedford lorries prevalent in Pakistan, with their high, wood-framed canopies and cabins painted in bright geometrical designs, adorned with silver frills and sequins. Its lights were off, even though the clamor of the motor would have woken the dead.

The Bedford came to a stop. Nick took his cue from the others, who waited under the cover of the trees instead of rushing forward. The cabin door swung open. A man climbed down, his face invisible in the dark. When he approached the trees, he cupped his hands to his mouth and said something in Pashto. The Afghans rose all at once and stormed into the truck without bothering to open the tailgate.

Nick hesitated, unsure whether this was *his* truck—the one he had paid Masood to arrange. He trotted over to the driver, who was already climbing into the cabin. "Are you going to Torkham?" he asked in a hushed tone.

The driver looked at Nick with confusion. He waved his hand in front of his ear to signal his nonunderstanding, and then started to pull away. "Hey, wait!" yelled Nick, pounding on the door.

Irate, the driver stuck his head out of the side window, and cursed him in Pashto. A glimpse of his face revealed freckled, splotchy-white albino skin and pinkish, mouselike eyes. His pure white *shalwar kamiz* and woven skullcap, even in the darkness, seemed to accentuate his genetic oddity.

"Stop . . . please," Nick pleaded. "I need to get to Torkham."

The albino driver braked, then he turned to a Pashtun sitting next to him. They spoke to each other briefly. "Engleesh?" the albino asked.

"American," said Nick after some hesitation. "I arranged transport to Torkham—through Masood."

"Masood?" he repeated, pulling on his mustache.

"Yes, yes, Masood!" Nick said. "You know Masood?"

The albino nodded ambiguously. "Okay, okay," he said, thrusting his thumb at the rear of the truck, a signal that gave Nick no assurance whatsoever this was the vehicle he was supposed to take. The truck started to leave. Nick hesitated before realizing he had no choice but to bolt for it. At a full run, he reached for the extended hands of the Afghans perched against the tailgate, who hauled him on board.

The cargo area overflowed with compressed bodies—fifty or sixty men packed in on top of one another. Nick made his way into the interior, unable to avoid crawling over the limbs and laps of other passengers. The men, however, helped him along, lifting and passing his weight from one to another, contorting their bodies in order to make room for him.

Nick settled in not far from the rear. He had a view out the back through a gap in the canvas that hung down from the roof, covering the otherwise exposed opening over the low tailgate. He pulled his bandanna low over his eyes and crouched, resting his elbows on his knees. As the truck sped through the archway of the caravanserai, rousing a donkey to bray, he stared at the ancient fortress receding in a blur.

The Bedford raced west through the narrow streets of the old city until they gave way to the dusty avenues of the modern outskirts, where the road widened. Vast cement-block apartment buildings lined the road. Accelerating rapidly, the truck turned north. Nick shook his fist in relief when he saw the sign that read partially in English AUTONOMOUS TRIBAL REGION OF KHYBER—40 KM—FOREIGNERS NOT ALLOWED.

A few minutes later, they reached the city periphery and the avenue turned into a roadway of broken tarmac. The Afghans clutched their blankets over their heads against the bite of the wind. A thick mantle of dust had accumulated on their shoulders and beards, so that only their eyes stood out. Nick held his head between his knees, the deafening drone of the motor crowding out all sensations but the cold cutting through to his bones.

Later, when the moon rose, illuminating the earth in dark grays and tawny browns, the road turned from fissured tarmac to potholed gravel and dirt. Occasional mud brick dwellings and emaciated livestock were the only signs of habitation.

Despite the wind and cold and the sickening diesel fumes, Nick was elated. He was speeding away from Peshawar, and all of the horrors there. If he survived, he vowed somehow he would find a way of repaying the one-armed Afghan beyond the commission he must have earned on the money Nick had paid. No price would be enough. But it would be a while before he could do so. After making the ATM withdrawals in Peshawar, he had under two thousand dollars left in his savings account, barely enough to buy a plane ticket back to America. Soon, he would be completely broke, having used up his entire savings, all that was left of the money he had earned from his days as a lawyer in America—a job to which he felt that he could never return.

He had arrived in Asia two years and four months earlier looking for something he could not define, knowing only that he needed to get out of his life in America, which, for reasons he did not fully comprehend, had been stifling him. He had practiced law in Boston for nearly seven years with a reputable firm that specialized in litigation and white-collar criminal defense. The long hours had not been difficult for him; he had worked from the age of twelve until college in his father's landscaping business, and as a former high school wrestler, he had acquired the competitive, brawler mentality that makes for good litigators. As he moved up through the ranks, he had built a reputation for being skilled in the courtroom and persuasive with juries—a regular guy who could relate to "the people." Though his firm did not pay the exorbitant salaries of the elite law firms on State Street, by the time he was a sixth-year associate, he had paid off his college loans and amassed the kinds of possessions that are supposed to make young lawyers willing to consume the prime years of their lives tucked away in sterile offices—a one-bedroom condo in Back Bay, an Audi, and a Whaler docked in Marblehead, which he never had time to use.

Though he had detested the research and writing aspect of legal practice, he enjoyed the rush of arguing before a jury in an expensive suit, exaggerating his otherwise slight North Shore accent so that they would know he came from them, beating up on arrogant, big-firm lawyers who could not touch his rapport with the jury and regretted not having settled before trial. In short, Nick had been the perfect associate, tough, hard-working, a shoe-in for partnership.

Then, within the span of a year, everything changed. His slide downward seemed to have started with his most successful courtroom victory, his defense of Leonard Hannon, one of the firm's wealthiest clients. Hannon had been the owner of a thirty-year-old Revolutionary War–themed amusement park called Libertyland outside Hyannis on Cape Cod, which he had bought out of Chapter 11 from its previous owners. The rides were outdated and rickety, the whole place a tort waiting to happen. When a seventeen-year-old boy was thrown off the Cannon Coaster, suffering multiple fractures and a severe concussion, the partners assigned Nick to defend Hannon at his trial on criminal negligence charges brought by the state for Hannon's alleged failure to keep the roller coaster in a safe working condition. The partners presented the case as Nick's chance to prove himself worthy of partnership, but in truth, it was a loser that none of them wanted to touch.

Nick, however, shocked them all. Through pure diligence and painstaking investigation, he found a witness, an off-duty police officer moonlighting as parking lot security, to testify that he had seen the teenager quite possibly ingesting hallucinogenic mushrooms with his friends before entering the park. Though he had no hard evidence to make any specific contentions, Nick was able to raise at least a question in the jury's mind about whether the teen might have recklessly unbuckled his safety belt and himself been the cause of the accident. No jury *wants* to side with some drugged-out teenager, especially when they suspect he is just after money. Nick pulled off a perfect case of character assassination, Hannon was acquitted on all charges, and he stayed open for business.

Then, exactly three months after the verdict, one of the cars of the very same roller coaster flew off the track, decapitating three patrons—Bob and Linda Cole and their eight-year-old daughter, Susie. A whole family wiped from existence in a fraction of a second. A grade school portrait depicting Susie's gap-toothed smile was emblazoned on the front page of all the local papers, burned into the memories of the state's citizens. Especially Nick's.

Nick was not to blame; he had only done his job well. All of the partners had told him so. His colleagues rolled their eyes at the obligatory news reports that had lambasted his "despicable" trial tactics, which, though perfectly permissible under the canons of professional ethics, had arguably prevented the park from being shut down by the state, thereby enabling the tragedy. And perhaps predictably, the firm's business only swelled after Nick's successful defense of Hannon made him the scapegoat of statewide antilawyer sentiment. Nonetheless, the partners began to note a decrease in his billable hours. He even missed a few filing deadlines. Nick promised the partners to get back on track, and indeed, he put in a few solid 250-billable-hour months in a row. But then his mother suffered her third stroke in two years, this last one finally sending her from a state of moderate dementia into a permanent coma. After nearly a month of indecision, during which all his cases fell to pieces, he finally signed papers to take her off life support. Then, a few days later, he smashed his Audi into a tree. Police arrived on the scene, and his blood-alcohol content tested at twice the legal limit.

After he pleaded guilty to driving under the influence and paid the hefty fine, he faced the mandatory state bar disciplinary committee's hearing on whether his license should be suspended for substance abuse. Suspension was not really a serious threat. It was his first transgression—mere probation and a few Alcoholics Anonymous meetings would have been in order. Indeed, better lawyers than he had pickled their livers through winning careers. Still, Nick approached the hearing with inconsolable dread.

Watercooler talk at the firm posited that Nick had gone soft, that he felt *guilt*—that nagging emotion inimical to the principles of zealous advocacy—for the Libertyland tragedy. But those deaths were only part of it (after all, he *was* just doing his job, and he *had* counseled Hannon to renovate the park). The obliterated family of three, his decision to let his mother finally die, the disgust he felt expending such a huge percentage of his waking hours and his talent to preserve the wealth and status of undeserving clients—all combined to render him rudderless and confused. The life he had built for himself, that he had worked so hard to achieve, suddenly seemed meaningless at best, parasitic at worst. He began to see his license to practice law as a crutch, even began to loathe it. He could envision his future before him, from partnership to death, and nothing about what he foresaw inspired him anymore.

Nick skipped the disciplinary hearing, and because he did not show, his license was suspended and then ultimately revoked. Without a plan or any desire for one, he resigned from the firm (sparing his partners the need to fire him), sold his condominium and all of his possessions, and with enough savings in the bank to travel for a couple years on the cheap, bought ten books of traveler's checks and a one-way flight to Bangkok.

As he crouched in the back of the overcrowded truck, that man he once was seemed no more familiar to him than the impoverished, hollow-eyed refugees crammed in around him.

* * *

The Bedford slowed as it approached the checkpoint into the Tribal Areas. The Afghans pulled their shawls up over their chins, transforming the entire flatbed into a clutter of turbans and caps. Although Nick harbored no illusions of concealing his foreign face, he stood out sorely without a blanket. As if discerning the reason for Nick's edginess, the man next to him offered part of his own. "*Shukria,*" Nick thanked him, pulling one side of the blanket over his face.

The checkpost was nothing more than a lean-to guardhouse with a couple of poles across the road. A single guard with an AK-47 slung across his shoulder approached the truck, while another sat in the guardhouse, asleep. They wore the uniform of the Frontier Guards—tan *shalwar kamiz* with black sweaters pulled over them and green berets. A third soldier sat in the hut on the far side of the road. From his standard-issue fatigues and darker face, Nick guessed he was Pakistani army.

The albino driver and the guard at the truck exchanged salaams and conversed briefly in Pashto. Their tone was friendly, but this did nothing to mitigate the tension on the faces of the Afghans sitting around Nick. The guard walked to the back of the truck. Peering in, he shined the beam of his flashlight from face to face.

As the beam hit the men in turn, they pulled down their blankets to show their faces. The guard continued down the line, examining each one. Nick waited breathlessly. Westerners were not allowed in this part of the Tribal Areas without a special permit. If the bribe had not been paid by Masood, he was finished.

Before he could think what to do, the flashlight was upon him. He hesitated, the beam blinding in his eyes. Then, without any choice, he pulled the blanket down. The light fell on his face. Bowing his head, Nick waited for the command to climb out into the cold.

He heard the grumble of the engine. The gate lifted. The lorry jolted forward, kicking up a plume of dust that obscured the road to Peshawar behind them. *God bless Masood!* Nick uttered in silent jubilation.

CHAPTER 15

The lorry turned off the road that led to the Afghan border. It bounced along a dusty jeep track for several miles before it arrived at a settlement of clustered mud-brick dwellings and weathered tents. The albino driver climbed out of the cabin and walked to the rear of the flatbed. Nick noted he was devoid of facial hair, with only a few thin, milky curls spilling out from under his skullcap. He hollered something in Pashto, and within a few moments, the whole truckload of Afghans had hopped down over the tailgate and disappeared into the desert night like ghosts, heading northwest toward Afghanistan on foot.

Nick looked around, unsure what to do. The settlement was dark except for a solitary gas lamp that illuminated the interior of a tent. "Hey, aren't you taking me to Torkham?" Nick called out to the driver.

"Come," he replied with a nod.

Nick followed the albino into the interior of an open tent where two turbaned Pashtuns sat around the table, smoking cigarettes and playing backgammon. A radio played Arabic pop music. Crates labeled with Chinese characters were piled to the roof. Nick presumed the men were smugglers.

The albino greeted the two Pashtuns in the traditional manner—gently bumping their chests while clutching the waist, one hug on each side of the body, left then right. To Nick, the ritual seemed too tender, wholly out of character with the fierce-looking Pashtuns. One of the turbaned Pashtuns waved Nick toward the table and pulled out a chair. "No, thank you. I'd like to get going," Nick said.

"Sit," he commanded, ignoring the urgency in Nick's voice.

Someone poured Nick some tea, which he warily pretended to sip, having heard stories from fellow travelers about being drugged and robbed in Central Asia. Nick was not sure that these were the men actually hired by Masood's contacts and could not take any chances. The conversation in Pashto continued, until the eldest, a gray-bearded Pashtun with hashish-inspired eyes, spoke to Nick in thickly accented, broken English. "You Mr. Nick?"

"Yes." Nick sighed in relief, for it meant they were indeed Masood's contacts. "Yes, I am."

"You pay. Two thousand dollar," said the graybeard.

Nick paused. "I think you've made a mistake. I already paid Masood a thousand dollars. We agreed I would pay the other thousand when I get to Gilgit."

"Two thousand dollar. You pay now," he insisted, this time more adamantly.

"Again, you've misunderstood. My agreement with Masood . . . you know Masood? When you take me to Gilgit, I pay you a thousand dollars when I change trucks."

"Truck? . . . Truck here." He pointed toward the vehicle in which Nick arrived.

"No. Not *that* truck. When I get to—"

"You pay now!" He slammed his hand on the table.

Nick wiped his face in frustration. At that moment the most important thing was to get as far away from Peshawar as he could, as quickly as possible. For all he knew, the police had already discovered he was missing, and each second lost increased his chances of being hunted down and sent to the gallows.

"Fine. I'll pay the remaining balance now," Nick submitted. The three Pashtuns watched Nick closely as he reached under his *kamiz* pants for his money belt. He handed over a wad of cash, the one thousand dollars that he had already segregated and expected to pay in Gilgit, to the gray-bearded Pashtun. The tribesman thumbed through the bills.

"No good!" he snarled. "I tell you two thousand dollar!"

Nick clutched his temples, turning to the others. "Please—doesn't anyone speak English?" he asked in frustration. "I have no money left," said Nick, turning his open money belt upside down. "See? All gone."

The men shifted their eyes back and forth between Nick and the gray-bearded Pashtun. The truculent elder began to holler at the white-haired albino. A flurry of sharp-tongued rebukes and angry retorts flew back and forth. Then the elder Pashtun reached for a Kalashnikov leaning against the card table.

Chaos erupted—furious shouting, the glint of gunmetal flashing under the orange glow of the lantern, a whirlwind of motion as pistols materialized from under cloaks. When the pandemonium stopped, Nick's hands were raised high in the air. The Pashtuns, however, pointed their guns not at Nick, but rather, in a confusing array of alliances, at each other.

After a tense moment, the graybeard mumbled something and casually lowered his Kalashnikov. The others followed suit, their tempers oddly subsiding as fast as they had flared. The graybeard grabbed Nick's hand and thrust the money back into it. He pointed toward the truck, glaring at Nick. "Go."

"Where?" Nick had no desire to revive the dispute, but he needed an answer. The old man pointed to the southeast, toward Peshawar.

The albino, who had not said anything to Nick since the dispute, shook his head. "Not enough. Must go back."

"No. I *can't!*"

The old graybeard, stronger than his years suggested, grabbed Nick around the elbow and began pulling him out of the tent. "*Please!* I paid already." Nick wrenched free of his grip and reached for his boot. The men grabbed for their guns. "Wait!" cried Nick. "I've got more money."

At gunpoint Nick cautiously untied his bootlaces and extracted his last five hundred dollars of reserve cash, which he had wrapped in a plastic bag. He held it out to them. In abstract, offering his last bit of money was a foolish thing to do, as there would be no banks of any sort anywhere near where he was traveling, except possibly Gilgit, where showing his face would be insane given that it was a Pakistani army post. But he had no other choice. "Here . . . here's another five hundred dollars. All together, I've given you fifteen hundred dollars on top of the thousand dollars I already gave to Masood. It's *all* that I have. I swear. *Please.*" Nick pleaded, joining his palms in supplication. "I can't go back to Peshawar."

The graybeard studied Nick a moment, and then haggled with the albino in Pashto. Finally, the graybeard snatched the money from Nick's hands, counted out what looked like two thirds of it, and handed the rest to the albino. "In Torkham, another truck take you to Gilgit," said the albino to Nick. "After that—finish," he motioned with a sweep of his hand.

"What about India? That was the deal with Masood."

"He does not care what you pay Masood. He cares what you pay *him.* In Gilgit it is not hard to find transport going east. Good luck, Engleesh.

Kuddah hafiz," said the albino, his white clothes billowing as he receded into the darkness toward his lorry.

A short while later, a beaten gray Toyota pickup pulled up. The old Pashtun stood and motioned for Nick. Behind the wheel was the second man, the graybeard's backgammon partner from the tent. He was stoned on hashish, clearly unfit to drive. Nick noticed a Kalashnikov resting on the front seat.

The elder pointed at the exposed flatbed and climbed into the passenger seat. There was no canopy and Nick worried he would be too conspicuous sitting out in the open compartment, especially in a few hours once the sun started rising. Nick guessed that it would take longer than that to drive over the mountains to Torkham, and they could run into army vehicles on the way.

"Out in the open?" Nick said. The driver pointed to a heap of dust-covered blankets piled in the back. Nick shook his head in exasperation and then, reluctantly, he climbed in. Pulling the blankets over his legs, he braced himself against the wind.

Though Nick could see nothing in the blackness but the dirt road winding under the wheels like an endless desert viper, an eerie feeling of familiarity came over him. He had explored the Tribal Areas a few times since he had been in Peshawar, each time visiting different regions, but the landscape had seemed to be the same everywhere. Scrubby sun-baked hills, dried riverbeds, scorpion-infested chasms—a lifeless moonscape of monochrome khaki. It astonished him how even vultures could survive in such arid bleakness, let alone the mangy goats that, along with their yield from smuggling, provided the Pashtun tribesmen with sustenance.

Just over a week earlier, he had traveled to the village of Darra Adam Khel, probably some sixty or seventy miles from where he was now, to see the gun factories of Darra bazaar with Yvette and Simon. Simon had recently shown up in Peshawar, and Yvette had wanted them all to do something adventurous together, a kind of kickoff to their reunion. Though she had no interest at all in guns, and would have preferred to do something else altogether, she eventually submitted to Nick's suggestion that they visit Darra. There had been an unspoken tension among the three of them since Simon's arrival, and she had felt a little collective adventure might help smooth things over. Through Masood, Nick arranged the transport and bribes for the tribal police, necessary because Darra was off-limits to foreigners.

Once they were there, the local tribesmen permitted them free rein to wander through the bustling gunsmith shops that lined either side of the road, which ran between steep cliffs at the base of the Kohat Pass. The men, Pashtuns from the Afridi subtribe, appeared to Nick like long-bearded Central Asian versions of banditos, many of them with pistol holsters and double bandoleers criss-crossing their chests and AK-47s slung over their shoulders.

The workers, some just children, used primitive methods of manufacture that had been obsolete and probably forgotten in the West for centuries. They cast steel parts in sand molds, pouring the molten metal into handheld crucibles, and used water and pedal-powered drills to bore rifling into gun barrels. Gunstocks were carved from wood, and metal parts meticulously engraved by hand with chisels and picks. But despite the crude tools, the impressive Afridis were manufacturing modern small arms of every size, type, and make by the hundreds, ranging from small pistols to heavy machine guns, all exact replicas of name brands from around the world.

The makeshift factories adjoined display shops, where weapons of all makes and vintages were openly exhibited for sale, many of them locally manufactured knockoffs. "Enough firepower to establish your own empire," said Simon. "And they're not even shy about it."

"Yes," said Yvette, unamused, glancing at Nick. "Your War on Terror is really working, isn't it, Nicholas."

There were early model Martini-Henrys, World War II–era M1 Garands, and even German Lugers and rare Schmeisser submachine guns. There were Vietnam-era Colt M16s, and the whole gamut of captured Soviet and Chinese-supplied weaponry dating to the war against the Soviets—Russian Krinkov submachine guns, Dragunov sniper rifles, and everywhere the ubiquitous AK-47. One store even sold derringers that fit into tailor-made belt buckles, and "pen guns"—they looked and wrote like ballpoint pens but fired a single .22 caliber bullet, designed specifically for surprise, close-quarter assassinations.

"You must try!" a lanky Pashtun named Arif said in heavily accented English, sweeping his arm wide through the hundred-gun display in one of the shops. "Any one you wish. You pick." He leered at Yvette and plucked a replica Uzi submachine gun from one of the shelves. "This little one good for the lady, I think."

"No, no," said Yvette. "If I'm going to do it, I prefer mine to be big, like that one." She pointed to a Chinese shoulder-fired rocket launcher.

"Very clever, madam," said Arif approvingly. "Crush all your enemies with just one shot. But, I am so sorry, that one is not allowed for testing. Big explosion might cause avalanche on people's houses."

"In that case," Nick said, "I say, when in Rome . . ." He pointed to one of the AK-47s, eager to try out the mujahideen weapon of choice.

After they had agreed to pay Arif for one hundred rounds of ammo at ten rupees a round, he led the three of them to a nearby street lined with crumbling dwellings. "Shoot there," he said, pointing to the ridge above the homes. They looked where he was pointing and saw an old man in a skullcap sitting on a wooden bench downrange of them. Arif handed Nick the Kalashnikov.

"But the homes?" Nick inquired.

"Nicholas," Yvette said. "It's not safe."

"It is no problem, madam," Arif insisted. "I show you." He snatched the gun from Nick's hands and in a single burst emptied the clip on fully automatic, the fusillade of bullets spraying into the hillside above the dwellings in an explosion of dust. A group of children playing nearby scrambled behind doors and dropped to their knees, holding their hands over their ears. To the old man on the bench, however, it was business as usual. He never flinched.

Arif, beaming from ear to ear, handed the gun back to Nick. "You go now."

"No, no, this is stupid," said Yvette, an uncharacteristic display of caution. "It could ricochet. We pay for the bullets, but no shooting. Look," Yvette said, pointing. "People are scared."

They all looked downrange at the dwellings again. Someone reached out of one of the windows, pulling shut a pair of wooden shutters. Nick and Simon shared a look, considering.

"It's okay, I tell you," said Arif, affronted by Yvette's indignation. "This is where we shoot. Aim high, no problem. I insist."

Yvette looked at Arif, and then glared at Nick. "I want nothing to do with this," she said and stormed off in disgust.

Nick watched her walk away. Then he turned to Simon, who was grinning. "Well, she's right about one thing," Simon said with sarcasm.

"They certainly have tight safety standards." He shrugged. "Like you said, Nick—when in Rome . . ."

Nick considered Simon's dare. Then, almost spitefully, he lifted the weapon to his shoulder and with one squeeze of the trigger fired a long, gratifying burst of lead high into the hillside, while Simon snapped photos of him with his digital camera. When Nick was through, he let out a hearty cowboy yelp. Simon then took his turn with the gun, enjoying it almost as much, and they even bought another hundred rounds over Yvette's objection, trying several different weapons.

Afterward, they sat down at a food stall where a barefoot, white-bearded old man in a lime green turban grilled minced goatburgers on a massive rounded skillet. There they waited for the transport arranged by Masood to pick them up and take them back to Peshawar. Yvette's mood had turned sulky and petulant, something that had been happening frequently in recent days. "I cannot believe you," she said suddenly to Nick. "You are such an asshole! What if you had killed someone?"

"Everyone had cleared out," Nick replied. "And that guy, Arif, he wasn't going to take no for an answer. So just relax. It was actually kind of fun—you should have tried it."

"Of course it was *fun* for you. You Americans love your goddamn guns."

"Hey, I wasn't the only shooter."

"Thanks for spreading the love, Nick," said Simon, who was clicking through his recent snapshots on the screen of his digital camera. He paused to examine one of them more closely. "Oh, man," he murmured, snickering. "From now on, you'd better watch your step with me, my friend."

"Oh, yeah?" said Nick. "Why is that?"

"I've got blackmail material on you." Simon turned the screen of his camera, revealing a snapshot of Nick firing a burst into the mountainside with Arif's AK-47. With his thick beard, Chitrali cap, and long *shalwar kamiz*, he could have passed for some kind of Caucasian jihadist. "All I've got to do is post this baby on the Internet, and you'll be marked a public enemy. The next John Walker Lindh. FBI will be waiting to arrest your ass as soon as you set foot on American soil."

"I don't think so," Nick scoffed. "Maybe I'd be scared if I were Muslim."

"How would they know that you're *not*? Becoming a Muslim is simple. All you've got to do is recite 'There is no god but Allah, and Muhammad is His messenger' in front of a couple of witnesses who are already members of the persuasion. The whole thing probably takes a minute or two. It's what comes after that's the tough part—no booze or premarital sex, praying at god-awful hours.

"If you want," Simon kidded, "I bet there are plenty of guys around here willing to stand up for you. By the looks of some of them, they might even be able to swear you into al Qaeda at the same time."

"Interesting tidbit of information, Simon," said Nick. "But not for me. I was born without the religion gene. And to tell you the truth, I don't really regret it."

"Suit yourself," Simon said.

Yvette, who had been ignoring their conversation, sighed with impatience. "Where the hell is our driver?" she interjected. "Guns everywhere. I fucking hate guns," she muttered, her gloominess transformed to angry frustration. "And I hate this fucking place. This Kalashnikov culture, it's . . . it's . . . not . . ."

"*Natural?*" Nick said, facetiously completing the sentence for her.

"Don't make fun of me," she snapped. "This place is a culture of death. Probably built by your fucking CIA. I want to go back to Peshawar now. Why did you make me come here?"

Nick looked at her, perplexed. "I did *what?* We talked about this, Yvette. You said you wanted to come. So we could all be together like—"

"Be quiet, Nicholas," she cut him off. "*Please* . . . just stop your mouth."

The three of them sat in silence and waited for Masood's transport to pick them up, while attempting to devour their goatburgers, an undertaking they soon abandoned due to their inability to prevent the swarms of ravenous, dime-sized flies from dive-bombing headlong, and at great speed, into the greasy meat. Yvette's outburst, coupled with their frustrated appetites, had caused such tension that they were almost relieved when a clean-shaven stranger wearing a Western-style tan chapeau sat down next to them in an obvious effort to strike up conversation.

"My name is Hassan Abdullah Ali Khan," the man had said. "But to make it easier on your Western ears, please call me 'Prince.'"

At nearly six feet, gaunt, with a pencil-thin mustache and darting black eyes, he explained he was a member of a "royal family" of the Kailash, a tribe of modern-day pagans who claimed descent from Alexander's Macedonian troops, isolated over the centuries from the spread of

Islam by the mountains. "Prince," nevertheless, was Muslim, and they guessed he had concocted his Kailash lineage to impress tourists.

"I am a guide, sir. I could not help but notice you are very good marksman. Would you like to buy the Kalashnikov you shot? I know the seller. I can get a good deal for you. Or maybe something you can carry in your luggage, like a pen gun perhaps? I can get you anything you want, sir—*anything* at all."

"No, thanks," Nick replied, wanting to get off the subject of guns. It was obvious to Nick the interloper was another of the ubiquitous charlatans looking to finagle a few bucks out of gullible foreigners. "We've got everything we want."

Prince leaned closer, undeterred. "Maybe you want to go to Afghanistan? Kabul, Jalalabad, Kandahar. Or maybe you want to see the battlefield at Tora Bora, where Osama outfoxed the Little Bush?" he offered with a humorous wink. "No visa, no problem. I can give you safe transport for very good price. You are the first tourists I have seen in months. I will outbid any competition."

"That's a first," interjected Simon. "Business must be quite bad."

"Terrible, sir. With America dropping bombs on Afghanistan, all of the Taliban have come here. We have car bombings weekly. The mullahs are preaching death to the government for supporting the West, and there are mujahideen camps only fifty kilometers from here. Tourists are very rare indeed these days. Which may mean you are—how should I say it—in the business of information?"

"Spies?" Simon replied, his tone sarcastic. "Him, maybe," he said pointing to Nick. "But have you ever seen a spy who looked like her?"

Yvette rolled her eyes at Simon. Normally, she would have been glad to see Simon showing some humor, which had been a rarity since he had arrived to join them in Peshawar a week earlier. But she was too irritable now, and Nick was sure her dislike of Darra's culture of guns was not the only reason.

Prince tossed his head in acknowledgment. "Good cover is essential, is it not?" He leaned closer. "I have eyes like an eagle and ears like a dog. And I have friends among the tribes on both sides of the border. I could be a valuable asset."

Prince's gaze fell back on Yvette, and Nick concluded that he was putting on a show for her. "Thanks, but we don't need your services," Nick replied.

Just then Simon intervened. "Wait a minute. It's really true you could get us . . . anything?"

Prince locked eyes with Simon, riveting his stare. "Ahhh." He tossed his eyebrows and nodded his head to the side—that peculiarly ambiguous Asian manner of saying yes that always hints at the possibility of a no.

"'Anything' is indeed something I deal in. Assuming of course you mean this . . ." He scanned the busy plaza. Satisfied that no one was watching, he pulled something out of his vest. Motioning them closer, he opened his hand under the table, revealing a dark resinous slab of hashish.

"I want to see," Yvette said, suddenly perking up.

Prince hesitated, glancing at Nick and then Simon. When no objection was forthcoming, he handed it to her. She held the chunk to her nose and sniffed. When she licked it, tasting to assess the strength of the oils, Prince's eyes sparkled lewdly at Yvette's tongue dappling the hashish.

"How do you say it? . . . A connoisseur," Prince said with an effeminate giggle. "What country you from?"

"Different places," replied Yvette, before handing the chunk to Simon.

"How much of that can you get?" Simon asked.

Nick gave Simon a surprised look. The one piece seemed plenty to him, at least for a while.

"My people are very choosy with whom they do large-scale business," he said. "If you want more, it must be done face-to-face. Not here. You will need to come with me, to a special bazaar. It is not near to Darra, and there are no tourists who know of this place. But for you, my friend, it can be arranged."

"How about now?" replied Simon.

"Not possible. It is very far. Tomorrow."

"I'll go with you," said Yvette, after a pause.

Nick shifted in his seat, uneasy at having been dropped from the discussion. "Yvette," he intervened. "This piece is going to last for a while."

Prince observed their banter, trying to work out the nuances of their relationship, registering the tension between them.

"It's okay, Evvie," Simon interjected. "You stay with Nick in Peshawar."

"I'll go if I want," she snapped.

"No, I insist," said Simon, his eyes locked on hers. "You said you were going rug shopping with Nick tomorrow. We can always go back again later, all together."

Nick reached for his money belt. "How much for this bit, then?"

"Please, it is my gift to you. If you like it, then you will give money to your friend to buy more. You do not like it, no problem," said Prince.

"I'd rather pay for it," Nick replied. But Prince was already standing.

"Hospitality is part of our culture, sir," he said, before turning to Simon. "I will pick you up at your hotel tomorrow morning at seven with my transport." He positioned his chapeau on his head with the air of a man crowning himself king.

"Oh, it's the Rose Hotel," said Simon, remembering he had not told Prince.

"Yes, sir, I know," Prince replied. "There are very few Westerners in Peshawar these days. People talk. See you tomorrow." He turned and walked away.

Though Prince struck Nick as too shady to be trusted, they were all glad to have finally gotten their hands on some good hashish. Nick and Yvette had been in Pakistan alone together nearly a month before Simon had arrived from Southeast Asia to rejoin them. The narcotic gold mine they had heard so much about seemed a myth. All they had been able to find in the bazaars of Peshawar was odorless, pale, and crumbly—the dregs of last year's harvest—not fit to be smoked by a toad.

Yvette, especially, needed something to help her mellow out. She had been on edge since they had entered Pakistan, even though she was the one who had insisted on coming. The drive down from China over the Kunjerab Pass on the Karakoram Highway had been long and rugged. The bus, a run down Pakistani jalopy with wooden benches for seats and a deafening sound system blaring shrill Indian pop, had blown out two tires at sixteen thousand feet. Each had taken over an hour to change, since there was only the driver to do the job. To make matters worse, Yvette spent much of the hair-raising ride vomiting out the window while Nick held back her hair. "I told you, you bastard," she berated him between gasps, angry at him for making her throw out their last chunk of hashish before passing through Chinese customs. She had wanted to stash it in her underwear to quell her stomach in anticipation of her motion sickness.

They had finally reached Peshawar after four days of hard bus travel. Nick had been enamored of the city's chaotic bazaars, serpentine walk-streets lined with crumbling alcoves, cornucopia of tribal peoples, and Dodge City atmosphere of frontier lawlessness. But Yvette had grown progressively dour. Nick wished he could have dismissed it as a temporary mood swing caused by the hardships of travel grating on her nerves—the dingy hotels, the frequent bouts of dysentery, the groping eyes of men not accustomed to seeing Western women. But he could tell the fact that Simon had not shown up was the real source of her malaise.

"We should leave," Nick had told her. "Simon probably got sidetracked. We could go to Ladakh, or go back and hang with the throwbacks and gurus in Rishikesh. Maybe even head over to Africa."

"No, a little longer," she had insisted.

When Simon had finally arrived two weeks later than expected, he had been awkwardly surprised to find Nick and Yvette sharing a room. After the initial enthusiasm of their reunion, he had shown little desire to spend time with both of them together, except for an occasional late-morning meal or evening tea. While Nick and Yvette continued spending their days wandering bazaars or taking day trips to villages in parts of the Tribal Areas not off limits to foreigners, Simon remained detached, uncharacteristically subdued, opting to spend his time alone. He had checked into a different hotel, an even cheaper boardinghouse than the Khyber, tucked into a hidden corner of the old city. Though Simon had pleaded poverty, Nick could only assume he was jealous.

"He's the one who left you," Nick had said to Yvette. "Not the other way around. So I don't know why he's got such a problem hanging out with us."

"It's not like you are going out of your way to make him feel welcome."

"That's bullshit. I invite him to do stuff with us all the time."

"He is going through a difficult time. You should have offered to pay for his room for a couple days, so he could stay near us. Instead, he is kilometers away."

"The Khyber's only five bucks a night—it's not like it's expensive. Besides, why should I pay for him?"

"You used to when we were in Nepal and Tibet."

"Only a couple times, when I wanted a hotel with a hot shower. I'm running low on cash, too. I've been paying for your room and board for over a month."

"I did not know paying for me was such a big deal," she had said to Nick, oblivious to how presumptuous she had sounded. "Can't we just forget about meaningless shit and have fun all together like old times? Isn't that what you keep telling me? To have fun?"

The night after they met Prince during their trip to the Darra weapons bazaar, Nick was roused from sleep by the muezzin. At first he had found the Muslim call to prayer exotic. Now it only rankled his nerves. A sign that it was time to leave Pakistan, he thought.

He sat up in bed. A thin shaft of moonlight sifted through the window, just enough to illuminate the room with a pallid glow, and to allow him to notice that Yvette was gone.

He called out for her, but there was no answer. He noticed that her shoes were missing, as well as the T-shirt she would set aside on the chair each night before bed, choosing to sleep only in her underwear. He felt some relief to see her backpack on the luggage rack along with her travel journal, dog-eared French translation of *A Suitable Boy,* even her tobacco pouch and rolling papers.

He mulled over her absence for several minutes before slipping on his jeans and hiking boots. He walked down the hallway, descended the stairs. For a moment he thought of rousing Shahid, who was asleep on the floor in his makeshift bed of piled Afghan blankets. But he decided against it, returning to the room instead.

He lay back down on his bed and felt overcome with nausea. Minutes turned into hours, until the orange light of the new sun glowed through the window. Roosters called in the alleyway. One of the homeless street people coughed and spat outside his window. The world of men was awakening.

When he could no longer stand it, he put on his boots once again and headed across the bazaar to look for her. When he arrived at Simon's guesthouse, to his surprise, he found her outside in the now vacant plaza, waiting. Her eyes were red with fatigue.

"I suppose you're going to tell me you just talked all night," Nick said.

Yvette sighed. "You want me to feel like a cheating wife or something?"

"I didn't say anything about cheating. Why do you mention it?"

"Shut up, Nicholas. If you need to know, yes, I was with Simon last night. And we did talk all night, okay?"

Nick kicked at a large roach scurrying for a crack between the cobblestones near Yvette's feet.

"Stop it, Nicholas. Stop acting sorry for yourself."

"I'm a lot of things, Yvette. But not sorry."

She paused, tapping the ashes from her cigarette. "Simon is going to leave for somewhere easy to chill out for a while."

Nick studied her for a moment. "You're going with him?"

She rubbed her temples, as if smitten by a sudden headache. "Look, it's been a long night. We'll talk this afternoon," she said, garbling her words slightly.

"You're high."

Yvette flicked her cigarette butt onto the ground and placed her palm on her forehead. "I smoked some of that hash, so what?" she said with her eyes closed. "I'll see you when I get back."

"From where?" Nick said. "Where's Simon?"

"He is sick. I am going to the Smugglers' Bazaar in his place."

Nick stared at her. "You can't be serious."

She replied with silence.

"Goddamnit, Yvette," Nick cursed. "You're not going to the Smugglers' Bazaar alone."

Yvette raised her hand. "Stop it, Nicholas. Go back to the hotel."

"Just you and that guy, Prince, going on a hash run to the Tribal Areas—that's about the stupidest thing—"

"Please . . . just *leave!*" she beseeched, her words riding a wave of frustration. "I can take care of myself."

Nick stood in muted silence. "Nothing you can say will convince me to let you go alone, Yvette . . . nothing."

These memories passed through Nick's mind as he looked into the blackness behind him, the wheels of the truck spinning him into a future he could only guess. He cursed himself for trusting Masood. He was broke, robbed of his last bit of reserve cash, and did not have enough left to buy his next meal, let alone pay his way beyond Gilgit. But he was moving, at least, away from Peshawar, each second increasing the distance between himself and the police.

CHAPTER 16

The pale glow appearing in the eastern sky dispelled any comfort Nick had taken in his mobility. *Why is the sun rising to the left?* he puzzled. *We should be heading northwest to Torkham—not south!* The conclusion was unavoidable. They were heading back toward Peshawar.

Nick rapped on the rear window of the cabin. When the gray-bearded Pashtun looked back, Nick thrust his thumb at the eastern sky. "Why are we headed south?"

The Pashtun cupped his hand to his ear and shrugged his shoulders. Nick pantomimed, pointing east and thrusting his arms to the side. "I said, why south?"

"No problem," the Pashtun mouthed, wagging a raised palm at Nick. The gesture was an instruction to settle down, but Nick detected smugness about it.

"No . . . stop! . . . Stop the goddamn car!" Nick pounded on the cabin window. He considered jumping, but they were driving too fast. He would break a leg, or possibly his neck. And even if he survived the jump, there was nowhere to hide. They would easily chase him down and shoot him. There was not anything he could do except wait for whatever they had in store.

Ten minutes later the truck sped over a rise. When they reached the crest, he could see orange lights flickering in the distance and the outline of a few mud-brick blockhouses and a cluster of parked vehicles. Nick felt an uprush of relief—maybe they were taking him to another truck, which would turn around and drive north?

When they stopped at the settlement, however, and the gray-bearded Pashtun hopped out of the truck pointing his Kalashnikov at Nick, all hope was shattered. *So this is it then,* Nick thought. *They are going to kill me—right here in the desert.* The Pashtun motioned him down with a sweep of his gun muzzle.

Nick stared at the barrel of the Kalashnikov. Two men came out of one of the buildings, joining the driver and the Pashtun holding the gun. He could not see their faces in the dark.

One of the newcomers searched Nick, found his money belt containing his only remaining ID, and took it with him back to the building along with Nick's backpack, leaving him with nothing but the clothes on his back. The other new arrival, a hulking man dressed in Western-style pants, said something to the driver, who handed him the cash Nick had paid at the previous stop.

As the men bantered in Pashto, one of the voices sounded familiar. It was the same voice Nick had heard booming off cement walls, the salty taste of blood in his mouth, staring into the whirling bright lights. A voice he would never forget.

Inspector Rasool Muhammad Akhtar stepped out of the shadows, holding the wad of Nick's cash. "You did exactly as I expected," he said.

"Expected?" replied Nick.

Akhtar scoffed. "As a barrister you should know, a suspect's flight is evidence of guilt. Sub-Inspector Shiraz insisted on giving you the benefit of the doubt. But I, for one, always suspected *you* should be facing the murder charges, not the English. You should have honored the bargain."

The gray-bearded Pashtun jabbed Nick with the gun barrel, prodding him toward a Japanese-made minivan parked behind one of the mud-brick buildings. Akhtar followed, counting Nick's money, then slid open the side door of the minivan. He fumbled in the dark, then handed Nick a pair of handcuffs. "Put them on."

Nick's hands shook as he took the cuffs from Akhtar. He dropped them.

He looked down at the cuffs lying in the sand, then back up at Akhtar. The graybeard poked the gun into Nick's back.

Later, Nick would not remember deliberately thinking about what he did next, though in retrospect, he must have done so. For one cannot act in the manner he acted without some forethought. Nick bent and scooped up the cuffs. But as he slowly jackknifed upright, he grabbed the barrel of the Kalashnikov with his free hand.

His small, futile act of defiance must have caught the Pashtun, still high on hashish, by surprise. Instead of yanking the gun from Nick's grasp—which he could have done easily since he held it by the trigger grip, a much firmer handhold than Nick's—he hesitated, glancing at Nick in disbelief. For a moment, the two stood transfixed, like guards standing sentry with the same rifle, until Nick dropped the cuffs and heaved with both hands on the barrel with all his might.

The Pashtun fell back on his heels, losing the tug-of-war before realizing it was on. Nick found himself holding the gun with two hands, the muzzle about shoulder height and pointing behind him. His hands trembled, but he did not drop it.

The Pashtun rushed him. Nick instinctively stepped into him, thrusting the heavy rifle butt down and across at the charging man's face. It hit him with a sickening sound, like someone stomping in a bucket of eggs. Then the Pashtun was on his back, legs kicking, as blood gushed through clutched fingers.

Nick stood in shock, not quite grasping what he had done. He feared the man would attack again, and wondered briefly whether he should just shoot him. But then he heard a throaty, gurgling groan, and thought the man was dying—until he realized the sound was coming not from the Pashtun, but rather from behind Nick. Only then did he notice the sharp scent of burned gases and the heat of the barrel in his hand. In his struggle with the Pashtun, the Kalashnikov had fired.

Nick swung around to see a figure lying on his back. It was Akhtar. He had a hole in his chest.

Nick stood over him. Black bubbles formed and popped on Akhtar's open lips with each labored breath. His eyes were wide with fear. Even as Nick felt a kind of satisfaction watching Akhtar struggle, he reflexively dropped to his knees and checked Akhtar's wound. It was hopeless. The bullet had entered below the heart, and blood was welling up through his punctured shirt in rhythmic spurts.

Akhtar's mouth moved in effort to speak. He raised an arm and motioned to Nick. Nick hesitated, but then felt an inexplicable impulse to hear the dying man's words. He bent closer until his ear was only inches from Akhtar's bloody lips.

Suddenly, Nick felt wet hands clamp around on his neck. He gagged, wedging the Kalashnikov against Akhtar's chest, pressing down in effort to pry himself free. Akhtar only squeezed tighter, strangling Nick with the desperation of a dying man bent on squandering his last bit of life on one final act. Nick could feel the vessels burst at the backs of his eyes. His head buzzed like a thousand cicadas trapped in his brain. He was slipping away.

Just then blood spewed from Akhtar's mouth. His grip fell slack.

Gasping, Nick fell back on the sand. Akhtar's broken body gave a final raspy wheeze before his chest sank and did not rise.

Nick stood, soaked in Akhtar's blood. He heard yelling, more cries of pain. He turned and saw the gray-bearded Pashtun rolling in the sand, clutching his bloody face where Nick had smashed it with the rifle butt. He heard more voices in the darkness, then the sound of footsteps kicking up gravel. He ran.

He heard a gunshot—like the sound of a rock shattering the surface of a thinly iced pond. The bullet whistled off to his left. He sprinted to his right.

More shots rang out, a vicious burst of automatic fire. He ran faster, blindly in the darkness, pouring all his strength into his thighs.

The ground disappeared beneath him. He fell forward and down. Gravel shredded his outstretched hands as he tried to break his slide. But it was futile. He tumbled downward, forever it seemed, until a jarring impact broke his fall. He lay still, his chest flattened against a boulder, his arms and legs scraped and bleeding.

Another fusillade of bullets whipped over his head. He heard a cackle of rocks above him—the sound of men trying to negotiate the slope—then the roar of a motor. The faded end of headlights beamed across a wide canyon.

Nick picked himself up. He continued down, searching for cover. The gradient plummeted steeply again. Losing his footing, he slid on his buttocks down a chute of scree, plunging into darkness. When he came to a stop, the men were high above, hollering across the canyon wall. He heard more shots, farther away, followed by the ricochet. He stood again and sidestepped down the slope, continuing for a long time, until his legs and lungs burned so badly he could only crawl. He had lost all track of time.

When he finally reached the bottom, he came to a shallow stream. He dropped to his knees and drank like an animal. Exhausted, his arms gave way. He fell to his stomach and rested with his face pressed against the freezing cold earth. When he caught his breath, he could hear only the gurgle of running water. He willed himself to his feet and staggered upstream, stumbling along the streambed.

Hours later, when the sun breached the horizon, the boulder-strewn canyon had opened into a desolate expanse of sand and rock. Nick fell to his knees and peered into the distance, too numb even to weep. He had escaped to an endless nothing. A vast gateway to oblivion.

PART II

CHAPTER 17

Tribal Areas, Pak-Afghan Border

Nicholas Sunder squinted the world into focus. He propped himself onto his elbows and struggled to get his bearings.

He had no clear recollection of events, only nebulous images he endeavored to string into some understanding—Akhtar's eyes, black and glaring into his own; the whistling of bullets over his head; the endless, panicked sprinting through the darkness; exhaustion, thirst, and infernal heat.

Nick's senses slowly attuned. He sniffed at the dry air. It was thick with soot and the sulfury smell of burning dung. Black smoke billowed above him. Like moons burning through a night fog, a pair of sun-parched, bearded faces was revealed as it slowly dissipated. Their cheeks smeared with grime, they stared at Nick from under their round *pakol* caps with curious, almost concerned expressions.

Nick's initial relief that they were not the well-fed, bureaucratic faces of police officers quickly gave way to alarm. He sprang to his palms, staring at them guardedly. The men backpedaled a few steps, then sat cross-legged on the ground. The pungent scent of their unwashed bodies pierced his nostrils like smelling salts.

"Salaam alaikum, sir," said one of the men. He had a familiar grin, stretching wide across an oval visage rimmed with a halo of long, fine whiskers. The other man looked equally familiar, with deep azure eyes that contrasted sharply with his black beard, blanketing his jutting cheekbones like a carpet of shaggy yak hair.

"You remember us?" queried the smaller of the two.

The wolflike larger man with piercing eyes leaned forward and struck a match, carefully placing it under a pyramid of sticks piled over a smoldering heap of dung chips. The other man—the speaker—sat cross-legged, his eyes riveted on Nick and his face fixed in a serene but dimpled expression, like a much leaner version of a laughing Buddha. "Fidali fixed your nose for you. You remember, sir?" he said, nodding toward his larger companion.

Still bleary-eyed, Nick rubbed his temples until finally he placed them—the two tribesmen from the holding cell where the police had locked him the night before his release. He was incredulous.

"Ahhhhh, yes—you remember!" said the man excitedly, the words rolling off his tongue in a jovial lilt, before his face abruptly turned grave. "But now you have much bigger problem, Ghulam thinks." He held out his upturned palms in supplication toward the sky and solemnly shook his head. Nick was too astonished by the strangeness of awakening to his two former cell mates to respond. His eyes darted about warily.

They were sitting in the shade of a high rock overhang—a massive boulder that slanted skyward, creating a natural refuge from the sun. Someone had gone to the trouble of constructing a wall of piled rocks across the open side, creating a pen for animals and a windbreak. Nick's eyes followed the long column of smoke curling up to the roof of the escarpment. The shelter appeared well used, judging from the smoky black deposits on the rock ceiling and the animal bones strewn on the sand. From the oblique angle of the sun, Nick guessed it was late afternoon. He must have been passed out since morning.

The tribesmen watched the fire burn down to embers. The one called Fidali placed a small kettle on the rocks encircling the glowing wood and dung and began digging through a rattan basket filled with sundries—cooking utensils, matchboxes, plastic bags of salt and sugar. Nick pretended to be engrossed by the fire while he stole cautious glances at the two of them, trying to discern their intentions. He was suspicious of their prior imprisonment. Though they had been kind to him that night in the jail, for all he knew they could be violent criminals. After what he had been through the last couple weeks, culminating in the setup by Akhtar, he felt certain he was being targeted for a robbery, kidnapping, or worse. Struck by sudden panic, he stood, surprised that his aching body had obeyed the dictates of his mind.

The gnomelike man shot out his hand and grabbed Nick's ankle. Startled, Nick jumped. "Please, sir," the man said. "Drink tea, eat food. You are our guest."

"No, I . . . really should get moving," replied Nick, aware of how absurd he sounded in light of his debilitated state and the lethal sun unleashing its rays outside the shelter. Even if he could tolerate journeying in such heat, where would he go? There was nothing but sunscorched sand stretching to the horizon.

"Too hot, sir, even for lizards. Very dangerous. You must wait until later."

Nick shielded his eyes and scanned the infernal landscape. The man was right. Nick's thirst was insatiable, his head throbbed, his legs were stiff, and his feet blistered. He would die out there. Necessity required that he take his chances with his hosts, at least until the sun sank lower on the horizon.

"You speak English pretty well," Nick said matter-of-factly as he sat back down, keeping a vigilant distance.

"Yes. Little bit, sir." He nodded to the side. "How do you feel?"

"Like I've been roasted on a spit." It was the truth. Nick's skin had been burned to a lobster red, and his eyes stung with dryness.

"Like kabob," he said, giggling. "English kabob! We found you alone, sir, two nights ago lying down against big rock. You had been cooked by the sun. Barely breathing. Not so very smart of you, English."

"No. It wasn't," agreed Nick, rubbing the back of his head.

"We brought you here, gave you tea. You sleep all day yesterday and last night." He pointed at Nick's *kamiz*. "Because of big problem, we think."

"*Yesterday?*" Nick repeated in disbelief, struggling to grasp the passage of time. He had thought he had been unconscious for a few hours, not almost two days. Nick looked down where the man was pointing and saw bloodstains on his shirt, splotches of Akhtar's gore now dried to a deep rust color. Reflexively, he covered the blood with his arms, but not before the men registered his effort with surreptitious glances.

"An accident," Nick muttered, making a tumbling motion with his hands. "I hit my head on a rock. I got confused, and then lost. Thank you so much for helping me," Nick added, hoping to divert their suspicion with gratitude. "I owe you."

"No problem," said the shorter one, who was doing all the talking.

The sound of boiling water drew the tribesmen's attention to the fire. The thick-bearded Fidali poured the steaming tea into three cups and passed one of the cups to Nick. They drank in silence. The tea was thick and sugary, and although it was sweeter and hotter than anything Nick would otherwise choose to drink in such a blistering environment, he could feel his body slowly rejuvenating.

Nick took a closer look at his hosts while they drank. The little man's wispy beard formed a full semicircle extending from both his sideburns around his chin. Although his face was round, he had high, angular cheekbones. Not entirely Asian and not entirely Caucasian, his visage spoke of a fusion of two races and two continents. When his face was fixed in a smirk, which was more often than not, his eyes gleamed, and he looked much like a child caught in a prank. He shoved a thumb into his chest.

"I am Ghulam Muhammad. And my friend, Fidali."

"Fidali?" After traveling in Muslim countries for so long, it seemed to Nick there were only so many Islamic names to choose from. But he had not yet heard this one, and first hearing it, it did not really sound Muslim to him at all.

"Yes. Same same as Fida Ali. But where we come from, we say 'Fidali.'"

"Oh . . . right," said Nick, recognizing the full version of the name. He remembered from his trip down the Karakoram Highway from China with Yvette that Muslim names of Arabic origin such as Fida Ali were often merged or otherwise altered when spoken in local languages. "Nice to meet you both . . . again."

"Ahhh, yes. Again," he said with a chuckle.

Fidali sliced potatoes with a long curved knife that looked more like a miniature scimitar than a culinary utensil, dropping the slices into the boiling kettle as he went. His hands were large and scarred, and he had a light complexion and thick, bristly black hair that stood up on his head like a crew cut despite its considerable length. Were he not dressed head to toe in Muslim garb, he could have passed for a Spaniard or a Greek.

Even though Fidali was sitting, Nick could tell he was powerfully built, with broad, square shoulders. But not until he stood did Nick see how massive he really was—the largest man he had seen since he began traveling in Central Asia, and indeed, big even by American standards, though his size was that of lean strength, endurance, and utility as opposed to the extraneous bulk of a weightlifter or the clumsy beefiness of an overfed Westerner. He appeared to be a foot and a half taller than his friend, with thick forearms and a wide, wedge-shaped back that stretched his *kamiz* tightly across his shoulders, a body forged by a life among mountains. With thighs like logs, he carried his weight in his legs, giving the impression of a man who was anchored to the earth, able to carry on his shoulders the full load of two sturdy bull yaks up steep, high mountains.

"And you, sir?" Ghulam asked.

"And me . . . ?" Nick repeated the question unnecessarily in order to buy time while his mind raced for an alias. He thought it foolhardy to give his real name.

Ghulam noticed Nick's awkward hesitation. "Ghulam means to ask, sir, what country you from?" he said, changing his query. "England?"

"Oh, um . . . no," Nick said, relieved Ghulam did not to press him for his name. "I'm, ah . . . I'm from Canada." He lied not only because he felt compelled to hide his identity but also because he feared an American might be considered as offering a better ransom. The reply that followed, however, seemed to frustrate that goal.

"Ahh yes, Canada—in America," Ghulam replied.

"Canada is different. Not the same as America," Nick clarified.

Ghulam looked confused. "Same same, but different?" he asked, shaking his outstretched hand in front of him in the universal sign of similarity.

"No. Just different," Nick replied. "And you? Are you from Afghanistan?"

"No, no. We are from Kashmir," he said—proudly, Nick thought.

"Kashmir?" Nick's ears perked. "What part?"

"From Kurgan," he replied. "You know Kurgan?"

"Haven't heard of it. Is it in the Pakistani- or Indian-controlled part?"

"On Indian side. Kurgan is a very small village, high in the mountains." He pointed skyward, becoming suddenly animated. "Very beautiful. Big snowy mountains and glaciers. We will be home soon, inshallah! It has been long time."

"And Fidali, too?"

"Same same."

"What are you doing here, then, in the middle of nowhere?" Nick asked, before suddenly regretting his nosiness for fear it might be reciprocated.

Ghulam scrutinized Nick a long moment, as if gauging Nick's trustworthiness. "This is the way we go home—*special* way," he replied. "We were in Pakistan for one year's time, looking for work. But we find nothing," he said, expressing his disappointment by tossing his head and clicking his tongue.

"What kind of work do you do?"

"Ghulam is cook and mountain guide," he replied in his habit of referring to himself in the third person. "That is how Ghulam learn

English—from British and German people who come to Kashmir to go trekking. Now, too much fighting in Kashmir. There has been no guide work for many years. So we go to Peshawar . . ."

"Why Peshawar?" Nick asked, trying not to sound probing.

"First we go to Skardu, to find work as cook for trekking expeditions. But not so many trekkers in Pakistan, either. Only jobs go to the local people . . .

"Karachi is no good—bad people there, very dangerous. So then we go to Peshawar to find work in cloth factories. But in Peshawar they do not like Kashmiri people. Police arrest us for coming to Pakistan with no papers. So now Ghulam go home, inshallah, to be with family," he said.

Nick nodded. "Looks like Fidali's the cook now."

"Yes, yes. Fidali also good cook," he replied.

Fidali scooped the hot potatoes and broth into cups and passed them to Nick and Ghulam. He unwrapped a slab of stale chapati from some newspaper and broke it into thirds. Nick thanked them both, accepting their generosity, then mimicked their method of dipping the rock-hard bread into steaming broth with their hands to soften it up, scooping down the potatoes with the soggy bread. The mushy substance was hot and salty, a welcome contrast to the stark sweetness of the tea. In silence, the three men devoured the food, except for the sporadic interspersions of "*Allah haq*"—"God is great"—muttered by Ghulam like clockwork between swallows.

"And you, English? Where do you go?"

Ghulam called all Westerners "English" regardless of their nationality— a habit Nick had found common in some rural villages of South Asia. "I want to go to Kashmir, too . . . inshallah," he added.

"Yes—inshallah!" Ghulam laughed at Nick's use of the phrase *god willing*. "You are Muslim?" he asked.

"I'm not really religious."

Ghulam pulled on his beard, tilting his head. "Not religious?"

"Well, my parents were Christian, but . . ."

"Ahh, People of the Book," he interjected approvingly. "You know, Isa bin Miriam is a prophet of Muslim people, too. But why do you say 'not religious'?"

Nick was still struck by the oddity of spontaneously launching into conversation about religious beliefs with strangers, even though he had found during his travels in Muslim countries that it was not uncommon for people to do so. In the West, Nick mused, discussing faith with random people would lead to suspicions of lunacy. "I just don't think that much about it," Nick replied. "I've never even been to church more than a dozen times or so, and that was mostly when I was a kid."

Ghulam considered Nick's words. "Allah not in church or mosque. Allah here," he said, pointing to his chest, "and Allah there." He swept his hand in a broad arch toward the hills on the horizon.

After Fidali refilled their teacups, Ghulam dipped a rag into the remainder of the hot water and handed it to Nick. "Here—wash face. It is better to be clean."

Nick wiped the caked dust from his face and hands. The feeling of the hot towel on his skin rejuvenated him. "How are you traveling? Are you going to catch a truck somewhere along the way?"

"Maybe. There are few roads the way we go. . . . If we find safe truck to ride, then okay. Otherwise we walk."

"*Walk!* How long would that take?"

"Three weeks, maybe four, inshallah. But maybe too much snow to pass. Many big mountains and glaciers to cross. You know Siachen?"

"I've heard of it. Isn't that the glacier near K-2?"

"Yes, part of it. Siachen is very long. We cross the border not too far from Kargil. Then we go to Kurgan by walking."

"Why don't you cross from Muzzafarabad? Isn't the terrain easier?"

Ghulam grabbed one of several large duffel bags lying on the dirt beside him and turned it upside down. A dozen cartons of cigarettes fell out. He pointed to them.

"These cigarettes we buy for cheap from Afghans to sell in Kargil. If we try to cross in the south, nearer to Muzzafarabad, the path is too open. Too many police. If we were gun smugglers, they give us no problem. But with cigarette, Pakistani police will take them unless we pay baksheesh. We have no money for baksheesh. So we go *special* way," Ghulam said, pointing toward the foothills on the horizon. "Smugglers' route. Very hard walking, very dangerous. But no police."

Nick paused. Now that he understood they were traveling this desolate stretch because it was along an established smuggling route, the fact that his former jail mates had stumbled upon him there began to strike Nick as less an impossible coincidence than a credible fortuity. "Where do you pick up the trail?" he asked, smelling an opportunity. Ghulam laughed, thinking Nick's question ridiculous.

"Sorry. It is too dangerous, Ghulam thinks."

"I'd like to know just the same. Please." Nick beckoned.

Ghulam looked at Nick, his eyes drifting to Nick's bloody clothes. He scooped up some potatoes with his fingers and chewed thoughtfully. "Ghulam does not know the way very good. Fidali traveled it many times. It is Fidali's way."

The men fell silent, sipping their tea. Then, after what seemed like an eternity to Nick, Ghulam spoke to Fidali in their native tongue. There was a brief discussion between them, and then Fidali nodded. Ghulam turned to Nick.

"Fidali says he will show you the way, inshallah."

"He will. . . . ?" said Nick, not quite believing in the possibility of his own good fortune. "But I have no money to pay you."

"No problem, English," Ghulam said. "It is very strange we meet again in this place, do you not think? Allah must have a good reason for it to be so."

"*Shukria*. I am grateful to you—again," Nick replied, the sincerity in his voice concealing his inner skepticism. He leaned toward Ghulam and held out his hand. Ghulam, perplexed by the gesture, clasped it awkwardly, and when Nick pumped it vigorously, Ghulam chuckled. Then, when he turned to Fidali and shook his hand as well, flinching at the compression of his knucklebones under Fidali's grip, Nick was surprised when even the stoic giant cracked a smile.

CHAPTER 18

"The solution to all problems lies in jihad." The slogan was drilled into them over and again during the "lessons in truth" they were taught at the training camp in Pakistan. As Kazim walked the line into his first brush with death, however, jihad was doing little to solve the problem the boy in front of him, Shari, had keeping his breakfast in his stomach.

Muzzafar Khan, their commander, scowled at the sixteen-year-old Shari, with whom Kazim had completed training only days ago. "You, boy, stop your damn retching!" he ordered in a hushed voice, fixing Shari in the sights of his Kalashnikov, which Muzzafar had adorned with gaudy primrose sequins, making it appear like a child's toy. Shari froze, spittle running off his chin. He was certain that Muzzafar intended to shoot him right there. A wet spot expanded down the leg of Shari's pants. Muzzafar shook his head in disgust. "Typical Kashmiri," he scoffed before moving on. "Softer than the fuzz on your little sister's cunt."

Muzzafar was a grizzled Pakistani born in the slums of Rawalpindi. He wore a long beard and turban in the style of the Afghani mujahideen. An eight-year veteran of the Afghan jihad, he was only fourteen when he killed his first Russian, a young conscript who, shot in the legs, had the misfortune of being too callow to know he should have rolled on his rifle instead of being captured. Muzzafar cut every square inch of the young infidel's body—"death of a thousand cuts," the Afghans liked to call it—and hung the bloody corpse, naked and dismembered, on a meat hook at a turn in the road for the next Russian convoy to chance upon. "That," Muzzafar would once tell Kazim, "is the real reason why we won the war against the infidels. Not the Stinger missiles given to us by the Americans."

Muzzafar was a fanatic who despised all breeds of infidel who ever had a grudge with Muslims—idolatrous Hindus, Russians, "godless" Chinese, American "crusaders," Jewish Zionists—and this was precisely why Kazim was assigned to his command. Kazim had manifested exceptional leadership qualities during his training. He was strong and intelligent, with a working knowledge of English he had picked up from his schooling, and from interacting with Western tourists in his home village as a boy. The last was a skill that could be useful down the line in the event Kazim proved himself worthy of advancement in the cadre of jihadis. A language barrier often separated the native Kashmiri insurgents, who mostly spoke local tribal dialects, and Urdu-speaking Pakistani intelligence officers. Since English was a common second or third language among Pakistani officers, a mujahid in a position of leadership who knew how to speak it could render a huge advantage over leaders of rival factions. As a Kashmiri, however, Kazim was presumed to be "moderate," religiously and temperamentally. The leaders of Lashkar-e-Tayyiba, the "Army of the Righteous," a pro-Pakistan faction of mujahideen Kazim had been duped into joining, hoped that some of Muzzafar's extremist fervor would rub off. The jihad in Kashmir needed to be radicalized, they felt, or it would collapse.

Ten mujahideen were chosen for the predawn attack, three of whom, including Kazim, were fresh from training. Their target was a *naka*—a guarded roadblock along the rugged supply road to Srinagar a mere few kilometers from the northern stretches of the Line of Control. Fortified by a bunker, the *naka* would be manned by a handful of *jawans*—guards belonging to the Indian Border Security Forces. It was to be a routine harassment under cover of darkness, perfect for inoculating the new recruits to the jitters of combat.

The mujahideen emerged from the thick pine forest. When they reached the section of road where they knew the *naka* was situated, Muzzafar split the group into flanks. His plan was to execute a blind-side attack while the other wing distracted the Indian gunners from afar with Kalashnikov fire. The northern probe was sent ahead to gain their position. It ran into an Indian patrol, however, that suspiciously had not been reported by the mujahideen's spy on the Indian side of the Line of Control. The attack quickly turned sour. "Fucking traitor!" Muzzafar cursed under his breath, as the sky suddenly exploded with the blinding light of red and white flares.

Kazim stared like a startled animal at the vivid flames bursting in the sky. A hail of gunfire ricocheted off the rocks around his feet. Before he could even hear the staccato of the Indian machine guns, four of the five mujahideen in front of him had been cut down, the bullets hitting their bodies sounding like a cricket bat slapping a side of beef. The fifth, one of the panicked rookies, ran for his life back toward where Kazim, Muz-zafar, and the three others had hunkered down among the trees.

It was an ill-conceived, perhaps cowardly, move on the part of the sur-vivor. He was taught to die a martyr, not run and lead the enemy to his comrades. But he was a boy who had been conscripted into the insurgency at gunpoint, and though all the lectures during his training about mar-tyrdom certainly had sounded noble to his adolescent mind at the time, when confronted with his mortality, life seemed much nobler. He was shot in the back while screaming for help—but not before he revealed his com-rades' position. When even Muzzafar muttered a prayer under his breath, suddenly it appeared to Kazim that his first combat would be his last.

The fury of battle. Orange flames of spitting gun muzzles, the deadly whis-tle of bullets tracing long arcs of startling light, the animal shrieks of the maimed and dying—all melded together in a kaleidoscope of violence.

Then came the mortars, firing in barrages of three or four rounds at a time. Kazim dove to the ground. Rocks thrown up by the bursting shells pelted him in the back. He buried his head in his elbows, unable to lift it to see through the torrent of debris.

He felt himself being hauled up by the back of his collar. He cried in fright, expecting a bayonet to plunge into his throat. But when he raised his head to look into the eyes of his killer, he saw that it was Muzzafar. His eyes were like furious black coals, his nostrils flared like an enraged bull's. With one glance Kazim knew Muzzafar loved this part of war more than anything.

"Get up and fight, shepherd boy! Or I'll shoot you myself!" he screamed above the chaos of gunfire.

Kazim believed him. Shaking, Kazim sat up on his knees and pointed his AK-47 into the night. He pulled the trigger without even daring to take the time to aim, expecting Indian bullets to rip into his chest. He could hear so much shooting all around him, he was sure some of it was his own. Until he felt a fist pound him on the back of the head.

"I said *shoot*, Kashmiri coward! Or I swear by Allah, I'll kill you right now!"

Confused, Kazim felt the barrel of his Kalashnikov. It was cold. Muz-zafar was right; he had not fired a single round. Did he forget to load the magazine? No. It was loaded. "It's jammed!" Kazim announced.

Muzzafar cursed him under his breath, before emptying a full magazine of his own Kalashnikov into the night with one long burst. He slammed in another clip before letting his weapon dangle by its strap and snatching Kazim's gun with his free hand. "You shit-for-brains! You've got the damned safety on!"

He threw the weapon back at Kazim's feet. Kazim picked it up, sure enough, this time it fired. Fueled by fear of Muzzafar as much as of the enemy, Kazim unleashed torrents of lead into the darkness. But the firing and flashes of light coming back at him continued unabated, bullets kicking up dirt and sand around his head. The Indians were a better-disciplined group of marksmen; they were aiming, while he and his comrades sprayed bullets blindly. Each time the enemy fired, the explosions of sand and rock came closer to hitting him.

Then it stopped.

"Hold your fire!" Muzzafar yelled, waving his arm.

The night fell into silence. Had they retreated? Kazim, Muzzafar, and the other mujahideen listened, peering into the darkness with their ears turned toward the front. But they heard and saw nothing.

Then came the pounding, slight at first and then louder, until it blared like a stampede of horses thundering toward them. "Shoot!" Muzzafar hollered.

A blinding white flare illuminated the sky over them, casting a phosphorescent glow over Kazim and his comrades. Instantly, the night opened up again with the clamor of firing weapons. Kazim, squinting under the bright light, crouched on his knees and shot haphazardly into the space in front of him. He could see nothing but shifting shadows, the shooting and explosions fusing into a single, indistinct roar.

Kazim felt the urge to run. He turned to his comrades. One howled off to Kazim's right, slumped over and clutching his chest. Another one writhed in the dirt, holding his intestines in his gut. Under the light of the flare, they had lost the cover of darkness; they were being slaughtered.

Then, the flares burned out. There was an ominous lull. Kazim heard a soft moan to his left. "Shari?" he called out to his young comrade.

"Shari!" Kazim cried again, louder, wiping the dirt from his eyes, as he moved from behind the tree trunk that had provided his cover. Before he could comprehend the shifting silhouettes around him, he saw a yellow flash where Shari had been, followed by a piercing blow against his shoulder that threw him backward, reeling on his feet. Still clutching his

AK-47 one-handed by its pistol grip, he fired a burst at where he had seen the flash. There was a guttural grunt, and then a great weight slammed against him, driving him into the dirt.

Fingers tore at Kazim's face and eyes. He struggled desperately, pounding his fists into the man's back and head. He could not see his assailant in the darkness, though he could smell the stench of cigarettes and, oddly, cologne. The man butted his forehead against Kazim's chin, and Kazim felt the fabric of a turban. Confused, he thought for a moment there had been a mistake, he was fighting one of his own—perhaps Muzzafar. But then he realized the man was a Sikh.

The Sikh dug his fingers into Kazim's eyes, and drove Kazim's head into the ground. Kazim rolled out from under him, but the Sikh punched Kazim in the face. Dazed, Kazim's head snapped back and smashed into a rock. His vision blurred. Only by stroke of fortune, Kazim's eye caught the glint of the blade as the Sikh cocked his arm back. With the strained cry of a wounded animal, he plunged the bayonet toward Kazim's chest. Kazim thrust his knee into the Sikh's groin. The man grunted and was thrown off balance, toppling.

Kazim rolled and grabbed for his gun. Before he could swing the barrel around, the massive Sikh was back on top of him, wrapping his hands around Kazim's neck. Kazim sank his teeth deep into the man's wrist, and his mouth filled with blood. But the Sikh did not release his death grip. Kazim was choking.

Kazim's arms flailed. He punched and clawed at the Sikh's body, catching hold of something fleshy below him. Kazim wrenched it with all his might. The Sikh shrieked in agony, the scrotum popping in Kazim's hand. The Sikh's grip loosened.

Kazim broke free. He hooked with his fist at the Sikh's temple. The Sikh grunted and rolled. Kazim fumbled in the dirt for his gun and swung it around just as the Sikh staggered back to his knees. He felt the gun jump in his hands. The Sikh's head burst open like an overripe fruit.

Kazim spun around just as another Indian was bearing down on him. Before he could react, a plume of blood spouted from the charging man's chest. The Indian slammed into him. They toppled, Kazim pinned underneath him as he bled out in spurts.

When Kazim pushed the body off him, Muzzafar was standing above, his eyes gleaming. The shooting had stopped. Nothing could be heard but the moaning of the wounded and dying and Kazim's own gasping breath. Clutching his bloody shoulder, Kazim turned on his side and threw up.

Muzzafar took an inventory of their casualties. Kazim had been shot in the shoulder, Muzzafar in the arm. The rest were dead except for Shari, who still moaned, barely conscious. "Come on, before they send up another flare."

"But we must carry Shari," Kazim replied. Shari was lying faceup with wide eyes, clutching the side of his bleeding head.

Muzzafar walked over to Shari, looked at him briefly, and then shot him through the temple.

Wiping the brains from his face, Kazim watched the life twitch from Shari's body, before following Muzzafar back into the darkness of the forest toward the Line of Control. Toward Azad Kashmir.

It was daylight by the time they had arrived safely at camp. Kazim went alone to the river to wash his *shalwar kamiz*. He rubbed the bloodstains with wet sand for hours, until his arms ached and his beard was drenched with sweat. Still, the blood barely faded. "So, that is what it feels like," Kazim thought later, as he doused his clothes in gasoline and then watched them burn. "A stain that will never be gone."

CHAPTER 19

They ate and rested, waiting for day to end and night to fall.

Ghulam announced they would travel only under cover of darkness. The obvious reason was to escape the lethal heat. No less grave a threat, however, were the units of Taliban fighters heading toward Afghanistan to press the fight against the American-backed government, as well as Afridi and Mahsud bandits, clans of Pashtun tribesmen who roamed these parts of the Tribal Areas. Both the Taliban and the bandits were equally liable to rob Ghulam and Fidali of their contraband, and worse, Nick of his life.

As they waited, Nick fretted over the manhunt certain to follow the death of Akhtar. Indeed, the search had probably started. He had no expectation of avoiding capture for even a day, let alone making it the hundreds of miles into Indian-controlled Kashmir. But what could he do but try? He certainly could not backtrack. Nor could he trek the desolate frontier alone without food, water, money, or a map. The first time he wandered into a settlement for supplies or transport, the locals, who would soon be warned to look out for him if they had not been already, would merely turn him over to the authorities. He had no money to convince them to do otherwise. Nor did he have any passport to suggest to those who might be inclined to harm him that some consulate would come asking questions if he were to simply "disappear." In fact, Nick did not have any identification at all—his driver's license and ATM card had been taken by the Pashtuns along with his money belt and provisions. He was alone in a hostile, lawless country with no way of proving that he, Nicholas Sunder, had ever even existed.

Though he was still skeptical of his guides' motives, in theory they appeared to have the same goals as he—to avoid the authorities and to escape into India. But, this was a thin basis for trusting them with his life.

*　*　*

Dusk had arrived. It was time to move. Ghulam and Fidali stuffed the dozen or so plastic bags filled with cigarette cartons into cheap Chinese-made vinyl duffel bags, stuffing these in turn into large rattan baskets with shoulder straps bound to the outside like makeshift rucksacks. Nick had no baggage, and he offered to carry some of their cargo with the hope of ingratiating himself. Out of either covetousness of their contraband or hospitality, they refused his offer, which was just as well. Even without a load, Nick would soon be struggling to keep up.

The two men slung the full baskets onto their backs. Then they strapped the few remaining, smaller duffel bags that had not fit into the baskets under their arms with pieces of twine wound elaborately around their necks and shoulders. Nick could imagine the great strain on their backs as the two of them huddled together, heads bowed and palms upturned, while Ghulam recited a *dua*—a Muslim prayer for safe passage. When they were through, all three men forged ahead into the vanishing twilight.

The bright moonlight illuminated the rocky ground under their feet as they hiked briskly toward the east. Taking the lead, Fidali set an aggressive pace, navigating in the darkness without uncertainty, even when there was no trail to follow, which was most of the time. His knowledge of the way seemed uncanny; his only map was the terrain passing under his feet, which he studied under the thin moonlight, reading each rise, hillcrest, valley, and peak as he moved.

They walked for hours on end, stopping only for quick swigs from Ghulam's canteen, and for Fidali and Ghulam to pray at the ordained times. Nick was weak and sore, having not recovered fully from his flight two nights ago. He quickly fell behind the others, who were compelled to stop and wait each time he dropped too far back. On top of his exhaustion, the night brought a cold, dry wind so severe Nick could not bear to stop for more than a few quick drinks from Ghulam's water bottle before the wind cut through him, forcing him to move again for fear of freezing. He lacked adequate clothing—all but his pile pullover had been with his rucksack. It took but a few hours before Nick's bare fingers cracked and curled, his hands transformed into frozen clubs. Ghulam and Fidali fared far better in Kashmiri wool pullovers, but even they shivered when the wind gusted.

After they had trudged through the wind for eight hours, the terrain changed from flat plains of sand and rock to barren hills. They came across no other people; the only signs of habitation were the occasional flickering of lamps far to the south, marking clusters of dwellings visible from the crests of the hills, and a few straggling goats that had lost their flock before nightfall. The walking was labored, with the constant ups and downs of the foothills. The air thinned with the gain in altitude, and although the troughs of the hills shielded them from the wind, the cold was even more penetrating than in the plains.

Cold and exhausted as he was, Nick felt relieved to be on the move, walking with the urgency and trepidation of an escaped convict. His fear of roving police patrols, however, never materialized. *Tomorrow they will find me,* he thought. For in the eyes of the police, he had murdered one of their own—far worse than merely killing a foreigner. They would see him hanged one way or another.

Fidali rushed ahead as soon as the pale light of morning diffused over the scrubby hills. "Let him go," said Ghulam, as Nick endeavored in vain to keep up with Fidali's sudden burst of uphill speed. Nick's suspicion of their motives unsettled him whenever he did not have both men in his sight. He would envision them lying in wait behind some outcropping, ready to stab him in the back or shatter his knees with a boulder, hoping that he might have some money stowed on his person that they could take.

Aside from mistrust of his companions, he feared solitude because it tended to make his mind wander, often to his impending capture, but mostly to Yvette. Her body had been dumped to rot in a similar, sun-baked hell. At times Nick's mind would play tricks on him, and he would find himself gripped by terror, convinced that just over the next rocky crest, or at the bottom of some approaching dried riverbed, he would stagger upon her half-naked corpse, pocked with bruises and bled out through the neck like a slaughtered goat, vultures feasting on her putre-fied flesh. These vivid and horrible images would never stop tormenting him, he thought. They were his punishment.

When Nick finally reached the top of the hill, he breathed a sigh of relief. Fidali was a half mile ahead waving them toward a stone shepherd's hut. He had only been scouting for shelter. "Good—Fidali find it," Ghu-lam said, some distance ahead of Nick. "There, we rest until night."

They dropped their contraband inside the hut, constructed of rough stones piled tightly together, crowned by a mud ceiling, and built into the face of a hill. Inside, the floor was heaped with dried animal dung, swarming with flies. Eager to smoke out the stench, Nick helped Fidali gather twigs and bits of branches for kindling from the adjacent hillside, while Ghulam placed some slabs of dung inside a circle of rocks to form a makeshift stove. He lit the fuel and started to heat water he carried in a plastic jug for tea and potatoes.

After refueling their tired bodies, they smoked, settling in for a long rest through the daylight hours. It was warming rapidly outside with the intensifying sun; within hours it would exceed 120 degrees, a huge swing in temperature from the freezing night. The hills appeared through the rough stone entrance of the hut like the grayish-brown humps of sitting camels, windswept and barren except for sporadic clumps of scrubby chaparral.

Nick was anxious, too ill at ease to sleep. "Where are we now?" he asked.

"We are still in land of Mahsuds. Very close to Afghanistan—the border is only five kilometers from here. Very dangerous."

"What's the danger?" he asked, with some hesitation.

"The people here follow Ayaz Ahmed Abassi. He controls all smuggling across the border. His people cross here with opium from Afghanistan, sell it in Darra, Landi Kotal, and Peshawar, and buy guns and bullets to sell back in Afghanistan. Abassi is a very rich man. If his people find us, they will kill us."

"What for?"

"Because we are not Mahsud. And because we smuggle not for Abassi but for ourselves. Ghulam is very sorry to put you in danger."

Nick paused, skeptical of Ghulam's sincerity. "I accepted the risk."

Ghulam smiled. "As you wish, sir."

"What about the army, or the police? Don't they patrol here?"

"You mean Pakistani? They do not dare. They would be shot."

"But there must be tribal police?"

Ghulam snickered, apparently amused by the question, and then said something in their mutual language to Fidali, whose lips curled under his beard into a wry smirk as he worked.

"Yes, sir, of course there are tribal police," Ghulam replied, his eyes twinkling. "Abassi is the chief."

Nick considered this—a bandit, gunrunner, and opium smuggler enforcing the laws of the land, and his companions' ability to find some kind of ironic humor in the sad truth of it. Were he not exhausted, scared, and facing his own imminent demise, he, too, might have found it in him to conjure a chuckle.

"So why do it if it is so dangerous? Why smuggle? Is the money worth risking your life?"

"We are all just mice running across a field filled with snakes. What will happen will happen, inshallah. Ghulam has seven daughters—seven dowries to pay. We do not like to do it, but we have no choice. . . . But Ghulam does not smuggle drugs or liquor—Allah forbids it."

"But he doesn't mind cigarettes?" Nick said, immediately regretting the inherent sarcasm of his question.

"Not so much, sir." Flashing a toothy grin, Ghulam pulled a cigarette halfway from his pack and offered it to Nick. Appreciative that Ghulam had not taken offense at his words, Nick took it, even though his last one had not yet burned down to the filter.

"Why not try to find work in India?" Nick asked. "Aren't there jobs in Delhi or Bombay? Isn't that safer than the Afghan frontier?"

"Safer?" Ghulam scoffed. His mood suddenly turned glum. "India is big problem for Ghulam. I went one time. I took the train to Delhi with one of my wives and daughters to find work in the Muslim quarter. As soon as we cross into Gujarat, Hindus with clubs come onto train and attack Ghulam. They pull me and my family off the train at next stop. It was a small village in Uttar Pradesh. They drag Ghulam into a field, beat me, and start to rape my daughters."

"No police around to help?"

"The Indian police saw. But they do nothing. They are too scared of the mob. Or else they are their friends."

"I'm sorry," Nick said.

He nodded somberly. "A Brahman from the village came to the field and stood between the bad people and Ghulam's poor frightened daughters. He must have been an important man, because he had some very big men around him, also with clubs. And they let us go."

"You're a lucky man."

"Luck . . . ? No, sir, Ghulam does not believe in luck. Allah willed it. The Brahman told me that Muslims had torn down a very old Hindu temple days before. Now the Hindu people were mad at the Muslims. He said it is too dangerous for Muslim girls in this part of India. So, Ghulam take daughters and wife on next train straight back to home. All the way, Ghulam fear for them. Thanks be to Allah, we made it back. Ghulam will never go again. Never."

Ghulam shook his head. "And you, English? How many children?"

"None."

Ghulam stared at Nick, perplexed. "But why not? You are from rich country. You should have given life to a whole village of little ones by now."

Nick shook his head. "I'm not married, so I never had any children."

Ghulam tugged on his beard. "No wife? No children? If you do not mind me saying, sir, when Ghulam was a younger man like you, he never even slept. My wives were fighting, fighting, all the time over poor Ghulam. In the mornings he was so sore he had to go out behind his house and dip his buttocks in freezing glacier stream just to wake it up from the dead, inshallah!" he said with a chortle. "You must make your parents very disappointed, with no babies for them to spoil."

"I'm sure they would give me a hard time about it, if they were still around."

"Allah . . ." Ghulam muttered. "But they are in peace now. . . . Ghulam has three wives. Two would be okay, but three is too many. Two of them are sisters. And they have two other sisters, too, who also live in my home, since their own husbands were killed in Kashmir fighting. So it is like being a cock in a coop full of hens—all the time, 'cluck, cluck, cluck' about something. I have to go find work away from home just to keep from becoming crazy man!" he said, not without nostalgia. "But they please me."

Fidali, who had left the shelter briefly while Ghulam and Nick had conversed, had just returned with large granite boulders tucked under each of his arms. Despite their obvious weight, Fidali hauled the rocks effortlessly in his upturned palms, before dropping them, with a deep thud, around the fire. Fidali then pointed to the rocks, inviting Nick and Ghulam to sit. Nick and Ghulam nodded their thanks and sat on the makeshift stools watching from a distance while Fidali knelt and blew a long, forceful gust of wind from his seemingly bottomless lungs onto the smoldering embers and dung, until smoke permeated the entire shelter. "I bet he could play a mean tuba," Nick remarked, eliciting a look of confusion from Ghulam. "He doesn't talk much, does he?"

"Fidali knows the true value of words," Ghulam answered without further explanation.

"How do you know each other?"

"He was the husband of my sister."

"Your brother-in-law."

"Yes. But my sister is in Paradise now, *Allah haq*."

"I'm sorry."

He held his palms up to the sky, a look of resignation on his face. "It is not our place to question what is written. . . . Ghulam told Fidali to marry one of my seven daughters or my five sisters-in-law, or one of my twelve cousins. I do not care which one. He can marry all of them if he wants. *'Please, take them,'* Ghulam says. The Qur'an says it should be so. But after Suraya, Fidali will not take another wife."

Nick considered this. "Maybe things will change in time," he said. "Maybe he loved your sister so much he thinks anyone else will just fall short."

"Maybe." Ghulam sighed. "Now his love is gone. And he will not speak to anyone but Ghulam. I am the only one," he said, his words resonating with melancholy.

Nick turned to Fidali, expecting a reaction from him, after all of their talk. But he remained expressionless.

"He does not understand English so good," said Ghulam. "But he understands life."

Nick looked at Ghulam curiously, then back at Fidali.

"Do not worry," Ghulam added, chuckling. "He is not listening, anyway. He hears only when he listens, and he listens only when he wants."

"I've heard that complaint before. Always from women."

"Yes, sir," said Ghulam, knowingly. "Sometimes a man's brain is like beeswax that clogs up his ears."

Nick rested his back against the inner wall of the hut, reflecting on the reticent Fidali as he watched him place a kettle onto the fire. It was hard to picture such a feral man being sensitive at all, let alone, as Ghulam described him, romantically in love. With his long black beard, penetrating stare, and muscular frame, he appeared every bit the stereotype of the fierce medieval Islamic warrior, but for the calm, almost docile composure.

As Ghulam watched Nick studying Fidali, Ghulam's face assumed a sad, contemplative expression.

"It is written in the hadith," Ghulam said, "that when Muhammad returned once from a victorious battle, he said to his disciples, 'We have returned from the little holy war to the great holy war.'

"'What do you mean, Great One?' asked the disciples. To which the Prophet replied, 'The little holy war is a war against the unbelievers. But the great holy war is the war against one's own self.'"

Ghulam stood and started toward the door. "You rest now," he said. "Tonight we start walking through the Hindu Kush. Do you know what *Hindu Kush* means?"

Nick shook his head.

"'Crusher of Hindus.' It will be very cold there—colder than last night. I will be back before nightfall."

Before Nick could ask him where he was going, Ghulam strode out into the hot sun and disappeared behind the hut.

CHAPTER 20

"Who are you to be barging into my house at this hour?" Raza rebuked the feral ragamuffin with the chest-length beard and deeply furrowed face who had invaded his living room at dawn.

"Salaam alaikum to you, too, Father."

"Father? I'm not your father." Raza barred the door with his arm.

"You old fool. It is me. Kazim!" his son exclaimed.

"Kazim? *Allah haq*! You look so . . . old."

"Thank you. I will take that as a compliment."

"It is not," Raza stated emphatically.

"Can I come in, please—to my own father's home?" Kazim said, growing irritated. Raza hesitated for a moment—too long, as far as Kazim was concerned.

"I suppose, so long as you promise not to bring ruin upon me. Stamp the mud off your shoes. Your mother does not need another reason to nag. And wash—you smell like a donkey." Cringing, Raza waved his hand in front of his face.

Kazim sighed in frustration, then he kicked the dirt from the treads of his boots—the brave mujahid who had for two years fought, killed, and watched men die, deflated to an admonished child.

After years of fighting for his country's freedom, Kazim presumed that he and his father would have much to talk about—things of which a father should be proud. But Raza was uninterested. He had never understood why Kazim left home. Kazim could have married into a good family and been set for life. Not necessarily rich, but far better off than Raza had ever dreamed.

Moreover, since Kazim had left him in the lurch, Raza had been forced to tend his herds alone. Without a son to take over the hard labor, as was the custom of his people, he had lost all hope for an easier life in his old age. He cursed the day he had let Mullah Yusuf dupe him into letting Kazim attend the madrassa, where his son's head had been stuffed like a *pakora* with all that nonsense about holy wars and freedom.

Luckily, Raza had a particular talent for ignoring his son. For had he listened, he would have learned much he had no desire to know.

Kazim had left for Pakistan when the passes cleared, around the same time Aysha had left for Delhi. By the time he returned to his father's home years later, he was a seasoned mujahid.

The jitters he had felt during his first firefight ceased to haunt him during the many more battles that followed. Though the "killing" part of war was not something that had come naturally to him, as had the other skills of soldiering, he had acquired a stomach for it, even if he could never acquire the taste. He had earned the "blood respect" of his peers, eventually even winning over Muzzafar, who had become Kazim's mentor despite their unspoken differences. By the time Kazim showed up at his father's doorstep, he had proven himself many times over and had been given command of his own cell of mujahideen.

The way of the Kalashnikov had transformed Kazim from a poor goatherd, whom no one had taken too seriously (not even Aysha, he thought), to a leader with power to shape the future. He would not, like his father, tend goats in poverty his whole life, while others moved into his land and siphoned its wealth. He would drive the Indians out or die trying. At the very core of his being, he was a freedom fighter; no one could ever take that away from him.

Raza, however, was unimpressed. "So, are you home to stay? No more of that stupid business of yours, running around in the mountains with a gun, trying to bring down the Indian elephant with a pinprick?"

"Stupid? I am fighting for people like you, who are too lazy to fight for themselves. I am fighting for your freedom, Father. For once, why can't you show some respect?"

"I do not want anyone to fight for me!" snapped Raza. "You should be tending my herd. It will, after all, be yours once my time has come, inshallah."

"Is that all you really care about? Goats?"

"I am a goatherder," he replied with a sardonic shrug. "What difference does it make to me whether Kashmir is independent or part of India or part of Pakistan or whatever else people are hollering about these days?

No matter what flag they fly in Srinagar, I will still be doing the only thing I know how to do—tending goats."

"That may be. But if Kashmir were independent, you would get more money for your pashmina because you would not have to compete with the greedy Hindus who pay you next to nothing. And one thing is for sure, we wouldn't have a goddamn Temple to Shiva in our village, with all its obscene fornicating idols."

"Bah! The Hindus pay more than my Muslim buyers do. Especially that stingy Naseem, whose daughter, soon to be a rich doctor, I might add, you should have married as I told you. And if the Temple of Shiva bothers you so much—and I don't believe that it does—then look away, you fool!"

"There is no talking to you," Kazim said, exasperated. "You are a simpleton."

"Yes. And the fruit does not fall far from the tree. You seem to have forgotten that these days."

To Raza's unspoken relief, Kazim did indeed tell his father he was home to stay. He did not bother, however, to mention what little time he would be spending in the pastures. In the ensuing years, the rebel leader who would come to be known to the Indians only by the villagers' moniker—"the Leopard Slayer of Gilkamosh"—became the nemesis of the security forces. He would lead his band of mujahideen in countless raids and ambushes: disrupting supply lines, stealing provisions, and showering deadly fire upon the terror-stricken, altitude-sick lowlanders of the Hindu rank and file.

The mule was old and diseased, its belly filled with tumors. Nevertheless, when Kazim spat on his hands, gripped the rope, and gave a mighty heave, the animal would not budge. It had brayed and reared on its hind legs in stubborn defiance all the way up the steep trail. Now that he had practically dragged it only yards from its final destination, the mule's resistance only became more vehement, as if it somehow anticipated what was in store for it.

Kazim peered down the trail at his two comrades. They had Kalashnikovs strapped on their shoulders and carried a heavy wooden crate on top of a handheld cargo stretcher. Kazim checked his watch and then shouted: "Hassan! Jamal! Help me get this old beast moving. The road is just on top of this ridge."

Hassan joined Kazim at the harness rope, while Jamal used a switch he had broken off from a nearby pine to whip the animal's flank. Pulled and flogged, the mule twisted its neck and grunted in ire before it reluctantly ascended the slope.

At the top of the ridge, they came to a jeep road, unpaved and rocky, which had been recently blasted into the mountainside by the Indian army for use as a supply route to posts on the Line of Control. Before, there had only been the mule trail that Kazim and his two mujahideen had slogged up, but the jeep road permitted more rapid deployment. The three men walked the mule and their supplies downhill on the road until it turned a blind curve—a spot where momentum coming down the mountain could easily cause a braking vehicle to slide. Kazim led the animal to the middle of the road. He nodded to Hassan.

Hassan held up his palms and muttered a prayer for permission before he swung his AK-47 to his shoulder. He shot the mule through its brain. It gave a shrill cry, almost like a squealing pig. It stumbled forward few paces, collapsed onto its front knees, and then rolled onto its side, kicking until dead.

Kazim retrieved a sledgehammer from the cargo stretcher. He smashed the dead mule's knees, the two facing up. With his hands, he wrenched the shattered forelegs inward, toward the belly. "Come on. We've got to move quickly."

The three mujahideen grabbed the harness rope and heaved at the carcass. It was heavy and dragged only slowly across the dirt. They left it several yards from the side of the road, just far enough so a truck or jeep could pass by without moving it further. The whole scene appeared as though the mule had been hit by a vehicle, euthanized by gunshot, and then hauled out of the way.

Kazim wiped the sweat from his palms, and then lifted a 120-millimeter artillery shell out of the crate. The shell, an unexploded one that had fallen on a village near the Line of Control, had been rigged with a fuse wired to a battery and a small radio receiver, all wrapped around the shaft with duct tape. Jamal pried open the mouth of the dead animal, while Kazim and Hassan thrust the elongated projectile inside, using the handle of the sledgehammer to plunge it deep enough down the mule's throat so as not to be visible. They then stuffed a burlap bag of ball bearings, rocks, and screws into the mouth, making sure the receiver antenna was not too obstructed.

Satisfied, Kazim nodded his approval. *"Kudah hafiz."*

Kazim watched Jamal and Hassan jog a ways up the road and then turn into the deodar forest covering the ridge. They were local boys. Like Kazim they had crossed the Line of Control at the urging of their mullahs to train in the camps in Pakistan. They had recently returned to their villages, full of idealism, eager to press the fight against the hated Indian occupiers upon Kazim's call.

Kazim had a fondness for these young, patriotic mujahideen, whom he considered kindred souls. In recent years, however, as his fighters had been killed or captured, more of the replacements sent across the Line of Control by Muzzafar and the leadership were of a different breed. They were pro-Pakistani in their leanings, often foreigners themselves—professional jihadis—from Pakistan, Afghanistan, even places as far as Saudi Arabia and Chechnya. They did not blend in or speak the local languages, so they lived the life of bandits, stealing livestock and looting villages, treating the more liberal-minded Kashmiris with disdain.

Kazim had little affinity for these radicals. For Kazim, establishing a "purist" Islamic state or merging with Pakistan was never the goal of the insurgency. His sympathies had always been with those fighters advocating *azadi*—independence, or freedom—from the corrupt Indian government and their brutal security forces, even though as a trainee he had been unwittingly steered by Mullah Yusuf to a pro-Pakistan camp, Lashkar-e-Tayyiba.

It was no mystery to Kazim that the Pakistanis—who had been funding the insurgency years before Kazim had joined the fight—had been pulling the strings. They were still doing so, even though America's War on Terror had shone a spotlight on Pakistan so it could no longer do it so openly. Of course, the Pakistanis would favor those groups advocating a merger with Pakistan and stock the ranks of the insurgents with the jihadis with whom they had forged alliances as far back as the Soviet War—people like Muzzafar, who cared more about fighting infidels than what was good for Kashmir. This aggrieved Kazim, but he was too smart to let it be known. Every week, it seemed, there would be news of some *azadi* leader being gunned down by one of the ever-splintering rival mujahideen groups, or captured by the Indians, a victim of betrayal by his own handlers. Kazim distanced himself from these power struggles emanating from across the Line of Control and decided he had better not change alliances until the time was right.

But as the political types had muddled the goals of the violence, so, too, had they changed the nature of the beast. The pan-Islamists did not just want to force a political settlement with Delhi, they wanted to "cleanse" Kashmir of the Hindu infidels. Thus, they adopted a strategy of terror, employing the special brand of barbarism they had practiced to perfection in Afghanistan. Beheadings, castration, skinning men alive, massacres, and rape were the tools of their kind of war. This, in turn, fomented equally brutal acts by the Indian security forces, which was exactly what the radicals wanted—a vicious cycle of violent action by the insurgents, countered by equally brutal reaction by the security forces— so that the war would finally take on a momentum of its own, a tornado of brutality sweeping all civility from the once idyllic land.

When Kazim took over his position of leadership, he did what Muzzafar had told him and excelled at it. However, as devoted as he was to the struggle against India, when he returned to Gilkamosh—his homeland, after all—he fought the war the way he wanted. The Indian military and police, and even civilians associated with the national government, were all fair game. But he had little tolerance for his men attacking innocents, and quickly meted out justice to those who did. Indeed, when Kazim witnessed three men who had been recently assigned to his command taking turns gang-raping a Hindu girl, a few weeks later he "volunteered" these same men for a frontal assault against an Indian position. They were shot to death instantly. In this way Kazim enforced his rules in a manner undetected by the leadership across the Line of Control. But the message to his unit was always clear. By avoiding harm to innocents, his men enjoyed the support of the people. In fact, to many, especially the young boys, Kazim and his mujahideen were heroes.

Nonetheless, Kazim feared the day would come when direct orders would be dispatched from higher up to fire into a crowd or bomb a temple. One time years ago, one of Kazim's mujahideen, acting on his own, strafed a bus full of military families, killing dozens of women and children. The command believed Kazim had ordered it. Hoping it would gain him time, Kazim played along with their misconception, letting their mistaken belief stand. But that was several years ago, and time would someday erode the goodwill he had stolen from the madman's act.

*   *   *

These dreadful thoughts flashed through Kazim's head as he worked his way to the top of the ridge. He scanned the trees across the canyon for any sign of Hassan or Jamal. Nothing. They must have taken their positions already, buried themselves in leaves or behind rocks. The boys had learned their skills well in Pakistan.

Kazim sat hidden from the road behind a thick tree trunk, giving him a bird's-eye view of the road. He checked his rifle and laid out his equipment. There was nothing to do but wait. He drew his knife and began to whittle a juniper branch.

As he worked the knife, his mind drifted to Aysha. He had thought of her often over the years, especially during the long down times between the acts of violence. He thought not just of her beauty and the times they had spent together but of how things might have been different had he not gone off to war. Surely, they would be married by now. He wondered what their daily lives would have been like together, how it would feel to make love to her whenever he wanted, how many children they might have. He imagined her pristine, girlish body and pictured how childbearing might have changed it by now, made her hips curve and her breasts heavier. Would he have been jealous of his children for stealing her attention?

At night Kazim would envision his lips pressed into her neck under the curtain of her satin hair, his body entangled in hers, her hard belly perhaps swollen with child, and concluded he would only desire her more this way, as the mother of his children. When these fevered moments subsided, however, he often was left not with the fondness of memory but with the pain of regret, and the near madness of his longing.

Kazim heard the distant grumble of the approaching Indian convoy. He stopped cutting and put down his knife. He wiped the sweat from his brow, then peered through his binoculars.

Several jeeps, a large personnel truck carrying at least fifteen to twenty soldiers, and two cargo trucks descended the hill toward the road below him. The leading vehicle, one of the jeeps, slowed to a stop some distance from the mule carcass. A soldier stood. He studied the dead animal through field glasses long enough for Kazim to think the plan had failed. But then the Indian soldier waved to the vehicles behind him. The jeep veered around the carcass, passing close to it. The other jeeps and trucks jerked forward and followed.

Kazim reached down for a black box with a joystick control laid out beside him. It was a transmitter for a toy model, a radio-controlled car or plane, perhaps. He rested the box on the ground between his knees. The truck filled with soldiers slowly approached the dead mule.

Kazim took a deep breath and closed his eyes. He focused not on the business at hand but rather on the vision that was still fresh in his mind—a woman's body, beautiful, laid out before him, the only one he had ever known.

His breath quickened as he found the pain. His fists clenched and unclenched. He pounded his thighs. Then again, over and over, harder and faster, his whole body shuddering with a surge of anguish that seemed to erupt from the deepest recesses of his being—until it released in one simple gesture.

Kazim jerked the switch.

The earth shook.

The truck exploded in flames and metal and torn bodies.

CHAPTER 21

Nick had dozed off while Fidali was praying. He had slept continuously for five hours until roused by Ghulam, who returned a half hour before sunset brandishing several blankets.

"Where did you get them?" Nick inquired.

"There are Hazara shepherds in the valley across the border. Good Muslims. They help us." Ghulam held his hand over his heart in a display of gratitude.

"You mean in Afghanistan?" asked Nick. "Weren't you afraid of border guards?"

"People here do not believe in borders. Why should Ghulam? Here, take these." Ghulam handed Nick two thick woolen blankets woven with piebald geometric designs. Nick thanked him, remembering the severe cold of the previous night.

"Tonight, we start to climb. We must be careful. Many mujahideen are moving through these mountains on their way to Afghanistan."

"They travel by night?"

"Yes," he said, thrusting a finger toward the sky. "They say Americans watch from the heavens. Safer for them to walk in the dark. And for us, too. If we give signal like this"—Ghulam waved his hand in front of him—"that means get down on the ground. And if we do this"—Ghulam stretched his arm out and spun it erratically in the air—"it means to run like ibex."

And climb they did. They trekked due north for three nights, straddling the border of Afghanistan, following a low valley along a milky tributary of the Chitral River. Then the path suddenly became more vertical than horizontal, ascending a grueling series of steep switchbacks up pass after rocky pass blanketed with dry scrub and strewn with endless fields of boulders. The dimly lit mountains loomed like sleeping giants under the glittering light of infinite stars, their snow-covered peaks illuminated with purple moonlight. The peaks of the Hindu Kush were smooth and bald, as if worked with a gigantic swath of sandpaper. The trail traversed the sides of the mountains, gaining and losing hundreds of meters at a cycle.

Nick struggled to keep a tight line behind his stronger, more fleet-footed companions. Despite the biting cold, sweat soaked through his clothing into the thick blankets Nick draped over his shoulders like an Afghan. Fidali moved quickly up the steep mountains, his relentless pace actually increasing uphill, his stride surprisingly agile given the trunklike thickness of his legs. Although Nick was a competent trekker, the physical labor, exacerbated by the thinness of the air, was grueling. His feet blistered and his exposed skin—neck, face, and hands—was frostbitten. He had no time to acclimatize, and his head throbbed painfully as they climbed.

They pressed on for hours without rest, hiking in silence, their senses on edge, peering into the darkness for any sign or sound of movement, hoping to detect any bandits or patrols before they spotted them. Several times Fidali signaled them and they ducked down, but each time it was a false alarm caused by an ibex or wild goat rustling in the bushes on the trail ahead.

Once, when they had reached the top of a high pass, Nick saw dull flashes of light far away on the western horizon. He mistook them for a lightning storm until he deduced from the lack of any thunderclouds and the distant rumble of a jet that they were caused by the bombs of a sortie, most likely American, dropped on some perceived target along the Afghan border.

Nick saw no evidence of roads or trails suitable for vehicles, only an ancient network of well-trodden foot and donkey paths. Relying on the safety of night, they continued to bivouac in the daytime—once in a cave, another day hidden within a thick stand of pines, and other times in the vacant shepherd huts randomly dotting the high pastures and hillsides. They were traveling late in the year, so there was little chance that shepherds would discover them, for their animals had all been herded into the valleys below in anticipation of the first snows. Bands of hunters, however, used the shepherd huts as bases for excursions to higher elevations to track ibex, Himalayan markhor, wild yak, snow goose, and the rarely seen snow leopard. If any hunters discovered them, Ghulam said, they would leave them alone. But Nick, fearing a price had been set on his head, had become obsessed with avoiding all people, even in these remote hinterlands where the indigenous population was completely cut off from Pakistani authority.

A more serious concern was the rampant militants—bandits with a cause, as Ghulam explained. To them the hefty load of cigarettes would be enticing booty. One day, while lying low in their daytime shelter, they spotted a caravan of a dozen men, several with Kalashnikovs strapped across their backs, moving northwest toward the Dorah Pass into the Afghan frontier. "Taliban?" Nick asked.

"No, sir," Ghulam said. "They have no turbans and their beards are still like feathers of a goose. Ghulam thinks they are young mujahideen recruits from Kashmir. Probably going to training camp in Afghanistan. If they run into any Pakistani army at the border, they will get a cup of tea and a meal before making their way across."

After three days of hiking north into the Hindu Kush, they passed to the west of the Kailash Valley, or Kafiristan—the "land of infidels," Ghulam called it—a series of isolated valleys populated by tribes of strange pagans, who by their dress and mannerisms seemed lost in time. "It is okay we walk in daytime," Ghulam announced. "Kailash people no problem."

Though Nick preferred to hike at night, the hermetic aura of the place relaxed him. The valleys were fertile and more populated than the windswept foothills from which they had come. The hamlets were laid out along slopes above streambeds; the abodes flat-roofed, made of mud brick and stone, clustered together like hives.

The Kailash men greeted the travelers warmly as they walked through their villages, and though many invited the group in for tea, Ghulam politely refused, preferring to move on. Unlike Prince, who had claimed, probably falsely, to be Kailash, these men had features that appeared European to Nick, many of them with striking blue eyes and reddish-blond hair. The women wore their hair twisted into tight braids dangling like horsetails behind their ears and were dressed in long gray or brown tunics with bright green and red fringes of woven yarn. Some went unveiled, while others paraded long, gaudy headbands of copper and bronze coins, red beads, cowrie shells, and mother of pearl buttons. "Very beautiful women," Ghulam remarked, and Nick agreed.

After passing through the Kafir valleys, they waded across a series of raging, ice-cold streams, and then headed northeast, forgoing the more heavily traveled Shandur Pass in favor of a northerly, higher, and more rugged offshoot of the Darkot Pass, which could only be traversed on foot. According to Fidali, Ghulam explained, this way over the Hindu Kush crest to Gilgit was relatively untrodden, and thus it was the safest way to cross undetected into the heart of Pakistan's Northern Areas—the part of the former principality of Kashmir that had successfully rebelled against Indian rule upon Partition and was administered by Pakistan.

The danger of bandits and roving mujahideen had lessened since they had moved away from the Afghan frontier, but as they headed toward the trailhead to the pass, they reached terrain even more daunting, too treacherous to be negotiated safely at night. Since they had to travel by day, they avoided the few roads along the tributaries of the Yarkhun River, opting instead to take the network of dangerously eroded footpaths that cut along the mountainsides before ascending the easternmost chains of the Hindu Kush.

When they finally neared the top of the pass, which ran alongside a deep, funnel-shaped canyon of ice and rock, they came upon a man and a young boy riding an enormous, shaggy-haired yak along a narrow trail bordered by a sheer cliff face. Large flaxen baskets filled with cordwood were strapped like saddlebags to the yak's flanks. Both father and son wore matching tall, cylindrical hats made of hair-fringed goat hide and long collarless button-down coats and knee-high boots made of tanned goatskin. Their faces, Mongolian in appearance, spoke of the lure of Inner Asia.

"Kyrgyz," Ghulam said. The man halted his yak, salaamed them, and force-filled their pockets with heaps of dried barley kernels that crackled in their teeth as they snacked on them. The language barrier impossible to bridge, the two Kyrgyz saluted the travelers by holding their right hands over their hearts and then moved on, happy enough to have exercised hospitality to strangers.

The mountains east of the Darkot Pass became massifs of black and purple granite; the *nallahs* deep and wooded, the stunted junipers, willows, and toothpick-shaped poplars of the lower altitudes giving way to dark firs and rows of birch, their leaves pure gold in their fall splendor. When they reached a mountain hamlet tucked in a valley north of Gilgit, they stopped to rest. Ghulam explained it was safe to venture into the village, populated by ethnic Tajiks. But Nick was still apprehensive of mingling with anyone, so he rested alone at the outskirts while Ghulam and Fidali went to stock up on *dhal*, rice, and fresh batteries for Ghulam's flashlight.

When they returned, the men cooked a meal of salted *dhal* and rice. Ghulam was uncharacteristically reticent. "There is big problem in Gilgit, the people say," he finally said.

"What kind of problem?" Nick asked.

"Sunni and Shia fighting. There is curfew. Too many Pakistani police. We must not go there."

"Does that mean we're not going to catch a truck in Gilgit?" Although his body had toughened up after weeks of walking, Nick would have welcomed taking a truck the rest of the way to the Line of Control and cutting another ten days off the journey. But at the same time, he feared the checkpoints road travel would present.

Ghulam shrugged. "We think maybe no truck. There is fighting on the border again, and there will be many army jeeps on the road. It is safer to go by walking."

Passing north of Gilgit by secluded foot trails, they delved into the western cordilleras of the Karakoram—the "Black Mountains." The Hindu Kush, formidable as they were, seemed tame in comparison to these giants. Nick felt hobbitlike, dwarfed against the immensity of the jagged, ice-capped spires surrounding them in vast rows like shark's teeth. Glaciers cascaded from precipitous mountainsides, filling whole valleys with white and black ice, grinding deep canyons between the peaks; the crash of avalanches rumbled from the great heights like sonic booms. An ever-present crescent moon loomed above them, juxtaposed against the azure sky. Coupled with the thinness of the air, it seemed they had entered the stratosphere; indeed, reaching points above fifteen thousand feet, they nearly had.

They trekked up acute steeps and down dangerous slides, along gigantic dry riverbeds, wastelands of nothing but dust and fissured sediment, surrounded by sharp peaks too vertical for snow. In the few places where water did flow, it was so thick with silt it looked like gray milk and tasted like mud. The only other travelers were clusters of itinerant Tajiks and Afghans returning from the fertile valleys of Hunza and Nagar, where they had found work picking the apricots, apples, and mulberries that grew there in abundance. But when they entered the rugged and dry highlands of Baltistan, the mountains and glaciers were too inhospitable for anyone other than bands of seminomadic goatherds, driving their flocks down from pastures dotting the high glacial basins in anticipation of the winter's snows.

"This land is home to our people," Ghulam explained. "Here it is safe."

"You are Balti?" Nick asked.

"Yes. Little bit Balti," Ghulam replied. "Fidali, too. Same same."

"But your faces are different. And Fidali has blue eyes," Nick said.

"Yes. That is because many years ago, Tibetan people come to Baltistan. Balti language is like Tibetan. Same same. Me—I am Tibetan Balti. You see?" Ghulam said, pointing to his Asiatic eyes. "Ghulam looks little bit like Chinese.

"Fidali is Balti, too," he continued. "But Balti people are all mix mix. His people come from the Dards."

"Who are the Dards?"

"Mountain people, too," said Ghulam, with a nod to the side. "Ancient people." He swept his head toward the peaks. "Dardic language little bit like Burushashki language people speak in Hunza. It is very old. Dardic people used to live all over Baltistan, Kashmir, and Ladakh. But then—Tajiks, Uzbeks, Pashtuns, Mongols, Turkmen, Hindus, all kinds of other people come in, too. Everyone, mix mix," he said again, rolling his hands. "Only in high mountain villages are true Balti people still found. Like Ghulam's village."

Nick found the discussion of Ghulam's and Fidali's ancestry a useful way to keep his mind off his physical exhaustion and his growing fear of the impending border crossing, which had once seemed too remote to worry about. "So the Dards were living here before Mohammad was alive?" he asked.

"Yes. Many years before Islam came to this land. Then we were infidels like Kailasha. We believed in many gods—some say 'same same' as gods of Skander."

"Skander? You mean Alexander the Great?" said Nick.

He looked uncertain. "Yes, I think. Then we learn Buddhism from the Tibetans. Now we are Muslim, inshallah. You see?—mix mix."

"Which of the invaders brought Islam?" Nick was oblivious to the cynicism inherent in his question.

"Islam did not spread here by the sword." Ghulam was emphatic. "It was brought by Sufis. They were scholars—people of peace."

When the trail turned a corner, they came upon a section that clung to the side of a vertical cliff, as though some mythic gargantuan had gouged it into the granite face with a gigantic pickax. Below, a sheer drop plummeted several thousand feet to a roaring river. Huge plumes of white water foamed over immense boulders, the sound of crashing water amplified against the cliffs, drowning out the sound of their footsteps. The trail was only a meter wide; one slip would result in certain death. The immensity of the cliffs on either side of the canyon, and the deep chasm in the earth, was at once awesome and frightening.

As if cued by their conversation, Ghulam pointed toward the cliff above them, yelling to be heard above the torrent: "There, Buddha!"

Nick scanned upward to where Ghulam was pointing. Implausibly high on the cliff face, embossed in the black rock, was a massive figure of the Buddha sitting in the Lotus position, eyes closed, one hand in his lap, the other with middle finger touching thumb, as if meditating to the eternal sound of the rushing river.

Nick froze in his tracks. He imagined the artisan, thousands of years ago, dangling like a spider from a piece of twine, with a simple hammer and chisel, carving the masterful tribute to his god, more detailed and impressive than Mount Rushmore, Nick thought, yet made thousands of years earlier, with more primitive tools. The artisan no doubt believed that by choosing that spot, so difficult to reach, and so inspired by the timelessness of the river and mountains, he was creating a fittingly indestructible tribute to the god of eternal truths. He would have been satisfied to know that passersby such as Nick were still able to marvel at his work thousands of years after he risked his life to etch it into the precipice.

"There we must cross," hollered Ghulam, snapping Nick out of his trance. Ghulam pointed ahead, toward the vast abyss.

CHAPTER 22

Nick stood at the top of the cliff and stared down into the chasm at the furious river, its waters opaque with silt, billowing in clouds of mist and gray spume.

"What do you mean cross *here*?" Nick had to yell to his companions standing beside him to be heard above the roar of the turbid water. "Impossible!"

"No, sir!" said Ghulam. "Look!"

Ghulam pointed to a pair of rusted metal cables spaced about a yard apart on the surface of the cliff beside them. Nick followed the cables with his eyes down into the canyon. They ran in a long arch, bowing downstream, and then disappeared from view underneath the murky, gray surface of the river, pulsing back and forth where they penetrated the swift surface. The cables reappeared closer to the opposite bank of the river, where they curved back upward and then disappeared from view over the top of the far cliff.

Nick then looked where they were standing and saw that the cables had been looped and knotted to several thick hemp ropes, which were, in turn, wound around two sturdy pine trunks driven like stakes deep into the ground, apparently some kind of primitive pulley system. From the tree trunks, the ropes ran to rock outcroppings on the mountainside above the river, where they twisted in a ganglion of knots and loops.

Nick gave Ghulam an inquisitive glance, still not comprehending how a couple of submerged cables, perhaps the remnants of an old bridge that had been swept away in floodwaters, were going to deliver them across the canyon.

"You see, sir," Ghulam explained, finding humor in Nick's confusion, "local people, they build bridge here so they can use pastures on other side of the river. But then mujahideen come and use bridge, too, for traveling back and forth from Kashmir to training camps. At first, local people were okay with them using bridge, because they treat people good.

But then, things change. More and more foreign fighters start coming—Afghan, Arab—they steal food and goats. So the villagers decide to destroy the bridge to stop them from coming. Now the bad soldiers have to go very far from here to cross, and do not come to people's village anymore."

"Makes sense," said Nick. "But how does that help us?"

Ghulam nodded down into the river. "It looks like the bridge was broken, maybe lost to the river, does it not? The local people make it look like that, but they never really destroy it. The bridge is just hidden. Underneath. You cannot see it because the water in this river is always gray with silt from glacier."

Ghulam turned and gestured to the tree trunks wound with the shabby ropes attached to the cables. "Those ropes, they look like they are no good. But they work. The people tie them to yaks to pull up the bridge when they want to use pastures on other side. It takes very strong yak. Sometimes two when the river is high. . . . Very clever, don't you think?"

Nick scanned the mountainsides. "I don't see any yaks around here. We're going to get some from the villagers?"

"No, sir. They will not let us borrow any yak. People here do not like foreigners knowing about bridge. That is why they hide it. Only Fidali knows. But he has kept their secret. As you must as well, sir. We would not want villagers to know that we know, because they would only live in fear that the bad soldiers would return to punish them. And they are good people, the villagers. . . . No, sir, we do not need yak. We have Fidali."

Nick glanced at Fidali, who had taken off his pack and was, for some reason Nick could not fathom, using the heel of his shoe to burrow a trench behind the first of the upright tree trunks. "You're telling me Fidali is going to pull up the bridge?"

"Yes, sir."

"With the pressure of all that water bearing down on it?" Nick said. "No way."

Ghulam thrust out his lower lip, a sign of concern. "The river *is* very high this time. Very hot summer, Ghulam thinks. Glacier melting more than normal. Could be very dangerous," he added.

Ghulam and Fidali conversed for several minutes in their dialect, until finally, Ghulam turned to Nick. "Fidali says we will try. We must pray that he is very strong today, inshallah. Otherwise, Ghulam fears we must walk all the way back over the Darkot Pass to go different way. If we are not pulled in the river."

Nick knew that backtracking all that way would consume at least an extra two weeks, time they could not spare with the first snows fast approaching.

Nick watched while his companions prepared for what he could only conclude would be an ordeal. Ghulam poured water from his plastic bottle onto the ropes where they were wound around the tree trunks in order to lubricate them. Fidali retrieved a spare length of rope he had brought in his pack, wrapped it around his shoulders and thighs to create a harness, and tied the rope into a double loop in front of his navel. Before he closed the loop, he threaded through the eye the ropes attached to the bridge cables, so that, in effect, he had locked himself to the bridge cables by a makeshift carabineer. He then wound the ropes around his waist two times. Nick thought Fidali foolhardy to bind himself in this manner, for in the event he could not handle the force of the current bearing down on the submerged bridge—a concern Ghulam had already acknowledged—he would be swept down into the furious river and would drown or die of hypothermia. Ghulam, however, told Nick that Fidali's method was the only possible way of getting enough leverage to raise the bridge.

When he finished tethering himself to the ropes, Fidali sat himself in the trench he had dug on the incline behind the trunk closest to the edge of the cliff, wedging his feet firmly against the wood. Then Ghulam instructed Nick to position himself behind, above, and slightly to the side of Fidali, in order to take up the slack as Fidali heaved at the rope. "Be prepared to pull, too," Ghulam said.

Ghulam then climbed up the mountainside behind the second tree trunk, spat in his hands, and grabbed the ropes as well, unwinding them from the pole until a single wrap of each was all that was left to stave off the pull of the river. Ghulam wound the loose end twice around his own waist and dug his feet into the sand. "Okay, we wait for Fidali now," Ghulam said.

Nick watched Fidali from his obscured vantage. Fidali breathed deeply for several moments, bent his legs at the knee, and adjusted his grip on the rope. Then he closed his eyes as if in meditation, uttered what Nick guessed was a prayer, and yelled loudly, *"Allah-o-Akbar!"*

Ghulam pulled the ropes up over the top of the tree post, and instantly, all three men felt the powerful drag of the river nearly topple them downward. At that moment Nick was certain all three of them would plunge into the torrent, never to be seen or heard from again.

As he struggled to hold on, Nick watched Fidali. His teeth clenched as the full force of the river pulled against him, yanking his body downward until his knees bent deeply, his feet wedged against the tree the only thing keeping him from careening into the river. For a suspended moment, Fidali and the river seemed to be locked in a stalemate, his back bowed, his massive thighs trembling, the tight, banded tendons of his neck popping out from under his skin.

Suddenly, Fidali grunted and his body buckled, his knees thrust against his chest.

"He's losing it!" Nick yelled, clutching the rope, sure Fidali was going to plummet headfirst to his death along with the whole apparatus, tree trunks and all. But somehow, his body bent forward, his face contorted in agony, Fidali held fast.

His lungs sucking in air, he slowly pushed his legs against the tree, which bent under the conflicting forces of Fidali and the river. For a few moments, the rope did not move. Then, slowly, it inched upward, and then stopped.

Fidali paused, hyperventilating to replenish his strength, as sweat dribbled down from under his cap and off the point of his beard. He heaved again, and the rope moved another inch. And then another. Until his legs were finally straight, locked at his knees.

"It is coming!" Ghulam hollered.

Nick looked down into the chasm. Though he could still see nothing under the murky water, a wave—more like an elongated hump—had formed across the river from some unseen, submerged obstruction, as if the long spine of some sea monster were starting to surface.

"Help him! Pull pull pull!"

Fidali cocked his knees again, quickly, so as not to lose momentum, allowing Nick to draw the slack from the last heave, which Ghulam wrapped around the second tree. Over and again Fidali squatted and pressed his legs against the tree, hauling the rope until his legs were straight. Nick and Ghulam pulled, too, but with Fidali taking the brunt of the weight, it seemed they were doing little more than taking up his slack. Each time Fidali's legs locked at the end of their press, the wave across the river grew larger, until it crested with white water and grayish foam.

Finally, Fidali gave a last growling heave, and a dangling mass of rusty cables entangling a series of waterlogged, broken planks suddenly burst free from the roiling surface of the river. Fidali, Nick marveled, had done what he had never imagined a man could do. He had beaten the river.

With the tension of the current no longer a factor, the pulling was easy, and within minutes of first surfacing, a mangled suspension bridge traversed the gorge, stretching a good 250 feet across a sheer drop of at least four times as far. Fidali collapsed in exhaustion, his chest heaving, as Nick and Ghulam tied off the ropes.

"Very close to swimming," Ghulam said, beaming. He slapped Nick on the shoulder and then approached Fidali, offering him a drink from his water bottle.

Nick studied the bridge, which showered the surface of the river below with streams of silty water. The ancient cables of the bridge were knotted together in places, as if the original sections were not long enough to reach, and separate additional sections were entwined like simple electrical wires to make the bridge reach across. The shoddy planks intended as footholds, blackened with water rot, were spaced at impossible intervals, some a meter or more apart, so that one would literally have to leap across the gaps from one footboard to the next. Some of them were so badly fractured that only the cable itself, like a circus tightrope, could provide any footing at all. Between the planks there was nothing to prevent a fatal plunge.

"After we cross, then just two days until border," said Ghulam, trying to encourage Nick, who, despite his awe at Fidali's ability to have raised it from the riverbed, stood petrified at the sight of the slick, mangled contraption.

"You can't be serious," Nick said, convinced Ghulam was joking. "I mean, when was the last time Fidali used it? It's probably rotted a lot since then."

Ghulam struggled to hold his laughter. But when Fidali, too, who had recovered remarkably from his exhausting struggle to raise the bridge, broke into an uncharacteristic smirk, they both burst out uncontrollably. Nick turned, deadpan.

"Sorry, sir. Please, it is no problem," said Ghulam, laughing. "Fidali and Ghulam will go first. Then you will see."

Before Nick could voice further objection, Fidali sprang out onto the first plank, and then the next and the next, until he was well out on the bridge. It sagged deeply, swaying precariously with each bound he took. A few steps further, and Ghulam followed suit. "Follow Ghulam!" he hollered.

"Wait!" But it was too late. Ghulam was halfway across before he twisted around. Holding a cable with one of his hands for balance, he waved Nick out onto the first plank.

"It doesn't look like it can hold all three of us," Nick said.

"No problem! Come come!"

Had there been more footboards, Nick might have found the bridge barely tolerable. But each step required a jump instead of a stride. And the rushing current, visible through the huge gaps in the planks and cables, created an optical illusion obfuscating Nick's perception of depth, throwing his eye-to-foot coordination wholly out of sync. It was like one of those three-dimensional drawings of a cube with one line drawn to connect in the wrong place—one cannot tell which line is in the foreground. As a result the water sometimes looked closer than the planks, deceiving his mind into wanting to step into the interstices instead of on the planks.

He envisioned himself being swept under, dashed along the riverbed, pinned under some subaquatic rock until he drowned or froze to death. Each stride was a struggle of will. Shaking with vertigo, knuckles white with tension upon the rusted and flayed cables, he shuffled, stretched, and clambered his way across from one slippery, rotten board to the next, between frozen moments of panic.

Fidali and Ghulam sat cross-legged on the far bank beaming prankishly. When Nick's feet finally touched solid ground, they broke out into a facetious ovation. Making the best of an embarrassing situation, Nick hammed it up, bending down to kiss the sand. When their revelry subsided, he joined them on the ground, where they smoked, staring across the vast chasm.

"You are very funny, English," Ghulam said, suddenly growing serious.

"Why? Because I'm chicken."

"Chicken?" Ghulam repeated, confused at the idiom.

"Scared," Nick clarified.

"No, not fear. Something else, Ghulam think."

"Oh? . . . Then, what?" Nick inquired, expecting a joke at his expense.

Ghulam tugged on his beard, assuming his pensive air, which Nick did not expect, given the preceding moment of levity. It occurred to him that Ghulam was a walking oxymoron—part clown, part prophet—capable of turning from one to the other like the flip of a coin.

"You are strong man, on outside, sir. Very . . ." He puffed his chest out and held his cupped hands, palms up.

"Confident?" Nick pitched in, helping him along.

"Yes. Con-fee-dent." He pronounced the syllables like a schoolboy learning a new word. "But you do not trust in *yourself*."

"I know. But you've got to admit—that bridge—it's sketchy to say the least."

"Dangerous? Yes, of course." He paused, drawing on his cigarette. "But if you trust yourself, there is no reason ever to fear."

"That river, and that bridge, those are reasons enough for me. I couldn't help thinking about falling," replied Nick.

Ghulam nodded. Then, after a few moments of thoughtful silence, his eyes lit up with inspiration. He fixed them on Nick's. "Thinking is why you are afraid. To be able to think is a gift—it separates man from the animals. But Allah places each man's foot *before* he steps. . . . We might believe we can control where the foot falls. But we cannot, sir. It is already written."

Nick contemplated this thought for a moment. "I understand what you're saying. You believe that people can't really control anything; we have no free choice. It's already determined, whether I fall or make it across."

"Yes and no," Ghulam responded. "A man is free to choose his path. This is why Allah has given us this power to think. . . . If a man chooses the right path, Allah watches out for him and will forgive him even when he strays, so long as he chooses to get back on the right way. If a man chooses the wrong path," Ghulam shrugged, "then he will surely fall. If not in this world, then in the next.

"But once a man has chosen, rightly or wrongly, he cannot alter what has been written for him to happen along the way. This is our destiny."

"Okay," Nick replied, drawn into the discussion not by Ghulam's words, which he might have considered trite were they spoken by anyone else, but by his fervor. "But how do you know you *have* chosen the right path? That's the question. Because if, as you say, I've chosen wrongly, I'm bound to fall. Therein lies the problem." Nick spoke rhetorically, not really expecting an answer from Ghulam, who he was fast learning had levels of depth far beyond Nick's initial impression.

"You know right now, sir."

Ghulam stared intently into Nick's eyes. His words and demeanor did not strike Nick as sanctimonious, but his intensity, the personalization of his sermon made Nick uncomfortable, even defensive.

"I think I know what you're saying. You chose Islam, and *that* is the right path. But, no offense, you can't expect everyone to share your faith."

"That is not what I am saying," Ghulam snapped. "Yes, I am a Muslim. But the way of Islam is not the only path. 'Had Allah pleased, He could have made of you one community'—so it is written. But He did not ordain it to be so. You see, it does not matter what path you take to Him, or what Ghulam thinks. *You* know you have not chosen well. That is the important thing."

"You read minds," Nick retorted, smiling to mask his sarcasm.

"No, sir," he said firmly. "I can tell by the way you step across the bridge, the way you do not trust your mind to guide your foot. . . . I can tell by the way you were lost when we found you by the big rock, with no will to live. By the lies you tell about the blood on your *kamiz,* and by the way you are too scared even to tell us your name. I can tell by everything you say, and everything you do."

Nick shifted nervously on his haunches, confronted with his lies. When he looked into Ghulam's eyes, he expected anger and insult, but could detect not a trace of either.

"We are simple people, sir. But we are not blind," Ghulam added.

Nick bowed his head, ashamed. Ghulam reached over and touched him gently on the shoulder. "You have nothing to fear from us. You need not tell us what you have done. Deeds are not any man's to judge. Only Allah can do that."

Nick searched for something to say, anything, but came up empty. They sat in silence, Nick stinging from Ghulam's words and disgusted with himself, and Ghulam, his ruddy face aglow under the setting sun.

Nick glanced at Fidali sitting off to the side. Cross-legged on the sand, Fidali gazed across the chasm and toward the great Buddha carving on the far face of the cliff, hovering omnisciently. Though Ghulam had said Fidali could speak only a few words of English, Nick was certain Fidali knew exactly what had just transpired, the import at least, if not the words.

Suddenly, Nick was gripped by a strong urge to leave them. But he was tired of the running and the lies. Ghulam said he and Fidali would do him no harm, and Nick believed them, it occurred to him, more than he had ever believed in anyone. Confronted with his own lies, he felt as though he had tasted genuine trust for the first time in his life.

"If you knew I was fleeing the police, why let me come with you this far?"

"You are no threat to us. Look at Fidali, you have seen his strength. He could kill you with one hand." Nick glanced at the massive Fidali and knew it was true. "And Ghulam thinks you are a good man, who has just chosen unwisely," he added.

"How can you say that? You don't know what I've done."

"Ghulam knows, because he can see you are fighting inside your head—fighting the great jihad the Prophet has foretold. You are mujahid. You may not know it yet, but that is what you are. And that, sir, is something . . . precious."

Nick's face contorted with confusion and shame. "I'm not sure what that means. But I lied to you, Ghulam, in a lot of ways. I don't feel right staying. I'm a burden to you. I should leave."

Ghulam frowned. "Only if you feel that you must. Allah is forgiving. And so should be man . . . *Mr. Nick.*"

Ghulam pulled a folded piece of newspaper from his pocket and tossed it on the sand at Nick's feet. Perplexed, Nick glanced at Ghulam, and then picked it up.

It was a report from the Peshawar *Daily Guardian*—one of several gossipy English-language newspapers ubiquitous in Pakistan that would run exaggerated articles covering the latest violent crimes. The title read AMERICAN SUSPECTED OF MURDERING INSPECTOR IN FATA STILL AT LARGE. Above the column was a mug shot of Nick, next to one of Simon. Nick guessed that Ghulam must have seen the photo during a supply run in one of the larger villages along the way.

"Ghulam does not read English," he said. "But Ghulam pretty much knew the meaning of what it says before shopkeeper tell him."

His suspicion confirmed, Nick read the article:

According to witnesses, Inspector Rasool Akhtar of the Peshawar Police Department was shot dead by American Nicholas Sunder in a remote region of the Kyber Agency in the Federally Administered

Tribal Areas (FATA). Sunder is a known associate of Simon Black, an English national charged by the District Criminal Court of the North-western Frontier Province for the murder of Yvette DePomeroy, a French national, whose body was found dumped some twenty kilo-meters north of Landi Kotal in the Tirah Valley. Peshawar police sus-pect that Sunder, a material witness and possible accomplice in the killing of DePomeroy, was attempting to flee Pakistan through the porous borders of the Tribal Areas when he shot Inspector Akhtar to death. Black awaits trial for the murder of DePomeroy. Sunder remains at large. The Chief Judicial Magistrate has issued a nonbail-able warrant for Sunder's arrest.

Nick covered his face in his hands, feeling the weight of not only Yvette's fate but now Simon's as well bear down on his shoulders.

After a few moments, he felt a hand clasp his shoulder. Nick looked up and saw Fidali. He was pointing at the newspaper clipping clutched between Nick's fingers. In his free hand, Fidali held a burning match.

Confused, but seeing no reason why he should not comply, Nick handed Fidali the article. Fidali burned it until its ashes fell to dust.

Ghulam and Fidali resubmerged the suspension bridge under the river by unwinding the ropes wrapped around the tree trunks on the near bank. Then, after resting about an hour, Ghulam summoned Nick. "Tomorrow we cross big glacier," he said. "Very difficult walking. Then, next day, if weather is clear, we climb over Kumba La—very high snow pass—nearly twenty thousand feet. Winter is very near. If the pass is blocked by deep snow, it will not be passable until next June. But if Allah wills it, it shall still be clear, and we cross into India in just a few days.

"If it is your decision to come along, you are welcome. We ask only one thing. If we are stopped at the crossing, Ghulam and Fidali know nothing about you. And you, sir, know nothing about us."

Nick looked into his eyes. "Thank you, Ghulam," he said. "And you, too, Fidali." Fidali gave Nick a subtle nod, in a rare display of acknowl-edgment.

"Someday I *will* repay you both," Nick promised.

"Please, no," said Ghulam. "It is not our way."

CHAPTER 23

"This is preposterous!" exclaimed Mrs. Mehta, a dark-skinned Hindu woman with thick brows that appeared arched in a state of constant indignation. She paced to and fro before a crowd of her sisters and cousins. She was beside herself, hardly able to push the words past her lips. "I raised my little Mitra to be virtuous. Why, she doesn't even know a male organ from a banana—do you, Mitra."

Although it was not meant to be a question, like a flock of hens spooked by a weasel, the women jerked their heads in unison toward the teenaged girl, still dressed in her wedding sari, black streaks of tear-smudged makeup running down her cherubic cheeks. She was sitting in the reception room of the first known medical clinic in the history of Gilkamosh—Aysha's clinic. Mitra blew her nose with the tissue Aysha had given her. "I do now," she said, shuddering with sobs.

A portly matron dressed in a gaudy orange and gold sari, flanked by her own legion of female kin, stepped toward Mrs. Mehta. "Liar!" she snapped. "That girl is no virgin. You . . . you . . . deceived us and brought dishonor to the Khoudari name. Why, if it were not for my keen powers of observation, my poor Rishi would never have known he had married such tainted goods. I have the evidence to prove it." She held up a bed-sheet, spreading it out with her arms. The women gasped in unison. In the center of the sheet, speckling the posterior of a green embroidered elephant, were several small bloodstains.

Aysha shook her head, trying her best to be diplomatic and hide her irritation. "Mrs. Khoudari, medically speaking, that does not prove a thing."

"Nonsense!" Mrs. Khoudari erupted. "There would be more blood on the sheet if I squashed a cockroach! I demand an immediate annulment!"

"I am not a judge, Mrs. Khoudari," Aysha replied. "And even if making such judgments were within my purview, I would rule, in any event, that it should be up to the newlyweds whether to petition for an annulment." Aysha, however, was well aware of the parents' rights according to tribal custom to challenge a marriage on the basis of a bride's lack of virginity, which would have rendered her unmarryable.

"See," said Mrs. Mehta, wagging her finger in the other woman's face. "That's what I told you, you nosy old witch. I never should have let my daughter—"

"Shut up, you fraud! You and your cheap husband, who paid a pittance for a dowry. Imagine, ten thousand rupees and three goats! If you claim she was a virgin like you say, then what are you afraid of? I insist upon an examination, right now."

"Ohhh, so that's what this is about? *Greed.* You are just trying to bleed more dowry out of us by questioning my daughter's virtue. And you call *me* a fraud? Your son should be so lucky as to have married such a jewel as my Mitra."

"Stop, please!" cried Aysha above the din, silencing the women. "Fine. I'll do the exam. Just stop bickering."

Aysha took poor Mitra into the private room and had Vilashni, Aysha's nurse, fix the girl tea. Taking her time, Aysha looked down Mitra's throat with a flashlight, checked her ears, and felt her tonsils. "If they ask, I checked you *thoroughly,*" she told Mitra, wiping the smudged makeup from the girl's cheeks. Then, without examining another inch of the girl's body, Aysha returned with her to the reception area, where the women waited on pins and needles. "Last night was her first time," she announced. "Without a doubt."

"I don't believe it. How do you explain so little blood?" said Mrs. Khoudari, indignant, and more than a little dubious.

Aysha paused. "Perhaps, Mrs. Khoudari," she replied, "it has more to do with the size of the banana than with the peel in which it fits—if you know what I mean. I would be happy to examine your son, if you would like me to investigate further. He might be embarrassed by my assessment, but sometimes a little modesty can be a good character builder in a boy."

Mrs. Khoudari declined, and after an exchange of apologies and a few more goats, the mothers put aside their grudge and reached an accord, finally agreeing to grant the newlyweds their privacy.

The news that Aysha was planning to open a clinic in Gilkamosh had preceded her return. The villagers were ecstatic, and not just because their favorite daughter was returning. As soon as it was announced, they quickly compiled a long list of problems and ailments they needed addressed, only some of which were medical. Indeed, it became apparent to Aysha during her first few weeks of service that many conditions had been concocted merely as an excuse for a social visit. In other instances, as in the case of Mrs. Khoudari's challenge to young Mitra's chastity, Aysha was trusted to act in the nature of an arbiter.

Though she preferred to recuse herself from such nonmedical matters, Aysha was for the time being content with the mundane nature of the genuine medical conditions she was called upon to treat. Since she came to Gilkamosh a fresh doctor with the bare minimum of clinical training, she preferred to hone her skills on non-life-threatening ailments before tackling the more serious conditions that she anticipated would eventually arrive.

Of course, she had completed the mandatory emergency-room training in New Delhi, but never before had she been the only doctor on staff. In Gilkamosh she had no one with more experience to consult or to discuss options with, or to second-guess her decisions. She would have to do it all alone and take full responsibility should anything go wrong. A tall order, and a scary one, for a neophyte physician.

Surprisingly, Naseem had tried to dissuade Aysha from moving back home, preferring that she stay in Delhi and open a lucrative practice there. Kashmir could be a dangerous place for physicians. Since the start of the insurrection, many had already fled for fear of being kidnapped by militants for ransom. Others had been harassed by the Indian security forces, who, not always without cause, accused Muslim doctors of secretly treating wounded militants. Several prominent physicians in Srinagar had disappeared over the years, perhaps at the hands of militants, but more probably murdered by death squads made up of off-duty soldiers dressed as Muslims. "Don't worry about us," Naseem had told her. "We have survived this long without a doctor. A little rebellion won't change things."

But Advani, who had the ear of the commissioner of police, as well as the commander of the regional Border Security Forces, assured Naseem that he had been promised Aysha's clinic would not be harassed by security forces, as some hospitals in Srinagar had been. This gave the concerned father a modicum of comfort.

In any event, Aysha would not be deterred. She had intended all along eventually to set up shop in Gilkamosh, not just because she felt compelled to repay the villagers for their generosity or to rekindle things with Kazim, whom she had not heard from in nearly eight years. She knew, quite simply, that it was her destiny to return.

So Aysha had prodded and pleaded for grants from the Indian government and from various Muslim charities, barely scraping together enough money to purchase the initial stockpile of equipment and supplies. But at the end of the day, Advani once again made the whole scheme possible. He had made a killing on the pashmina wool business over the past decade, through all its ups and downs, and out of his sense of charity, a devout belief in karma, and not a little egoism, he posted a substantial infusion of the initial seed money.

With the aid of the best carpenters the village had to offer, the clinic was constructed on the outskirts of Gilkamosh, in a small, forested *nallah* segregated by a single ridge of mountains from the larger Gilkamosh river valley where the town was situated. The clinic was close enough to the village to allow one to commute quickly on the badly potholed dirt road, but far enough to afford the patients privacy and to avoid the roving eyes of the Indian security forces stationed in the village.

After the clinic had been running for nearly a year, it seemed Naseem's worries had been misplaced. Not a single casualty of war had come through Aysha's door, even though the fighting had spread beyond the Vale years ago to such remote areas as Kargil and Doda, which were not so far very from Gilkamosh, but which were easier to access. It appeared the insurgency, which itself seemed to revolve between cycles of brief but intense violence and long periods of apparent dormancy, would completely miss Gilkamosh altogether. In fact, things were pleasantly relaxed at the clinic, and Aysha even had some time to herself for the first time in years. But this was something, she discovered, she preferred to do without. For time alone meant opportunity for her mind to wander, dredging up the dormant sentiments of her youth.

CHAPTER 24

Fidali moved deftly through the vast talus fields atop the ridge of glacial moraine, his tattered brown *shalwar kamiz* rippling in the hot wind that moaned a melancholy baritone over the vast heaps of black rocky rubble. As he receded from Nick's vision, even Fidali's massive form was dwarfed against the immensity of the sheer spires surrounding the glacier.

The whole morning Fidali and Ghulam had maneuvered their way through the incessant pitfalls of shifting boulders, slick ice, and scree slides, as only men born to such terrain can do. They were not regular men, Nick fathomed, but human ibex, naturally selected through an evolutionary process spanning thousands of years of Dardic and Tibetan ancestry to leap and bound tirelessly at intolerable altitudes over rock and ice, crevasses and streams. Like horses smelling the barn, they raced at an incredible pace, hoping to beat the first snows of winter expected to fall any day and block the passes, impeding them from their homeland.

When Nick ascended the top of a ridge over which the two men had vanished, he froze in awe at the astounding view. Great fields of coal black ice flanked each side of a wide frozen river, slashed through the middle by a wider band of pure blue-white icebergs scintillating in the sun. The glacier stretched as far as his eyes could see, like a great, black-and-white-striped serpent coiling its way through the peaks toward the east, striking at the rump of China. Suspended in the magnificence of the display, for a fleeting moment Nick was consumed by an ineffable sensation of timelessness, as though all that had transpired in his life to that day had been swept into the oblivion of eternity by a single pure vision. The glacier appeared to him like an endless sea of possibility, where new ice, pristine and white, was reborn from the freezing night, while the old and sullied melted away, or was thrust underneath the frozen mantle with the slow march of time.

But then, as suddenly as it came to him, the notion escaped.

*   *   *

Baffled, Nick paused briefly, trying in vain to regain the inexplicable moment, before descending the steep slope of moraine to where Ghulam and Fidali sat waiting.

By the time Nick reached his guides, the sun was nearing its hottest, and the glacier creaked like the hull of a great ship. He could hear the hiss of running water from every side of him, and it unleashed his thirst. Stopping to drink, Nick noticed his water bottle was almost empty. He glanced around, but saw no stream.

"Ghulam?" he hollered ahead. "I'm out of water. Where's the stream?"

Ghulam pointed down to the ice under his feet. "Underneath!" Ghulam replied. "And over there." He pointed toward the distance where a huge, craterlike depression in the rubble gave way to an emerald green pool of ice melt. "But wait. Here it is black ice. Very dangerous."

"Dangerous?" Nick replied, his voice straining to be heard.

"Yes. Glacier moving. Better place for water in two hours' more walking." Ghulam pointed in the direction of the white ice forming the center of the glacier.

Nick's thirst was almost unbearable, and he was not sure he could wait that long before hydrating. But he heeded the warning, deferring to Ghulam's judgment, for Nick knew nothing of the nature of glaciers.

"Guide knows best," Nick replied, with a tinge of disappointment.

Ghulam waved for Nick to follow, then continued after Fidali, who was climbing up and out onto the gravelly black ice. "Stay close!" Ghulam added at a holler.

Fidali forged the path across the glacier ahead of the other two, probing the ice and rock with his walking stick, stopping occasionally to assess the safest way across as he moved. Nick trailed Ghulam at a distance, up and down icy ridges hidden deceptively under a thin layer of scree, stopping on occasion to catch his breath and once to stare in bewilderment at the immensity of Fidali's footprints, wide and set deeply in the slushy top layers of melted ice, appearing as if they could have been made by a mythical yeti. The going was slow and treacherous, with massive boulders, easily capable of shattering an ankle or shin, shifting dangerously on the slick black ice with the mildest disturbance caused by their footsteps.

The surface of the outer band of the glacier had been strewn with boulders perched implausibly atop thin stems of ice, appearing like surreal patches of giant mushrooms. But when they reached the white ice at the spine of the glacier, it was devoid of debris. Here the ice was segmented into huge seracs lined up like great crystalline dominoes, dripping like ice cream melting in the sun. Despite the circuitous path Fidali took to circumvent the seracs, the white ice provided better traction than its black counterpart, and they traversed it in a fraction of the time.

When they had crossed onto the second, farther band of black glacier, however, Nick heard a distinct popping sound, followed by a deep, ominous groaning under his feet, as if someone had roused a giant from slumber.

"*Allah haq!*" Nick heard Ghulam mutter.

When he looked up, Nick saw Ghulam frozen stiff, like a mannequin. Carefully, slowly, Ghulam craned his head toward Nick, searching for the hand that Nick was too far away to give. Unable to reach each other, the two men locked eyes for a moment. Then, Nick thought he saw Ghulam raise his palm as if in resignation, before the ice fell apart beneath him.

Nick screamed Ghulam's name as he scrambled up to the point where he had vanished. Where Ghulam had been, the glacier had caved into a funnel-shaped slide. At the bottom of the slide was a furious torrent of white water that sliced through the glacier, plunging straight down into a gaping hole. The mouth of the hole, wide enough to consume a man, was bottomless black. The water jetting into the hole was powerful and fast, like a precision drill that bored cleanly through the ice to the core of the earth. Anything that fell into the furious water, including Ghulam, would disappear in an instant, swept down deep under the glacier to drown in terrifying blackness.

"Ghulam!" Nick yelled. Only the roar of the water replied.

"Ghulaaaaam!" But he was nowhere to be seen.

Then, when Nick had lost all hope, he heard a feeble cry above the din. "Here!"

"Where?" Nick yelled, desperately scanning the abyss. At last he spotted a pair of white-knuckled hands about ten meters below him, clenching the base of a small boulder at the junction of the chute and sheer ice wall leading into the sinkhole.

What Nick did next was beyond foolhardy. Facing the slope, he lowered his feet and began to climb down the icy chute. Digging the toes of his boots into the thin layer of stones covering the ice, he clutched with his fingers to any handholds he could find—rocks, ice ledges, fissures—all the while praying he could maintain the critical friction that kept him from sliding uncontrollably to his death and knocking Ghulam down into the sinkhole along with him.

Loose rocks dislodged under his feet as Nick descended the chute. Ghulam turned his head as the rocks showered down on him, his arms shaking with his effort to hold on to the boulder, and his legs dangling uselessly. Hand over hand, toehold by toehold, Nick managed to crawl on his belly the ten meters down to where Ghulam's hands clung for his life.

When he finally made it, Nick was at a loss. He had no leverage to haul Ghulam up, and he was too precariously balanced on the steep, icy slope himself to do anything more than reach down with one hand and brace Ghulam's wrist. This alleviated some of the strain on Ghulam's own hands and arms, but it was only a delay of the inevitable. Ghulam was going to fall.

"Hold on!" was all Nick could think of to say. Stupid, it seemed, for what else was Ghulam to do?

Nick cursed. He was locked in a futile labor of contracting muscle and stretching sinew. Without a boulder or rope upon which to leverage himself, he could not pull hard enough to haul Ghulam up, for Nick himself would have tumbled off the face if he tried. Nor was it likely, even if Nick were to let Ghulam go, that Nick could climb back up. Descending was one thing, but the ice chute created by the collapsed glacier was too slick to ascend without crampons. In trying to save Ghulam, Nick had doomed them both. With their eyes the two men urged each other not to lose resolve. But each knew their combined effort was useless. The critical mass was approaching.

"It's okay," Ghulam said through his clenched teeth.

Nick held fast, his arm trembling with exertion, but the futility of the struggle was sapping his ability to resist. He was *losing*. He was going to die if he continued to hold on. Letting him go, ceding Ghulam to his death, was Nick's only chance of surviving himself.

"Let go!" Ghulam implored him again. His eyes were strangely calm.

Sweat dripped from Nick's forehead, stinging his eyes. He could feel his hand loosening around Ghulam's wrist.

"Allah!" Nick heard Ghulam shout, barely audible.

Then Nick felt a lashing sensation at the back of his neck. Twisting around, he saw a rope dangling in his peripheral vision, its end tied in a wide loop. High above, Nick could barely make out Fidali's face, peering over the icy ledge.

Nick wound the rope around the crook of his elbow, then dropped the loop for Ghulam, who snatched it like a gecko pouncing on a fly, wrestling it under his armpit while his legs swung like a pendulum. The wild swinging motion wrenched them both off the face. Ghulam plummeted, taking Nick with him.

There was a chaotic blur of falling rocks, as Nick's stomach lifted into his throat, then a violent jarring accompanied by an excruciating pain tearing at Nick's bicep where the rope dug into him like a tourniquet. He slammed hard, shoulder-first, into the ice face, Ghulam jackknifing below. But the rope held fast.

Minutes later, collapsed in a heap at the top of the ice chute, when their lungs at last settled, Ghulam looked at Nick, Fidali, and then the sky, and he smiled.

"So it is written," he said.

CHAPTER 25

There is a silent understanding between human beings when they have seen the same thing, felt the same thing, and acted. Neither Ghulam nor Fidali ever mentioned the episode on the glacier. Perhaps in their worldview, there was nothing to say. Their lives, quite simply, had not been fated to end. And in light of Fidali's incredible rescue, Nick, too, began to wonder about the existence of destiny.

Even assuming a twist of fate, the three men had acted together in a near-death crisis, peered over the precipice as one, and delivered themselves to safety. Nick had probably saved Ghulam by what he had done, delaying his fall long enough for Fidali to be able to rescue them both. But still, he felt no pride in his action. True, he had risked his own life by crawling down to reach Ghulam, but he could not help feeling that he would have dropped Ghulam in the end to save himself, had Fidali not prevented him from making the choice. Nick wished the thought of self-preservation, as natural and logically justifiable as it was, had never crossed his mind. But it had.

Ghulam seemed oblivious to Nick's self-doubt. Perhaps he assumed Nick had heroically resolved to hold on until the end. More probably, however, he understood there was no sense in both of them perishing and did not hold Nick's wavering against him. He *had* urged Nick to drop him, after all.

Regardless of what Ghulam thought, and Nick's own nagging disgust with himself, from that day a bond was forged between Nick and his two companions that transcended Nick's ability to rationally comprehend.

Because of the dangerous conditions of the ice, they did not make it across the rest of the glacier until nightfall. With darkness fast approaching, they bivouacked behind a wall of moraine heaped on the southern bank of the glacier. The night was arctic cold, the wind howling between the ice seracs in an eerie screech. Their blankets inadequate to stave off hypothermia, they huddled like children hiding from a thunderstorm, swaddling themselves together. In this way they maximized the heat from their bodies, and although they shivered violently, unable to sleep from the cold and their combined, pungent stench, they survived the night.

Before sunrise the three men packed their things and started trekking southeast. Their load was lightened by six bags of cigarette cartons Ghulam had lost down the sinkhole when he plummeted. The loss irked Ghulam, seemingly more than his flirtation with death. Nick chided him about this, until Ghulam explained that the cartons would have earned him enough rupees to sustain his family for a year—nearly as long as he had been in Pakistan looking for work. Now Ghulam had to go home to his wife and daughters almost empty-handed, and would have to make the long trip back to Pakistan again the following spring. As far as Nick was concerned, however, none of this explained how Ghulam could be so nonchalant about nearly dying.

Equally perplexing was their willingness to assist him in fleeing Pakistan in the first place. Given the harshness of Islamic law, the charge of aiding a fugitive, especially a murderer of a police officer, would carry a severe penalty, possibly death. They were not saints or soldiers but itinerant workers of small means struggling to piece together an existence for themselves and their families. They had no reason to help Nick—it was by now clear he had no money—and many substantial reasons not to do so. Still, they guided him hundreds of miles and shared their meager provisions at great risk to themselves. Nick began to feel more ashamed than ever that he had mistrusted them.

Fidali mystified Nick most of all. Hardened by poverty and the extreme elements of the Himalayan environment, yet humble to the point of submission, he seemed devoid of any interest other than looking after his friend's every need. Fidali not only served as Ghulam's guide through the treacherous frontier and mountainous backcountry, using his mysterious photographic memory of the landscape, but he cooked every meal for him, and clearly would risk his life to protect his friend if anyone raised a hand. And despite his reticence, he was far from the simpleton Nick had first taken him for. Nick was certain Fidali somehow intuited the bulk of his conversations with Ghulam. Some mystery was behind Fidali's behavior that Ghulam had not disclosed, and during the long hours of trekking, perhaps to keep his mind off his own dire predicament, Nick had become obsessed with finding out what it was.

Not until the aftermath of the incident on the glacier did Nick feel comfortable enough to press Ghulam.

"Tell me something, Ghulam," Nick said during a rest stop, while Fidali was away fetching water. "Why is Fidali so loyal to you?"

Ghulam gave Nick a curious stare, apparently confused by the question. He shifted on his seat and drew his knees up under him, resting casually as he chewed a stem of grass. "Why is anyone loyal to anyone else? He is like a brother to Ghulam."

"A lot of brothers do nothing to help each other. Hell, Cain and Abel were brothers. Fidali does *everything* for you. He's . . . like your servant."

"The ways of Allah are as many as the breaths of human beings. Who are we to question the how or the why?"

"But don't you think it's, well . . . a little *odd*?" Nick said. "I mean, you never ask yourself what makes him act the way he does?"

Ghulam sat up in alarm, as if challenged. Nick suddenly regretted raising the topic of Fidali at all. But when Ghulam spoke, he was not angry. "There is a Sufi saying: 'When a thief sees a saint, all he sees are his pockets.' A man can watch, question, and judge. But this only keeps him from seeing things for what they are."

Nick crinkled his brow with skepticism. "What about 'an unexamined life is not worth living.' That's what Socrates said."

"I do not know this man. He is Muslim?" Ghulam said, pulling on his beard.

"No. He lived before Islam."

Ghulam gave a blank stare. "That cannot be. Islam has existed always."

"What do you mean? How could there have been Muslims before Mohammad?"

"We do not worship the Prophet—to do so would be the sin of *shirk*. We worship Allah. And just as Allah has always been, so has the way of Islam. Islam means 'to surrender.' We surrender ourselves to Allah without question."

"But if you never question your beliefs, doesn't that lead to a blind faith?"

Ghulam shook his head. "I think you have it wrong, Mr. Nick. If you question always, you will always be blind. Only if you submit do you begin to see."

"I'm not sure about that. Asking questions, thinking—that is what makes us men. You said so yourself. Without it we'd be no more advanced than apes."

"Do apes kill each other with bombs?" said Ghulam, tugging on his beard.

"You know what I mean," Nick rejoined.

Ghulam stared off at the horizon. As he searched for words, his eyes sparkled from behind the weathered wrinkles of his sun-browned skin, reminding Nick of a Tibetan monk.

"Thoughts and ideas, Mr. Nick, are tools—like this." He picked up Fidali's ice ax and held it in front of his face. "It helps me test for holes in glacier, to find safe way across. But just as Ghulam can use his ax to split another man's head"—he swung the ax down on a stone, sending a shower of shards through the air—"thought is man's *curse*, at the same time it is his gift."

"A curse? Why?"

"Because thoughts and ideas are not *real*. They are made up in man's head. That is why all ideas, no matter how good they seem up here"—he pointed to his head—"lead man to sin: to hate, to fight, to steal, and to doubt. . . . Like countries—Allah did not make India or Pakistan or Russia or America. These are all the ideas of people. And no matter how righteous people may think they are, they are like a plague. They always lead to death, sooner or later. *Always*."

"But isn't religion just a bunch of ideas, too, wrapped up in claims of some divine inspiration? I mean, there's not a religion in the world that hasn't been changed a thousand times over by people interpreting and postulating and theorizing about what is and isn't the true word of some god or another."

Ghulam thrust out his lower lip. "Perhaps. But I cannot say what others do. *Ghulam* never uses thought when he speaks to Allah. Ghulam uses love. And love is not thought. It is the absence of thought. Thoughts are just theories of men, and theories are never beautiful."

Nick considered Ghulam's words in silence, not fully grasping them but impressed just the same. "I appreciate what you say. And no offense. But, for me, if something is not rational, I just can't believe in it. I don't see any logic in religion, or God for that matter. Not yours or anyone else's. Not in this world."

Ghulam tugged his beard one last time. "One man may see logic in

Allah, another may not." He shrugged. "Just as you may or may not see logic in Fidali's way. But if you try too hard all the time to make sense of him, one thing is true: You will miss his beauty."

After lunch they trekked along the periphery of the glacial valley until they reached a steep slope leading to a vast frozen basin, like a great snowy lake. From there they could see to the south the Kumba La Pass snaking its way over a narrow ridge between two lofty peaks. Once over the nearly twenty-thousand-foot pass, Ghulam explained, it was a straight, steep hike down to the village of Shingri, about twenty kilometers from the southern branches of the Siachen Glacier, forming the Line of Control. By evening they reached the snow lake, where they rested for the push over the pass.

Since they were above the tree line, there was no wood. Fidali made a fire from dried yak dung he had carried from the lower elevations, while Ghulam hiked a half mile down into a side valley to gather some juniper branches for fuel to keep the fire going through the freezing night.

Nick took Ghulam's goatskin water sack to fetch runoff from a nearby stream. When Nick returned, Fidali poured the water into a kettle, which he propped over the flames on a tripod of rocks, in order to brew salted "mountain tea" from flower petals he had plucked from an alpine meadow earlier in the day. Nick began to help Fidali tear the petals into tiny pieces and saw Fidali wince as he stretched his arm over the fire to adjust the kettle.

"You okay?" said Nick, pointing to a large bloodstain on the right sleeve of Fidali's *kamiz*. The stain, covering the entirety of Fidali's forearm, must have been concealed by Fidali's sweater for Nick not to have noticed it until now. Fidali shrugged, then shook his head—his way of saying "no problem"—and began to drop the fragmented flower petals into the boiling water.

Nick paused, studying the bloodstain. It certainly did not appear to be a trifling wound. Without thinking it through, he reached over and pulled up Fidali's sleeve. The whole thing seemed to catch Fidali by surprise.

Nick cringed. Fidali's thick forearm was shredded with deep lacerations. Still glistening with ooze, the cuts must have been caused only the day before, when Fidali had wrapped his rope, weighted with Nick's and

Ghulam's bodies, around his arms in order to save them from falling into the sinkhole. "That looks bad, Fidali. You need to wash it," Nick said, pointing to the goatskin of water he had just retrieved.

Fidali nodded curtly, tugging his sleeve back down, but not before Nick saw the grayish white of exposed tendon, or possibly even bone, on the blood-caked underside of Fidali's wrist, where the rope had cut him deeply like a knife. He was lucky he had not lost his hand.

The sight of mangled flesh made Nick think of the grisly wound across the throat of Yvette's corpse. Averting his eyes, he felt a familiar heaviness in his chest, as if his lungs were filled with lead. What right did Nick have at all, he thought, to put Fidali and Ghulam at such great risk to themselves, when they did not even know what he had done?

Suddenly, Nick felt a wave of anxiety. His pulse began to throb behind his ears, louder and louder—just like the day Akhtar had made him identify Yvette's corpse—as if the crescendo of his rushing blood would burst his eardrums if he did not somehow stop it. Before he even knew what he was happening, the words were blurting from his mouth.

"It was my fault!"

Fidali looked up at him, surprised at Nick's outburst. He put down the bag of tea and stared at Nick intently.

"The article . . ." Nick said. "The one that you burned . . . about the murdered French girl, Yvette. I . . . I did a terrible thing. . . . *I'm* responsible."

Nick, shocked to hear his own words, turned from Fidali and clamped his eyes shut. His lungs heaved, as if his body were somehow trying to flush itself out with cold, pure air.

A moment later Nick felt a firm grip on his shoulder. He turned back around to find Fidali's eyes peering at him—*into* him. Nick held his breath, paralyzed, as though he could not break free from Fidali's stare, even if he had wanted to.

Finally, after what seemed like a long time but was probably less than half a minute, Fidali nodded, and then released his hand from Nick's shoulder. Nick knew instantly that Fidali had understood every word he had said.

Nick's lungs at last let go of his breath. The pungent odor of the brewed mountain tea pierced his nostrils as Fidali handed Nick a steaming cup. He took a sip, and just as soon as the hot liquid warmed his throat, he felt his chest, his whole body, somehow grow lighter. When he looked up again, Fidali was stirring the fire, his silent self once again, as if nothing of note had transpired between them.

Minutes later, when Ghulam returned with more wood, all three men drank their tea in silence, holding their feet and hands close to the flames to ward off frostbite. Then, wrapped in their blankets, braced against the arctic cold of the wind, they waited through the night for the early hours of morning, when they would break for the pass in darkness in order to reach the top before the sun harassed the ice, causing the first of the day's avalanches.

They began the long, brutal slog up the Kumba La under a ceiling of effervescent stars that flickered white, silver, and gold.

The snow on the pass was cast blue with starlight. Waist deep and crusty from the cycle of daily melting and nightly freezing, it crunched like peanut brittle under their feet. Nick's lungs sucked at the stratosphere like a punctured balloon unable to get its fill. As they approached midway, each footstep began to feel like his last. He stopped every few meters while Fidali and Ghulam pushed onward, the chunks of ice dislodged by their feet pelting him in the face. The incline was steep, and without crampons or a rope, a minor slip would have resulted in an uncontrollable, deadly slide. Were it not for the crusty old snow to provide traction, and the fortunately late onset of any new seasonal snowfalls, they could never have made it.

But providence was on their side, and after ten hours of climbing through the night and morning, they reached the top just before dawn. When Nick caught his breath, exalted warmth formed in his chest and spread through him like a drop of oil on water. All around were huge mountains, mantled with ice, extending toward every horizon as far as he could see, blushed pink with the new sun. Visible far to the northeast, the highest peaks of the Karakoram stood like majestic gods—the nearly perfect, classic pyramid of K2, the arching Broad Peak, and the Gasherbrums I and II. The Siachen Glacier stretched east to China. And to the south, beckoning him like a siren, was India.

Nick heard a jubilant shriek reverberate off the rocks. Before it dissipated into the vastness, he realized it was his own.

CHAPTER 26

When Aysha returned to Gilkamosh from Delhi, she noticed that much about the village had changed during her eight years of medical college and internships. Some of the differences were manifest: police and *jawan*s patrolled the streets; barracks had sprouted up on the outskirts of the village; the road into town was barred by a checkpoint; the crowds at the bus station were checkered with the khaki and green of Indian army men coming and going.

Other changes related to the depressed economy caused by the dearth of tourists—closed shops, abandoned looms and craft factories, more restless and idle people mulling about the streets, squatting on the curbsides and smoking. Once nonexistent in Gilkamosh, beggars now worked the village streets—Hindu untouchable migrants from Bengal or poor Muslims rendered jobless by the eviscerated economy.

Still, Aysha detected other differences, less palpable but no less out of the ordinary for Gilkamosh. More women than ever, and even young girls, were wearing head scarves or burqas, whereas before, only a handful of women had chosen to cover themselves. Aysha would learn that this Islamic dress had been imposed by edict of Mullah Yusuf and upheld by his protégé when Yusuf departed. The edict was not backed by any official law but by an undercurrent of fear fomented by newspaper reports of attacks on unveiled women in Srinagar. The end result was that the more religiously conservative families, and the paranoid as well, heeded the mullah's edict without voicing objection. More than a few women, however, including Aysha, partly out of stubborn defiance and partly out of womanly vanity, chose to ignore it. Gilkamosh had been tolerant as long as anyone could remember, and the actual enforcement of such tyranny would have been unheard of.

The most poignant difference of all, however, was that Aysha had returned to a Gilkamosh without Kazim.

It had been more than eight years since they had parted ways. During her first years of study in Delhi, Aysha had written Kazim frequently, sending letters to his parents' home in Passtu. But after the second year had passed without any reply, she became convinced he had been killed. So, when she came home during her breaks, she anxiously paid a visit to Raza, who told her he, too, had not received any news from Kazim. He did not even have an address to which he could forward Aysha's letters, so he had kept them for Kazim at the house.

But Raza had assured Aysha that Kazim was alive. Raza had gone to the village about nine months after Kazim's departure and inquired after his son from the new mullah who had replaced Mullah Yusuf, who had apparently left to plunder another village of its youth. The mullah had said that although he was forbidden to discuss the whereabouts of Kazim, he promised to notify Raza if he was killed. To Aysha, however, knowing Kazim was alive, although a burden lifted, meant only one, almost more painful thing: Kazim had intended to shut her out of his life.

Having lost all faith in Kazim's ever returning to her, Aysha tried to drive him out of her mind. After so much time had passed, no one could fault her for presuming her engagement to Kazim void. But still, he had been her first and only love, pristine and forged in innocence. To truly grasp that such a love is destined never to be fulfilled is to suffer deeply, not just the loss of the joy once shared, but the loss of the essence of one's youth.

At the insistence of cousins and friends from the Kashmiri expatriate community, she went out on a handful of dates with young men. They were educated, kind, and from good families, and more than one had been handsome. But she found that she was simply unable to give herself to anyone other than Kazim. Certainly, she longed for the erotic affections of a man, at times to the point of suffering, and the fact that she was able to trigger amorous stares from otherwise desirable mates by doing no more than crossing their field of vision in modest, Muslim clothes served as a constant reminder of this painful void in her life. But just as Kazim had unleashed her desire when she was a youth, he wholly defined it now that she was a woman.

And even if she could learn to compromise and submit to the want of another, what would she tell such a future husband on their wedding night? Would he forgive her if she told him her heart had belonged to another? Would it even be fair for her to ask? Finally, she told her classmates her parents had accepted an arranged marriage offer from a man in her hometown, thwarting all further potential suitors, if not their wandering eyes, for the rest of her schooling.

With time, through an almost monklike devotion to her studies, she managed to bury her memories of Kazim deep within her. They would resurface only when she was alone at night, lying awake after a hard day of hitting the books. To her relief she had succeeded, she thought, in relegating her love to a sentiment. But the sentiment, nonetheless, was one of longing and emptiness.

Despite coming to the conclusion that she and Kazim would never be together, Aysha had kept abreast of the myriad rumors that had circulated in the village at different times over the years—that he was in Azad Kashmir; that he was in Afghanistan; that he had given up fighting and emigrated to London; that he was in prison being tortured by the Indian security forces. The list went on. Many of them were silly, others plausible, and others too terrible to consider.

Then, between her last year of medical college and the start of her internship, she had discovered that Kazim was back in Gilkamosh. Specifically, she heard that Kazim had been spotted in the village, definitely, this time, by the butcher Faruq, a reputable witness. Upon further inquiry, her father, Naseem, reluctantly told her that he had learned from his goatherd friends that Kazim had indeed moved back into Raza's home in Passtu. He was said to be a mujahideen leader now, a local folk hero of sorts. Though no one would ever think of turning him over to the Indian authorities, he tended to keep a low profile, coming into Gilkamosh only once or twice every few months.

This knowledge first had caused a small, fleeting smile to pass across Aysha's face. Later, however, it filled her with sadness, even grief. For it had proved that Kazim now knew about her letters and visits to Raza during the early years of her studies in Delhi, and yet he did nothing to contact her at all, let alone reconcile with her. This could only mean he had fallen out of love with her, and not simply, as she had done, repressed his love to pursue a higher calling. Or worse, it meant what she feared more than anything, for if true, then the walls behind which her passion had been imprisoned, which she could never tear down, had been constructed on a lie: that he had *never* loved her.

CHAPTER 27

The three men descended the Kumba La Pass and then followed the trail down a series of forested slopes to Shingri, a tiny village populated in winter by Gujars, a seminomadic community of Muslim goatherds. Ghulam explained that although most stayed neutral in the Kashmir conflict, some Gujars served as mountain guides for the militants infiltrating across the Line of Control. Shingri was a major launching place where they could obtain information on the safest routes, which changed depending on the Indian border patrols. It also served as a supply depot for Pakistani regulars stationed along the Siachen Glacier—the world's highest war zone—where daily exchanges of fire between Indian and Pakistani forces dug in around the glacier took almost as many soldiers' lives as did altitude and avalanches.

Ghulam told Nick that with so many Pakistani soldiers around, they would avoid the village, opting instead to stay in a vacant "safe house" outside the village used by mujahideen awaiting orders to cross from their Pakistani "launch commanders." From the safe house, they could venture into town for supplies and information, minimizing their exposure. Fidali knew where the safe house was located, as well as the way across the Line of Control, so they had no need to hire a Gujar guide.

A few kilometers before reaching Shingri, Fidali turned onto a trail heading due east, roughly paralleling the Line of Control, but still far enough north of the village to avoid the Pakistani military caravans shuttling ammo and other supplies to the front. The Pakistanis were not a threat to Fidali and Ghulam, though they would be inclined to pilfer their remaining bundles of cigarettes. If the army were to spot Nick, however, they would be compelled to investigate.

The trail followed a long *nallah*, thickly wooded with spruce and thin-barked aspens. Streams of glacier runoff cut across the trail. Although shallow, the current was swift, and they crossed with their shoes on in order to avoid slipping on the slick rocks and being swept downstream. When they were drying their cold-numbed feet and shaking out their wet shoes, they heard voices. The three men grabbed their belongings and ran barefoot into the forest.

Hunched down behind a stand of large pine trunks, Nick recognized the clip-tongued intonation as Urdu. A few moments later, a half dozen grimy and bearded Pakistani mountain troops tramped by, their uniforms camouflaged in white to blend in with the snow, their waists appearing almost as gaunt as the long rifles slung on their shoulders. Large white-covered helmets rode clumsily atop their heads, seemingly too big and heavy for their bodies. To Nick's relief, they passed without hesitation, oblivious to their presence.

Fidali, Ghulam, and Nick continued along for a few kilometers until they came upon a simple *bahik*—a stone-walled hut with a log roof. There was a hole in the ceiling to let out smoke and a wrought-iron stove under the ventilation hole, around which stood several thick logs for benches. There were no signs of mujahideen anywhere, and the stove did not look recently used, the charcoal in it without any luster or odor. This was a relief, for Nick was not sure what the mujahideen would have thought of him—a spy maybe, or some idiotic adventurer. Perhaps, after two months in the mountains, he could pass as a mujahid himself, with his long beard, tattered *shalwar kamiz,* and round *pakol* cap, his face and clothes sullied from living outdoors.

"It is very late—winter has come," Ghulam said, peering out the door at the sky, as if trying to divine when the first blizzards would arrive. "Two, three weeks ago the shelters were full with *mehmaan* mujahideen . . . Pakistani, Afghani, some Chechnyan and Arab. More foreigners than Kashmiri. They fight against India—but not for Kashmir."

"What do you mean? Isn't that what they're fighting for? For Kashmir to be independent?"

"Pakistani mujahideen want Kashmir to be part of Pakistan. They do not care what Kashmiri people want," said Ghulam. "Other *mehmaan* mujahideen just want to fight the Hindus. They treat local people just as bad as the Indians."

"Wouldn't you prefer to be governed by Muslims rather than by Hindu India? Isn't that what the fighting is about?"

Ghulam's face flushed red. It was the first time Nick had seen him really angry. "Those people are not Muslims!" Ghulam snapped, his voice filled with venom. "If independence means sharing my country with them, I do not want it."

Without saying another word, Ghulam stormed out of the shelter in the direction of Shingri, leaving Fidali and Nick. Surprised by Ghulam's reaction, Nick stared at the fire in awkward silence. When Nick finally looked up, the orange firelight flickered on Fidali's face. Nick's eye caught the gleam of a single tear as it broke free from Fidali's eye and found refuge in the cover of his beard.

As Nick sat perplexed over Fidali's display of emotion, a jarring clap of thunder exploded outside. He went to the door and examined the sky, but saw not a single rain cloud. It sounded again, this time followed by a swooshing echo that seemed to travel from place to place. Then the distant, secondary rumbling gave it away.

"Pakistani," Fidali said. "Indian boom coming."

Nick turned to Fidali, at that moment shocked more by the fact that Fidali had spoken to him directly for the first time than by the exploding artillery shell. Then, as Fidali had foretold, Nick heard another barrage, this time off to the south.

For three days Nick waited in the safe house while Fidali and Ghulam went to check with the Shingri launch agents on the status of Indian patrols across the Line of Control. Each day the launch agents said their Gujar spies on the Indian side had reported patrols. On the fourth day, the sector was clear.

It was common knowledge that roving Indian patrols never stayed more than three nights in the same vicinity. This was especially true given the lateness of the season. Few mujahideen risked the high passes under the threat of lethal weather. Consequently, the Indian Border Security Forces were always thinned out along the northern reaches of the Line of Control starting in mid-October, and were transferred to the western portion, around Poonch and Kupwara, where the altitude was not so great and passes were usually open year-round. So, at last, the launch agents gave them the go-ahead to cross.

They left three hours before sunrise. It had snowed earlier, just a dusting, but enough to cover the pitfalls of the glacier, rendering the trek treacherous and painstaking. To make matters worse, the dim partial moon made for poor visibility, but it was just as well, for there would be insufficient light for Indian marksmen to get a bead on them from a distance. After an hour of sluggish trekking, they had carefully picked their way across the glacier to the ridge of moraine on the far side of the ice.

They slowly climbed the ridge and stopped at the apex, where they hid behind boulders. On the other side, there was an exposed, rocky alluvial plain. Somewhere out in the open boulder field was the "zero line," the actual line dividing Pakistani and Indian-held territory. This was the riskiest stretch of the crossing—a no man's land—kept clear in the warmer months by the intermittent exchange of mortar and machine-gun fire from both sides. On the far side of the open terrain was a forested area. Once in the haven of these glades, there was a trail, Ghulam had explained, that led up a long *nallah* into the relative safety of the mountains.

For nearly an hour, they crouched behind the rocks, silently peering out over the dimly lit boulder field toward the dark clusters of conifers and brush. The safety of the trees was just four hundred meters away, and they saw no sign of Indian troops. Nick, charged with exhilaration, kept glancing sidelong at his companions with mounting impatience.

Finally, Fidali nodded to Ghulam and Nick, and then slowly shouldered his bags and disappeared into the darkness. Ghulam waited for a few moments, then followed suit. Then, at last, Nick took Ghulam's cue and climbed over the boulders that had provided their cover.

The three men descended the ridge and stepped out into no man's land under a faint gibbous moon. Nick's senses were on edge. Dark shapes seemed impossibly sharp. He was painfully conscious of every sound, including the gravelly crunch of his own feet shuffling on loose scree.

As on the night that he had fled through the dark streets of Peshawar many weeks before, safety appeared so close, so tangible, that Nick felt the urge to sprint. But he resisted it, knowing that the pounding of his steps, and the danger of stumbling, would jeopardize stealth. He walked cautiously, hunched at the waist, so fixated on the woods across the exposed space that the distance seemed to actually lengthen as he moved toward the trees. He began to doubt they would ever make it across to the glades unseen.

Finally, they made the thicket. Relieved to find no Indian patrols waiting for them, Nick felt like shouting in triumph. What he had dismissed as impossible one month ago, he had achieved against all odds— he had made it out of Pakistan alive!

Then, suddenly, Ghulam reached out and pressed his palm against Nick's mouth, stifling his excitement. *Had he heard something?*

As they crouched under the trees, the three men scanned the heavy darkness. Nick could hear nothing but the distant cacophony of ice crackling on the glacier. But he knew from the intense expressions of his companions that his jubilation had been premature. They were not out of danger yet.

Fidali whispered something into Ghulam's ear before rising to his feet and scuttling briskly through the woods, his heavy bags shifting under his arms with each step. Ghulam watched and waited for thirty seconds, until Fidali was about forty meters away. Then he looked at Nick, placed his forefinger to his lips, and waved Nick forward, indicating he should follow quietly behind Fidali. And so Nick did.

Nick cleared the thicket when it happened.

He had just crossed into a small open meadow between the pine groves. Fidali was far in front of him, out of Nick's sight. He assumed Ghulam was still moving through the trees behind him, though he could not hear any footsteps other than his own. Nick was trying to step softly; otherwise, he might not have noticed when he stepped on something. It did not roll or compress under his foot like a stone or a stick. Rather, it slid into the ground with his weight, squawking slightly, like metal sliding against rusty metal. Instinctively, Nick froze in his tracks.

He looked down, straining his eyes in the darkness to see what had caused the odd sound under his foot—rusted metal and plastic ribbing, and a pin with a wide flat top that had barely caught the heel of Nick's boot.

Curiosity slowly gave way to terror. Nick clamped his eyes shut, and waited for the explosion to end to his life.

But nothing happened.

Maybe it is a dud, Nick thought. *Should I leap and run? Yes—on the count of three . . .*

Wait! Nick thought, suddenly stopping himself. *What if it explodes when I take my foot off?*

Unable to decide what to do, Nick stood paralyzed, cursing God— the very God he had never believed in. He was so absorbed by his lament, he did not see the big man until he felt a gentle tap on his shoulder. Fidali's sudden appearance was uncanny. The last time Nick had seen him, he was more than fifty meters ahead, disappearing into the darkness of the trees. Nick had not cried out for help, and yet suddenly Fidali was there.

They locked eyes, Fidali reading the hopelessness on Nick's face. Fidali's stare was calming, almost fatherly.

"No move," he said to Nick in a whisper. Even in his panic, Nick was surprised to hear Fidali speak to him, now for only the second time.

Then, Ghulam's voice piped in from behind, from where he had just emerged from the woods. "What is it?" Ghulam said to Nick, his voice urgent.

Fidali squatted. He clasped Nick's knee in one hand, his ankle in the other, holding them firm in order to keep Nick from shuddering.

"I think I've stepped on a mine," Nick blurted.

Ghulam's eyes widened with alarm. "Don't move!"

"Easy," corroborated Fidali, his tone soothing. Fidali examined the ground under Nick's foot. *He's too close,* Nick thought.

Nick's comprehension of what happened next would always be clouded. He saw Ghulam approach closer, lean down, and speak quietly to Fidali in their native tongue. Fidali grasped Nick's knee in his firm grip, while his other hand probed under Nick's foot. "What are you doing? You're going to make it blow up!" Nick cried with hushed exclamation.

"No problem," Fidali responded, still composed. He gently slipped his hand underneath Nick's heel, digging around the mine with his fingers. "Okay, okay," he added.

"What do you mean okay?" Nick said.

"Fidali mean, you step off now," Ghulam interjected, his voice uncharacteristically tense. "It is okay."

"But if I step off, won't it blow up?"

"No no. Fidali say it no blow up," replied Ghulam.

"Are you sure?"

Ghulam and Fidali spoke again in their dialect.

"Yes, yes. Fidali say if you step off now, no problem. He has disarmed the mine," Ghulam reassured Nick.

"Okay, okay," Fidali said again, nodding.

"But . . . *disarmed*? . . . How did he . . ."

Before Nick could finish his thought, Fidali had thrust hard against Nick's hip. Nick stumbled backward and fell to the ground. When he looked up, Fidali still crouched there, one hand still manipulating the device.

"No problem," Fidali said again. He gave Nick a sideways nod. "Okay, you go now. Quickly . . ."

Nick stared back at Fidali, perplexed. One second he had been condemned to die; the next, he was freed from danger. But what about Fidali? What was he doing?

Nick felt Ghulam grab him by the elbow. He pulled Nick to his feet and rushed him back. Then, Ghulam stepped in front of Nick, toward Fidali. But Fidali shouted something, raising the palm of his free hand.

Ghulam stopped. He thrust his hands out by his sides, words rolling off his tongue in what sounded like a string of desperate questions.

Fidali was silent. He stared upward, toward Ghulam, or beyond him, perhaps, at the moon. This seemed to agitate Ghulam, and he spoke again, this time, with even more urgency.

Again, Fidali did not reply.

The third time Ghulam spoke, he was hysterical.

Then everything disappeared in a blinding flash.

The next thing Nick remembered, he was lying on the ground with no memory of getting there. There was smoke and the pungent smell of burned sulfur. A monotone ringing in his ears had usurped his hearing. His mind was foggy from the smoke and concussion.

When his vision finally settled, Nick saw Ghulam on the ground in front of him. But where Fidali had been, he could see only smoke.

Ghulam crawled, inching slowly on his hands and knees, to the source of the smoke coiling up from the earth. When he was at the edge of it, his elbows and knees gave, as if he had been cut down with the swing of a sickle. The side of his face pressed to the dirt, he stared into the thick cloud of smoke before him. Ghulam uttered something, but Nick could not hear his words.

Seconds later, the smoke shifted and Nick could see where Ghulam was looking. Fidali, on his back, was propped up by his elbows, looking down at a smoking hole where his legs should have been. His lips quivered, as if praying. Oddly, his Chitrali cap was still neatly perched atop his head. But below his abdomen, there was nothing—no feet, no legs, no waist—only smoke and dust. There was not even much blood, at first. It was as if he had been ripped apart so suddenly that his body had not time to bleed.

Ghulam rocked back up on his knees and slid over. He lifted Fidali's head onto his lap, cradling it. Fidali looked up at the sky, his face aglow with yellow moonlight. He raised his hand back and upward, until Ghulam clasped it in his own. All the while, he continued his silent praying, and by the movement of Ghulam's lips, Nick could tell that Ghulam was doing the same. Fidali's eyes changed from glossy to dull, his face whitened, and his lips moved slower and slower, until they were still.

When it was over, Ghulam closed the eyes of his friend. He held his hands high, palms turned up toward the heavens. At that moment, Nick's hearing came back, as if turned on by some switch beyond his control, and he heard Ghulam chanting alone, over and over, what they both had been chanting together.

Though Nick knew not what those words meant at the time, he would carry them always.

"... *la ilaha illa Allah* ... *la ilaha illa Allah* ..."

CHAPTER 28

Late September. The time of year in the Himalayan regions when the sun still emits a sweltering heat through the day, yet the crisp evening air gives its first hint of the harsh winter to come. Skeins of migratory snow geese had spangled the cloudless skies, and the aroma of impending harvest had wafted through the open windows—freshly cut hay, winnowed grain, and rotting leaves.

Aysha's clinic had been open for just over a year. She had been busy that day with the usual mundane conditions of a rural medical practice: a boy with a cut finger that had become infected; an old woman with gallstones; a few cases of dysentery; a man with a bulbous tumor protruding under his arm. By early afternoon, most of the staff had gone home. Hamid Mohammad, an elderly farmer, was the last patient of the day. Hamid had sliced his shin while cutting wood and had come in to get the sutures removed. As Aysha dressed the wound, there was a loud rap on the door.

"I will get it, Madam Doctor," said Omar, one of Aysha's assistants, in the formal tone of a soldier addressing his superior. Omar, a sixty-five-year-old Kashmiri Muslim, had worked at the Indian army medical clinic outside Kargil for many years before retiring to idyllic Gilkamosh. His wife had died less than a year ago, and he had been living alone in the village on a meager military pension when Aysha, who pitied him for his loneliness as much as she desired an experienced medical assistant, hired him. As Omar passed Aysha on his way to the door, she could not keep from smirking at the brilliant orange-red of henna coloring in his normally gray hair, beard, and mustache—a sure sign he was in the market for a new wife. Hamid, the patient, caught her amusement.

"Madam Doctor see Omar with new look. You like?" said Hamid, a trace of mischief in his voice.

"I can't say it's . . . very natural looking. But it certainly catches one's eye."

"Ahhh! Madam better look out. When old man paints hair with henna, he looking for young wife!" he taunted impishly, waving a finger of admonishment.

"I hardly think Omar is courting me, Hamid, if that's what you are implying."

"Don't be so quick to say, madam," he teased. "Old Omar, he very sly. Like snow leopard, he sneak up on lamb, and . . ." Hamid curled his fingers into claws.

"I don't think orange hair is particularly 'sly,' Hamid. Buffoonish, maybe. He rather looks like a baboon." Aysha and Hamid laughed irreverently, fortunately undetected by Omar, whose pride was easily bruised.

"Madam Doctor," Omar called from the entrance of the clinic. Aysha turned toward the cone of light beaming through the open door.

He was about forty feet away, and still from that distance the sight of him froze her. As he stood under the lintel of the doorframe gazing back at her, it amazed her how easily she could recognize him after so many years. He was thinner—almost lanky—his beard thicker and his eyes now sullen. Gone, too, was the boyish gleam she had found so alluring. But everything else about him was the same—the proud nose, the squareness of his shoulders, the straight black hair that cascaded down across his brow, always threatening to conceal his melancholy eyes.

Omar left the visitor at the door and approached Aysha at an axious pace. "Madam Doctor, the man wants so speak to you. I asked him what about, but he will not tell me. He says it is an emergency." Omar leaned in, whispering quietly. "I think maybe he is mujahid. I will tell him to go?"

Captivated by the visitor at the doorway, Aysha did not register Omar's words.

"Madam Doctor . . . ? Shall I tell him to leave . . . ?"

"No," Aysha replied finally. "Finish Hamid's dressing, please. You are very expert at it." Aysha took several deep breaths. Then, trying her best to remain calm, she rose to her feet.

"But Madam Doctor," Omar objected.

"I said it's okay, Omar." As Aysha walked toward the entrance, she felt as though she were being lured by a force more powerful than her own will—one that she could not overcome any more than she could have when she was just a girl.

The sun on the western horizon shifted, backlighting the doorframe, so that only the silhouette of the man she once loved stood there, silently waiting for her to approach. He stepped outside as she neared him. Aysha followed, closing the door behind her, never knowing what traces of emotion, if any, might have been revealed by his face.

Kazim had studied her pensively, unsure of how she would handle seeing him after all these years. He had chosen not to see or write her since they had parted so many years ago, as much for her benefit as for his own. Since his first bloody combat, he knew the turn his life had taken left no place for the love of a woman, let alone marriage. One either martyred himself for the jihad, or abandoned the struggle and pursued the normal life of men. There could be no half sacrifices or middle grounds, and trying to pursue both would result in failure on both accounts.

But still, for all the unspoken resentment that now separated them, he could tell by his first glimpse that she was pleased to see him. For a fleeting instant as her eyes met his, he felt the same disarming pull of her radiance that used to afflict him, as though nothing—the war, the intervening years, their separate ideals—had changed things between them. She was every bit as beautiful as when they had parted, except that now she was more graceful as a woman than she had been as a girl. But the brutal exigencies of his reality drove him onward to do what he had come for.

"Aysha," he said calmly, at once an acknowledgment and the onset of an inquiry. She was silent, at a loss for words.

"I heard about a clinic run by a Muslim. I did not know it was yours," he lied. In truth, he had known all along that she had returned to open the clinic a year ago. It was only out of necessity that he had come to her now.

Aysha's eyes, glassy with moisture, stayed locked on Kazim's, as the edges of her mouth curled, too slightly for him to tell whether it was the hint of a smile or a frown. "Well," she replied after several moments. "Now you do."

"I have wounded. Anyway, I don't expect you to treat them."

Aysha had known the day would come when the carnage of war would be dropped at her doorstep. The reaction of the Indian security forces, she knew, could be severe if they found out she had treated mujahideen. Nevertheless, it was more the shock of seeing Kazim that gave her pause.

"The only distinctions made here are between the sick and the healthy," she said.

Kazim hesitated, as if teetering on a moment of reconsideration. Finally, he replied. "They are just inside the trees. I needed to make sure it was safe first."

"How many?"

"Ten."

"Ten!"

"I probably should have put one or two of them out of their misery. But I am not very good at that. The others might live, I think, with your help."

Aysha flinched. The callousness of taking a life, even in euthanasia, repulsed her. The Kazim of her memories would never have considered such a thing. "I have only one assistant here," she said, intimidated by what she was about to confront.

"One who asks for charity has no right to expect miracles. If you only do what you are able, we would be very grateful. Otherwise, they will all be dead by the morning. There is nowhere else to go."

"Bring them quickly," she snapped, rushing back inside. "Omar!"

Just as that night out on the Line of Control many years ago had been Kazim's baptism in fire, so, too, this night was Aysha's. Only one doctor and ten trauma victims—her brief stint of emergency-room training in Delhi had done nothing to prepare her for the carnage Kazim brought her. Her little clinic, so clean and comely before, soon resembled a butcher shop. The wounded—just boys mostly—cried out in blood-curdling pain, even after being shot up with morphine. One of them, riddled through the abdomen, had been shrieking so loudly on his way to the clinic, his comrades had gagged him. Another mujahid, no more than fifteen years old, had had his legs blown off by a grenade, his hips reduced to mangled meat. Barely breathing, he had already lost too much blood— he died before Aysha could do anything.

A man whose arm had been torn off by machine-gun bullets walked into the ward, amazingly on his own, clutching the disembodied limb to his chest like a child protecting a toy. When Omar tried to take the arm, he cursed and kicked Omar so furiously his comrades had to pry the arm from him. Another boy had been shot in the gut. "I can't feel my prick," he kept announcing in a panicked voice, until his lungs filled with blood and, without sophisticated pump equipment, he choked to death.

All night, Aysha and Omar labored tirelessly, elbows high in blood and guts, cutting and severing and sewing, uttering quick prayers over the ones that died on the table. It was all she and Omar could do to keep from slipping on the bloody floor, so Aysha recruited Kazim to cart sand in from outside and spread it around their feet for traction. She took command, barking out orders even to Kazim.

"You got them into this, so now you help," she admonished him, holding out her hand. "Antiseptic!" And Kazim jumped. This was her world—not his.

When Aysha and Omar had done all that they could to patch the wounded, it was morning, though still dark. The mujahideen who had carried the wounded to the clinic began to load them back onto makeshift stretchers of logs and canvas.

"What are you doing?" Aysha demanded.

"I am taking them away from here," Kazim replied.

"Absolutely not. They will stay here until they recover."

"If they stay, the Indians will capture them," Kazim replied.

"So what? They can't fight anymore. If you take them, some of them may die."

"That's a chance I will take."

Appalled, Aysha challenged him with her stare, stepping in front of the wounded men. "They are in my custody now. They go when I say they are ready."

"Think of what you are saying, Aysha. Think of yourself and your staff."

"I am a doctor—I am neutral. They will not bother us," she said, doubting her own words.

"If they find out you treated mujahideen, in their eyes you won't be neutral. How many hospitals in Kashmir are treating Muslim fighters?"

"I don't know."

"None—officially. In Srinigar, doctors have been murdered by the Indians for treating the mujahideen. If they stay, it will put you in danger."

"Don't play games with me, Kazim. You came here, didn't you?"

Kazim paused. She was right. He had indeed known he was putting her in danger by bringing his men to her clinic. But he also had known she would treat them. "I am taking them. If they die, they die. That is a risk they took when they became mujahideen."

"It is better for them to stay here and get captured than to die out there with you," Aysha insisted, flustered by his indifference.

"No. It is not." Kazim lifted his *shalwar* over his chest and turned around. A grid of deep scars was etched into the musculature of his back. Covering her mouth, Aysha looked away. She had just been elbows-deep in the blood of men, but still, she had to avert her eyes from the mere remnants of Kazim's suffering.

"That was many years ago," said Kazim. "Things have changed. If it were now, they would not have stopped. Go on and ask my men. Every single one of them would rather die out there than be tortured into giving up his comrades."

Aysha fell silent. Kazim read the anguish on her face. He regretted bringing his wounded to her, even though he felt it was just a matter of time before she would be dragged into the fire. "It was a mistake to come. I won't do it again."

Kazim motioned to his men, who started to trudge with the wounded back into the forest. Resigned that there was nothing more she could do to keep them, Aysha handed out packets of morphine, bandages, and antibiotic serum, which the able-bodied gratefully stuffed into their rucksacks and pockets.

"We will be across the Line of Control by nightfall," Kazim said. "They will help us at the Pakistani army hospital."

After his men hobbled into the woods, Kazim turned to Aysha. She was exhausted from the labor of mending torn bodies, and strings of her jet-black hair were matted to her cheeks. The glistening of moisture on her skin reminded Kazim of the time in their youth, when they were caught in a downpour near the river.

That day they had surrendered their purity to each other was imprinted indelibly in Kazim's mind. For years, he had recalled it alone at nights, often on the eve of battle, using the memory to relive what he could of the pleasure, only to feel guilt for defiling it when he was through. At such times, he wondered whether that impression of Aysha's breasts through her wet clothes, the fleeting first brush of his hand, the ineffable radiance of her body under his, would be his only foretaste of Paradise before he died. And though he eventually concluded that this was so, he had come to terms with being deprived of another such moment. It was not the realization that what he had done had broken Allah's code, and all of the strictures of their culture, that had caused him to abstain from other women. Nor did he think he could somehow purify himself in His eyes through the punishment of deprivation. Rather, that moment in the rain with Aysha was so perfect, so sublime, he had concluded it could never be captured again—and he feared that whatever came after could only taint the memory of it. Such beauty should be taken to one's grave alone, preserved upon the pedestal of the soul.

Still, he knew what he had done was wrong, for by taking her virtue he had rendered her unmarriable. This often pained him, despite his feeling that he was justified in leaving her to fight the jihad. But at the same time, the fact that the two of them were forever forestalled, each in his or her own way, from moving beyond the transgression of that day cemented the act's ultimate significance for the rest of their lives, rendering it impossible for their love to be overshadowed. For this reason, he knew that no matter what happened to them, that moment by the river would always be remembered as sublime.

"I am sorry, Aysha," he said.

"Sorry?" she replied, her eyes glazed with exhausted frustration. "Damnit, Kazim. I am a doctor. This is why I came home."

He paused briefly. "That's not what I meant."

He opened his mouth as if to say something more. But then he bit his lip so that no words might escape, lowering his head as he walked off toward the trees. When he had reached the thicket, Aysha took a few involuntary steps, as if drawn by him without wanting it so. But then she stopped. He had already gone too far.

CHAPTER 29

A volley of bullets whistled over Nick's head within minutes of the explosion. A megaphone blared some incomprehensible command.

Dazed, Nick did not react at first. But when he saw Ghulam's silhouette, caught in the searchlight, with raised hands, Nick figured he had better follow suit.

Moments later, about a dozen helmeted troopers of the Indian Border Security Forces approached through the darkness, rifles snug to their shoulders and pointed at Nick and Ghulam. They staggered around, eyes darting nervously between the woods and their captives, ready to unleash fire at the slightest sign of an ambush.

As Nick focused on the approaching soldiers, he felt something hard shove into his back—a knee or a rifle. He toppled to the ground, his face grinding into the dirt. A boot bore down painfully against his spine, while hands groped under his clothes. Out of the corner of his eye, he could see they were doing the same to Ghulam.

Having assured themselves that Ghulam and Nick were unarmed, the soldiers barked questions in a language Nick could not understand—Hindi, Punjabi, or even garbled Urdu, for all Nick could tell. When Ghulam and Nick failed to respond, the soldiers kicked them in the ribs with their hard-soled army boots. Wincing, Nick glanced at Ghulam. He appeared too shocked to feel pain, or even to care he was being beaten. Nick, however, was not inured to their blows.

"Stop it! Please!" he hollered, protecting his head between his elbows as he rolled up into a ball on the ground. But it was no use. They continued kicking and jabbing at Nick and Ghulam with their rifle butts and boots.

Finally, Ghulam began murmuring to the soldiers in a low, doleful voice. Nick guessed Ghulam was trying to convince the Indians that they were not mujahideen, an assertion they no doubt found dubious.

The soldiers did not halt their fruitless beatings until a young lieutenant with dark skin and a black mustache approached briskly from the trailhead leading from the woods. The officer calmed the soldiers down with an acerbic command. After briefly examining the body of Fidali, he spoke into a handheld radio. Then, he ordered Ghulam and Nick to stand up and place their hands on their heads. The soldiers marched them both toward the trail.

"What about Fidali? We can't just *leave* him there!" Nick protested.

"Let it be," Ghulam said in a hushed voice. Nick read the trepidation on Ghulam's face and fell silent.

Ghulam and Nick were marched for fifteen kilometers, rifles fixed at their backs, along the wooded trail running the base of the *nallah*. When they finally came upon a rocky path, two weathered Russian-made jeeps waited, manned by another platoon of soldiers. The Indians herded Ghulam and Nick into the canopied back of one of the jeeps, and they were driven away.

They tossed violently along the rough dirt road. Nick and Ghulam had to struggle to maintain their balance and keep from toppling off their seats. Though the back of the jeep was open to the road, a soldier sitting in the passenger-side front seat had his assault rifle fixed on them. They were driving south, away from the Line of Control, and away from Pakistan. Nick guessed they were being taken somewhere for interrogation—to some kind of jail, most likely.

As they bumped along the road, the orange effusion of the morning light penetrated the mountains to the east, but still it failed to ward off the deathly chill. To his dismay, Nick realized that he had been so focused on escaping Pakistan that he had never worked out a plan in the case of his arrest by the Indians. He was loath to tell them the truth—that he had fled Pakistan under suspicion of murder, killing a Pakistani detective in the process. He feared they would surely send him back as a matter of diplomacy, if not "justice," despite the bad blood between the two nations. Nor would the Indian authorities ever believe he was a tourist who had lost his way *and* his passport. No tourist would be so foolhardy as to attempt to cross the Line of Control. In any event, to verify Nick's nationality, they would trace Nick through the American embassy, which would likely reveal the warrant for his arrest in Peshawar. Though Nick had made it out of Pakistan and was moving away from the border, all paths, it seemed, led him back to trouble.

CHAPTER 30

Three days after Kazim had appeared at Aysha's clinic with wounded for the very first time, two patrolmen of the Border Security Forces had walked into the ward. They were enlisted men, and they had spoken in slanged Hindi.

"One of our guard posts was ambushed forty kilometers to the south of here. An informant saw the bastards heading off toward this place. They were carrying their wounded. If you've got something to say, you'd better start talking."

"I have nothing for you," said Aysha. The soldiers eyed her with suspicion. She could smell alcohol on their breath.

"We'll have a look," said the leader, a dark-skinned Bihari sergeant.

"This is a private hospice. You have no cause to search." Aysha stepped in front of him, challenging him with her eyes.

"Shut up!" the sergeant snapped, shoving her aside.

The two soldiers ransacked the ward, going through drawers and closets, even dumping out the garbage, while Aysha and her staff watched nervously. Luckily, despite her strenuous objection at the time, Kazim and his men had carted away all of his wounded. And she and Omar had thoroughly cleaned up that morning, so there was no proof to be found. "You better pray we don't find out you treated any of those animals," the Bihari said with contempt, when they were through searching.

"Healing people is not a crime. Now, leave us alone." Aysha turned her back to the soldiers and started back into the clinic.

The Bihari sergeant snatched Aysha by the hair, wrenching her neck backward. He twisted her around by the hips, thrusting his face into hers, his eyes black and wide with rage. Omar stepped toward him, but the other soldier drove the muzzle of his rifle into the old man's side. With a feeble cry, Omar crumpled and fell. The patrolman raised his rifle, holding him at bay.

"Muslim cunt!" said the sergeant gripping Aysha by the hair. "Those murderers killed half of my platoon. Two of my friends were taken alive. We found their bodies yesterday. Their heads this morning."

He pulled her hair harder. Aysha, holding her scream, clenched her eyes shut.

"If I find out you so much as gave one of those Muslim pigs a single bandage, jail will be the least of your worries." With his free hand, he gripped one of her buttocks and squeezed it, so hard she felt her tissue tearing. He moved his hand under her pubis, pushing hard up into her. She winced in pain, pounding his chest, trying to writhe free. But he was too strong. He held her fast and spat in her face before he shoved her hard to the ground. By the time Omar and the others could help her up, the two soldiers had climbed back into their jeep and were already driving off.

Aysha never told Kazim about the assault, so as not to deter him from bringing his wounded for treatment. She had, however, paid Advani a visit as soon as she had regained her senses. Advani had been livid and had vowed to ensure it would never happen again.

Weeks later, Aysha would learn that the two soldiers responsible for the attack had been transferred to a post at eighteen thousand feet up on the Siachen Glacier—the most feared and miserable assignment in the entire Indian armed forces. Advani claimed credit for pulling the strings. It did not matter, however. Aysha would have continued to treat whoever walked through her door, regardless. And that was exactly what she continued to do, as the war raged on that year, and for several thereafter, until the day the valley would become a crucible of destruction.

CHAPTER 31

Nick sat in the Indian army jeep, broken and demoralized. He struggled to come up with some kind of story to tell the Indian authorities, but his mind was numb, wiped clean of its capacity to reason. He was oblivious even to the gun muzzle the Indian soldier had been pointing at his chest for the last hour.

He glanced at Ghulam, whose face was expressionless, his eyes lowered. Gripped by a deep-seated guilt for the death of Fidali, Nick felt compelled by an irrepressible urge to apologize to Ghulam for stepping on the mine.

"Ghulam . . ." he said, evoking no response. "Ghulam, please . . ."

"*Chup raho!*" The Indian soldier barked in Hindi, accentuating his order to shut up by jabbing the barrel of the gun into Nick's chest.

Nick met the soldier's stare, an act he took as insolent, perhaps threatening. The soldier raised his hand over his shoulder, preparing to strike. Nick did not even care enough to duck his head.

Then, just as the soldier's arm was about to swoop down at Nick, a deafening blast rocked the jeep. In a shower of sand and rock, the vehicle swerved sharply, wrenching Ghulam and Nick off their seats. Only their hands clutching the roll bar prevented them from being thrown clear out the back.

The jeep veered again, accelerating, and then slammed into an embankment. The impact knocked Nick's legs out from under him. He flew into Ghulam, both of them toppling into the rear wall of the vehicle.

The first explosion was followed by another, closer this time, the concussion of the bomb spinning the jeep on its axis. Nick ducked his head under his arm, pelted by rocks and debris raining in through the tailgate. A man cried out—a long blood-chilling shriek. Then there was another explosion, a little bit farther off, and when the dust cleared, an eerie silence.

After what seemed like a few minutes, Nick began to think that whoever had ambushed them had called off the attack. But then the silence was interrupted by sharp popping sounds. The jeep rattled as if struck by a hailstorm. A loud burst of gunfire exploded near Nick's head—the driver firing back.

Startled, Nick poked his head out from under his arm. His face was greeted with a shower of blood. The driver jerked sideways off his seat, his brains splattered across the windshield. The stench of burning oil permeated the air. Orange flames jutted out from the hood, sending a long spiral of black smoke into the air.

Another maelstrom of gunfire hit the jeep, imploding the windshield into tiny shards of bloodstained glass. Nick pressed his body against the flat bed, bracing for the pain of a piercing bullet, praying he would be hit cleanly—an arm or a leg, or if it had to be fatal, the head, so it would be over with quickly.

When the fury died down, he felt stinging pain in his legs and back. Lying flat on his stomach, not daring to move, he could not see whether it was caused by shards of glass or bullets. He looked over at Ghulam. He, too, was pinned, unable to move for fear of being hit by the bullets zipping over their heads.

"Ghulam!" Nick cried. Ghulam twisted his head slowly and looked at Nick. "Ghulam, am I shot?"

Ghulam's eyes surveyed Nick prone body. "I think not, Mr. Nick. But I fear I am not so lucky."

Nick looked down at Ghulam's legs. His *shalwar* pants were soaked in blood.

Ghulam craned his head and glanced at his shredded legs. "*Allah haq!*" he exclaimed, wincing in pain.

More gunshots exploded nearby, sporadic at first, then increasing in frequency until a full-blown firefight was raging again. The rest of the Indian troops, it seemed, had finally mustered the gall to shoot back at whoever was ambushing them.

Nick risked lifting his head to look beyond the confines of the jeep. The engine fire had worsened, the flames now bellowing from under the hood in orange tongues. Through his clothes, he could feel the metal of the vehicle getting hotter. The thick black smoke caused by the burning oil was choking him.

"I don't think we can stay here," Nick yelled to his wounded companion. Ghulam's eyes were clamped shut and he was breathing through his teeth.

Just then the canvas top over the flat bed caught fire, transforming the cargo area of the jeep into a furnace. They were going to be incinerated. "We've got to get out now!" cried Nick. "Can you move your legs?"

"Yes. . . okay," Ghulam replied, his voice raspy and broken.

Nick looked out the tailgate. The jeep was lodged nose-forward in a rocky ridge. The road was littered with dead or groaning soldiers. There was only sporadic fire now, coming from the hillside above them and opposite the road. If they tried to scramble up the slope, they would be easy targets. Behind the jeep stretched about thirty meters of open ground, leading to a cluster of boulders by the side of the road—the only cover. From there, Nick thought, they could make a dash for the woods. It was their one hope.

"See those boulders behind us? We'll both go together."

"Okay," Ghulam replied, wincing.

"On the count of three. You sure you can do it?"

"Yes."

"One . . . two . . . three!"

Nick rose to his knees and slid out of the back. In the fraction of a second it took him to realize Ghulam had not followed, bullets tore into the sand around his feet. Nick jumped back into the burning jeep, out of sight of the shooters, who would probably rather they burn than have to waste more bullets. The flames were leaping off the canvas of the jeep, transforming the interior into an inferno, the metal frame scorching Nick's skin.

"Ghulam?" Nick shook him.

"You go," he replied.

Ignoring his response, Nick hooked his arm around Ghulam's torso, pulling him toward the lip of the tailgate, determined to drag him out if necessary. Dangling his feet outside, Nick was greeted by another fusillade, spewing sand and ricocheting off rocks. They were pinned.

Nick wracked his brain to come up with some way out of their trap, but he could think of nothing other than throwing themselves at the mercy of those bent on killing them. He pulled off Ghulam's cap. Although it was long past white, it was all that they had. Extending the cap out the back, he waved it for a good twenty seconds, all the time he could spare, as the jeep's heat became lethal.

And then came the moment of truth. He probed with his leg, hanging it over the tailgate, half expecting it to be shot off. When no bullets came, he held his breath and lowered his body, holding his hands high as he faced the slope from where the shooters had been firing. Then, slowly, he reached in, clasped Ghulam's arm, and slid him out of the jeep. Nick took him by the shoulder, and they staggered together, away from the burning hulk. When they were a safe distance, Nick helped Ghulam onto the ground, both of them mercilessly exposed to the ambushers' guns.

Ghulam's pants and shirt were drenched with blood. Bullets had entered the flesh near his groin. Though Nick's knowledge of anatomy was inexact, it looked as if he had been hit dangerously close to his femoral artery. Ghulam clawed at the dirt. Nick ripped a long section from his tattered pant leg and wound the cloth tightly around Ghulam's upper thigh, doubting his attempt at a tourniquet would do any good.

"*Allah haq!*" Ghulam moaned.

"It's not so bad. You hang in there, you hear me?"

"No, no, Mr. Nick. Ghulam not good."

"Yes, Ghulam. You're going to make it."

"Allah's will . . ." he said, his words drifting under his breath.

The mujahideen slowly filtered down from the heights, sifting through the trees. There were over a dozen of them. Some carried AK-47s strapped over their shoulders, with their muzzles pointed at the ready; others clutched light machine guns with belts of ammo draped across their torsos. Two men carried spent shoulder-fired grenade launchers, which presumably had caused the explosions that had destroyed the jeeps.

Like Ghulam, they, too, wore the ubiquitous round and flat *pakol* caps, and *shalwar kamiz* with woolen sweaters pulled over their gaunt bodies. Others wore *pherans*—long shirtlike Kashmiri overcoats. Most had beards, long and thick, but a few were mere teenagers, their youthful faces barely sprouting fuzz. Their clothes and faces were smirched with dust and smoke, appearing as though they had been living off the land for months.

When the rebels reached the road from the slopes on either side, they silently approached the Indian dead, collecting their weapons and looting the bodies. One of the Indian soldiers was still alive, writhing on the ground in pain as he held his hands over his head in surrender. A thin, boyish-looking mujahid who appeared to be no older than fifteen pulled a knife from his belt, stooped over the helpless man, and as if slaughtering a goat, slit his throat with one swipe of his hand. Afterwards, the boy wiped the knife clean on the soldier's brown uniform, then proceeded to take the dying man's boots, even while he bled out onto the dirt.

Nick turned his eyes from the lootings and executions, dreading the implication for him and Ghulam. Strangely, however, the mujahideen went about their murderous business without paying any attention to them.

Being ignored would have suited Nick fine, but for Ghulam's dire condition. Ghulam was drifting in and out of consciousness, and Nick knew he would bleed to death soon. The rebels were going to either help them or kill them, Nick figured, and leaving the two of them to their fate was commensurate with the latter.

"Please, my friend needs to get to a hospital," Nick said in English. "Can you help us?" But they ignored his pleas. Only when they had finished plundering all of the bodies and equipment did they approach.

A tall man with a dark beard and an air of authority stepped forward from the group. He looked to be in his midthirties, and he had large, chocolate-colored eyes. His somber visage, with its roughly hewn lines and prominent brow, was that of a man who had witnessed more than his share of killing. Even so, something about him gave Nick the impression the man's character had been forged not by what he had seen, but by what he had lost.

The man held Nick in his stare, and though Nick did not expect he would understand his words, the import of what Nick was saying should have been obvious. But then, to Nick's surprise, the man spoke in a thickly accented English.

"Where did you come from?" he said.

"Thank God," Nick said under his breath, relieved to be able to communicate with someone. "We crossed this morning, from Shingri. They arrested us. My friend has been shot—by your men. He was just trying to go home. Please, all I want is to get him to a doctor. He's going to die!"

"Trying to go home?" the man replied with skepticism.

"Yes," Nick insisted. "He is from near here. Please . . . help him. He's got nothing to do with your war. This is all a mistake."

"But you?" he scoffed. "This is not *your* home. . . . So what are *you* doing here?" He lifted his rifle and pointed it at Nick's chest. Nick raised his hands, as he searched for a safe explanation.

"I was trekking. I got lost, wandered over the Line of Control. I ran into this man here . . . on the Pakistani side. He offered to guide me back across. Please. He's my friend."

"Trekking? Here? *No*," he said. "You and he work for the Indians."

"No, I swear to you!" Nick pleaded. He felt the need to come up with something more credible to be believed. "Okay, look. I got into trouble in Pakistan. I got caught carrying some . . . hashish in my backpack. I didn't know it was there—it belonged to a guy I was traveling with. You know the penalties in Pakistan. I had to get out. I met this man and his brother-in-law in the desert. They helped show me the way. The other man—the brother-in-law—he was killed by a land mine earlier. The Indians left his body up at the border. You can go see for yourself if you don't believe me."

The tall leader turned to a shorter man with a red beard and blue eyes, and said something in their language. Then he turned back to Nick. "We saw one dead," he said. "But we cannot know he was with you. You could have heard the explosion, like we did."

"Why would I lie? He was from the same village as my friend here. It's called . . . Kurgan, I think. His name was Fidali."

There was a brief pause. "From Kurgan, you say?"

"Yes. Yes, that's right."

The leader frowned, then he barked some commands to the others. "Okay," he said to Nick. "You come with us."

It took two men to carry Ghulam despite his diminutive size. Nick held his torso under the armpits, while one of the mujahideen hauled his legs below the knees, like handles of a wheelbarrow.

The mujahideen had two wounded of their own. One was gut-shot and in serious condition, unable to walk. He, too, was being carried by human stretchers, and like Ghulam, would die if he did not get a blood transfusion soon. The other insurgent had an arm wound and could walk on his own, but the bullet had shattered his bone, causing enormous swelling. In their unhygienic condition, gangrene would take the limb without immediate treatment.

The trail was rocky and steep, and each of the porters tired quickly under the strain of their human cargo. As a result, they had to take turns carrying the wounded to keep up the relentless pace. They hiked with a sense of urgency, up and down slopes, crossing streams and talus fields, traversing mountain ridges and tree-lined valleys. Even on his rest shifts, Nick refused to leave Ghulam's side, afraid that if his attention lapsed for a moment, Ghulam would die. Nick had tied the makeshift tourniquet tightly, doing the best he could to stem the bleeding, but still the color in Ghulam's face paled as he continued to slip in and out of delirium. Nick talked to Ghulam constantly to keep him awake, despite his pessimism that each spell of unconsciousness would be Ghulam's last.

Then, suddenly, Ghulam had an unexpected stint of lucidity. "Mr. Nick!" he called out, unaware Nick was just a few feet away.

"I'm right here, Ghulam."

Ghulam's eyes opened, though his head bobbed limply on his shoulder, as Nick carried him. "You must know . . ." he said, his face contorting with effort, mustering all of his energy just to speak.

"Know what, Ghulam?"

"Fidali . . ."

"Yes, Ghulam," Nick said, thinking that Ghulam's memory had slipped. "I already know him. I'm so sorry."

"No. You must *know* . . ." he said, appearing to drift off again.

"What must I know, Ghulam? . . . *Ghulam?*"

There was a long pause. Then, "I never would have let him," Ghulam mumbled.

"I understand," Nick consoled him. "I was the one who stepped on the mine. It should've been me."

"No. Don't you see?" Ghulam muttered, his voice rasping in his dry throat. "He told me the mine would not explode. But he *knew*."

"Knew *what*?" Confused, Nick craned his head down to the wounded man's mouth. "Ghulam—what did Fidali know?"

" . . . that the mine . . ." Ghulam's words drifted off again.

Nick's mind struggled to complete Ghulam's sentence. Only one possibility surfaced in his head, but it was too disturbing to contemplate. "Ghulam. . . . ? I can't understand what you're trying to say."

"He *knew*!" Ghulam said forcefully, waiving his finger with sudden animation. "He told me the mine was pressure release . . . that he could disarm it. But after he pushed you off, he said the mine also had a timer. . . . He *knew* that it was going to blow up before he could stop it. Yet he surrendered his life . . . to save *you*, Mr. Nick."

Nick stumbled, nearly dropping Ghulam. The mujahid holding Ghulam's feet glared back at Nick, berating him with a stream of Kashmiri expletives, which Nick did not hear. Ghulam's face turned away.

"Ghulam, stay with me! *Ghulam!*"

But Ghulam's eyes started to flutter.

"My God . . . Why!" Nick cried, almost angrily, at the mystery of Fidali's final act, as much as at the gravity of Ghulam's condition.

It was not God, but Ghulam who answered. "It was his way . . . *Fidali's* way . . ."

Ghulam did not speak again. Nick, fighting back tears, handed Ghulam off to one of the mujahideen, then sprinted up to the leader of the group, who was hiking at the front of the line. The man was silent as he moved, with long strides that spanned two steps of another man of the same stature.

"How much farther?"

"Maybe ten minutes more." After weeks of hiking with Ghulam and Fidali, Nick knew perfectly well that ten minutes in tribesmen's terms could mean hours.

"Goddamnit! He won't last that long. Lend me two of your men to help me run him ahead." Nick's tone was more a command than an inquiry.

The leader looked at Nick, devoid of compassion. "If he dies, he dies. He will not be the first, or the last, to die in this war. One more life is nothing."

Nick did not have the temperament to debate. "You want to save your own man, too. Don't lie to me!" Nick said, pointing to the injured mujahid being lugged along in front of Ghulam.

"Only so he can kill more Indians before he dies another day."

"I don't believe you. If you felt that way, you wouldn't have agreed to help us at all."

The mujahid tossed his head with indifference. "When you ran out of the burning jeep, I thought you were foreign jihadis—captured by the Indians trying to cross the Line of Control. Most of the *mehmaan* mujahideen I could care less about. But with some, we have a pact to help. So I told my mujahideen not to shoot you. Then—when I saw that you were a Westerner—I knew I was wrong. I should have killed you right then," he added, his eyes fixed on the distance ahead of him.

"Maybe I still will. But for now, I see no reason." The bearded warrior turned his eyes on Nick, as if looking through him. "I suggest you not give me one."

Not knowing whether to run from him or to thank him, Nick chose silence.

"There . . ." said the mujahid, nodding toward the horizon. "You can see the hospital now."

PART III

CHAPTER 32

Nick sprinted ahead to forewarn the doctors of the incoming emergency as soon as the leader of the mujahideen had pointed to the clinic.

The building appeared more akin to a barracks than a hospital. The structure was elongated, its walls made of roughly hewn planks. Large timber beams jutted out at yard-wide intervals, over which stretched a sloping roof of long wooden shingles. A mud-splattered Toyota pickup truck was parked in the dirt road in front. Two stretchers were battened down to the flatbed, a canopy suspended over them to keep out dust, forming a makeshift ambulance. The whole compound was tucked into the trees, not clearly visible from the surrounding mountainsides, so that one had to know it was there in order to find it. A large red crescent painted on the front door was the only indication it was a hospital.

Three huge metal sinks lined the outside wall. Nick cringed to think what instruments of butchery were washed in the industrial-sized sinks, the blood and other bodily fluids piped into the nearby glacial stream that ran along the floor of the small valley where the hospital was situated. As primitive as the "hospital" appeared, however, it was Ghulam's only hope.

Nick knocked and, without waiting for a reply, barged into the clinic, nearly stripping the hinges off the wood-planked doors. He entered a small anteroom that served as the reception area, its wooden benches now occupied by a few listless, glassy-eyed patients. The anteroom opened into the long, spacious ward lined with two rows of beds, one on each side, running the full length of the space. A small operating area stood on the far side of the ward, and two additional rooms adjoined the southern wall, apparently an office and a supply room. The walls had recently been painted a pastel green, rendering the interior pallid and gloomy.

Wounded men and women in various states of decline or recovery lay in the beds, some patients swathed in blood-speckled body bandages, others with faces silently contorted in pain, and others lay still, apparently unconscious. A few nurses scurried up and down the aisles handing out pills or checking the flow of intravenous mixtures into several catatonic patients. The air was foul with a stiff odor of blood, sweat, and stale antiseptic.

Nick's eyes were drawn to the doctor at the far end of the ward, visible through the half-closed muslin drape cordoning off the hospice's surgery from the recovery beds. The eyes of the doctor, an old man in a bloodied smock with a long carrot-colored beard dyed extravagantly with henna, were fixated upon a gaping wound in his patient's thigh. Holding some sort of surgical clamp, he was flanked by a nurse. She was also smocked and bloodied, her hair up in a cap, probing at the wound in front of them with a gloved finger. In stark contrast to the rest of the interior, the light over the surgery was incandescent and bright, drawing all attention to the grisly procedure.

Nick ran down the row of recovery beds, dodging a female nurse with silver-streaked hair and a bright purple sari. The woman glowered at Nick disapprovingly, as if she had never seen a Westerner before and had no desire ever to see one. Of course, she probably *never* had seen one who looked and smelled as bad as Nick did at that moment. After weeks in the mountains without a bath, he was haggard and filthy. Nick hurried over to the henna-bearded doctor in the smock. "Doctor!"

The man looked up blankly at Nick.

"I need your help—my friend's been shot!" Nick cried.

The man shrugged and then looked at his nurse, who was equally unfazed as she took the clamp from him and carefully fastened it to some torn tissue inside the open wound. Nick figured the doctor did not speak English, though he thought this unusual. Many medical schools on the subcontinent were taught at least partially in English, he had been told. The inability to communicate with the physician wracked Nick with frustration, and indeed, panic. He started to mime, trying somehow to impersonate a gunshot victim.

"My friend is coming. . . . He is shot very badly. . . . He needs help now!"

Without making eye contact, the doctor tilted his head to the side. Nick took his gesture as one of unconcern. The nurse, eyes unwavering from the patient's open leg, said something to the doctor in Kashmiri. Nick's face reddened with anger.

"Damnit! It's an emergency! Doesn't anyone speak English, for Christ's sake?"

The nurse slapped the clamp down, her eyes still fixed on the groaning man's thigh. "Yes, I speak English," she said curtly through her the surgical mask.

Nick advanced toward them, while the medical team continued with their work. "Well, can you explain to the doctor here that there's an emergency coming?"

The woman finally looked up at Nick. Even in Nick's state of exasperation, he could not help but notice the green of her eyes above her surgical mask. Annoyed at his persistence, she pulled the mask down so she could speak unimpeded.

"This man is not the doctor. That is Omar—my assistant," she snapped. "Second, it should be obvious to you we are in the middle of surgery. You will have to wait until I have finished with this patient before presenting your problem to me for diagnosis. There are many wounded here. All of them are emergencies. Your friend will be treated in turn, according to priority of injury."

"Priority!" Nick exclaimed.

"Yes. It is called triage. That is what we do in war."

Nick struggled to keep his temper in check but did not succeed. "Just give me some fucking morphine and a sewing kit and I'll try to save him myself!"

"Behind you," she said with a straight face, "the young man with the crushed skull and missing legs. He's hooked up to our last morphine IV. Why don't you take it? I don't think he can put up much of a fight."

The next thing Nick knew, he was lunging at her.

He never intended to hurt her, nor did he believe he would have touched her at all. Nonetheless, before he had the chance to find out for sure, a large hand swooped around Nick's chest, yanking him back. Nick looked over his shoulder and froze, confronted by the severe eyes of the mujahideen commander. He and his men had just entered the ward, carrying Ghulam and their wounded.

"What is this?" cried the mujahid. Nick bridled his rage, heeding the arm that barred his chest. He turned to the woman doctor and pointed to Ghulam.

"There he is. *Please.* Can't you see he's dying?"

She sighed, then put down her instruments and walked to Ghulam. A grim look came over her. She barked an order to her assistant—the man she had called Omar—who began to clear one of the beds of another patient with the help of the heavyset nurse. Omar motioned to the mujahideen bearers, who carried Ghulam, unconscious, to the now-vacated bed. But for Ghulam's slight chest movement, Nick would have thought him dead already.

The mujahideen commander turned to Nick. "You—wait outside."

"No, I'm staying."

"She wants you out. If you want your friend to live, then do as she says."

Nick waited restlessly under a giant fir tree outside the clinic for hours. The afternoon sun sank behind the massif to the west. Though it was still light, the shade permitted the chill of evening to descend before its time, causing his breath to spout from his mouth and nose in long, curling white plumes that lingered like cigarette smoke before slowly dissipating. He did not know what to do to pass the time, and his mind inevitably succumbed to worry over Ghulam and regret for having reacted so rashly toward the doctor.

The mujahideen and their leader filtered out of the hospital within a few hours of Nick's expulsion from the ward. As they prepared for their trek back into the forest, Nick approached the commander.

"Hey, there, excuse me," Nick called out. The man stopped. "I just want to say . . . thank you for bringing me here. No matter what happens. If you didn't speak English, I don't know what I would've done back there at the ambush," Nick added. "How'd you learn it so well?"

"We have schools," he said, his tone sardonic. "And we used to have tourists. But mostly—from her." He gestured toward the clinic. Nick glanced back at it.

"Whoever you are, I tell you this one time," the mujahid continued. "You and your friend—if he lives—never saw me or my men. If you mention us to anyone—I promise you. You will pay with your life. Don't make me regret not killing you this day."

"Like I said, it's not my war," said Nick, taken aback by the man's words. "I have no business with the police—not if I can help it."

"Not just the police—*anyone*. Leave Kashmir. The *mehmaan* mujahideen have a habit of kidnapping Westerners like you. Some years ago, three foreign trekkers were beheaded not far from here. There have been no Westerners since. Believe me, your presence has already been noticed."

* * *

A while later the doctor came out to wash her blood-splattered arms. Nick watched her from afar as she walked to a metal sink propped against the outside wall of the clinic and methodically scrubbed her hands with a brush and some abrasive powdered soap.

After she had washed to her satisfaction, she removed her surgical cap. A mane of raven black hair sprang from under the cap and cascaded down her back, standing out against the bright green of her medical smock. She must have sensed Nick's scrutiny from a distance, and when she turned to look at him, her eyes, which had since transformed to a bright blue-green, again startled him. Juxtaposed against her complexion and silky hair, they were so captivating Nick had forgotten to speak.

"Are you going to attack me again?" she inquired with offhanded derision. Nick flushed with embarrassment, as much from her insinuating words as in the face of her beauty.

"I wasn't going to do anything . . . back there. I was shaken. I just didn't think. One of my friends stepped on a mine when we crossed the—"

"Stop," she snapped, cutting him off. "I don't want to know who you are, or what you were doing."

"I was just trying to explain why I behaved like I did."

"Don't explain anything."

Nick was perplexed, unable to fathom why she would refuse an explanation. The sudden appearance of a grimy, desperate Westerner accompanied by a band of mujahideen was strange by any standard. Yet she acted as though she were not the slightest bit curious. "Well, I'm sorry anyway," Nick replied. "I didn't mean any harm."

She nodded her forgiveness. "We are in a war. I am used to much worse." She wiped her hands with a towel and untied her bloody smock.

"How is he?" Nick inquired with hesitation.

"Your friend has suffered severe internal bleeding," she said matter-of-factly. "The body can only live so long without a sufficient blood supply to the brain tissues. He is patched up now, but he is still unconscious. We just have to wait and see if he wakes up."

"How long until we know either way?"

"It could be hours, it could be days. Or it could be never. He is in Allah's hands now."

CHAPTER 33

So Nick waited while Ghulam struggled with death. Despite the muja-hideen commander's warning, Nick could not bear to leave, even if he *had* somewhere safe to go. Ghulam had become Nick's responsibility—the kind of responsibility one does not think about.

After Nick spoke to the doctor about Ghulam's condition, Omar, the henna-bearded old man whom Nick had mistaken for the clinic's physi-cian, called Nick in from the evening cold. Nick sat on a bench in the anteroom and quickly fell asleep, only to awake in the morning to a stiff back and the painful groans of a patient.

The doctor, who Nick had discovered by eavesdropping was named Aysha, told Nick she wanted him to leave the clinic, suggesting he wait out Ghulam's struggle in the nearby village called Gilkamosh, which was over the ridge of mountains to the south. "I am not in the habit of billet-ing itinerants," she remarked. "With any luck, you should find at least one guesthouse in the village that has not closed for the lack of tourists."

But Nick pleaded poverty, offering to work at the clinic, doing what-ever she asked of him, in exchange for room and board. To his surprise, she accepted his offer, despite his poor first impression. "I suppose, for a few days," she agreed.

In pondering her response, Nick thought she must have understood from the suspicious circumstances of his arrival that he needed to keep a low profile, and for some reason, sympathized with his predicament. Or else, she really needed the help at the clinic, even though he had no nurs-ing or other experience that might be useful. She did insist, however, that he not sleep in the ward anymore, which was just as well. That evening, Omar led Nick to a small, private room adjacent to the clinic's office, where staff members would sleep on nights they did not go home.

The quarters were stark—a cubicle with a bunch of carpets and blan-kets thrown over the floor for bedding. There was a wood-burning stove in the center of the room for heat. The bathroom and shower facilities were in clustered outhouses behind the ward, standing separately so as to avoid the stench of the one from deterring the use of the other. Showering, nonetheless, was not a pleasant experience. The water came directly from the icy stream running through the small valley where the clinic was situated. The water was silty and unbearably cold, tolerable only in brief dousings to rinse off the granular powdered soap. It took Nick a torturous hour to scrub the thick layers of dirt from his skin. Only later did he discover he could have heated water in a big cauldron using the wood-burning stove in his quarters, pouring it into the shower reservoir. Though a time-consuming and tedious process, the task would soon be necessary, he thought, given the impending onset of winter.

Nick's clothes, which he had worn all the way from Peshawar, were tattered and worthless, so Omar gave Nick one of his own *shalwar kamiz* outfits to wear. Nick did not shave, however, wanting to remain as inconspicuous as possible, in a land where nearly all the men other than Hindus were bearded.

On the fourth day after their arrival, Aysha told Nick that Ghulam's vital signs and complexion had slightly improved. At the same time, she cautioned him that it was simply too early to tell whether he was on the road to recovery. Ghulam was still unconscious, and the decreased blood supply to the brain during the several hours it took to get him to the hospital might have caused brain damage precluding his return to consciousness. Time would tell.

Meanwhile, there was no shortage of work to meet Nick's offer of assistance. Once he was rested, he was eager to begin, simply to keep his mind off Ghulam's grim condition and his own uncertain future. The clinic was terribly understaffed given the number of patients that it treated, and always looming in everyone's mind was the ever-present possibility of a sudden influx of casualties. With only Omar and two other orderlies to tend the dozen or so patients and the daily maintenance of the clinic, Aysha and the others wasted no time in assigning Nick mostly menial tasks. Nevertheless, he worked hard at them, earning the appreciation of the orderlies, if not Aysha. Soon, more than a week had passed without any indication from Aysha that Nick had overstayed his welcome.

Besides Omar, the stolid and dignified, if unintentionally amusing, chief orderly, Aysha's other assistants were named Aroon and Vilashni, a Hindu man and woman respectively. They spoke broken English, as did Omar. Aroon was a waiflike, wiry man, his shortness of stature masked by his thinness, with teeth stained reddish-black from his nasty habit of chewing *paan*, a semi-intoxicating mixture of betel nut, tobacco, and various spices. It was a habit Aysha justifiably forbade in the confines of the clinic, as it necessitated frequent expectorations of a vile color, unbecoming an environment aspiring to sterility. Aroon had a peculiar manner of snapping to attention upon his receipt of an order from Aysha or Omar with an unabashedly martial air, a vestige, Nick would learn later, of his much younger days as a medic in the Rajput Guards.

Vilashni was a widow in her mid-fifties with a dark complexion contrasting strikingly to the brightly colored saris she wore. Though Nick could not understand her words when she spoke Hindi, she had a habit of lecturing the patients as if they were her children, wagging her finger at them incessantly. She would even lecture the other orderlies, and sometimes Aysha, perhaps feeling it was her right, as the eldest woman— the matron of the clinic. In any event, her manner was more endearing than annoying. Vilashni did the bulk of the cleaning required in the operation of the clinic, at least before Nick's arrival, scrubbing the surgical instruments, mopping floors, and changing bedsheets and bedpans. Omar told Nick there had been in the past other orderlies beside himself, Vilashni, and Aroon. But the clinic subsisted primarily on grants, and it was all Aysha could do to pay Omar, Aroon, and Vilashni.

Nick helped any way he could, eager to repay his room and board and make up for his impetuous behavior upon his arrival. He assisted in washing patients' wounds, changing dressings, handing out pills, fetching instruments, and performing a host of maintenance duties, such as scrubbing sinks and mopping floors, burning the waste, and anything else asked of him. Despite all the efforts at sterilization, the smell in the ward was pungent—ammonia-based antiseptic mingled with the odor of blood. But he got used to it. And the whole time he kept close watch on Ghulam, pulling for him silently and talking to him with the perhaps foolish hope he would hear and be compelled to awaken.

As the days passed into weeks, Ghulam's last statement before he slipped off into unconsciousness began to haunt Nick. He could not comprehend why Fidali would deliberately choose to kill himself to save him. Fidali hardly knew Nick, and what little exposure Nick had to him consisted of Nick's confession that day at the snowy lake that he was responsible for Yvette's death. Nick had no difficulty believing Fidali was capable of facing death per se; his bravery had been palpable. However, it was the illogic of his *choice* that perplexed Nick.

Ghulam, Nick thought, would help him understand Fidali's choice and tell him everything he thirsted to know about the quiet man's life. As much as Nick wanted Ghulam to live out of deep affection for him, Nick *needed* him to live. For understanding Fidali, he intuited, was a key—to what, exactly, Nick did not know.

"*Allah haq!* That's cold," a cantankerous voice reverberated across the ward.

It was early morning, and Nick was helping Omar move a gunshot victim, one of the mujahideen who had originally arrived with Nick at the clinic and seemed to have weathered the brunt of his injury, from one bed to another. Along the opposite aisle of beds, Vilashni was attempting to wash a petulant patient.

"Stop your crying, it's good for you, old man," Vilashni retorted.

"If you think I'm old, my angel, then show me your respect," the voice bandied back, followed by an uncharacteristically girlish squeal, as if Vilashni had suffered a pinch. When Nick looked up, he nearly dropped the young mujahid he and Omar were moving.

"Ghulam?" Nick said, incredulously. "Ghulam!"

Omar and Nick set the young man down on the bed and raced over to Vilashni's side. Despite the banter between Vilashni and her patient, only when the others arrived did she grasp the remarkable—that indeed it was *Ghulam* she was washing, Ghulam who had spoken.

Aroon followed suit, until all four of the clinic's assistants were huddled around Ghulam's bed, staring down at him in an effort to confirm signs of life. Sure enough, Ghulam's eyes were open, though clouded with confusion.

"Allah! Why do you stare at me so? Do you think I am dead?"

Vilashni bent over him, peering into his pupils. Ghulam looked back inquisitively. "Where am I?" he asked.

"Why, you are in Gilkamosh," replied Vilashni.

"Gilkamosh?" Ghulam's mouth dropped open in astonishment. "*Allah-o-Akbar!* I *am* dead. And you . . . ? *You* must be the Angel of Gilkamosh!"

CHAPTER 34

In time it became clear that Ghulam had not suffered damage to his brain, although he was virtually incapacitated by exhaustion, sleeping almost the whole of each day. His femur had been shattered into pieces by the bullets and his legs had atrophied badly due to loss of circulation. Unbearable pain shot through his legs and lower abdomen whenever he tried to move them even slightly. Aysha told Nick that, after the required period of motionless rest necessary for his bones to heal had passed, Ghulam would have to force himself to endure the pain of exercising his legs if he were to have any hope of ever walking again.

Still only intermittently lucid, Ghulam required continued hospitalization for at least several more weeks. Although Aysha was eager to free bed space for potential emergencies, her clinic was the closest hospital to Kurgan, Ghulam's remote village. The only other alternatives were the hospitals in Srinagar and Leh, several days away by jeep, and Ghulam could not afford to pay for them in any event. So Aysha really had no choice but to permit Ghulam to stay. And she agreed to let Nick continue at the clinic as well in order to help Ghulam with his physical therapy regimen. This way, she spared the rest of her paltry staff the time and effort of rehabilitating Ghulam, while Nick continued absorbing his share of the remaining workload.

It took a full week after he had first regained consciousness before Ghulam could frame coherent thoughts. He was aware of his surroundings, but he was still incapable of conversation beyond rudimentary expressions of need. When Ghulam had finally reacquired a preponderance of his faculties, Nick asked him if he wanted Nick to send a message to his family in Kurgan. Ghulam, however, responded that his family expected him to stay in Pakistan until the following spring or summer anyway, and he did not want to worry them now by telling them he had been shot and hospitalized.

As much as this struck Nick as surprising, it dawned upon him what a great burden it would indeed be on his wives and children to grapple with the possibility of their breadwinner's becoming a permanent cripple. On this level, he understood why Ghulam would not want to inflict such traumatic news upon them until he had a better idea what his condition would be. It was common for men in Asia to be apart from their families for years while they traveled to find work, and Nick figured a man knew best how to handle his own family affairs.

However, the situation of Fidali's death was different. The following day, Nick asked Ghulam whom they should notify about his death. Surely, his next of kin would want to retrieve the body from the Indian authorities and hold some kind of burial ceremony. "Forget about it, Mr. Nick," Ghulam told him. "There is no one to tell. And by now, Indians give Fidali's body to local Kashmiri police. They are Muslim. They give Fidali proper Muslim burial already. Ghulam is very sure." This confused Nick. Fidali had been married to Ghulam's late sister; surely, he must have had relatives still in Kurgan—Ghulam's own family, at the very least.

Ghulam, however, not only rebuffed Nick's suggestion but was loath to speak of Fidali at all, or the subsequent ambush, or anything else relating to their journey. Nick attributed this to Ghulam's trauma over the loss of his friend, and decided to drop it for the time being, until Ghulam's presence of mind improved.

Nick continued his work while Ghulam remained bedridden. Soon the mountains, and thereafter the valleys, started to take snow, and the whole world was painted with an exquisite mantle of pristine white. The cold lost the disarming bite of November, as if the frequent snows somehow attenuated the earth's elements.

In contrast to the warmer months, when wild animals could rarely be seen, the valley was teeming with wildlife. In the mornings, rare Hangul deer came down from the mountains to drink at the stream, until chased away by a red fox or a Himalayan lynx, bounding at them through the deep blanket of snow. One evening, Nick spotted a brown bear, which had apparently chosen to forgo hibernation, trudging brashly across the snow until it disappeared into the piney glades. A single golden eagle reigned over the valley, at dawn and dusk drawing majestic circles in the cobalt sky in search of unsuspecting hares or alpine weasels traversing the snowfields.

Because Nick was a foreigner, many of the patients assumed he was an international aid doctor and treated him with great deference, only to be confused by the menial nature of his tasks and his apparently inferior position in the staff hierarchy. However, as time went on and the other orderlies and Aysha got used to Nick, his work became more variegated and challenging. On occasion, he even assisted Aysha during surgical operations. Nick learned how to suture and cauterize ruptured tissues, and the correct way to dress different types of wounds. Aysha taught him how to impede lacerations with clamps and pressure points, and to administer IVs and local anesthetics. The blood and gore of surgery took some getting used to, but after delving elbows-deep a few times, he grew somewhat accustomed to it.

Aysha remained inscrutable to Nick. She worked tirelessly and appeared to have little life outside the office. It seemed unusual to Nick that such a beautiful woman, whose youthful appearance gave Nick the impression she could still be a year or two shy of thirty, had not married, in light of the intense social pressure to do so in her culture. He wondered if her lack of a husband, or any discernible suitors, was the result of a personality hardened by the emotionally taxing effect of her occupation. Indeed, he found her distant, at times abrasive. He could count on one hand the occasions upon which she spoke to him that first winter.

On one rare morning when the ward was almost empty, Nick yawned in front of her. "Just you wait," Aysha said, annoyed by his show of lassitude. "Sure, it is quiet now. This war is like that—months and months of nothing. Then, just when the security forces start bragging about how they have defeated all the insurgents, something bad happens. When the passes melt, a fresh crop of brainwashed fools will cross over from the Pakistan side to cause trouble. We'll see how long you last then," she said, with more than a tinge of cynicism in her voice.

"We'll see," Nick replied in a challenging tone, inwardly relieved that she might at least be open to letting him stay until springtime. Other than giving orders, that glib exchange was the closest they had come to a conversation during the whole first two months of Nick's tenure at the clinic.

The fact that Aysha never questioned Nick about the unusual circumstances of his arrival at the clinic especially surprised him. Perhaps she feared discovering something that might be construed by the security forces as potentially incriminating to her. But Nick had proven himself not to be associated with the rebels at all, aside from having been ambushed by them. He began to suspect she genuinely did not *care* where he came from, or what he was doing in such a remote part of Kashmir, or anything else about him. Nick, it seemed, served a purpose at the clinic—he was a volunteer worker by default—and that was all that mattered.

Indeed, the clinic *was* Aysha—it was her alter ego. She poured all of her energy into *it* and nothing else. Starting at dawn, she would make her rounds, checking each patient, before walk-ins arrived. Sometimes there were injuries caused by accidents, but most common were the various, often deadly third world illnesses—cholera, diarrhea, tetanus. By the time the outpatient sessions were completed, it would be late afternoon, when Aysha did her evening check-ups, visiting each of her in-patients again, which usually took until dinnertime. Dinner was prepared by Vilashni, typically rice, *dhal,* potatoes, naan, sometimes chicken and on rare occasions, mutton. Afterward, Aysha sometimes drove to the village where she would spend the night at her parents' home. But more often than not, she collapsed in her office, falling asleep on carpets strewn across the floor, until five in the morning when she would start all over again.

"Poor Madam Doctor," remarked Vilashni, who had a penchant for gossip, in a mournful voice one evening after Aysha had retired to her office in exhaustion. "She so beautiful, she could have any man she want. I tell her, 'no man, no good.' But she no listen to Vilashni. You know what she tell Vilashni?"

"No, what?" replied Nick, eager to glean whatever snippets of information about Aysha he could.

"She say she married to whole village." Vilashni shook her head in disapproval. "I tell her it is okay for woman to be mother to many. But she should be a wife only to one. The heart that only gives can never be full. But she no listen. No one listen to Vilashni."

In early February Aysha insisted it was time for Ghulam to begin exercising his legs. "I'm beginning to suspect he'll never lift his bony backside off my cot unless someone gives him a boot," Aysha told Nick.

"He does seem to be enjoying all the attention from Vilashni. Not to mention the three meals a day."

"Well, you brought him here, in quite a tizzy, as I remember. Which means the honor of preparing him for expulsion falls on your hopefully able shoulders. If you wait much longer, he'll lose too much strength and may never recover. So, chop chop."

Aysha had no particular background in physical therapy to pass on to Nick, so all Nick could do was improvise and do his best to motivate a recalcitrant Ghulam.

"Please, Mr. Nick, it is still too painful," Ghulam protested.

"You've got no choice. Doctor's orders."

"Oh, that doctor-woman will be the death of me," Ghulam said, shaking his head. "Just tell her Ghulam has walked. Please, Mr. Nick."

Nick hesitated. Ghulam was not averse to *any* hardship, so Nick knew that Ghulam's obstinacy could only mean the pain was practically unbearable. Yet he forced his friend nonetheless. "No, Ghulam, I won't tell her that, because it would be a lie. And lying is a sin, remember?"

Ghulam's eyes opened to the size of silver dollars. "Yes, Mr. Nick. But he who lies to do good for another is washed of the sin. And sparing your poor friend Ghulam much pain—*that* is the most noble, righteous kind of lie."

"Nice try, Ghulam. Now, sit up."

"But, Mr. Nick, this is *Ghulam* speaking to you," he rejoined, holding his hands in supplication. "After all I have done for you, how can you do this to your good friend?"

"Don't try to guilt me," Nick replied, trying his best to keep a stern face. "The doctor says your legs will rot and fall off unless you start using them today, as in *right now*. You don't want that, do you?"

He paused, pulling on his beard. "She didn't say that," he said dubiously, yet frowning with concern.

"Yes, she did. She didn't want me to tell you, but I figured it's for your own good to know. Look how skinny they are, Ghulam. I've seen thicker legs on chickens. My God, they've already almost vanished."

"*Allah haq!*" Ghulam exclaimed, looking down at them.

"So let's have it. I'll take your shoulders and help you down slowly."

"Eeeehhhhh!" Ghulam's face contorted in agony when he stepped down onto the floor, his eyes tearing as he let out a painful shriek that alarmed the entire ward. He teetered, his knees wobbling. He would have collapsed like dead weight on the floor were it not for Nick propping his slight frame up by the shoulders.

That first day Ghulam was able to take only a few steps before the pain overtook him, and only with Nick supporting him. Then, after about ten days, they slowly graduated to walking abreast, in baby steps, across the ward, Nick taking most of the pressure off Ghulam's legs by holding him under the shoulders, leaving just enough weight on Ghulam's own two feet to make it hurt tolerably. "The pain is necessary, the doctor said," Nick explained.

After the excruciating walks, Nick would soak Ghulam's feet in a steaming bucket of heated glacier water and Ghulam would finally relax. The daily exercise behind him, it was Ghulam's favorite time of the day. From their comfortable corner of the ward, they would talk and drink tea together, sometimes joking with Omar, or watching Aysha in quiet contemplation, as she checked patients. Nick noted that when Aysha interacted with her patients, she would shed all of her sober aloofness, and though he could not understand what she was saying, her voice would take on a tone of hopeful warmth, and her demeanor would be cheerful, even humorous.

"*She* is the Angel of Gilkamosh," Ghulam said one day, his feet tingling with the pure ecstasy of the foot bath, as they sat watching Aysha feed juice through a straw to a boy suffering from lockjaw. "No insult to Vilashni, who is angel in her own way, Ghulam thinks," he added.

Nick looked at Ghulam. Though he had missed the significance of the reference months ago when Ghulam first awoke from his coma to find Vilashni peering into his eyes, now it came to him—the memory of their discussion of djinns that night in the Peshawar jail when Nick had first come across Ghulam and Fidali. *"Allah sent down a beautiful angel,"* Ghulam had said, *"to tend to the wounded."*

So much had happened since then. The horrors of the interrogations and beatings, his flight, the tragic death of Yvette, and the slaying of Akhtar—all felt distant and vague, yet no less real. "Lucky for you," said Nick. "Lucky for us both."

CHAPTER 35

The Himalayan winter had passed its peak and soon it was late March. Though the thaw of spring was still at least two months away, the noontime sun had started to warm the air just enough to allow one to sit outside comfortably at midday. Nick had just finished coaxing Ghulam through his exercises and had decided it would be good for him to get some fresh air after being cooped up in the ward for so long. He set out two chairs in the sun, looking out over the valley and the snow-covered peaks beyond. Then, helping him outside, he lowered Ghulam into one of the chairs.

As a pair of hawks soared by overhead, a sense of promise lingered in their wake. For the first time in a while, Nick felt consumed by a feeling of well-being, caused purely by his surroundings. So, too, Ghulam's face began to glow, as he silently absorbed the beauty of his homeland. Nick seized Ghulam's solace as an opportunity to raise the matter he had been mulling over all winter.

"Ghulam, do you remember what you told me about Fidali right before you passed out from your wounds?"

Ghulam became sullen. "I do not think so," he said evasively.

"You said that Fidali sacrificed his life . . . just to save me."

"Please, Mr. Nick. I do not wish to speak of this," Ghulam replied.

Nick kicked at the slushy snow at his feet. "But, Ghulam, it's very important to me. I need to understand why he did it. I mean, do you think he knew for sure the mine would explode? That it was a deliberate trade of his life for mine?"

After a long pause, Ghulam nodded. "Fidali was expert in explosives. He knew it could not be defused when he pushed you off the mine."

"He was in the army?"

"Fidali was mujahid. An expert in explosives. During the war against Russians, mujahideen become very good at disarming mines. So, Russians put timer on them to make them blow up a minute later, even if foot is not taken off. This way, if someone feel mine under foot but does not make it go off, they can sometimes kill two enemy—the one who steps on the mine, and the one who comes to help.

"After Fidali pushed you off the mine," Ghulam continued, "he yelled at me to get away, that there was no time to defuse. So you see, he *knew* mine was going to blow up. But he held the pin down, long enough so you could get away."

Nick paused, considering this. "And Fidali learned all this . . . fighting the Russians?"

"No, sir. He fought Indians, here in Kashmir. But Indians are friends with Russians, they buy their weapons from them." Ghulam fell silent, his face forming a pensive frown. Nick cupped his hand over his forehead, trying to make sense of things. Then, after a long silence, Ghulam began again.

"When Fidali married my sister, Suraya, he was a 'big man' in Kurgan. His father was leader of our clan. And Fidali was the first son. He was big and strong. Everyone give him very much respect. . . .

"And Suraya was beautiful. Every man in village wanted to take her as a wife. But none was match for Fidali. Ahhhh, so beautiful Ghulam's sister was," he said with a rueful sigh. "Her hair was black as night, her skin pure white and delicate as spring snow—just like the good madam doctor here." Ghulam shook his head sadly. "But Fidali, he served two great loves—not just my sister, peace be unto her, but *azadi*, too."

"*Azadi*?" Nick asked.

"Yes, *azadi*, Mr. Nick. That worthless whore you English call 'freedom,'" Ghulam replied, waving his hand in disgust.

Nick could not help snickering at Ghulam's irony. He had never heard such a cynical interpretation of man's most cherished ideal. And it seemed all the more odd coming from Ghulam, a man so carefree and persistent in his optimism.

"Fidali crossed into Pakistan to become mujahid—holy warrior—to fight to free Muslim people from Hindus. When he come back, even stronger than he was before, he fought against Indians for two, maybe three years. He was very brave, Fidali was. Respected by his people, feared by his enemies.

"But, in time, Indians find out who Fidali was. Someone talked for a handful of rupees." Ghulam shook his head, not in sympathy or disgust, but in an expression of inevitability. "Where the whore is for sale, there is always a customer.

"Because Fidali was 'big man,' the Indians are needing to make an example of him. One night, when he was away fighting, Indian soldiers, dressed like Muslims, come to Fidali's house. His father was home, his wife, Suraya, and Fidali's son, Abdul. We could do nothing. They took them away. All three.

"Their bodies were found by a farmer, washed up by the river. Suraya had been raped and shot. Fidali's father and son had their throats slit. Like goats."

Nick released a long, reflective breath. Ghulam's story jogged from his memory the response of the mujahideen commander who had escorted them to the clinic. *"Fidali from Kurgan?"* the rebel commander had asked him. Clearly, the man had recognized Fidali's name when Nick identified Fidali as his friend who had been killed by the mine. At the time, the connection had escaped Nick. But now, it was apparent that the rebel leader had known of Fidali, by reputation at least, as a fellow mujahid. Perhaps *that* was why the man had decided to guide them to Aysha's hospital.

"Only that which cannot be lost belongs to a man," Ghulam continued, after a long pause. "Suraya, Abdul, his father—they were *everything* to Fidali. After the Indians murder them, he was taken by hatred. Hatred aimed not at the killers—but at his own demons. Fidali took his gun and hid it under his *pheran*.

"He waited at the bus station for the big buses filled with families of Indian soldiers coming from the south. When one came, he walked into bus and shot them all. He slaughtered so many people before he ran out of bullets, the dead were all piled up on top of each other. Mostly the wives and childrens of the soldiers. Some villagers, too, he killed by mistake."

Nick shook his head in shock. "Fidali? I can't see it. He saved my life. He was . . . so . . ."

"Good," Ghulam said. "But demons, Mr. Nick, are part of every man." Ghulam paused several long moments before continuing, his eyes fixed upon the black and white peaks thrust against the sky.

"After he did this, Fidali quit fighting. He gave away everything he owned to the poorest people in our village. Then, he shut himself in his house, refusing to come out. He just waited."

"Waited for what?"

"To die," Ghulam replied. "Maybe he hoped the Indians come and kill him. But they did not. Maybe the Indians never found out he was the one. Or maybe they decided he was already just like dead, and letting him rot and put a bullet in his own head was better punishment than making him a martyr by killing him with their own hands.

"He stayed in his home for almost one year. He ate almost nothing. He grew so thin he almost starved to death if Ghulam did not take him in. Ghulam brought him into his home, make sure Fidali eat something. And instead of dying, Fidali lived. . . .

"But he was different, he changed. He was no longer same Fidali— proud, always talking big ideas. He became the Fidali you knew. Still brave, of course, but he never think of *himself* after that. Not for one second since he shot all those people. It was as if he did not even know Fidali existed anymore . . . or that he had *ever* existed.

"His fate is in Allah's merciful hands now. Ghulam hopes He judges my good friend worthy, inshallah," said Ghulam, with his palms outstretched to the sky.

For several minutes, Nick contemplated Ghulam's story of Fidali's past. "So then it was guilt," Nick said at last. "He wanted to make up for the bad he had done."

"No!" Ghulam cried, so sharply his voice echoed across the valley.

Startled, Nick turned to face him. Ghulam's eyes were wide with fervor. When he spoke, his voice was charged with emotion. "If you believe this, you do Fidali the greatest of all injustice!"

Nick was so taken aback by Ghulam's outburst, he did not notice how thin his voice sounded when he replied. "I'm sorry. I don't mean to insult Fidali's memory, Ghulam. That's the last thing I want to do to the man who saved my life . . . but if he didn't act out of guilt for what he had done, then I don't get it. Why else would he do what he did?"

Ghulam's eyes fixed again on the snow-capped serrations on the horizon, as if their jagged, angular shapes constituted some god-written cryptography that only Ghulam could interpret. He studied the mountains and the angle of the sun, turning his head on its axis like a perplexed child. When he spoke again, his voice was calm.

"It is not for us to say why another man does what he does. But guilt, Mr. Nick, has *nothing* to do with what Fidali did for you. You *must* know this. Of all people."

"What do you mean? . . . Why me?" Nick said, perplexed.

Ghulam stared at Nick. "Because *you* received his gift."

"Then whatever his reason for giving it," Nick said under his breath, "I don't feel . . . that I deserve it."

"Then change!" said Ghulam. "If not for yourself, for the sake of the giver."

Nick's face grew somber. "A lot has passed under the bridge, Ghulam. They say once a man's made his bed, he has to lie in it—until he dies."

Ghulam flashed Nick a fleeting look of alarm. The two men sat in silence for a long moment, each absorbed in his own thoughts. The peaks, now blushed with rose-colored light, were so clearly delineated in the crisp air they seemed almost surreal. For the first time, Nick permitted himself to notice the clarity of the external world, and it served only to contrast the maddening obfuscation of Nick's inner mind.

"You must remember one thing, Mr. Nick," Ghulam said. "Seeking redemption is a man's biggest mistake. Man cannot redeem—only Allah. Your job is to change the path you are walking on. Not try to make up for all the bad things you have done. That will only lead back along the same path, so that the past will become destiny. What is written, Mr. Nick, can never be unwritten."

The winter's snowfall had been heavy, and the high passes to and from the Valley of Gilkamosh were blocked. The time passed slowly, Nick's work at the clinic consuming the bulk of each day. To the others' curiosity, Nick had not yet ventured to the village, forgoing the weekly supply runs. Like a criminal on the run, he had come to know what it was like to be in constant fear of capture, and the more isolated he was from any authorities, the better he felt.

He used the short breaks in his work schedule to wander alone in the valley and along the surrounding mountain ridges, borrowing from Omar a pair of old-fashioned snowshoes fashioned from wood and twine. He spent this time in the wilderness thinking, sometimes about what he was going to do when Ghulam recovered and he would have to leave the clinic, other times about Fidali and the life of tragedy he had led, but mostly about Yvette.

The recurrent nightmares he had experienced in Peshawar and during his flight over the mountains had returned. Yvette haunted not only his dreams, but his waking thoughts as well. He tried to combat his remorse by convincing himself that *she* bore primary responsibility for her death, *she* had made all the crucial choices that got her into trouble. But no matter how much he churned the events and rehashed them in alternative lights and degrees of inevitability, nothing could absolve him of his guilt.

At times, when the grief was unbearable, he would walk across the high ridges above the valley and look down off the deadly precipice at the miniature trees below. He considered how easy it would be to simply step off, and more than once, he stood with his toes extended over the edge, the wind howling in his face with mocking encouragement, convinced that it was the right thing to do. A fury of gravity sucking him downward, perhaps a momentary flash of panic, followed by a single blot of terminal pain. Then, relief. And who could not seriously contend that the world would be a better place without him? Yvette, Simon, even little Susie Cole—the girl killed at the amusement park owned by Nick's client when he was a lawyer years ago—all these people whose paths he had crossed spiraled toward death or demise. Having come to the unavoidable conclusion that he was a negative force in the world, Nick scoured his conscience for any reason to persist, only to come up empty.

But there was one—*Fidali*. Nick became even more obsessed with Fidali's choice than before his conversation with Ghulam. His insatiable need to comprehend one man's selfless act—not simply to have it explained abstractly in terms of logic but to apprehend its very essence— urged him to carry on. Quite simply, Nick could not make that final step off the ledge, until he fully grasped why a stranger had felt compelled to die for what Nick was so willing to throw away himself.

Ghulam's revelation of Fidali's past merely compounded his befuddlement. That Nick's own life had been saved by a murderous terrorist turned his worldview on its head. Notwithstanding Ghulam's dogmatic assertion to the contrary, Fidali *must* have acted out of a desire for redemption, Nick concluded, or at least a sense of utter resignation induced by his guilt. Why else would a mass murderer who had shown such total contempt for human life, one callous enough to slay a busload of innocent women and children, have chosen to die to save Nick, a man whom he barely knew, and to whom he had no tangible duty or sense of loyalty? In Nick's mind, the conclusion was inescapable. Fidali's action was not in essence a gift to *Nick*, but rather, a desperate act of guilt-ridden suicide. *Still*, something about Ghulam's words stirred him deeply, making Nick question whether Fidali's act was really that simple.

Soon the air began to warm and the aroma of melting snow hinted of spring. The seclusion of winter was a haven he knew would not endure.

CHAPTER 36

Abdul sat cross-legged on the carpet blanketing the dirt floor of the cellar underneath his home, admiring its finely embellished geometric stitching—twelve knots of silk per inch. It was a Turkmen carpet, given to him by a friend and brother-in-arms, Mahmud, brought back from Hotan—an oasis city in what Mahmud would never admit to be Xinjiang Province of China. When Mahmud had bestowed it on Abdul, he had been choked with emotion, for he had been the recipient of few gifts in his life. "Please, I cannot accept it," Abdul had told his friend. "Take it back, for I have nothing of value to give in return."

"No, my friend," Mahmud had replied. "When both our lands—Kashmir and Turkestan—are finally free from infidel rule, inshallah, you may give it back to me. But until then, you keep it."

Now, Abdul beamed with pride, silently musing that the special significance of Mahmud's gift made it a fitting implement to coddle the asses of the great holy warriors sitting around him in his basement.

The cellar was a large, dank chamber where grain and rice would typically be stored for the long winter. Currently, however, it served as a safe house for insurgents. Across from Abdul, sipping tea in long, noisy slurps, sat Muzzafar Khan and two grungy mujahideen who had accompanied him across the Line of Control two nights before, arriving in Gilkamosh only hours earlier. Their beards were dusty from the journey, their unwashed bodies filling the cold air with the stench of stale sweat.

Abdul, once the boy who had driven the cricket ball into Kazim's face on that fateful day so many years ago when Kazim first met Aysha, was Kazim's trusted lieutenant. He and Kazim were of the same mold, both sons of goatherds, students of Mullah Yusuf, and zealots in the armed struggle for freedom. Kazim had been Abdul's inspiration to join the movement, and their friendship was such that once Kazim had crossed the Line of Control, it was only a matter of time before Abdul followed suit. When Kazim spoke, Abdul's eyes were filled with respect, if not, on occasion, a tinge of brotherly jealousy. Nonetheless, throughout their lives, neither harbored a doubt that they were shoulder to shoulder to the end.

Abdul's basement, though gloomy and cold, was a good place to meet. Kazim did not feel the least bit vulnerable meeting with his men in the village. Abdul's basement was ideal precisely because it *was* so exposed— where the police would not think to look—and especially because it was in Abdul's abode. Unlike Kazim, who through his charisma and stature looked the part of a rebel commander, no one suspected the diminutive, freckle-faced, red bearded Abdul of being an insurgent. And Kazim did not worry about any villagers turning himself or his men over to the police. Although the financial incentives offered by the Indian counterinsurgency agents had great allure to a people plagued with poverty, creating the persistent risk of informants throughout much of Kashmir, in tightly knit Gilkamosh no one would ever consider snitching on their own fabled "leopard slayer" and his boys, who were heroes even to those less than enthusiastic about the war.

Indeed, while Abdul and the visitors waited impatiently for Kazim to arrive, he was walking casually down the main street of Gilkamosh. He salaamed Faruq, the butcher, and stopped briefly to chat with Ashfaq, the shopkeeper, who still had Kazim's stuffed snow leopard displayed in his store, although having shed most of its fur and shrunk quite a bit, these days it looked more like a shorn goat.

Leaving Ashfaq's shop, Kazim casually waved to a group of Indian *jawans* climbing out of their jeep on their way inside to buy cigarettes, probably on their way to their posts on the Line of Control. They looked sorely out of place, with their dark, tropical skin, and torsos bundled with layers of clothing even though Kazim found the weather quite mild. As he smiled and nodded, he wondered whether he would someday slay these men, who wanted nothing more than to leave Kashmir and never come back.

By the time Kazim finally arrived at Abdul's home, the men in the basement had said all they wanted to say to each other. Muzzafar, who considered Abdul a sycophant, was already irritated by his drivel. To Muzzafar, Abdul was a typical Kashmiri, a people he loathed, cowardly women in men's bodies, soft and all too willing to make concessions. Indelibly polluted by the blasphemies of Sufism and Hinduism, Kashmiris were a weak race of dancers and poets, goatherds and weavers, altogether lacking the fire of Wahhabi fundamentalism so necessary to fuel a successful jihad. It was no wonder that they permitted themselves to be disgraced by a Hindu yoke. Abdul in particular, Muzzafar thought, was the worst form of ass-kissing toad, though he was adequately stringent in his religion, and thus had his uses. It even remained to be seen whether Kazim, who was by far the pick of the lot, had enough spine to carry out what the jihad now demanded.

Once Abdul sensed Muzzafar's irritation with him, he sat nervously in the corner, afraid to say another word, praying for Kazim to hurry up and arrive from Passtu to alleviate the tension. As much as he desired to please his guests, he feared Muzzafar and his henchmen—and rightly so. They were powerful men, who had risen through the ranks not because of diplomacy, but by ruthlessness.

Despite his unease, however, when Kazim finally arrived, and Muzzafar dismissed Abdul from the meeting, Abdul felt a profound disappointment. He had wanted so much to be part of the planning that he sensed would take place. To be dismissed from the meeting in his own home was deeply humiliating.

After embracing Kazim, Abdul left the cellar with a disgruntled frown, leaving Kazim alone with Muzzafar and his retinue. For his part, Kazim watched Abdul retreat up the stairs, wondering what Adbul's dismissal could mean. His ostracism did not bode well for one of them, though he could not tell whether it was he or Abdul who had incurred their wrath.

"Salaam alaikum, Kazim." Muzzafar embraced his former foot soldier. "You look well rested. Taking it easy this winter, I see."

"*Wah alaikum salaam,* Muzzafar. We have been keeping the Indians busy along their northern supply routes. Has word of our activities not reached you?"

"I hear mixed reports," Muzzafar replied soberly.

Kazim took his commander's criticism in stride. It was common for Muzzafar to belittle his soldiers' achievements, not only because it was in his personality to criticize, but in order to motivate his men to do more. "I am sorry to hear that," Kazim replied. "If you could spare us a little more of that American hardware pilfered by your Taliban brothers in Afghanistan—a crate of grenade launchers, night-vision goggles, some more of those fusing devices we can use to make IEDs—we'd turn the tide of this insurgency in a year. Anyway, whatever brings you here must be important. I know you don't prefer to spend time in my homeland unless it is to kill Indians."

"You are right." Suddenly, Muzzafar's mood changed, his avuncular demeanor becoming more cool and detached. He spoke in clear, deliberate language, tinted with his Pashtun accent.

"Kazim, we've known each other for ten years. I was with you during your first fight that night on the Line of Control. When that fat Sikh nearly strangled you to death, and you wet your pants like a little girl."

Muzzafar's compatriots chuckled as Kazim stewed. Even after redeeming himself many times over, Kazim still was subject to embarrassment about his first day of combat. And it was just like Muzzafar to hold on to something like that and use it at just the right time to belittle a man's masculinity and gain the upper hand. Muzzafar held up his palm, silencing the others.

"There is a candor between men who face death together," Muzzafar continued. "I will not dishonor that bond with words of warning left open to ambiguity. My aim shall be true. Keep this in mind as you consider my words."

Kazim nodded in feigned appreciation of Muzzafar's forthrightness. Meanwhile, his thoughts shuffled anxiously.

"You've served the jihad well," Muzzafar added. "You've made many bold strikes on the infidel army and police forces. Taken your share of enemy lives. You eliminated that spineless pro-Indian politician Mustaq . . . what was his name?"

"Mustaq Bhat," one of the others added.

"Yes, him. But this jihad, Kazim, is about more than skirmishing with the Indian army and a few random attacks on authorities. It is—as it *must* be—about taking back what is rightfully Muslim land. This is *your* homeland they are violating, for Allah's sake. That is why we gave you a command. But you have *not* been doing your part, my son."

"But, Muzzafar—"

"Don't interrupt me." Muzzafar raised a finger, silencing Kazim. "Remember the goal of this jihad. It is to purge Kashmir of all Hindus and their collaborators. Killing soldiers and police here and there is not going to do it. India is a country of more than one billion infidels—it will always have hundreds to replace every one of the soldiers that we kill. No, Kazim. The only way to win is to instill fear in their hearts. Do you think that the Afghan jihad against the Soviets was really won by butting heads with their army? We would have never stood a chance."

"I understand," Kazim replied with deference.

"No. I don't think that you do," Muzzafar snapped. "I once skinned a villager alive for giving a bandage to a Russian soldier. Another time I ordered my mujahideen to shoot all the men in an entire village, when I found out they were selling goats to the Russians. We used to deliver the testicles of the Russian soldiers we had captured to their commander in a box. The Soviets had the largest army in the world, but we bathed them in blood until they ran away in terror. If only you Kashmiris would put half that heart into this war, you would be free by now."

He paused for a moment, letting his passion subside. Then he continued. "I like you, Kazim. I always have. You are clever, brave, a good leader to your men. But we thought you would be a *great* leader. You have let us down. We are no longer confident that you have what it takes."

Kazim wet his lips with his tongue, about to speak. But knowing exactly what Kazim was going to say, Muzzafar lifted his hand.

"I do not want to hear any more lies about that busload of infidels that was shot to death a few years back. You have hidden behind your false claim of credit for that attack for far too long. Do you think I am stupid? I know you had nothing to do with that."

Kazim sat with his head hung low. He had nothing to say. He had indeed taken false credit for an attack with his handlers across the Line of Control, which in reality had been committed by a man from Kurgan named Fidali. It was uncanny that Muzzafar knew about his deception, Kazim thought silently.

"The time has come, Kazim. Because I am a generous man, and consider you like a son, I have obtained permission from our beneficent leaders to give you one last chance to prove yourself. I know that you have plenty of boys eager to give their lives for the jihad. Choose three. Prepare them for martyrdom. We will advise you of the date sufficiently in advance of the attack."

Kazim waited in silence for a moment, letting Muzzafar's words sink in. He was tempted to ask Muzzafar to specify the plans now, but he knew that was not how it worked. No information would be divulged until a few days before the attack.

"Of course," Kazim said in the most determined voice he could muster. "I thank you, Muzzafar. And await your orders."

CHAPTER 37

"Ghulam Muhammad seems to be progressing nicely," Aysha said to Nick one day after a grueling session of physical therapy. Aysha had just started to decrease Ghulam's painkiller dosage, and Ghulam had been struggling so much that Nick felt like a bouncer lugging a recalcitrant drunk as they walked together across the ward.

"Right," Nick replied, indulging her perceived sarcasm.

"I mean it. You're doing quite well with him."

Nick made eye contact with her and held it—for the first time in months. Detecting her sincerity, he nodded. "Thank you. He helped me when I was down. It's the least I can do for him."

She returned her eyes to one of her ubiquitous charts. "He'll probably be fully mobile in another month. Then you both can go back home," she added.

"And if I wanted to stay a while longer?"

She looked up at him, her brow knit in consternation. "But your family must be expecting you."

Nick shrugged. "I have no one close, really. I'm not in any hurry to leave."

"I find *that* hard to believe, after getting caught up in this mess?" She swept her hand across the row of beds and patients.

"You're caught up in it, yet you keep carrying on."

"It's different. Gilkamosh is my home. This place is my life. You? You can go back to America, buy a house and a big gas-guzzling car, eat at Pizza Hut every day. Becoming a plump, rich American sounds pretty nice to me. It seems lots of your countrymen these days are willing to die for that."

"And kill," Nick added.

She paused, sweeping her hair from her face, as if noticing something about Nick for the very first time. "Goodness, a cynical American?" she said. "Perhaps there's hope for the world, after all. Are you a disillusioned soldier? When you showed up here a few months ago, you looked like you might have walked all the way from Kabul. Smelled like it, too."

"Thanks for your brutal honesty," Nick replied. "No, not a soldier. Not the kind who carried a gun, anyway. But I used to do my share of fighting for rich Americans. Some of them even plump. It was my experience that the ones who already *are* rich, they stay that way by getting the ones who want to be like them to fight their dirty battles."

"Well, then," she said. "It must be the same everywhere. It's the promise that kills you.

"I appreciate your help and your candor, Mr. Sunder," she continued. "And I hope you have found whatever it is you came to this corner of the world looking for. Unfortunately, when Ghulam is able to make the journey to his village safely, I will not have the resources to keep you on at the clinic any longer." She turned, starting to walk away.

"I didn't say I was looking for anything," Nick called out after her.

She stopped. "No. I suppose you didn't," she said. She lifted her chin slightly, studying Nick's expression. "Then, perhaps I should have said, I hope you have escaped what you were fleeing."

CHAPTER 38

"I have fear, Abdul."

"Fear? What for, Kazim?"

"For the path our leaders are taking," Kazim confided to his friend after Muzzafar and his cohorts had slipped out of the village after dark.

"Why would you say that?" Abdul's voice was filled with concern.

"I have always felt to succeed against the Indians against such great odds, we must keep the people on our side. And we have done so. They have never turned on us. But what if that changes? It will be the death of our struggle. Of our dream."

"Why would that change, Kazim? What did Muzzafar say to you?"

Kazim hesitated. If he were speaking to anyone else, even one of his other men, he would never be so open about his reservations about Muzzafar and the Lashkar leadership. But Abdul had been his trusted friend since childhood. If there was anyone in the world he could confide in, it was he. "You know, Abdul, I never envisioned us staying with Lashkar-e-Tayyiba for as many years as we have done."

Abdul's face went blank with confusion. "I do not understand." Abdul could not have cared less about the complexities of the fractious mujahideen groups and their internecine rivalries. Ever since he was an impressionable student at the madrassa, eagerly absorbing the fiery sermons of Mullah Yusuf, he had been inspired to fight against the Indians first and foremost by religion—not by politics. As long as he was fighting jihad, what did he care for the nuances of political affiliations?

Kazim, in contrast, understood that war was in its essence a political endeavor, and that all the rest—especially religion—was simply a matter of how the leaders spun the filthy business of killing humans. It was for this reason that the heart of the leadership was crucial. "This village, these mountains and valleys, this small corner of Kashmir, it is our watch. It is our homeland, and we are fighting for *our* freedom. We know our people better than any foreigner."

"Of course. That is why you are our leader. The people love you. The boys in the madrassa, they cheer your name. You are their hero," Abdul said, his voice charged with admiration.

"Listen, Abdul. There's no reason why we should have to take orders from across the Line of Control. From Pashtuns, Arabs, Punjabis."

"But Muzzafar is a Muslim; we are all brothers. He gives us direction. Inspiration to continue our fight."

"Inspiration? Abdul, trust me. I know his methods better than anyone does. He inspires nothing but fear. How can we expect to convince the people we're fighting for them, if they fear us?"

"But they should fear us. They *must*. We are His warriors, the army of the pure." He glanced at Kazim with alarm. "You worry me, Kazim. You used to be . . ." he stopped himself.

"Used to be what?" Kazim pressed him, studying his friend's eyes. Abdul shifted uncomfortably. He looked at the floor. "Say what's on your mind, Abdul."

"It's nothing, Kazim. You seem . . . distant these days. You are my leader. Always. So . . . just tell me what you want me to do."

Kazim opened his mouth to speak, but something in Abdul's eyes, a glimmer of doubt or a furtive batting of the eyelids, gave him pause. "I will, Abdul. When I receive the word. The insurgency is about to change. I just need to know if you are ready for it. That's all."

"I am ready, Kazim. I promise. I am ready for anything that you ask of me."

CHAPTER 39

The truck groaned with labor as it climbed the steep, rocky switchbacks on the road to Gilkamosh. The rugged, unpaved jeep path was typical of rural Kashmiri roads; although roads were not typical at all in that part of Kashmir. In fact, it was the *only* road in the area, dynamited into the mountainside by the Indian army as a supply route to the northern stretches of the Line of Control. Except for the few military settlements through which the road passed on its way north, all other villages within a 120-kilometer radius of Gilkamosh were reachable only by foot.

The secluded side valley in which Aysha had established her clinic was accessible by a short jeep trail off the road. From the intersection, it was thirty kilometers up a seemingly endless series of acute switchbacks to the top of a rocky ridge, where one could view the verdant Valley of Gilkamosh sprawling below, surrounded by peaks. As the crow flies, the clinic was only about fifteen kilometers up and over the ridge of steep mountains separating it from Gilkamosh. But engineering limitations required the road to take its longer, more circuitous route. There was also a footpath leading directly to Gilkamosh, comparatively shorter than the jeep road, but it took longer to walk it than to drive along the road because of the steep and treacherous uphill climb.

The road had yet to be repaired after its winter erosion, and the driving was slower than usual. It took Aysha nearly an hour to drive just to the top of the ridge. Dusty and potholed, the road was bisected with a thick stripe of rocky rubble down the middle between the wheel ruts, which had been too deeply cut by persistent use to drive with the wheels in them. To avoid bottoming out, Aysha had to drive with one set of wheels on the uneven lump of rubble between the ruts, and the other perilously close to the edge of the road. At the more precipitous curves of the roadway, one had a clear view straight down sheer cliffs dropping off into the torrential, gray-blue river.

Nick sat tensely in the passenger seat of the Nissan pickup truck, which doubled as the clinic's ambulance and supply truck, peering down into the precipice. "Wouldn't it have been much easier to build the hospital in the village?" Nick asked, trying to shake off his vertigo.

"More convenient logistically. But inconvenient in other ways," she replied.

Nick looked at her briefly. "Other ways? Trying to avoid someone?"

"Hah!" Aysha replied. "Heavens, no. There is no avoiding people around here—it is too small. We are all in each other's business. But I don't mind that. It's the outsiders I have to worry about."

"Outsiders?"

"The police, the security forces. Where the clinic is now, I can run things the way I want. Under their noses, that would not be possible. They would never stand for it."

"So you sacrifice convenience for autonomy."

"Yes, I suppose. Around here, autonomy is the only way to keep your neutrality."

"What do you mean?"

"All sick are the same to me," said Aysha. "Their blood is red, whether it flows from a villager, a soldier, or a rebel."

"I see," Nick said with a nod. "You mean they don't know you treat mujahideen?"

"Of course they do. But so long as I do not flaunt it, they have been willing to turn a blind eye. There was an incident in the past, but that was nipped in the bud. We are lucky. The authorities have not been so deferential to the Hippocratic Oath in other parts of Kashmir."

"Still, don't the villagers suffer? As a result of the distance?"

"A little bit. But we are mountain people; we are used to walking much farther every day just for basic errands. And if there is an emergency, we pick patients up with our trusty ambulance," she said, patting the dashboard.

Aysha downshifted with her thin-fingered hands, the truck's motor sputtering to ascend the steep switchbacks. Nick peered down again. He saw far below the carcass of a vehicle pinned against the thick bole of a pine tree. It was a minibus—mangled and rusted in a twisted hulk at the bottom of the ravine.

He wondered what had gone through the doomed passengers' minds the moment they felt the wheels give way and felt the rush of gravity—those few seconds of terror before the jarring impact. Were they thinking of God? Loved ones left behind? Profound disappointment they had run out of time to do good? He felt a flash of shame for contemplating a similar death at his own hands only weeks ago.

"Don't tell me you're going to toss the vindaloo?" Aysha said.

Nick pulled his pale face back in from the window. "The *what*?"

"Vilashni's chicken vindaloo," she said teasingly. "You ate it for lunch. She'll never forgive you if you spit it up."

"Oh . . . no, I'm fine. It's just . . . a long way down."

Nick had been ambivalent about spending time alone with Aysha. He envisioned the awkwardness of two people not speaking to each other for an entire three-hour round trip. Mostly, she approached people, including Nick, with clinical detachment, as if each human were a condition to be analyzed, rather than a person to be communicated with.

Over the last month, however, Nick had started to detect little flashes of personality seeping through the cracks—a deadpan sarcasm, a fleeting hint of a smirk at one of Ghulam's ridiculous anecdotes, or a subtle swallow when a patient took a turn for the worse. Nick wondered whether she had walled herself in from necessity, given the bombardment of tragedy that accompanied her occupation.

But somehow he detected there was more to her than a walled-up bleeding heart. He had become intrigued by her. It was not just her physical beauty. Certainly, she was stunning and sensual, despite her rare use of makeup, jewelry, or any other feminine accoutrements. But Nick was drawn more by her mystery. He had been traveling long enough in Muslim countries to know a woman doctor in a traditional Islamic culture was unique in and of itself. The fact that she was such a beautiful one, unmarried, running a strapped-for-cash trauma clinic in an isolated war zone, however, made her an anomaly of anomalies. The trip to her home village played into Nick's inquisitiveness, so he agreed to accompany her despite his reservations.

The reason for the expedition was to pick up their monthly shipment of blood for transfusions, and other supplies, which had arrived from Srinagar. Aysha needed someone to help her load the boxes and accompany her on the rough drive, which always presented the risk of a breakdown or blown tire. Nick was selected for the task by process of elimination. It was a Friday, the Muslim day of prayer, and Omar's typical day off.

Vilashni had a weak back and was incapable of lifting heavy boxes, and Aroon was needed at the ward to watch the five or six patients, including Ghulam, who had just started to walk on his own with crutches.

Now that Ghulam was mobile, he was a "bloody nuisance," Aysha proclaimed. He was hobbling about and getting in the way, diverting everyone's attention with his rantings. Aysha had threatened to "release" him if he did not start "behaving." He seemed well on his way to recovery and probably could go the extra length at home, nursed by his multiple wives and daughters. But when Aysha suggested this to him, he panicked. "What? Are you crazy, Madam Doctor? My family is eight women! Ghulam would be back in a week—with *head* problem to go with his foot problem!"

The real reason might have been Ghulam's reluctance to return to his village empty-handed, having lost his smuggled cigarettes, and with only the bad news of Fidali's death to report. Besides, he seemed to like living at the clinic, indulging in his newfound proclivity to tease Vilashni no end, entertaining everyone with anecdotes from his myriad occupations and past misadventures, and his erudite quotations from the Qur'an. Despite his mischief and her better judgment, Aysha let him stay for no compelling reason other than that the staff was amused by his presence.

As Nick had expected, Aysha talked very little on the ride to the village, and this was just as well. She was an atrocious driver, and the road was treacherous enough without the distraction of small talk. She drove excessively close to the edge of steep drop-offs and had an uncanny ability to hit each bump, boulder, and divot squarely, even when the obstacle seemed more difficult to hit than to avoid.

When they had finally descended the mountain, reaching the floor of the Gilkamosh Valley, Nick's feeling of relief turned to awe. The lush green of the valley, surrounded on all sides by stark spires of black basalt woven with frozen cataracts of glacier, stood out like an alpine oasis. Spring flowers blanketed the hillsides leading up to the heights in brilliant reds, yellows, and whites. Apricot and apple trees lined the edges of the road, their branches sprouting fledgling pink and white blossoms.

As they neared the outskirts of the village, clusters of well-kept homes lined the road, constructed of mud-brick walls. Some of the dwellings had sloping roofs made of long planklike shingles, while most had flat roofs in the style of homes in Baltistan and Ladakh, with dung and hay stacked on top to serve as insulation. Each house had its own plot where vegetables were grown and animals kept. Many large fruit trees surrounded the homes, providing ample shade.

The center of the town consisted of several general stores, craft shops, a Hindu temple, and two mosques, Sunni and Shia, on opposite ends of the street. Boisterous children darted around, chasing balls or playing cricket, the eyes of the toddlers outlined with coal-black eyeliner to keep away bad demons. Girls, some veiled and others not, walked in groups toward their respective schools, one Muslim and near the Sunni mosque, the other a secular school administered by the government. The Muslim boys wore white *shalwar kamiz* and some had skullcaps. The students at the public school wore blue pants and button-down shirts. Wood smoke billowed from chimneys, and a few jeeps and miniature pickups drove up and down the street.

Though the village was far from affluent, Nick noted only a few signs of poverty. Occasional mendicants squatted under the trees, cooking naan in makeshift ovens. Just beyond the village center was a squatters' camp tucked into some empty stretches of land along the river, where low-caste Hindu migrants had made their slipshod shelters of wooden planks, sticks, and canvas. Their ranks would swell at the end of the summer in anticipation of the harvest, but a few hundred lived in the camp year round, enduring the harsh winter in their congested, flimsy abodes.

"That's nothing," Aysha said, when she saw Nick's attention drawn to the shanties. "Next week the entire village will be filled with them. Each year at this time, Hindus come up from the south—Jammu, Punjab, and Gujarat—for a pilgrimage through the mountains to the north. Gilkamosh is one of the main stops on the route. Thousands will come."

"Where do they all stay?" Nick asked, surprised by Aysha's uncharacteristic loquaciousness. He noted her face had become more radiant, her eyes gleaming.

"They camp around the squatters' village, but during busy years they fill up half of the valley. They stay for just a few days before they move into the mountains, trekking up the foot trails to Passtu, the next village on the circuit, before moving west. There will be a big ceremony at the Hindu temple here in town, where they will receive the blessings of the god Shiva and make offerings for two days before walking up to Passtu in a big promenade."

"It must be quite a spectacle."

"Yes. It's like a big, moving festival, really."

"Ever any problems—sectarian violence?"

"No, nothing serious. This is Gilkamosh. Before I left to study medicine in New Delhi years ago, there was never a single problem between Muslims and Hindus I can remember. Sure, there were little incidents, arguments and things, but nothing violent, even while the troubles were raging in Srinagar. Since then, we have had fighting in the mountains between the mujahideen and the army, some of it severe. But still, there has not been any violence here in the village."

"That's a relief."

"Certainly. There is one difference, though, that is troubling. The so-called Islamists have become more influential. They speak out against the Hindus, and against other Muslims who do not agree with them. I know for a fact that the mullahs at the madrassa openly disapprove of me."

"Why?"

"I am a doctor *and* a woman. Those things should not go hand in hand in their view."

"Are you ever scared of them?"

"Why should I be? I was living here long before they were. Besides, they may stare at me in disgust, preach against me, or whatever they do, but it would turn the whole village against them if they tried to run me out of Gilkamosh.

"Of course, people elsewhere have been less fortunate," she continued. "Innocent Hindus have been kicked out, more liberal-minded Muslims have been beaten into obeying *purdah*. But here, we have an understanding."

"Understanding?"

"The mujahideen target the national government like everywhere else—police and army posts and the like. But their commanders grew up in this area. Like everyone else who hails from this village, I do believe, they have kept a fondness for the place."

"Couldn't that change?"

Despite shaking her head no, Aysha's face grew austere. "I know their leader. I have confidence."

"The one who brought Ghulam and me to your clinic?"

Aysha started to reply, but stopped herself. "I don't know why I am telling you any of this."

"Because you can," Nick answered. "They say it's a lot easier to be frank with strangers. Because they're not involved."

Aysha turned and looked at Nick, trying to read his sincerity. "One can never be sure enough, under the circumstances."

"I'm just a backpacker who ran into some bad luck. That's the truth."

"So I was told," she replied.

"Told?"

"One does not survive, walking the thin line that I do, without ears in the field," she rejoined.

"I was wondering why you never pressed me on my background," Nick said.

"Why ask the one most likely to lie?"

Nick nodded. "Point well taken." They had passed through the sporadically settled village outskirts, into the thick of town. Nearer to the concentrated village center, groups of ruddy-faced children in blue school uniforms skipped along after the truck as they drove. "Hallo, hallo!" they hollered, as they chased the vehicle. Aysha smiled back at them, but when the truck turned a corner, and they passed an army jeep with a machine gun mounted in the back, she sighed.

"I will tell you, I am far more concerned about the Indian security forces than the mujahideen," she said. "The army is a bunch of criminals. They use force as a matter of course against everyone. For years, they have tortured people in the Vale, sometimes to death, for information. So far in Gilkamosh the Indians have acted with restraint. But not too far from here, in Kurgan several years ago, a rebel's family was murdered by army thugs dressed as mujahideen. The security forces of course denied it."

Kurgan? Probably Fidali's family, Nick thought, remembering the story Ghulam had told him. "So what makes Gilkamosh so lucky?" he said.

"Not luck. Politics. Our village leader, a Hindu, is as well connected and politically savvy as he is wealthy. He is close with the local army and police, and has been able to keep the security forces in check. He is quite effective at it. We have a deal—as long as I continue to treat Indian soldiers when they need it, Advani keeps the security forces at bay, and they honor my neutrality."

"How does a civilian keep the *military* on a leash?" Nick asked.

She paused, considering whether to continue. "For one thing, Advani has an inside track with powerful people in New Delhi. The army does not dare snub him. And for another, he is a shrewd businessman. One could surmise that a few rupees changed hands somewhere along the line."

"Corruption," Nick said reflexively.

"Hardly. Can one call money that saves lives 'corrupt'?"

"No. I suppose not."

"It's been our way in this village as long as anyone can remember. People save just a little bit of compassion for the neighbor who is different, and somehow, Allah willing, everything else falls into place. That is the way we have learned to survive."

CHAPTER 40

Aysha parked the truck at the side of the road in front of the largest home on the street. "Here is where we pick up our supplies," she said, before checking her appearance briefly in the truck's mirror. Nick quietly took note of this small display of female vanity, a trait he had not seen her exhibit at the clinic, where she was clad in the armor of her profession.

The flat roof of the home was barely visible over the tall mud-brick wall that surrounded it, forming a compound. A gate made of metal posts opened into a courtyard threaded by a dirt walkway that led to the front door.

The home itself was well kept and indicative of wealth, but far from lavish or ostentatious. The walls were wood-framed and made of plaster painted with new whitewash. There was an alcove in front surrounded by a modest lawn of wild grasses fringed by pink Himalayan rosebushes forming a circular arbor around some lawn chairs. The rose garden, buzzing with hummingbirds and bees, was impeccably manicured.

"Tasteful," Nick remarked.

"The home of Advani Sharma. Our clinic's primary benefactor."

Nick nodded in acknowledgment. "So *he's* the one with the funds. As you said yourself, it pays to be well connected."

"It pays *me* nothing. All the money goes to supplies and maintenance, and there's not even enough for that."

"I was kidding. After five months at the clinic, I've noticed how there's barely enough cash to scrape by."

There was a covered shed on the far side of the compound, in which a pile of boxes stood stacked on top of one another. Aysha pointed at the boxes, indicating they were the clinic's supplies. Then, after tucking a few stray hairs behind her ears, she knocked on the dark wooden door, while Nick remained behind to load the truck.

A short, light-skinned Hindu man with a potbelly, a mustache, and a bald head greeted Aysha with a wide grin. After they exchanged some pleasantries, he invited Aysha inside, but before closing the door behind them, he peered out at Nick and waved him in as well. Nick politely refused, gesturing to the boxes of supplies.

When Nick had finished stacking the boxes in the truck, Aysha returned along with Advani. Nick had hoped to avoid meeting him. Always in the back of his mind was the threat that the authorities, even here in Indian-controlled territory, had been alerted of his escape from neighboring Pakistan, or that the border incident with the Indian army had implicated him with the rebels. The police could be looking for him, and might have put out the word to civilian officials like Advani. But there was nothing Nick could do now—he was trapped.

"Mr. Sunder," he called Nick by name, surprising him. "So very pleased to meet you." He spoke in a lilted, animated voice, and his sharp, intelligent eyes seemed incongruous in light of his jovial demeanor.

"Likewise," Nick replied, avoiding eye contact in an effort to avoid making an impression.

"Aysha tells me you are a volunteer at her clinic. How very beneficent of you. Thank you, sir, for your service to our community."

Nick glanced at Advani quickly. "Pleasure's mine." In attempt to curtail the conversation, he turned back toward the truck, but Advani was not finished.

"How interesting that you are here in this part of Kashmir. We have not seen a Westerner in Gilkamosh in, oh, three years. Other than the occasional adventurous journalist doing some piece on the world's highest-altitude military conflict," Advani continued, adding a chuckle.

"I love mountains," Nick said, fumbling for what to say.

"And you are from the United States?"

"Canada," Nick said, repeating his usual lie.

"But Aysha told me you were American."

Nick felt heat spread across his face. He had forgotten what he had told Aysha. "Well, um, I'm *both*. Canadian on my mother's side, American on . . ." Caught in his lie, Nick jumbled his words.

"Your father's."

"Right." Nick's eyes shifted to Aysha, who detected his evasiveness. She decided to cut in.

"Clearly I didn't get the whole story," she said. "Thank you, Advani.

I should say hello to Father quickly, and then get back to the clinic. Things are starting to pick up now that it's spring."

"Yes, I know—farming injuries. Very well. I just wanted to welcome Mr. Sunder to our humble village. You must come, sir, for tea some afternoon. Please."

"Thank you," Nick replied, walking away briskly, at the risk of being rude.

They left the loaded truck parked in front of Advani's home and walked along the sleepy, tree-lined road away from the village center toward Aysha's father's home. Nick's nerves, agitated by his meeting with Advani, were soothed by scenes of domestic tranquility—children cavorting in front of homes and young mothers, fine-featured beauties dressed in brightly colored *shalwar kamiz*, peering curiously from open doorways at Aysha and the strange foreigner as they passed by, some waving, others smiling coyly.

The home in which Aysha had been raised was modest in size, much smaller than Advani's, but cozy. Chickens and goats wandered freely about the yard, oblivious to their bondage to humans. Aysha's numerous brothers and sisters had built their homes adjacent to her father's, and all the houses shared a common plot where the extended family grew vegetables and grain. The door was open, and Aysha walked in, waving to Nick behind her.

The interior consisted of a large room with a metal wood-burning stove in the center. Near the stove was a wooden table with pots, pans, and teakettles. And to the right of the main chamber, set off from the scullery, were two sleeping rooms in which bedding and pillows were strewn about the carpeted floor. An adjoining room to the left of the main chamber and devoid of furnishings served as the tearoom where guests were hosted, so essential in Muslim households. On the wall hung a picture of the late Mirwaiz of Kashmir.

The home was empty. Aysha motioned for Nick to follow her past the smoldering stove in the center of the main living room and out the back door of the house, which opened onto the common plot. There they found Aysha's father, Naseem, stacking logs of firewood at the far end of the field.

With one quick glance, Nick could tell Naseem, a white-bearded barrel of a man with large, rugged hands and a chiseled profile, was a man who had spent a far greater part of his life outdoors than in a domestic arena. Nick guessed he was in his late sixties, though he could have been much older or younger, for the mountains have a way of either aging one rapidly or preserving youth, depending entirely on the individual. He had the same high cheekbones as Aysha, and the kind of full, silvery hair that results only from that which was once pitch black.

At the sight of his daughter, Naseem's eyes lit up. He hugged her with warm affection across each shoulder then kissed her on the forehead, before Aysha introduced Nick. Because he spoke only a few words of English, they did not graduate beyond a cordial handshake. Naseem escorted them back inside the house, and they sat cross-legged on the carpet around the stove, while Aysha poured tea into porcelain cups. She heated a dozen or so samosas, deep-fried dumplings filled with potatoes and vegetables, as Aysha's numerous relatives gradually filed in through the front and back doors, having been given word of Aysha's arrival by Naseem's loud, excited talking. Aysha introduced Nick to each one as they arrived—her various sisters, brothers, in-laws, and cousins—but there were too many of them, and their names largely went in and out of Nick's ears without registering.

Aysha's sisters, all of them older, resembled Aysha, but they were more matronly and, though fetching in their own way, not as stunning. As with Naseem, none of them had Aysha's mesmerizing eyes, which Nick saw to be an anomaly. The sisters joined Nick and Aysha around the stove, while their rambunctious children—Aysha's cousins, nieces, and nephews—too numerous to keep track of, ran about the room, giggling and stealing playful glances at the strange foreigner.

Soon, the entire Fahad clan, nearly twenty of them, had packed themselves in around the stove, chatting and laughing. Though Nick could not understand a word that was said, he was uplifted by the joyful inflections in their voices and their excited expressions. Aysha's sisters shot glances at him and made faces at one another, telling secrets with their eyes, and Nick felt flattered to be considered a novelty. For unlike Aysha, the others had not spent much time away from Gilkamosh; a foreign man at such close quarters was a rare curiosity.

Being the focus of so much female attention, however innocent, was a flattering privilege Nick had not expected. For the few times Nick had been invited into people's homes as a guest during his travels in Muslim countries, the women of the families had not been permitted to even be seen by Nick, a nonrelated male, let alone interact with him. But the

Fahads did not follow the same strict code of *purdah* adhered to by some Sunni and Shia sects, adopting a more liberal attitude toward certain social aspects of their religion, something Aysha later explained was not uncommon among Muslims in Gilkamosh and other parts of Kashmir.

Aysha's brothers marveled at Nick's beard, insisting that he *had* to be Muslim to own such a wondrous crop. Their exposure to Americans had been limited to boyishly clean-cut Hollywood movie stars; they never knew that an American could grow a beard at all, let alone one that would make a mullah snarl with envy. Aysha's twin brothers, Khaliq and Nabir, stood out in Nick's mind above the others, not just because of their similarity in appearance, but for their obvious reverence for Aysha. He could tell by the way the boys gravitated to her that Aysha had been a kind of second mother to them. They were no older than sixteen, with large brown eyes that exuded a callow innocence. They sat silently, in deference only to Aysha and their father, the latter reveling in the attention afforded him as head of the clan. Khaliq and Nabir were healthy and lean, their beards still downy with youth and their faces handsome, with Aysha's high cheekbones and straight black hair. Once they mustered the mettle, they were eager to befriend Nick and use their schoolbook English.

"You have wife in America?" Khaliq asked, casting away all shyness with a single question. Aysha's sisters, hands over their mouths, tried to stifle their chuckles. The public school in Gilkamosh endeavored to teach their girls English with as much vigor as it did their boys, and the Fahad clan was certainly a beneficiary of this rule.

"I don't," Nick replied.

"Why not?" he probed.

"Khaliq, that's not a polite question," Aysha interjected.

"It's okay." Nick chuckled. "I guess I haven't met the right person."

"You have not been in love?" Kaliq bandied gleefully. The girls giggled. Naseem frowned, his curiosity piqued by the commotion, but unable to follow it.

"Do you have any American love stories to tell us, please?" Khaliq's twin brother, Nabir, chimed in.

"Nabir!" Aysha admonished. Everyone laughed. Nick could not fathom two teenage boys being as fascinated with something as seemingly girlish as love stories. "I'm afraid I can't think of any right now," Nick replied. "Maybe next time."

"I like love stories very much," Nabir said, disappointed. "Is it true

American women wear clothes in public that look like underwear?" he followed.

"Nabir, what did I say?" said Aysha.

Nick snickered. "Well, yes," he replied. "I guess that's true, in some places . . . like at the beach."

After three cups of sugary tea and far too many samosas, Aysha announced it was time to leave. As a final gesture, the twins invited Nick to go trout fishing with them someday, and then the process of hugging good-bye started. To Nick, this seemed to last nearly as long as the visit, especially since he, to his embarrassment, was drafted into the ordeal. Finally out the door, he and Aysha left for the ride back over the mountain to the clinic, feeling aglow.

Walking the road back to Advani's house where the truck was parked, Aysha and Nick passed the temple and the mosque. It was evening and the road was deserted, most people having returned home for dinner or for evening prayers. When they had nearly reached the truck, they came upon a slight, wiry man dressed in a solid white *shalwar kamiz* and skullcap. He had a long, thin nose, freckled skin, and a sparse, tangled, reddish-brown beard hanging down to his chest. The man recognized Aysha from afar and stopped in their path.

Aysha fell silent, her staid expression now devoid of the warmth that had been brought on by the visit with her family. The red-bearded man stood glaring at her with hostility. He shifted his gaze to Nick, then back to Aysha again. He spoke in local dialect, though later Aysha told Nick what was said.

"Salaam alaikum, Aysha." Despite the Qur'anic greeting of peace, his voice was filled with contempt.

"*Wah alaikum salaam,*" Aysha replied curtly.

"I see you have again disrespected our village by violating Mullah Sharif's edict."

"Mullah Sharif does not speak for the village. Nor does he speak for me."

"Yes, I know. The infidel Advani speaks for *you.*" By now, he had stopped right in front of them, impeding their path to the truck.

"No, Abdul, I speak for myself. Now shut up and get out of my way."

"Stupid slut!" he said.

Aysha stopped in her tracks, challenging him with her stare. Though they were about the same height, she seemed to tower over him. He quailed back a half step, intimidated and disgusted at the same time, as if she were afflicted with some loathsome disease.

"I will pretend I did not hear what you said," she retorted. Without understanding the words, Nick sensed the building tension. He instinctively took a step forward. Abdul's eyes scanned him from head to foot.

"So you are bedding *infidels* now? You disgrace the *ummah* as much as you flout the Qur'an."

"It's none of your business what I do. Now get away from me or I will have you arrested. Or have you forgotten how powerless you really are?"

She walked by him, Nick following suit. Some curious bystanders—two Muslim youths—had heard the hostile voices and gawked from a distance. The red-bearded man followed Aysha like a wolf stalking prey, even more incensed by her snub.

"You think you're better than the rest of us, don't you," he said, his fury now turned to exasperation. "You better watch your step. Soon enough, you may have no one left to protect you."

They had reached the truck. Aysha climbed in. Nick waited, standing between her and the man until she was safely inside. The man challenged Nick with his glare. But something about him, the way he consciously cocked his chin, perhaps, led Nick to suspect that underneath all his puffery, he was afraid.

"Nick, get in," Aysha said, as she started the truck. Not wanting any trouble himself, Nick obliged, backing off slowly to make sure the angry man did not rush him. As soon as Nick climbed in the passenger side, Aysha started to pull away.

"I tell you for your own good!" Abdul shouted at the receding truck.

CHAPTER 41

The peculiar confrontation with the red-bearded man, so at odds with the rest of the day's experience, soured the drive back to the clinic. Nick and Aysha sat in awkward silence, their eyes fixed on the perilous road. Halfway back, Nick decided to break the tension.

"Jealous ex-boyfriend?"

Aysha winced. "You would accuse me of such poor taste?"

She chose not to follow up with an explanation until Nick pressed her. Since he had witnessed the transgression, Nick felt somewhat entitled to a response.

"His name is Abdul," Aysha said. "I have known him since we were children. He is a literate man—not ignorant. Like a lot of the boys from this area whose families cannot afford the public school, he studied at the madrassa. The mullah who taught him was an extremist and never liked me. I guess the teachings went to Abdul's head."

"How could the mullah have a problem with you? You were just a girl."

Aysha turned her eyes from the road and peered at Nick. He felt as though she was assessing him, trying to decide whether to open up. "This may sound unusual to you as a Westerner. When I was a girl, I served a special function in the village. I was a sort of 'village healer.' People believed that I had . . . curative powers."

"You do. I've seen it."

"Now? I should hope so. I am a trained physician. But that is not what I mean. When I was a child, my status as a healer was based purely on superstition. That's partly what the mullah objected to."

Nick paused. "Like a shaman?"

"Something like that. Though shamans are men. Anyway, I was an impressionable child. I took my role very seriously. Like everyone else, I actually started to believe that I had special powers," she said with a chuckle. "You know, in a very traditional community like Gilkamosh, there is nothing for a girl to look forward to other than getting married

254

and having children as soon as she is physically mature enough to do so. So it made me feel special, proud actually.

"Because I was trusted by the people as their healer, they opened up to me in ways that were unheard of for a child. I became, in effect, a very rudimentary type of psychologist. People would tell me all their problems, temptations, and fears. I was so young, I did not know what to *tell* people. More often that not, I said nothing—I just listened. But I think it made them feel better just to get things off their chests."

Unable to help himself, Nick laughed.

"What is so funny?"

"I just . . . I can picture you as a little girl, sitting wide-eyed, while the village women reveal all the skeletons in their closets. I bet it could have been quite useful, in a small town, to have all those secrets handy at your fingertips."

"Yes. But it was more of a huge responsibility. To this day I have *never* breached a single trust."

"You were nobler than I would have been at that age. Or any age, actually."

"It was not nobility. I knew once I let one secret out, no matter how small, it would travel through the village like wildfire. I would never be trusted again."

"I still would have let at least one slip," Nick said.

Aysha sighed. "Well, that settles it. If you are not good at keeping secrets, I shouldn't tell you anything more," she said.

"Come on, Aysha. Who am I going to tell? You are the only person who speaks English at the clinic well enough to hold a conversation. Except Ghulam, and he's too busy driving Vilashni crazy to care about anything right now."

She flashed a smile. Nick felt pleased to humor her.

"Do you think Ghulam is *flirting*?"

Nick scratched his chin in consideration. "From what I can tell, definitely. But I'm sure it's all in good fun. He's married already, a couple of times over."

She laughed. "A Muslim man may marry as many women as he dares. In fact, it is encouraged. I'm afraid monogamy is a Christian value."

"True. But then again, so are chastity and fidelity. The whole system's rigged to keep people sinning," Nick said, surprised to see Aysha blush. He entertained the possibility that she was a virgin—almost unheard of, at her age, in the Western world, but very possible given the local mores.

"Anyway," he continued, "that guy back there almost attacked me. What's his dark secret? I deserve an answer, I think."

"It's a sad story. Are you sure you want to hear it?"

Nick nodded. "I'm sure."

"When Abdul was just twelve, his mother, Yasmeen, confided to me that she had committed adultery with a Hindu man. It happened before I was born, so I did not know the man. But when she spoke of him, I could tell she was still in love. He was handsome, she said—a soldier— and very kind to her.

"Yasmeen's husband, by contrast, was a brute. He treated her like a slave—she would labor for long hours in the fields, and at home catering to him and her sons. He also beat the children, including Abdul. Yasmeen said he did it to discipline them, but more probably, it was simply because he was cruel.

"Whenever Yasmeen voiced her disapproval of her husband's treatment of the children, he would beat her terribly as well. Several times, she came to me with her eyes blackened with bruises, and once with broken ribs. I was a young girl. There was nothing I could do," she said, a trace of guilt in her voice. "The man of course claimed that disciplining his wife by beating was sanctioned by passages in the Qur'an. And no one would dispute him."

"It amazes me how anyone takes something written down over a thousand years ago so literally."

"The fundamentalist philosophy cannot allow for such things as anachronism. Every word must be the true word of God, timeless, written down exactly as recited. Because if one word is false or considered obsolete, then it's possible that it all might be false. There's no arguing with them.

"Anyway," she continued, "here comes the secret. Abdul, Yasmeen told me, was the son of her Hindu lover—*not* her husband. She never told the boy. How could she? And from what I know, Abdul does not know, even now."

"Do you think she will ever tell him?"

"She cannot. She is dead."

"Husband killed her?"

"He and some others. And I suppose, she was also responsible in a way. You see, it was what I call an indirect suicide. I have seen it several times. She could not stand her life, married to that despot, with all the beatings, being treated as a beast of burden. So, she told her husband about the affair. And then her husband and his brothers stoned her to death."

Nick fell silent, staring out the window. Aysha glanced at him. "Are you *sure* you don't get carsick?" she asked, jarring the wheel to keep from wandering too close to the edge. "I know my driving can sometimes be erratic."

"Yes, it can . . . but, no, I'm okay. It's just . . . why stoning?"

"The punishment for adultery under the *sharia* is death by stoning. The family, the ones who are affronted by the crime, carry out the sentence."

"This is India. Isn't the law supposed to be secular?"

"In theory, but people administer what law they see fit in the remote villages. And once a sentence has been carried out, the authorities are reluctant to arrest anyone. This was especially true during that period, at the start of the rebellion, when the government was sensitive about appearing religiously intolerant."

"Intolerant? A stoning to death seems intolerant—*not* preventing one."

"I could not agree more. But if the government throws people in jail for carrying out the judgment of a village mullah, then everyone screams Muslims are being unfairly treated. Which would not be entirely untrue, since village councils in Hindu villages condemn women to similar punishments, and rarely is anything done to intervene. You see, brutality against women has nothing to do with being Muslim or Hindu. It is the same across the board. Although in these parts such extremism has always been very rare, at least until recently."

"How does this all fit into what happened today?"

"With Abdul? I don't know, really. Maybe it doesn't at all. Or maybe Abdul hates all women, and therefore me, for his mother's adultery and ultimate abandonment.

"The regional mullah has issued an edict requiring all Muslim women to wear veils. The Shia, of course, don't care what a Sunni says, but they've typically been on the conservative side anyway. There are many like me, however, who—although Sunni—never wore a veil, and simply do not want to be told what to do. This man Abdul—he acts as a kind of religious enforcer. Few listen to him—myself included."

"He seemed awfully violent over such a small infraction."

"*That* is something new. He has said fanatical things in the past, but never has he been so . . . unrestrained in his hostility," she replied.

"Why don't you tell Advani to do something about it? If he's as influential as you say, he must have the power to silence him."

"Oh, I can handle Abdul. He has always been nothing more than an insignificant nuisance of a man."

"Well, he certainly looked to me like he was capable of some damage."

Aysha considered this a moment. "Yes, I suppose he did, didn't he? I can't help wondering," Aysha contemplated aloud, "if he knew who his real father was—that he is half Hindu himself—whether he would be so fanatical. I mean, it's pathetic, absurd really. He is always preaching hatred against Hindus. Yet they are his own people, and he does not even know it."

"Maybe you should tell him."

"No. I can't do that."

"Why not? It may help him to see things differently. For the better."

"He wouldn't believe me, Nick. People blinded by hate only hear what they want. And as I said," she added, "the village's trust in me depends on my keeping their confidences. If I let one secret go, I betray them all. They deserve better. I am their investment. They paid for my medical training. I have a responsibility to them all."

"You're the village doctor. Maybe you have a responsibility to him as well—so he knows the truth—for his own good? And everyone else's, really. As tightly as he was wound, who knows, telling him might save someone's life someday."

Aysha sighed. "Therein lies my conflict. You see now my position is not one to be envied."

It was evening as the truck descended the steep ridge on the way back to the clinic. The sun sank low on the western horizon, causing the snowy mountains to emit a pink luminescence. Despite the somber talk and biting chill, as they finally arrived at the approach to the clinic, Nick felt flooded with warmth.

CHAPTER 42

Kazim walked into Abdul's basement to find Abdul waiting for him with three boys—Gani, Tariq, and Aatef. Not one of them was more than eighteen years old.

Kazim greeted them in turn, looking each of them in the eyes. He felt that same unsettling mixture of resignation and empathy as when he stared at the body of his first kill, the Sikh whose skull he had crushed with his rifle butt in his first battle on the Line of Control so many years ago. On that night, his mind had fought to suppress its intuitive resistance to violence in order to do what he had to do. Still, he could not vanquish completely his compassion for the man he had sent to his grave. He wondered if that was what a justifiable killing must always feel like—done reluctantly, in the face of compassion for one's victim.

If so, perhaps he could convince himself he was acting in self-defense now, he thought. Anything, to make the decision to send them to their deaths lighter to bear.

"Salaam alaikum, my friends," he said finally.

"*Wah alaikum salaam*, leader," the youths replied with enthusiasm.

"Abdul, do you have the robes in store?"

"Yes, Kazim," Abdul answered. "Here is the map." Abdul unrolled a hand-drawn map of the village of Gilkamosh.

"Good," said Kazim, pointing to it. "Abdul and I scouted the area this morning. The best place for your approach is here, at the junction of the road and the courtyard of the Hindu temple. At exactly one hour before they start the procession, you must be in your places.

"Triq and Aatef will take this position here," Kazim said, pointing at the map. "And across the street, Gani, you shall be posted here, near the entrance to the temple. From the two vantage points, it will be more difficult for the police to pinpoint you, and you will have more time to do what you must before you are . . . martyred, inshallah."

Kazim stopped and looked into their eyes.

"Are you men ready for this?" He called them men, knowing they were still boys. Children aspiring to be men, he knew from experience, make the best warriors, combining the optimal mixture of viciousness and desire to please.

"Yes, leader," they replied, staggered, each waiting to make sure the other concurred.

"Make sure you double-check each other's guns, and that each is working smoothly. Have four clips each. Forty-shot magazines, taped together in pairs top against bottom, so you can flip each pair quickly, the two extra clips under your robe."

"Yes, leader," they responded again.

Kazim hesitated, trying his best to muster a tone of upbeat sincerity for what he would say next. Instead, he feared he sounded apologetic.

"As martyrs you will not have to wait for Judgment Day to enter Paradise. You are privileged men!" Kazim exclaimed, his voice falling flat.

"These last days, be good to your parents, so they will have a fond last memory of you. They will be proud of you. Remember your ablutions— you want to go to Him cleansed and pure. Try to clear your mind of everything but the task at hand, so you have no distractions. And when you are hit and can no longer fire your guns, think only of Him. . . .

"If you follow the plan, do exactly as you have been told, nothing more and nothing less, eternal glory surely will be yours. I have faith in your courage. You are mujahideen. Go with Allah—inshallah."

Kazim embraced each of them in turn, tenderly, as if they were his own children. His eyes welled up. But he wiped them quickly, for no tear should be shed for the privileged.

"Thank you, sir," the boys said, touched by their commander's emotion.

"*Allah-o-Akbar!*" Kazim said forcefully, trying to dispel the quavering from his voice. As he turned and walked out of the room, he caught a trace of surprise shining across Abdul's face. *He didn't think I had it in me,* Kazim thought.

CHAPTER 43

The trip to Gilkamosh had bridged the distance between Nick and Aysha. Nick, for his part, shared what information about his past he felt he could. He did not mention Yvette or Akhtar, or the real reason he had risked the crossing into Indian-occupied Kashmir. And Aysha continued not to press him on his past.

Had Aysha not exuded utter honesty, Nick would not have believed her claim that she never had any love interest, either while studying in Delhi or thereafter. When he probed whether she *ever* had a boyfriend, she admitted she once was engaged to a boy from a nearby village, but they had "grown apart" during her time in Delhi. Her tight-knit family saved her from loneliness, but the lack of romance in her life imbued her with an aura of sadness. This singular vulnerability only enhanced her beauty in Nick's mind.

Soon after the trip, Nick found himself coveting her presence. Though his feelings often were buried under recurrent waves of worry and remorse over Yvette's death, Nick became aware of his longing to complete that part of Aysha that was missing. The seeds of attraction had been planted from the start. Before their trip to Gilkamosh, however, her indifference toward Nick had thwarted his affection for her. Now, a feeling that they had grown closer made her allure much stronger.

It was not such a purely sexual attraction as with Yvette, but a deeper desire. At times, everything about Aysha seemed in stark contrast to Yvette, so much so, it surprised him that he could be attracted to such opposite personalities. Yvette's blatant mannerisms drew men like dogs. Her sexuality had been her lifeblood, a goal to which she had not needed to aspire, but still had attained, a ticket to lead the hedonistic life of her choosing, before it ended so violently. Aysha's sexuality, in contrast, was the embodiment of mystery; her tall, shapely body was merely hinted at beneath the loose, traditional garb she wore, but this only made Nick long to unveil what lay beneath. Yvette had invited men to possess her and drove them mad when they ultimately could not. To love Aysha, one would need first to earn a place in her life, which seemed far too consumed by her devotion to her people to allow room for anything else.

Nonetheless, Nick could not help but feel Aysha's melancholy gave away a desire for intimacy. He wondered, however, whether the *drive* to attain it had been irretrievably squandered on the one man she had mentioned from her past.

Two weeks after the supply run to Gilkamosh, a gray-bearded goatherd named Rasheed rushed into the clinic. He was breathless and panicked, having run five kilometers of mountain trail from his outlying hamlet. He said his "girl," presumably his wife or a daughter, was in labor. He feared she was having bad complications, and it was too late to walk her to the clinic.

"Is there no midwife with her?" said Aysha.

Rasheed shook his head.

"What were you thinking, old man?" Aysha cried. "Don't you know to bring her here before she starts to give birth? Why is this the first I am hearing of this?"

As Aysha hurried to retrieve her traveling kit, she muttered in English, so that Rasheed would not know what she was saying. "Damn these stubborn old goatherds. They never tell me when their wives are pregnant. No matter how many times they are told that I don't charge the poor, they all think I'm going to demand a year's worth of their wages. So they roll the dice with their wives' lives.

"Look, Nick. You better come with me," she said. "Omar is off today. And I might need a pair of strong arms to stretcher her back her to the clinic, if there's a problem."

Nick drove Aysha and Rasheed along the winding road toward Gilkamosh Valley, but instead of proceeding all the way to the top of the pass, they pulled into a turnout at the head of a rocky foot trail. The three of them climbed out of the truck and began to hike up the steep mountain trail. Nearly an hour later, they arrived at a small hamlet consisting of a dozen or so stone huts nestled at the foot of a majestic expanse of green pasture, shaded brightly with the spring's first growth. Outside the perimeters of the pasture, the base of the mountains was thickly forested with pine and spruce. A rocky stream ran through the pasture, disappearing into the woods. "Come," said Rasheed, who had rushed ahead, waving them toward his home.

Aysha was surprised, however, when Rasheed did not usher them inside, but instead, took them around back, where he pointed toward a ramshackle, stone-walled structure. It was a shelter for livestock.

"Rasheed," Aysha reprimanded, "don't tell me she's in there! A woman giving birth needs it to be clean."

Rasheed dropped his chin in shame. He swung open the wood-paneled door of the shelter, dimly lit by thin shafts of light coming through cracks and holes in the stone walls. Lying on her side on the straw-covered dirt floor, her bloated belly rising and falling rhythmically with forced breaths, was not a woman—but a nanny goat, bleating in a low, painful baritone.

"You made us run five kilometers for a goat?!" Aysha exclaimed, not without anger. "I'm not a veterinarian, Rasheed. I treat people! You know . . . they have two legs and no hooves!"

Rasheed looked at her with apologetic eyes. He spoke to her in dialect.

"I am sorry, madam. This is my girl, my best breeder. She has given me so many fine baby goats. Look at her. She's in trouble. Please, don't let this litter be her last. I cannot afford to lose her."

Aysha stared at the poor beast and shook her head. "As old as you are, Rasheed, I should have known something about this pregnancy was fishy."

The nanny goat's breaths were quickly paced, her grayish tongue protruding and dripping with saliva. Nick could see why Rasheed couldn't bring her to the clinic. Her belly was huge, and her water sac had already broken, spilling thick, viscous liquid out onto the floor.

"You're the goatherd, Rasheed. You should know how to do this better than I do."

"I tried, Madam Doctor. The baby is stuck. I need your special talents. Goat, people—are they not same same?"

Aysha sighed in frustration. "No, Rasheed. Not same same."

Rasheed, deflated, bowed his head, stroking the animal tenderly. "Sorry, madam. I thought you could help her."

For a moment, Nick could not tell who appeared to be in a more pained, sorry state, Rasheed or his goat. Aysha sighed, then looked at Nick, who shrugged his shoulders. "Don't look at me," he said. "I don't know anything about goats."

Rasheed peered at Aysha with sad, pleading eyes.

Aysha gave an exasperated sigh. "You're lucky my father kept goats."

She set down her bag, reached inside it, and pulled out a pair of rubber gloves and forceps. She stepped to the backside of the goat. "I need both of you to hold her legs so she doesn't kick my face off," she instructed. As Nick and Rasheed pinned the writhing animal, she carefully pried open its cervix with the forceps and looked inside.

"Goodness! Twins . . . no, triplets . . . wait, no!" she looked up at Rasheed in amazement. "You're right about one thing, she certainly *is* fertile. Congratulations, Rasheed. Your girl is having quadruplets!" She smiled at Nick and held up four fingers.

"No wonder she's stopped up," said Nick, amused.

"I think I'd better give her a C-section, or she's liable to hemorrhage."

Aysha instructed Rasheed to shear the wool off the nanny's belly, while she dug into her bag and pulled out her surgery set, extracting the largest of her scalpels. Nick and Rasheed held the animal down as she carefully cut the long, curving incision in its womb and pulled out four slimy, bleating kids, permitting Rasheed to sever the umbilical cords as she delivered them. After sewing her back up and cleaning her off, she gave the animal, still hysterical from the trauma of being pinned to the ground and sliced open, a small shot of morphine and antibiotics.

The procedure seemed even messier than the delivery of a human baby, and Aysha's clothes were completely covered with blood and fluid. After she and Nick had swaddled the kid goats in a blanket, Rasheed, who was beside himself with delight, left and came back with a wooden tray of tin cups filled with a clear liquid, potent moonshine made of fermented mulberries. Nick gave Aysha a cheeky look as she accepted one of the cups.

"What is with that look?" she said to Nick defensively, a glimmer of mischief in her eyes. "'Gilkamosh water' has been part of our culture for centuries, since we were drum-beating pagans. Besides, more and more villagers these days are calling me a heretic, so what's the difference?" She held up the cup toward Rasheed, and then to the four kids, still slick with amniotic fluid and now suckling intently on the mother's udders. "Here's to bringing our four new woolly friends to Gilkamosh," she said. "May you elude snow leopards and lynxes, and forever be spared from Rasheed's butcher block."

Aysha pressed the cup to her lips and took a single sip before putting it back down on the tray, while Nick and Rasheed downed theirs with gusto. Then the three of them watched the mother goat nurse, feeling elated, until Aysha, without explanation, dismissed herself and walked outside.

Nick threw back a couple more glasses of moonshine with Rasheed, then, starting to feel a little drunk due to his empty stomach, he gave Rasheed a congratulatory nod and stepped outside to wash the instruments. "I've got to wash these."

Rasheed intuited what Nick meant to do and pointed him to the thicket, where a brook ran through the trees. Nick thanked him and carried the tools, bloodied from the operation, into the woods.

Nick sat down by the bank, feeling warmed by the liquor, and began to rinse the tools in the clear water, when a movement through the trees caught the corner of his eye. He looked up and saw nothing. Wary of being stalked by a bear or a leopard that might have picked up the scent of the bloody medical tools, he stood, craning his neck as he stepped away from the brook to get a better vantage.

At first he saw only her back. But as she unfastened the drawstring of her *shalwar* pants, she turned slightly, compelling Nick to step behind a tree trunk.

Nick closed his eyes and breathed deeply. The mere glimpse of her bare skin made him shudder. He struggled to gather his composure, then started to step away, softly so as not to be heard, not so much to hide his indiscretion as to save her the embarrassment of knowing she had been seen.

But then, suddenly, he stopped. Resting his hands against the tree, he turned, forestalled by temptation. He raised his eyes.

She was about twenty yards away, the light dimmed by the canopy of trees, which grew thicker near to the stream. She had turned her torso toward Nick to receive the warm sunlight. Her breasts were ample and firm, the dark circles around her nipples partially veiled by her long black mane flowing down across her shoulders, and when she pulled her hair back with both hands, lifting her chin, they rose like perfect cones, splayed toward her shoulders. Then, with a quick, nimble movement, like a child struck by whimsy, she spun around and bent gracefully to wash her forearms, still red with the animal's birthing blood, in the brook. Her buttocks, two smooth half moons parted by a twist of downy hair, gave way to long legs of flawless brown skin.

Nick felt a heat rush up from his legs. His palms moistened with sweat. He knew he should turn and walk away, and his boldness was not unhindered by shame. But he stood his ground, mesmerized, permitting the pure beauty of her naked body to burn into the recesses of his memory.

Then, suddenly, she sensed a presence and turned. For some reason, Nick made no effort to step back behind the tree. Maybe he was too distracted to react, or perhaps subconsciously he wanted to be caught. Regardless, her expression, when they locked eyes, was something that he would revisualize in his mind over and again, each time embellished, perhaps distorted, by his own erotic subconscious.

First, there was shock—that much was clear when she blanched and quickly stepped backward. But then she stopped herself, perhaps out of resignation, but quite possibly, as Nick would later surmise, captivated by being so helplessly exposed, having a man relish her most intimate self, her very sex. For she could have crossed her arms over her chest or placed a concealing hand between her legs. But she did none of those things. She simply stood there, looking directly at him with her lips slightly parted, granting his eyes their desire for what seemed like several long, blissful moments, before finally picking up her clothes and vanishing unhurriedly behind the tangled stand of willows lining the stream bank.

Feeling dizzy, Nick propped his forehead against the tree and watched beads of sweat drip off his chin onto the dark forest floor.

Aysha made no mention of the incident during the hike back to the trailhead where the jeep was parked. Clearly, she was angry, Nick thought, and embarrassed by what had happened. He was sure that she would banish him from the clinic immediately upon their return. And who could blame her? Though on one level he was intrigued by how she had responded to his voyeurism, he was mortified by what he had done. He had not only violated her privacy by not averting his eyes, but also had likely destroyed their burgeoning friendship just when he had finally earned her trust. He felt compelled to at least attempt an apology. The incident was, after all, wholly his fault, so the obligation to rectify it fell on his shoulders, not hers.

"Aysha . . . I'm sorry," he said. She was walking in front of him, and he could not see her reaction. There was a long silence, during which Nick guessed she was searching for a response.

"Why are you apologizing?" she said, finally.

Nick sighed. Yes, she was indeed angry. And, as punishment, she was going to force him to suffer the embarrassment of expressly admitting what he had done. "The stream, Aysha . . . I'm sorry about what happened by the stream."

"I don't know what you're talking about," she said abruptly, without turning to look at him.

Nick opened his mouth to speak further, but then stopped himself. If denial was the manner in which she chose to handle the situation, why should he not honor it? Was it not her prerogative?

Later, during the silent drive back to the clinic, he would come to doubt whether she had seen him watching her at all. He *had* been standing a considerable distance from her. His view, and surely hers, had been largely obstructed by thick foliage and tree trunks. And being a nondrinker, might not that tiny sip of mulberry moonshine have affected her powers of perception? Perhaps her look of recognition, her voluntary submission to his gaze, had all been a figment of Nick's libidinous imagination, which had been painfully deprived since the death of Yvette, and all that had ensued from it.

Despite these doubts, however, Nick found himself poised at that intoxicating threshold of either pure ecstasy or black despair, a point where anything seemed possible, as easily as it was entirely unfathomable.

After several days had passed, Nick became, on some level, disappointed that Aysha had not at least acknowledged the incident in the woods. Nonetheless, he knew he should count her failure to do so as a blessing. And he was, in fact, relieved not to have incurred her wrath and been forced to leave the clinic. Aysha and Nick continued to work under the same roof as if nothing had happened, cordial, friendly, generally enjoying each other's company.

The time Nick and Aysha spent together did not go unnoticed by the staff. Vilashni, in her matronly way, voiced her approval of the time Nick and Aysha were spending together. "You good for Madam Doctor," she told Nick one morning. "You no leave her," she admonished, suspecting he would someday leave for America.

Ghulam, too, was tickled by the prospect of a romance in the air. With his penchant to translate everything into spiritual terms, he felt compelled to lecture Nick and Aysha, to her great embarrassment, that their "union" was mandated by Allah.

"Mr. Nick," Ghulam said to Nick one afternoon. "Ghulam knows. You like Madam Doctor. And Madam Doctor like you," he said.

"We're just friends."

"Friends? *You and me* are friends, Mr. Nick. You listen. Ghulam knows."

"Shhh!" Nick held his finger to his lips, fearing that Aysha might hear him.

"Let me tell you, Mr. Nick—to allow a woman like Madam Doctor to go through life with no husband—*that* is the worst sin a man can commit. Almost worse than *shirk*! Allah commands man must take wives. It is written!" He lifted his palms in supplication.

Nick paused a moment. "So then, what about you and Vilashni?" he replied, trying to turn the tables.

"What do you mean?" he replied, acting uncharacteristically coy.

"You know what I mean, Ghulam." Nick said, now teasing him.

"Ghulam does not understand," he said, his eyes shifting bashfully.

"You like Vilashni. So why don't *you* take a wife?"

"Ahhhh! Ghulam sees what Mr. Nick is trying to do. You think you can trick Ghulam? You want to change the donkey in middle of the path. But they are different animals. They go different places."

"No. It's *same same*." Nick bandied, using Ghulam's characteristic phrase.

"No *same same*. Different."

"How is it different?" said Nick.

"Ghulam has two wives already. And eight daughters. Ghulam has already reaped his share of the grain. It is sinful to be greedy. But Mr. Nick has not taken a wife at all." He wagged his finger, jutting out his lower lip shamefully.

"Maybe I don't want to get distracted. As you yourself said, Ghulam, I've got to concentrate on changing. You know, finding my 'path,'" Nick said, somewhat facetiously, proud to exploit Ghulam's own words against him.

"Ha!" Ghulam wagged his finger. "A young student once asked his mullah for guidance in becoming one with Allah," Ghulam said, his eyes twinkling. "The mullah said to the student, 'I can tell you have never walked down the path of love. Go away and fall in love. Then come back and see me.'"

Nick stared back at Ghulam blankly. He shrugged. "So . . . ?"

"So, Mr. Nick, the path to Allah, to find peace and love in Him, one must marry a woman."

"But Ghulam, it could never work. I am from America. Her life is here, in Kashmir," Nick said.

"No problem. You move here—Ghulam will help you build house. Then you go to America, then come back, and go, then come back. Ghulam does the same when I leave my home to find work. Ghulam is not home for one or two years at a time. But he still loves his wives and daughters. Even more, when Ghulam is away from them. See? No problem."

"Well, I'll consider what you say," Nick conceded, purely in an effort to end the conversation. But Ghulam took it as a victory, as he hopped around on his crutches in glee.

"Oh, yes, Mr. Nick, you think about it! Think, think! But don't take long. 'For every sin but the killing of time there is forgiveness.' It is—"

"It is written." Nick interjected. "I got it."

Ghulam hobbled over to Vilashni. "Mr. Nick is going to think about it!" he told her, before they both broke into conniving laughter.

Of course, Nick was just humoring him. He had no clear idea how Aysha truly felt about him. He knew that she enjoyed his company at times, but he doubted that she harbored deeper feelings toward him, and this was especially true after her outright denial of what had transpired that day in the pine glade behind Rasheed's goat hut. In addition, though she was moderate in her religious views, she was nevertheless a devout Muslim—she never missed a prayer session, and with the exception of her small toast of Gilkamosh water after helping Rasheed's goat give birth, she refrained from drink and smoke. In the back of his mind, Nick felt that she would never accept him, a nonbelieving Christian with little knowledge of her people or her customs. Perhaps, he wondered, *that* was why she was so quick to deny the incident at the stream that day.

Still, Aysha gave Nick something to look forward to, where there had been nothing for so long but grief and fear. The fact that there was at least a rumor of romance, even if it was just a ruse, lifted everyone's mood, making the staff giddy like a bunch of school kids. It was an enchanting spring—a final celebration of life, before everything changed.

CHAPTER 44

Within the span of a few days, the once sleepy village of Gilkamosh had been transformed into a swarming throng of humanity.

Thousands of Hindu pilgrims from all over India proper had congregated on the outskirts of the village, setting up makeshift encampments in nearly every square foot of the Gilkamosh Valley, except for the village center itself. Smoke from countless campfires obscured the mountain air with an asthmatic haze. The tumult of the shouting, laughing, and arguing multitudes could be heard throughout the valley, during all hours of day and night.

Each year, the teeming *yatra*—a miles-long human parade—would wind its way through the Gilkamosh Valley, stopping in a handful of villages to receive blessings at temples along the way, until it reached a great cave high in the mountains, where, as myth would have it, Shiva's phallus penetrated the great womb of Mother Earth, from which Life was born. Gilkamosh marked the start of the human convoy. As in each previous year for as long as anyone could remember, the pilgrims arrived gradually at first in sporadic clusters at the beginning of August, then in more massive numbers a few days before the opening ceremony held at the Gilkamosh Temple to Shiva. At the temple, the pilgrims were blessed by the resident holy men before parading en masse, flanked by long-haired saddhus in loincloths and swarms of painted holy men donning saffron-colored robes, through the village of Gilkamosh on their way to Passtu, the next major village on the pilgrimage circuit. After the parade had left, the village would settle back into its normal sleepy state of tranquility until the following summer.

That year the gathering of *yatris* was particularly prodigious. The pilgrims were mostly poor Hindus from the subcontinent—entire families, from infants to elderly great-grandparents. The women were smartly dressed in gaudy orange, pink, and red saris and lavishly adorned with nose rings, colored *bindis* on their foreheads, and thick stacks of brass bracelets from wrist to elbow. Some carried rattan baskets of aromatic red, orange, and yellow hyacinths, marigolds, azaleas, and hibiscus blossoms as offerings; others held their infants in their arms, swaddled in brightly colored cloth, sleeping, wailing, or suckling at their mothers' bare breasts. The men, most of them gaunt vegetarians, sat cross-legged in small clusters and smoked rolled bidis, waiting for the morning hour when they would rustle their families into the procession to receive the holy blessings at the temple before starting their strenuous week-long hike into the mountains. For ten days they would trek through some of the most daunting and breathtaking terrain, camping as they went. When they had completed the *yatra* circuit, they would begin the long journey home, by truck, bus, or train, to their villages in India proper.

Over the years, the villagers had become accustomed to chaos during the weeks from when the *yatris* started to assemble until they left. The pilgrims were a well-behaved, joyful group, interested only in their worship and some harmless revelry. Many villagers, Hindu and Muslim alike, were proud that their village had holy significance. The village vendors made bundles of money off the pilgrims, selling them provisions, locally grown flowers for offerings, and supplies for the trek. The police and army, quadrupled in size by units called in to reinforce the permanent missions, cordoned off the village center so the residents' daily lives would remain somewhat intact while the *yatra* passed through.

At the same time the swarms of *yatris* were preparing for the opening ceremony at the Temple to Shiva, Kazim was meeting with Abdul in his basement, going over the final preparations.

As the leader of the cell, Kazim's place was, of course, not to die with the attackers. He and Abdul would have to forgo the honor of martyrdom so that they could coordinate the attack, and the next attack thereafter, and so on, learning from their successes and failures, until the entire land was enveloped in so much bloodshed that the Indians would throw their hands up and leave. Such was the theory, anyway, of waging a war of terror. And such was Muzzafar's plan.

The three martyrs—the ones who had volunteered to die—were not present. They were engaged in solitary prayer, cleansing their minds and bodies in preparation for their ascendance to Paradise, which, if everything went as planned, would happen as soon after seven o'clock on the following morning as it took for the security forces to gun them down and for the Archangel Jibreel to guide them on the way.

Kazim and Abdul were supposed to be envious of the three. In reality, they were not, though they would never openly admit it. As for Kazim, he pitied them, even though all three went willingly. The fact that Kazim had known one of them, Gani, since he was a child, made the thought of sending him to die intolerable, and Kazim had to block it from his mind. Gani, a new recruit who had yet to see battle, was from Kazim's own village of Passtu. His father and Kazim's father were friends. They often kept each other company during summers in the mountain pastures, grazing their goats for months at a time. The other two boys were foreigners, but they had been in Kazim's cell for over a year—Tariq was a Pakistani from Rawalpindi, and his friend Aatef was an Afghan refugee from the Peshawar area who had served with distinction under Kazim's command during the first raid of that year's fighting season, after the snowmelt. Kazim would have preferred to spare Aatef from the suicide mission, because he was so valuable as a fighter. But Aatef had insisted.

They were good kids, Kazim told himself, even if Aatef was the only natural soldier among them. He wondered what would become of their lives if tomorrow never came—would they eventually grow out of their desire for martyrdom and jihad, and someday lead normal lives? Or were they destined, regardless, to be victims of the war? Kazim would have liked to think the latter—that they would inevitably be taken in the prime of their youth—but he knew the boys too well. They were not like Muzzafar, to whom killing was innate. There would have been hope for a different fate if they were permitted the tempering of time. Perhaps they would have fallen in love and had children, learned a trade, and forgotten all about jihad and martyrdom.

When Kazim and Abdul finished with their checklist of final preparations, Kazim looked at his friend, perplexed. Abdul had changed in the last few weeks. Kazim could not put his finger on it, but there was something different in the way Abdul carried himself. He had a quicker temper, but at the same he seemed a little less eager to respond to Kazim's orders—there was less jump in his step. Though days before Kazim had dismissed the possibility, he wondered now whether Abdul might be having feelings of doubt.

"That's it, Abdul. It looks like we're ready," Kazim said, staring at the rough sketch of the village laid out between them as they sat on the floor.

"Inshallah," Abdul replied.

"Yes, inshallah . . . how do you feel, my friend?" Kazim probed.

Abdul nodded. "Like you said—everything is set," he answered, missing or perhaps evading the point of the question.

"No, I mean, are *you* prepared? In your own mind?" said Kazim, trying to find some sign in Abdul's eyes. "You know this will change everything."

"Yes. Of course. And you, Kazim?" Abdul rejoined, turning the tables.

Kazim hesitated. "Abdul, we've been like brothers since we were children. I have confided to you before my beliefs about killing noncombatants."

A darkness came over Abdul's face. His voice deepened and reverberated. It was the voice of a stranger. "What are you saying, Kazim? Are you not prepared to go through with it?"

"I am not saying that," Kazim replied, taken aback by Abdul's haughty tone. "Of course I am prepared. I'm just suggesting perhaps there's a different way—a *better* way—that we haven't thought about."

"What, then . . . ? Muzzafar said nothing else has worked. We cannot bring the Indians to their knees by killing a few *jawans*. Like Muzzafar said, there will always be so many to replace every one that we kill."

Kazim paused. For the first time in his life, he felt unsettled about his friend, sensing an almost intimidating aura about him. Where was the Abdul he had trusted with his life? But now was not the time to waffle.

"I've listened to what Muzzafar has to say for years now. What does he really know about our country? What if we did call off the attack?" Kazim said. "We can devise our own strategies—our own method of waging the war—one that uses our good favor with the villagers to our advantage, instead of squandering it forever. One that the people will support. Can't you see, if we can get more people on our side—"

"You mean betray our leader?" Abdul snapped. "Is that what you are saying? I cannot believe you would even think such a thing." Abdul's eyes flashed, causing Kazim to hold back his words. He had underestimated Abdul's loyalty to Muzzafar. And perhaps, it seemed, overestimated his own influence over his friend.

"I was just thinking aloud. It is just that I care so much for the boys.

They remind me of you, Abdul, when you were younger. So full of . . . that will to fight. And you know I could never send you to your death. Even though I know how much you would relish the opportunity to martyr yourself."

Kazim locked eyes with Abdul and searched again for any trace of uncertainty. But now there was nothing.

CHAPTER 45

By dawn, the pilgrims had swarmed the street in front of the Temple of Shiva. They were packed shoulder to shoulder and back to chest, the children stuffed between legs and under arms, so tightly that they formed a veritable human wall blotting out the road, extending from the foot of the temple all the way to the far edge of the squatters' encampments four kilometers from the village center. On the curbsides of the road, lining the periphery of the procession, stood Hindu holy men, bare-shouldered in saffron robes, spaced randomly apart, but no more than ten meters between them.

From his perch on the flat rooftop of Abdul's house, Kazim had a bird's-eye view of the multitudes. Throughout the village, many residents were doing the same; watching the spectacle from the comfortable distance of one's rooftop had become a yearly pastime of sorts for the people of Gilkamosh. But none was watching with the same profound sense of dread. It would have been easier if he had been one of the martyrs, Kazim thought. But it was too late now to do anything more—or differently.

Before the sun rose over the mountains to the east, everything had been dull, sheenless gray. But instantly, as if some transcendent force had turned a switch, the vibrant colors of the pilgrims' clothes struck Kazim's retinas in a wave of dazzling pinks, reds, indigos, purples, and yellows— all the more brilliant juxtaposed against the rich, dark skin and blue-black hair of the masses. Every man, woman, and child held handfuls of bright flowers, and the sweet aroma of flora and incense so saturated the air that Kazim could smell it from where he was, over two hundred yards away, squatting in nauseated anticipation.

As much as he had come to resent Hindu India since he was a boy—for its oppressive arrogance, idolatry, hatred of Islam, and relentless greed—he could not help but feel moved by the magical display before him. They were a filthy, miserable swarm of *infidels*, he observed, but beyond all the wretchedness, and their irrational faith in false idols, the vibrant masses of chanting, elated pilgrims, absorbed in their timeless ritual, somehow touched him. No man alive could help but feel the life force in the Hindu hordes that morning. The sight was spellbinding.

But to Kazim, this sudden, unexpected onslaught of compassion only exacerbated the anxiety that gripped the very roots of his being, constricting his lungs until his breaths were but shallow gasps. He had not wanted what was about to transpire. He had weighed his options, over and over. But in the end, he had made the only decision he felt he could take to his Judgment.

Knowing this, however, relieved nothing. And suddenly, he felt a driving compulsion to flee, to avoid watching it all unfold. But he was a man too modest to flee the consequences of his own folly, and he also knew that there was no *wudu* that could remove the taint of his complicity. He had fated himself, as a boy, when he chose to fall in love with *azadi*. But it had been a temptress that wasted his love. And now, he felt the terrible inevitability of a man lost in the woods who realizes he has spent his final reserve of strength circling back to the same exact spot.

The ceremony of the blessing of the *yatra* commenced when a group of five saffron-robed holy men carrying metal tridents emerged from within the temple. They were bearded and barefoot, their faces decorated with white and ochre paint. Their lips moving inaudibly, they floated trance-like down the stairs of the temple. Stepping onto the promenade of the temple, they approached the edge of the multitude, cordoned off by a line of police from the temple courtyard. When the holy men reached the throng, the faithful began to shower them with flowers. They threw handfuls, by the bushel it seemed, toward the arcade where the priests stood to issue the blessing, and for a moment everything—the crowd, the priests, the temple arcade, even the sun—was blotted out with a deluge of dazzling color.

But Kazim's eyes quickly turned from the ceremony, concentrating on the periphery, where his boys had positioned themselves. There, he could see Aatef and Tariq, on the side of the street opposite the temple. They looked like every other Hindu holy man, though while the others swayed to the rhythmic chanting of the throng, they stood rigidly. Only a perceptive eye would have noticed the slight bulge under their robes. On the other side of the street stood Gani. In contrast to the others, he looked conspicuous, anxious, even from where Kazim was watching.

Kazim scanned the crowd and saw two or three uniformed policemen scattered behind Aatef and Tariq. But the position of the police was way off kilter—there were hundreds of revelers packed in between them and Kazim's men. If the police laid down fire from where they stood, *yatris* would be cut down like wheat. "*Idiots!*" Kazim murmured. They could not even get a basic principle of security right   cordon off the victims from the possible points of attack.

Kazim glared down at his watch, swallowing at the fist-sized lump in his esophagus. There was one minute to go—an interminable minute before the point when all he had done in his life before would be tainted by that which came after.

His eyes shifted over the throng of *yatris* until he found Gani again, struggling to keep steady. He could tell the boy's nerves were failing him. Kazim had anticipated this would happen. In contrast, Aatef and Tariq were solid. It would be easier for them, each having the other by his side, and Kazim felt a chill when he noticed the row of women and children in front of the two boys.

Ten seconds! Kazim saw Tariq and Aatef reach under their robes and pull something out. He squinted to bridge the distance. "*Grenades?*" Kazim heard himself utter with dread. His young killers, bent on carnage, had improvised. Their elbows thrust back as they pulled the pins and held the bombs under their robes. On the other side of the crowd, Gani grappled maladroitly for the AK-47 concealed beneath his robe, hypnotized by the masses swarming away from him.

Five seconds! Aatef and Tariq swung their grenades out from under their robes. At the same time, on the other side of the road choked with *yatris*, Gani stumbled to one knee. Then, with an awkward swinging motion, he swooped his robe behind, his gun bare and hanging low below him. He wobbled to his feet. And when he rose, his fingers fumbled, scrambling to find the grip.

"Allah help me!" Kazim cried out loud, covering his face.

In the end, though he had killed and watched so many men die in his life, Kazim could not bear to look. But he heard. Not many, but one ear-piercing scream, as if the entire mass of India's wretched poor were a single organism that, at once, had cried out in pain.

Gani

Abdul Gani Dar had been awake for forty-eight hours before he found himself standing in front of the horde of chattering *infidels*.

He could not sleep. So instead, he had prayed, breaking only for the rice and chapati that his worried mother, Rukhsana, had prepared for him. Rukhsana had asked him what could be so wrong, that he would not come out from his room and eat around the stove with his father. Gani told her he was sick. So, being the devoted mother she was, she brought him his food in his room.

Gani's father, Mohammad Sabir, had protested. "Make your little mamma's boy come out to eat!" he yelled at his wife, loud enough so Gani could hear him through the mud-brick walls of their small abode. Gani was an only child and he blamed Rukhsana for babying him badly. According to Sabir, Rukhsana had made Gani soft. "*Sissy,*" Sabir would always say in disgust, in front of Gani, with the hope that his constant belittling would motivate his son to become a man.

When his mother brought Gani's food into his room, he wept. "Oh, my little Gani," she said with anxious concern. "Don't let your father hear."

Soon she would be unable to care for him anymore, and this made Gani sad. He was so filled with sorrow he spat up every swallow of food. But now at least he could find some consolation in the fact that he *was* actually sick; he was not lying to his mother anymore, at least not about that. Kazim, Gani's mentor and leader, had told Gani and the other boys to be good to their parents their last days, and Gani did not want to go to Judgment having lied to his mother.

The sting he felt, that degrading look on his father's face whenever he called him a "sissy," had compelled Gani to the spot where he stood on the day of the *yatra*. As far as his eyes could see, dark-skinned people dressed in wild, vivid colors, perfumed with the nauseating scent of hibiscus and incense, chanted in unison, their grimy children wailing and tugging with greasy fingers at their robes and saris. He was captivated by them. And terrified. So many open mouths with stinking breath and inflamed eyes. They were no longer individuals—just one massive *entity*—one giant *infidel* that threatened to swallow him whole, just as it had swallowed each *yatri* in its path as it crawled toward the temple. He feared that even he, a believer, would become part of it, chanting and marching and sweating and throwing flowers at idols like a heathen. He could shoot and shoot and he would not even dent it. One burst from his gun would barely peel the skin. The second burst and it would only be closer, swooping around him, hundreds of black eyes glazed over with rage, until they swallowed him like an amoeba.

His knees shook. He reached down with a hand, as if to steady his legs, and felt that his thigh was soaked. The saffron color of his robe had turned to a deeper red. He had lost control of his bladder. *How stupid I must look,* he thought, with his skinny bare legs wobbling like reeds blowing in the wind, covered by nothing but a wet rag. He had wished to go to Allah in clean clothes—*Muslim* clothes. *That* would have been proper. Now his parents would have to see his body dressed as an *infidel,* and know that he had wet his pants. Tears welled in his eyes. He had wished to be a martyr to prove himself, but even in his final gesture, he would be ridiculed.

Then, all of a sudden, Gani was kneeling in the dirt, vomiting. He did not remember his knees collapsing, nor did he care. He just wanted to lie there and curl up. *Why has my life come to this?* The question flashed through his mind with a profound sense of injustice as he saw a wall of *infidels* glowering at him. He tried to remember the decision that led him to that spot, or any decision at all, for that matter. But it seemed that everything that had happened in his insignificant life, from the first time he suckled his mother's breast to wetting his pants just moments ago, had been out of his control. He was a boy who had never known choices; only reactions to the demands of others. But as Gani knelt, startled by the frenzied hordes closing in on him, he saw the image of his father scorning him. Humiliation, that most underestimated and dangerous of all human emotions, gave him the strength to go on.

He rose to his feet. "*Allah-o-Akbar!*" he heard himself cry in his quivering, adolescent voice. Forgetting all preparations, he reached with his right hand for the edge of his robe, and with a rubbery arm slung the fabric back around his shoulder, exposing the stockless Kalashnikov dangling from its shoulder strap. He reached for the grip. But his fingers, slick with sweat, slipped off it. The gun dropped from his hands, suspended by the strap.

Again, he reached, and finally, his clumsy, shaking hands found the trigger. He braced the gun under his arm as they had taught him at the camp and leveled the muzzle at the phalanx of wide, black eyes and gaping mouths rushing toward him now, churning up dust that hovered in the light like orange haze. Then, a shrill, mindless clamor shocked the entirety of his senses; not only did he hear it, but he felt the sound hit him with the force of a charging yak.

The skin! Shoot the skin! Gani thought at last, before he felt a sharp jolt. He looked down with wide eyes and saw the wet robe clinging to the bones of his sunken chest. And by the time he raised his eyes back up, hundreds of hands were tearing at his flesh.

Aatef

Aatef Jalladin Khan stood with his chin raised. He had deserved to be a sahid. He had earned it.

Two months ago he had killed three *jawan*s in his first fight. They were holed up behind some sandbags, pouring machine-gun rounds out at the hillside where he and his comrades were hidden behind high boulders. He snuck around the back of the post and waited until they reloaded. Then he pulled the pin, counted to six, and ran fearlessly to the front of the post, dropping the grenade. One loud bang and he was showered with body parts. Some blood had trickled into his mouth, reminding him of the undercooked donkey meat he sometimes was forced to eat as a boy.

He had loved the sound of that grenade. A sound of pure power. One more time, he wanted to hear that sound before he died. That was why he had decided to bring it. And when Tariq found out his plan, he insisted on having one, too, not wanting Aatef to have any kind of bragging rights over him. He and Tariq were good friends, so he could not refuse. They made a pact to pull the pins under their robes ten seconds before the ordained time, and then throw them into the crowd together, as equals.

The pride he felt killing those Indian soldiers was one of the most blissful feelings of his short life. But there would be more good times to come. He had been taught that in Paradise there would be wine and virgins and music and dancing, and all the other pleasures that were forbidden in this life. And as a martyr, he would get to Paradise without waiting for Judgment Day like all the rest. That way he would have first pick of the prettiest girls.

The crowd is thick! This will be easy, he thought, staring into the horde. The little children milling about under the waists of the adults reminded him of himself ten years earlier. His father would grab him by the scruff of the neck and drag him into a *tuk tuk* and they would ride through the endless sea of refugee camps to the city. There, his father set him to work the crowds in the bazaar. He would position himself, just like those little *infidels*, needling his way between legs and under arms and tables, and with deft little hands, he would grope for loose rupees, watches, jewelry, and anything else he could snatch up. But the people eventually wised up to his game and the pickings became scant. Then his father made him start doing other things for money—to old men, behind the goat stables, in the alleyways, and in the stalls of the public toilets. Later, the mullahs would tell him it was immoral, what the men had made him do. But he did it only because it paid. And when he ran away from his family to live on the street, he continued to do it, because it was the only way he knew to survive. That, and picking through garbage. But when the Muslim charity finally took him in, he stopped doing those bad things. There is always a way to redeem yourself, the mullahs told him. Allah is merciful and forgiving. Especially to his warriors.

Yes, he could have done a lot of damage in this crowd, he thought, oddly nostalgic. Just as he was going to do a lot of damage now, but of a different sort.

With just seconds left before the designated time, he looked over at Tariq and their eyes locked. Tariq looked serious, detached, almost peaceful. But then, Tariq was a religious boy. He believed in martyrdom and jihad and all that. Aatef did, too, but with Tariq, it was different. Aatef loved to *fight*; Tariq loved only Allah. Aatef smiled at his friend, and though Tariq did not smile back, he still knew his friend was with him. He pulled the pin of his grenade and watched Tariq do the same. When Aatef looked up again, it seemed the crowd was backing away, stumbling over each other. *Strange,* he thought. He moved forward so he could reach them. Ever since he broke his arm in training camp, he could not throw well, and he was never much of a bowler in cricket.

Just then, Aatef heard a shot crack the air off in the distance, and then another burst of fire, closer. He looked to where the sound came from and saw Tariq, his arms flung backward above his head, as if surrendering in the face of a tornado. He paused like that, suspended in air, twisting slightly, before falling back onto the ground.

Something flashed off to Aatef's left. A man, one of the saffron-robed holy men, hunched low, pointing a weapon. Suddenly, Aatef wished he had his own gun in his hands, and not his grenade. He cocked his arm back to throw it at the gunman. But before he could sling it forward, a sharp pain pierced his upper shoulder and his whole side lost all feeling. He felt something heavy drop onto his bare foot, and his body shuddered uncontrollably, as if he were a puppet being tugged in dozens of directions at once.

His head, like a heavy weight, dropped down to his chest, so that just as he fell, the last thing he saw beneath him was his cherished grenade. There was a white-hot flash that bore into his gut. And then there was nothing.

Tariq

His senses were sharper at that moment than they ever had been.

He felt the rocky earth under his sandals, like an extension of his legs. He saw the teeming multitudes of sweating half-naked bodies, and smelled the musky odor of their perspiration. He could taste smoke from the burning incense in the air with the tip of his tongue. And his ears rang with the ceaseless chanting of the infidels, the clanging of their bells, and the stomping of their filthy, unshod feet on the earth.

All these things he saw, he smelled, he tasted, and he heard. But none of it converged with his mind. For that part of him was wholly detached from his senses, consumed by only the One—Allah. And he was in bliss.

Tariq's bliss was *real*—as real as the earth under his feet, the blue heavens above him. And as real as the sweating mass of infidels before him. He felt it in his mind, his body, and his heart, pulsating through him, warming his core.

This is it! The revelation struck him like a bell. He had finally achieved that which he had longed for—the culmination of a lifetime of faith, starting with the madrassa outside Rawalpindi where his father, a civil engineer, had sent him and his five brothers for schooling. Ever since he was eight, when he was first taught about martyrdom and jihad, he had been fascinated by stories of the "holy intoxication" felt by a sahid moments before death. He knew it was to be his calling. And from that point on, his entire life had been leading to this moment.

And now at last he had achieved his one true goal. Facing martyrdom, concentrating only on Allah, he had at last achieved detachment from his senses, so that even his own self was obliterated. He harbored no concepts, thoughts, or sensations other than the blissful energy of Allah's love coursing through his mind and body. And though he could not think, for there was no room for thoughts in his brain, he was fully aware of everything. It seemed as though he had been gifted with a new consciousness from Allah, and from this, he could act.

Without even looking at him, he was aware of his friend Aatef standing in line to his left, and the warm smile Aatef had flashed at him that was his signal. And he was aware as he pulled the pin from his grenade and waited, meditating on Allah and his infinite greatness. He reveled in the privilege of feeling the holy ecstasy surging through him. How he wished he could proclaim to the world what he now knew—that the bliss of martyrdom was Truth! For then millions would flock to follow in his footsteps, and His kingdom would be restored.

Suddenly, the crowd started to stumble and sway. Tariq did not know the cause of the sudden movement, but it did not matter. He simply stepped forward. But then they moved still farther away, and again he moved after them, until he found himself starting to chase the retreating enemies. Calmly, Tariq pulled the grenade from under his robe and cocked his arm. With a wide underhanded arch and a cry of jubilation, he swung his arm toward the infidels.

The next thing he knew he was staring at the sky. *Paradise?* he thought. But when he heard screams of pain, he knew it could not be so. For there is no such thing as pain in Paradise. Disappointed, his eyes darted around until they settled on his own chest. A great pool of bright red blood seeped up through a hole in his shattered sternum, flowing onto his neck and chin. He was cold. All sounds diminished, until he could barely hear his own rattled breath.

Then he knew. He was being martyred, right there on the dirt. He closed his eyes and reached one last time for the bliss. But before he could recall it, his grenade exploded and ripped him apart.

Sergeant Ravindra

Sergeant Kaushal Ravindra of the Border Security Forces Special Operations Team watched, waited, and sweated. The bulky flak vest under the saffron robe made him look and feel like a great fat yam, roasting in the sun.

He had meticulously studied his orders three times that morning. He was *sure* he was standing in the right place—between the fifth and seventh holy men along the eastern periphery of the procession, directly across from the temple courtyard. In fact, he *was* the sixth holy man. But nothing around him seemed suspicious.

The orders specified an "operative probability" that the *yatra* would be attacked, possibly by "terrorists" disguised as holy men. "Operative probability" translated to a 10 percent chance, rather low, which meant that the source of the warning was not a proven "cat," or police informant. But nonetheless, upon the insistence of a local politician, he had been posted there, dressed as a holy man, assigned to keep an eye on the other holy men and shoot them if necessary. But all the holy men around him seemed genuine. *It figures,* he thought, *another false alarm.* "Politicians!" he grumbled with disdain.

Bored, Sergeant Ravindra wished he could have a cigarette. But procedures forbade it. He did not understand why. In the regular army, where he had served for fifteen years, they never cared about stupid regulations like that. Good soldiering was all that mattered. And expert marksman as he was, Sergeant Ravindra always shot better when he had nicotine buzzing through his brain. It sharpened his vision, as though transforming his pupil into human peep sight—dead-center straight, from eye to target, like the beam of a laser. *Bastards!* he thought, spitting a stream of saliva and *paan,* cursing the BSF for their bureaucratic stupidity.

Sergeant Ravindra scanned the crowd with lizard eyes. The first dozen passes he noticed nothing suspicious. But as 0700 approached, he noticed something off about two holy men to his right. Perhaps it was their light skin that made them stand out. Or their youth. Or the fact that they were not chanting like the others. When he saw them reach under their robes, his mental alarm went off. *What are they doing?* he thought, feeling a jolt of adrenaline. Slowly he reached under his own robe and found the safety lever on his carbine, switching it from off to semiautomatic. He watched them standing silently, calmly, hands under their robes, for what seemed like ages, until the youngster closer to him swung his hand out from under his robe. He was clutching something round. In an instant, Sergeant Ravindra knew what it was.

In a blur, he swung the stock to his shoulder, drawing a bead on the closer. Just as his finger tensed on the trigger, a shot rang out from across the road. The crowd teetered. He flinched, losing his target. He cursed. When he searched again, the man had vanished.

His neck craned like a stork, trying to spot his target. Then, in his peripheral vision, he caught a second "holy man" running toward the *yatris*, clutching something. Sergeant Ravindra's eye beamed its imaginary laser exactly one meter in front of the man, who was really a boy. He squeezed the trigger. The bullet ripped into the middle of boy's saffron robe, sending a spurt of blood out his back.

An inhuman scream emanated from the mass of *yatris*, high-pitched and piercing like an ear-shattering chorus of cicadas. The shrill wave of sound startled him. But he was a hunter of men, and his mind quickly returned to spotting his quarry. It took only a moment, and perhaps a little luck, for Sergeant Ravindra to find the first "holy man," also a boy, only yards away, staring right at him through the frantic crowd, his eyes filled with hatred. *He's coming right to me*, the sergeant thought incredulously. The boy's arm was cocked, ready to throw. But this did not stir Sergeant Ravindra. In his mind, his target was already dead. He held his breath and squeezed, so smoothly it surprised him when the gun jumped in his hands.

The youth dropped the grenade, but he was still standing. So Sergeant Ravindra put three more rounds into his chest. He twisted, then slumped and fell, belly down on the dirt, before rolling over. A fraction of a second later, a muffled explosion hurled him five meters high, and he landed in parts.

Later, when it was clear it was over and the *yatris* had rushed out of town, Sergeant Ravindra lowered his gun and had his cigarette.

Kazim

The clamor from the street chilled Kazim's blood. But when he finally forced himself to view the carnage, it was not what he had feared.

He saw a swarm of *yatris*, blood smeared on their faces, tearing a body into pieces—Gani, he assumed. On the other side of the mob, Aatef and Tariq were lying in the dirt, a halo of black blood coloring the dust around their remains as a few soldiers encircled the bodies with guns at the ready. Police were running around chaotically, unable to control the mob from pushing its way out of the village. The mayhem risked a stampede more dangerous than the thwarted attack had been. But the police were smart enough not to impede the crowd, and the swarm muscled its way northward toward the mountains without trampling too many of its own.

He counted only the three deaths—his three mujahideen. A few more *yatris* rolled around in shock, probably hit by the shrapnel of exploding grenades, though none of them looked critical. He felt a surge of relief. He had succeeded in assuring his own failure.

But at the same time, he was filled with terrible dread. The precision and flawlessness with which the police had terminated the attack would implicate him. Had the police swept the area, as he had hoped, with uniformed officers instead of undercover specialists, making it appear more like a routine operation, Kazim's betrayal of his own boys might have remained masked. But now, all would be revealed, and it was only a matter of time before Muzzafar would come for him. His struggle for freedom had just become his own struggle for survival.

CHAPTER 46

Abdul stood on a rocky ridge as he watched the procession flood out of the village and snake its way along the road leading into the valley. He was amazed by its fluidity. Like water rushing through a gutter, the mass of infidels flowed faster once constricted by the narrow canyon. As they ran below him, thousands squeezing their way through the winding pass in which only half of them should fit, he was close enough that he could see the fear on their faces.

Kazim had posted him there as a lookout, with orders to radio back if he saw any army units approaching the village. But Abdul knew Kazim really just wanted him out of the way. What did Kazim expect to do if more army arrived? Call off the attack? It was a *martyr* strike, after all. Nonetheless, it suited Abdul just fine to be sitting atop that ridge. From there, he had a bird's-eye view of the frightened *yatris* fleeing into a trap. *His* trap, coordinated by Abdul, under Muzzafar's orders, which he had been instructed to keep secret from Kazim.

What a genius, that Muzzafar! Abdul gushed, *to plan a secondary ambush in case the first one failed.* He felt great honor to have been chosen to coordinate it, on his own. Muzzafar was a real mujahideen leader, Abdul mused. Not like Kazim, who seemed to have become too soft-bellied.

Indeed, Abdul had been confused by Kazim's lack of resolve of late. He had always been the bravest of fighters—the beacon to which all the boys in the madrassa had aspired, including himself. But somewhere along the way, Kazim had lost the conviction to do what was necessary. He had even become preoccupied with blasphemous thoughts of treason against Muzzafar.

Muzzafar had told Abdul, before Kazim had arrived at the safe house that day, that Kazim lacked nerve from the outset, that he had simply fooled everyone for years. Maybe Muzzafar was right. Certainly, Kazim's attempt to claim credit for the attack by that man Fidali years earlier supported his assertion. Indeed, the unfairness of Kazim's false claim of credit alone justified Abdul's telling Muzzafar about it.

Perhaps that whore, Aysha, had put a spell on him, leaving Kazim weak and unprincipled. After all, Abdul, too, felt her lure, often wondering whether he would have the will to fight jihad at all if he, instead of Kazim, had been chosen by her when they were boys. Abdul could not even mention her, let alone her despicable violations of *purdah*, without Kazim defending her in anger.

Nonetheless, when Muzzafar said the Gilkamosh mujahideen might need a new leader, Abdul could not believe it. Now, after thinking about it for weeks, Abdul saw the great wisdom in Muzzafar's statement. Determined to meet Muzzafar's test, Abdul had meticulously made sure everything was done as he had asked. If Abdul was fated to lead in lieu of Kazim, it was because Allah had chosen. So be it.

Abdul responded to the shots and explosions from the village echoing over the hill with a mixture of relief and disappointment. He was relieved that his friend had not backed down from ordering the attack. At the same time, had Kazim *not* done as ordered, Abdul stood a better chance of being given command of the cell than Kazim.

Still, by the few shots fired, Abdul surmised the attack was not a success. Whether Kazim was to blame or not, Abdul could not know until later, when Muzzafar made his assessment. Until then, there was still hope. But that did not matter now. Abdul needed to take care of his own job and everything else would fall into place. Even so, the prospect of outshining Kazim made him delirious. He could almost taste the power of his own blossoming greatness.

In the valley below, the swarm of stampeding *yatri*s reached the crest of a steep hill and then proceeded down toward the narrowest neck of the road, surrounded by steep mountainsides, where they would surely bottleneck. They were running for their lives, away from the shooting in town. As he had hoped, there was not a single policeman or soldier to guard them, for they were all in the village where the shooting had been. Just as planned, where the canyon narrowed, the column of men, women, and children bunched together even more tightly, piling up like logs.

Suddenly, a flash of light ripped through the midst of the crowd, followed by a jarring explosion. Cries of pain, amplified by the canyon walls, were punctuated only by more explosions, as fire and smoke erupted among the helpless masses. Body parts wheeled through the air. Women and babies screamed. Explosion after explosion. Ten, twelve, fifteen grenades—so many, Abdul lost count.

Then four men—*Abdul's* men—wearing black hoods over their heads emerged from the forest on either side of the road, Kalashnikovs in hand. They fired, unleashing torrents of bullets, round after round, clip after clip, into the helpless pilgrims. Abdul could hear the sound of the bullets smacking into flesh as the *yatris* scrambled and crawled on top of each other, seeking cover under the dead and dying. Some struggled up the slope toward the gunmen in an attempt to reach the trees, but they were quickly mowed down, their bodies rolling back into the bloodbath.

When the gunmen finally ran out of ammunition, they climbed over the crest and slipped away into the trees, leaving the slaughtered behind them, drowning in a river of blood. It flowed downhill, just like the spring rains.

CHAPTER 47

The morning the *yatra* commenced in Gilkamosh, Khaliq and Nabir had picked Nick up at the clinic shortly before dawn in Advani's jeep, which they had borrowed with his permission. They drove south, winding through a series of valleys and crests, arriving at the trailhead just as the sun was rising. The road was devoid of *yatris*; all the pilgrims by now had congregated in the village for the blessing that would mark the beginning of the pilgrimage circuit.

After so many years of witnessing the *yatra*, it was no longer interesting to Khaliq and Nabir—only chaotic—and for this reason they chose to spend the morning fishing in lieu of staying in town. Nick, for his part, would have liked to witness the spectacle but decided to accept the offer to go fishing with Aysha's brothers instead, thinking it better to avoid the police and soldiers called into the village for security.

Khaliq pulled the jeep off the side of the road near the trailhead that led to the stream, and the brothers grabbed the fishing poles from the back of the jeep, along with two aluminum cans full of hoppers they had gathered for bait from their fields.

"Today shall be very hot," said Khaliq, as they began the slog up the *nallah* toward the stream head. "Good thing we start early."

Nick, still groggy from waking before sunrise, stumbled along in a sleepy stupor, following the more nimble brothers up the boulder-strewn canyon. As they gained altitude, however, the hike invigorated Nick. The crisp air was thick with the sweet smell of pine. Warblers and finches twittered in the thick conifer boughs.

"Big bear very close!" said Nabir, the shyer of the two boys, pointing to the bole of a pine tree recently stripped of its bark. "Be very careful." They saw no bear—only its droppings—though they did spot a small, big-eared lynx scampering across the trail ahead of them.

Soon the gradient leveled out and they could hear the sound of running water. The air became cooler and heavy with moisture, the pines thicker, and when the trail wound its way over a last crest, they came upon the water. It was a gem of a stream, with clear, spring-fed waters tinted the color of turquoise, pocketed with deep pools and swift runs. "Many big trout fishes," said Khaliq, pointing toward the deepest of the runs, its surface smooth and shiny like polished glass. "We try below."

"I'd better watch first," replied Nick. He had fished as a boy, but had long forgotten the proper technique and was unsure what to do with the primitive-looking equipment the brothers had brought.

"No problem. I show you," said Khaliq. Nick followed Khaliq and Nabir down the steep and rather treacherous embankment. They descended the slope with alacrity despite the loose footing, filled with excited anticipation.

When they reached the water's edge, the brothers spoke briefly in dialect, and Nabir departed, disappearing upstream. Nick followed Khaliq downstream, until they reached the tail-out of the deep pool that Khaliq had spotted from the riverbank. The run was shallow near the bank, but formed a deep funnel toward the far bank, where the water flowed fast over a series of sunken boulders that shone reddish under the morning light. Khaliq nodded decidedly, and laying his own pole on the bank, stepped into the water, shoes and all, waving for Nick to follow.

Nick flinched at the shock of the freezing water. After a few seconds, the pain numbed, and he followed Khaliq in up to their thighs. Careful not to stumble over the submerged boulders, they waded to the edge of the run, where the slow backwater made a seam with the rapids that carved a deep groove into the riverbed.

Khaliq took the fishing rod Nick was carrying, an ancient one-piece bamboo pole seated with a rusty metal spool wound unevenly with string. He rigged a crude bait hook onto the unweighted, monofilament leader, then tucked the rod under his arm to free his hands. Khaliq pulled a bait can from a wicker creel strapped over his shoulder and cautiously uncapped the plastic cover. He reached into the can with his fingers and plucked out the largest of the hoppers—three inches long, bright green, and squirmy. Khaliq worked the hook shank through the insect's abdomen with a slight popping sound. Then, he tossed the frantic insect out into the water.

He took the rod by its grip and stripped line from the reel, letting it play out in the current. Flipping the rod upstream, he cast the hopper out into the swifter water. The current swept the insect downstream, its legs thrashing frantically, trying to fly away, but bogged down by the barb and the adhesion of surface film.

"See boulder? Good place for trout fishes," said Khaliq. He flipped the rod tip again, causing the hopper to skate across the surface until it was in line to drift toward a partially submerged boulder at the base of the run. "Okay. Now you take." He handed the rod off to Nick.

The two of them followed the hopper closely with squinted eyes as it drifted downstream, becoming smaller as it receded, until it reached the front of the boulder, where the water bulged and split into forks around it. When it hit the bulge, the hopper teetered, spinning at the swell of conflicting currents. Then it disappeared.

"Pull!' Khaliq yelled.

Nick raised the rod tip. It bowed deeply, and then stopped. For a moment, Nick thought he had snagged the rock. But then the rod began to throb violently, doubling the stiff bamboo to the base of the grip.

The fish shook its head furiously, then plugged deep along the bottom, dragging the line over the rocks in an effort to break free. It held in the fast water for several long moments before turning downstream, stripping line off the clamoring reel. In a tumbling leap, the fish rocketed high out of the water and landed in an explosion of spray, before peeling off more line, until there was nothing left on the spool but a crude knot holding the fish at bay. "Follow it down!" Khaliq yelled. Nick stepped downstream toward the running fish, in order to keep it from snapping the line. When the trout torpedoed out of the water again, Nick tripped.

"Mr. Nick!" Khaliq yelled, as Nick was swept underneath.

Nick flailed with his arms and swung his legs forward, trying to dig his heels into the riverbed as the rushing water drove him downstream, his shoulder and knees slamming into submerged rocks. Finally, the river cast him upon a large boulder, slowing his momentum long enough for Khaliq, who had been wading after him, to grab hold. Khaliq pulled at the scruff of Nick's *kamiz*, holding him fast in the current, until Nick regained his footing. To Khaliq's surprise Nick was still holding on to the rod. When Nick lifted it back up, the fish was still hooked. Nick turned to Khaliq, who stared back in disbelief. They burst into laughter.

Twenty minutes later, the five-pound brown trout was flopping on the bank, too big to fit in Khaliq's creel. Nick and the brothers toasted his first trophy Gilkamosh trout with stiff nips of "Gilkamosh water." When pressed, the boys admitted that their father, Naseem, had concocted it, clandestinely, of course, given the Muslim prohibition against alcohol. Naseem was a connoisseur of sorts, and had passed on the art, which had its origins in their ancestors' pre-Islamic past, to his sons.

Nick's trout was the only fish caught that day, but it was plenty of fish—enough for a feast. He offered it to the brothers, but they insisted he keep it. "No no, you swam for it!" This suited Nick fine. Vilashni would make a fine meal of it for the staff, and he relished the chance to provide food for once, instead of only consuming it. Full of cheer from the Gilkamosh water, they dropped Nick off at the turnoff to the clinic, planning to pick him up again soon for another try. They sped away up the mountain toward Gilkamosh, leaving Nick to lug his quarry home.

As soon as Nick strolled into the clinic proudly brandishing his trout, they heard the first truck. Even the labored moans and hollow coughing of its motor seemed to portend something terrible. Aysha, Nick, and Omar stepped outside to investigate, following it with their eyes as it raced down the mountainside, throwing up a cloud of dust. It appeared to be a military cargo truck. They might have thought it was an expected delivery of supplies, were it not for the breakneck speed at which it was driving.

In a cloud of dust, the truck skidded to a stop at the point where the dirt roadway ended in a turnabout in front of the clinic. The driver, a middle-aged Hindu man dressed in a pilgrim's robe, stumbled out. Since they were not expecting any trucks that day, they waited for him to explain the meaning of his visit. Speechless, all he could do was point, his eyes wide with terror, thrusting his finger frantically toward the back of the truck. Nick, Aysha, and Omar went around to the tailgate, where they were joined by Vilashni and Ghulam.

What they saw was unimaginable. People, some dead, others alive, but most somewhere in between, were packed into the truck like butchered animals, piled one on top of the other, in grotesque heaps. Mangled body parts and crying infants were strewn on the floor in thick pools of blood. The maimed were in shock, staring into space, their bloody bodies coated with a film of black dust from the roadway; others groaned or cried in agony, while still others just sobbed. Most were too far gone to swat at the swarms of flies eager to lay eggs in their gaping wounds.

The sheer magnitude of the carnage was medieval. The smell of blood and entrails, and the chorus of the dying, dropped Nick to his knees. Vilashni wept. Ghulam, who had hobbled out of the ward along with the others, held her under the shoulders for support. "*Allah haq,*" Ghulam muttered over and over again under his breath, while Aroon withdrew into himself, staring at the ground. For a long moment, they stood frozen in time, stunned by the grotesque display. Their dumbstruck stupor would never have lapsed had Aysha not managed to snap herself into action.

"Omar! Aroon!" she shouted, her voice coming in exasperated bursts. "Clear all the beds now! Vilashni, pull out all the blood supplies onto the floor . . . and I will need all the morphine we have!"

"Nick! Help me get them out of the truck. We will do triage as we go. The dead and dying stay outside. There will be no room for them in the ward."

"But there are more coming," said the driver, his voice fraught with despair.

Aysha turned to the driver, her faced screwed into a look of incredulous horror. "What have they done?"

The driver thrust his arms out in hopeless confusion. "I . . . I do not know, madam. They shoot many people . . . so many people."

Aysha teetered, rubbing her temples, as if struggling to put it all into some kind of perspective.

"Aysha?" Nick stepped over to her, thinking she might topple.

Suddenly, she snapped back. "Put the dead over there!" she said in a commanding tone, pointing to the left of the ward. "Terminally wounded on the other side. Give each a quarter shot of morphine to ease their way. It's all we can spare."

"What can I do, Madam Doctor?" asked Ghulam.

"With that leg? Inside, to assist surgery."

They began to haul the wounded off the truck, placing each one on the ground for Aysha to examine. "Inside" meant the patient was destined for immediate surgery, "Right wall" meant hopeless, and "left wall," dead. The first victim evacuated from the truck was a toddler—a "left wall"—about three years old, with no palpable wound. When Aysha pulled up his shirt, she saw that his tiny rib cage had been crushed—the first of many trampling victims they would see.

The first dead child set the tone, and things did not improve. Victims were torn, pierced, crushed, and disemboweled with every kind of shrapnel and bullet wound imaginable. Legs and arms were blown clear off, head wounds spilled brains onto the floor, and flesh was ground to hamburger. Others had severed arteries that had already bled out completely. They slipped and slid on the gore, their clothes soaked in blood within minutes, racing against time to clear the victims still warm with life. No matter how they rushed, patients were dying in droves just waiting to be taken off the truck. Ignoring Aysha's instruction to wait inside, Ghulam disregarded his crutches and climbed onto the truck to help heave and lift, despite the intense pain bolting through his legs with the exertion of hauling the wounded.

The amount of surgery was far too much for the lone doctor. Omar, Aroon, Ghulam, Vilashni, and Nick all found themselves, out of necessity, doing the work of a surgeon, though none of them had the required training, and still there were not enough hands. There was no time to sort out qualms about their lack of training. With no assistance from Aysha, Omar and Nick clamped a woman's femoral artery just in time to save her life—cutting into the muscle to access the hemorrhaged vessel and then clamping and tying it with a ligature, while Vilashni came by with antiseptic and the IV to feed her fresh blood. Aysha checked their work quickly, making sure the bleeding had been stopped and the vital signs were sufficient, and that was all she could do—the cauterizing, suturing, and dressing would have to be left for later.

One man had rolled his spilling intestines into a ball, cradling them like a baby to keep them in one place. Ghulam and Nick stuffed them back in his stomach with ungloved hands after they shot him with morphine. But his insides were too scrambled, and he died minutes later. Another woman was shot through the back. She did not appear to be bleeding to death, so they gave her a shot and moved on, leaving her surgery for later, when Aysha could cut her open and dig out the lead.

The ward was filled with the gut-wrenching shrieks and moans of the maimed. The cries of the youngest children were particularly hysterical, for they did not understand what had happened. One little girl with a mangled leg was wailing uncontrollably until Nick injected her with morphine. The foot and shin were too shredded by shrapnel to salvage, and she was losing too much blood too quickly to waste any time trying to patch up, one by one, her many hemorrhaging wounds.

"Cut it!" Aysha yelled at Nick, while she was hastily patching a man's skull. "Here!" She grabbed a bone saw and thrust it in front of Nick.

Nick took the saw with shaking hands. He looked up at Aysha in disbelief.

"Either you or Vilashni, but decide now!"

Vilashni shook her head. "You do it, Mr. Nick. I cannot!" she said in a panic, her eyes welling with tears as she stared at the child. Vilashni shot the girl with another dose of morphine and then quickly gathered hemostats and ligature thread. She wrapped one of the clinic's old-fashioned trauma tourniquets, still bloody from the last patient, around the girl's shin just below the knee. She pulled the belt until the pressure was sufficient, causing the girl to wince. Finally, she pinned the girl's small shoulders to the table and looked at Nick. "Okay . . ." Vilashni said weakly, before turning her head away.

Nick stared at the girl, horrified. When he placed the saw above her ankle, the child let out a blood-curdling scream, her body arching, throwing her whole weight into the force of her wailing lungs. When she finally ran out of air, she lay still, staring at Nick with terror-stricken eyes the color of dark chocolate. Nick could not cut.

"You've got to do it now! The leg's already gone!" Aysha hollered from across the room when she saw Nick struggling with the task. Gripping the slippery, blood-soaked limb, Nick closed his eyes, held his breath, and sawed. The girl screamed and writhed in agony, and her young blood spilled onto the floor. But the blade merely sliced through skin and flesh, barely cutting into the bone.

"Can't we give her more morphine?" Nick implored, struggling to hold her kicking leg while he worked the saw.

"No, damnit. She is too small—you'll kill her. Just cut harder, Nick! You're torturing her!"

Nick cursed under his breath, shut his eyes for a moment, clenched his jaw, and bore down harder. Furiously, he cut, pushing downward with all his strength. Blood sprayed Nick's tear-streaked face, as the little girl's screams reached an inhuman frequency. When the girl's leg finally dropped to the floor with a thud, Nick fell with it.

Nick woke up outside minutes later to Ghulam splashing water on his face. He took a drink, washed the blood from his arms, and went right back in. There was no alternative. For another truck had come, and then another, until the victims overflowed the ward, their broken and bleeding bodies strewn haphazardly about the clinic grounds. The rows of dead and dying had grown so that the charnel wall to the left of the ward was lined with piled corpses, swarming with green flies, and some already starting to bloat.

Inside, patients had to be moved to the office and Nick's bedroom—anywhere there was space—where they were placed on the floors for lack of beds. The electric fans buzzing on the ceiling did nothing to ameliorate the stagnant, humid air hanging over the rows of groaning patients. Thin shafts of light played on pallid faces contorted with pain, some of them convulsing so violently that they had to be bound to their beds, each patient's individual shriek, whimper, or moan merging into a single, incessant death cry.

In the early afternoon they ran out of bandages, so they cut up bed sheets to use in their stead. Moreover, the morphine was nearly gone, and the new arrivals, many worse off than the original patients, had to bear their agony on Percocet and codeine. Many passed out from the pain. Most crucially, the blood supply was fast depleting, so they had to skimp on patients who appeared to have suffered less bleeding. It was grim to deny a patient ample blood, but there was no other way.

By late morning, volunteers from the village, Muslim and Hindu alike, had made their way out to the clinic to help, including Aysha's brothers. They brought blankets for bedding, fresh water, and food. They helped move the dead and nursed the dying, setting up more tents for the hundreds of hysterical, grieving relatives. A hotel in town brought down stacks of beds. And they radioed all the nearest hospitals, none of them closer than a day's drive, begging for assistance and supplies.

By morning the following day, the patients had all either been stabilized or died waiting for treatment. Only then did some ambulances and helicopters arrive from Srinagar, Kargil, and Leh, and the various army hospitals near them. They brought much-needed blood, morphine, and hydration solution, and took with them as many of the most critical patients as they could carry, returning in long cycles until the remaining cases with life-threatening injuries had been moved to the larger, better-equipped facilities many kilometers away.

Forty-eight hours after the eighth and last truck had arrived, Aysha finally rested. Nick was sitting under a pine tree, exhausted, smoking, when she sat down next to him. She looked as though she was summoning all of the strength she had left just to keep charge of her shattered nerves.

"I don't smoke," was all she said. From this, Nick knew to offer her one. They sat together in uneasy silence, drawing on their cigarettes, staring off into the mountains, now purple in the fading light. As Nick wondered how such beauty could endure in the face of such suffering, Aysha inhaled deeply, as though the cigarette fumes somehow could fill the void the pain had bored into her. But when she exhaled into the still air, thick with the smell of death, she wept. Nick hesitated a moment. Then he took her in his arms and held her until she was through.

PART IV

CHAPTER 48

Gilkamosh had transformed overnight from a peaceful utopia into a police state. The villagers existed in a state of shock, closing shops and holing up in their houses while the Indian security forces swept through the village, searching homes and cars. Truckloads of machine-gun-toting troops arrived from the south, setting up roadblocks and bunkers and imposing a curfew. Anyone who walked the streets after nightfall was jailed as a suspected militant, regardless of age or sex. Ordinary citizens were hauled into police stations for questioning for no reason, pressured to point fingers and act as informants. The witch hunt for suspected militants had begun, with no end in sight.

The full scale of the massacre did not become clear until days later. Aysha's clinic had received more than 218 men, women, and children. Seventy-one of those brought to the clinic had either died on arrival or expired on the operating table. Nearly five dozen more were left for dead at the scene of the massacre. Altogether, the total number of people confirmed killed in the terror attack was 129, and the number of the wounded, though it would never be known for sure, was estimated to be no less than 240. The relative civility of the insurgency in Gilkamosh had been shattered in an apocalyptic way.

There was a great deal of work yet to be done in the weeks following the attack. The ward was still filled far beyond capacity, and many of the severely wounded would require weeks of recovery before they could be moved. A relief agency had delivered truckloads of crutches and prosthetic limbs, along with wheelchairs for the paraplegics. They were dumped in big, unsorted piles outside the ward, and the staff started slowly to sift through the heaps and fit the patients. The limbs varied significantly in size and quality, and once the patients discovered the cache, several of them nearly came to blows over the choice pieces. The emotional turmoil of mourning relatives, depressed paraplegics, and angry cripples beleaguered everyone, patients and staff, but especially Aysha.

Aysha had fallen into a deep depression. Nick had thought his comforting of her in the aftermath of the massacre held the promise of an emotional connection. But she retreated into herself. Whenever he tried to talk to her about what had happened, she would hold up her hand, stopping Nick short, as if she were a dam that could be shattered by words, and once broken, everything would spill out along with her grief.

Her extreme reaction to the massacre, though certainly understandable, was also surprising on another level. The sheer amount of carnage that day was more overwhelming than anything that any one of them had witnessed before. But Aysha had always been the beacon of strength. No one had anticipated she would be demoralized so profoundly, to the extent that it appeared she had lost all passion for her work and, indeed, her life. A pervasive worry for her well-being put the whole staff on edge. Despite the telltale signs of fatigue, she refused to take a break, even for a few hours, instead going through the motions of her surgeries and treatments like an automaton.

As the days passed and her spirits did not improve, Nick felt the need to do *something* to bring her back. At the first opportunity, he resolved to go to town and speak with Aysha's father with the hope that once he imparted to him the urgency of Aysha's condition, Naseem would rally her whole family to join in the staff's collective effort to bolster her morale.

A few days later, when Omar received a call that a shipment of medicine had arrived at Advani's house, Nick volunteered to make the pickup. He asked Ghulam to come along as a translator. Ghulam was well on the road to recovery now, and though he walked with a limp, he had regained his normal, useful self.

As Nick and Ghulam descended the mountain ridge and approached the outskirts of the village, they came to a newly built BSF roadblock, or *naka,* about a mile out of town. A wooden gate barred the road, fortified by a bunker made of sandbags covered with a corrugated iron roof. A porthole in the bunker held a machine gun strategically facing the road, and the whole fortification was draped with camouflage netting to keep out grenades. A half dozen *jawans* stood around the gate, peering at them with their rifles trained at the approaching truck.

As Nick steered into the path of the guns, he began to think he had doomed himself by volunteering for the trip. Luckily, however, a local policeman from Gilkamosh accompanying the *jawans* recognized him as a worker from the clinic and waved them through without hassle. By now Nick had visited the village on errands many times, and most villagers, apparently including the local police, presumed he was a foreign aid worker. Nick assumed Advani was the source of this bit of misinformation, and he welcomed the cover it provided him.

When they reached the main row of shops in the town center, it was devoid of the haggling peddlers and gossiping neighbors typically clogging its dusty walkways. Only occasional men could be seen briskly running their errands. Patrols of helmeted, mustachioed Indian soldiers walked abreast, their elongated FN assault rifles strapped across their chests, eyeing the few passing Muslims with suspicion.

The security forces had constructed a large bunker with two gun ports in front of the Hindu temple, now cordoned off with a barbed-wire fence. At various intersections in town, jeeps armed with mounted machine guns were strategically positioned. Nervous soldiers sat behind the guns, scanning the street for the first sign of trouble. As Nick took in all these changes, sadness overcame him. Gilkamosh had become part of him over the past year and some months. Now, the idyllic microcosm he had grown to love seemed lost forever.

Before heading to Advani's complex to pick up the supplies, Nick decided to stop first at Naseem's. Nick's concern for Aysha was gnawing at his nerves, and he was far too distracted to delay the visit any longer.

They parked in front of the Fahad home. As soon as Naseem opened the door, appearing pale and sullen, Nick and Ghulam sensed he was deeply troubled.

Naseem invited Ghulam and Nick inside, where two of Aysha's older sisters sat solemnly around the hearth, glowing with embers. To Naseem's right was Fatima, her raven hair appearing somewhat more streaked with gray than the last time Nick had seen her. Her eyes were bloodshot, as if from sleeplessness.

"What's the matter?" Nick asked.

Naseem shook his head, staring mutely into the smoldering fire.

"Naseem?" Nick pressed.

Naseem inhaled deeply, and then spoke. "Indians take my sons."

"They did what?"

"Nabir, Khaliq . . . Indians take them."

"Why?"

Naseem's minimal English skills were overstretched. He turned to Ghulam, speaking in a Kashmiri dialect Ghulam barely understood.

"He say his sons were walking home from mosque," Ghulam said. "Indian soldiers pull them into jeep, drive away. He does not know where they take them."

"What did the local police say? Don't they know anything?"

"The army take them—not police. The army do not tell police anything—they do not trust them. The army say to Naseem his boys are mujahideen. But Naseem tell them they are not," Ghulam said.

"They are good boys. They are no problem," Naseem interjected, his voice burdened with despair.

"What about Advani? Can't he do anything to get them released?" Ghulam translated Nick's question for Naseem, who tossed his hands and responded.

"Advani went to army base and pleaded. They do not listen," said Ghulam.

"Did Advani at least find out where they are?"

"He tried. The army tell Naseem the boys are being questioned somewhere. But they would not say where."

"What grounds do they have to accuse them?" Nick inquired. "I was with them the morning of the attack. Can't I vouch for them?"

Ghulam's face turned grim. He shook his head in silence. "It does not matter. We are Muslim. We are all suspects. I have seen this happen before," Ghulam said, placing an arm on Naseem's shoulder.

Nick sighed. "There's got to be something we can do. Does he know a lawyer?"

"Lawyer?" Ghulam said. "There are no lawyers in Gilkamosh."

Naseem's glazed eyes remained fixed on the smoldering hearth, his head clutched in his hands in a display of utter hopelessness.

"I'm sorry. Is there anything I can do?" Nick asked.

Naseem reached over and clasped Nick's hand. "*Shukria*," Naseem said, nodding in a show of gratitude. "Inshallah"—it's in God's hands—he added, before speaking in dialect again to Ghulam.

"He asks why we have come, Mr. Nick. We should tell him, I think."

Nick hesitated. He was reluctant to heap another problem onto Naseem and his family. But his concern for Aysha won out.

"We've come about Aysha. She's been in a very bad way since the attack. Everyone at the clinic is worried. We thought maybe she could use a visit from you and your family. She won't leave the clinic to come here herself."

While Ghulam translated Nick's words, Naseem silently stirred the fire with a wooden stick, his mind seemingly on his sons. Nick began to wonder whether Naseem had been listening at all. When he was through, Ghulam touched Nick's elbow, and whispered, "We should go, Mr. Nick."

"I hope your sons will be returned to you soon, Naseem," Nick added as he turned to leave.

It was not until Ghulam and Nick had reached the door that Naseem replied. "Tell Aysha we come soon."

"Thank you, Naseem. Salaam alaikum."

Nick and Ghulam, demoralized by Naseem's bad news, walked through the village to Advani's house. On Nick's prior visits, the gate into the compound had always been open, leaving the house in plain view from the street. In a sign of changed times, now it was locked.

Nick knocked loudly on the corrugated metal doorway. An elderly Hindu man with a bushy white mustache wielding a World War I–era Lee-Enfield rifle swung open the gate. "Who are you, sir?" he said to Nick in thickly accented English.

"We're from the clinic. We came to pick up some supplies—medicines and things—that were delivered to Mr. Sharma's house."

"Wait, please." He locked the gate behind him and they heard the sound of his footsteps receding toward the house. In a minute, he came back, unlocking the gate. He held it open for them, standing rigidly, with a military air, as they entered.

"Mr. Sharma would like for you to give Dr. Fahad a message. He wishes for her please to come see him. As soon as possible."

"I'll tell her," Nick replied, wondering whether Advani had some urgent news about her brothers.

"Come, please. The supplies are this way." The old man led them to the shed adjacent to Advani's home. They loaded the boxes into the truck, and as they pulled away, Nick noticed Advani peering at him through a window. When Nick caught his stare, he quickly slipped behind the curtain.

*   *   *

When they returned to the clinic, Nick found Aysha in the ward. She was examining a twelve-year-old girl who had suffered several gunshot wounds in the massacre. Aysha was stroking the girl's hair. Unable to speak, she was staring at Aysha with a questioning frown. She was wan, and her eyes appeared empty, distant.

When Aysha finally sensed Nick's presence, her gentle expression instantly gave way to the burned-out depression that had been plaguing her since the massacre.

"How do you do it?" Nick said, after he had deflected her attention.

"Do what?"

"Work like this. I mean, when was the last time you slept, Aysha? Or ate, for that matter?"

She turned her back on him, ignoring the question. "This little girl," she said, "she's taken a turn for the worse. I don't think she's got much time left."

Aysha carefully unwrapped the dressing on the girl's belly, revealing deep, oozing wounds. "Her parents must be dead—no one has claimed her," she said as she blotted the wound with a cotton swab. "She's not said a word since she was brought here. I don't even know her name. I'm calling her Supriya—'well-loved.'"

"Aysha," said Nick. "If you don't take care or yourself, you're going to become a patient yourself."

She replied without looking at him. "I'd rather run *myself* into the ground than have someone else do it for me."

Nick furrowed his brow. "That's fatalistic."

"I am Muslim," she replied.

Nick sighed. There was an awkward silence as he struggled with the necessity of plunging the knife of her grief even deeper with the news of her brothers.

"We went to see your father today."

She turned to him curiously. "What on earth for?"

"I was . . . concerned about you. We all are."

"So, now you worry him, too? That makes a lot of sense," she said.

"He's your *father*, Aysha."

"Mine and ten others'. He's got enough on his mind. I don't want my family involved in any of this mess."

Nick hunched his shoulders, staring at the floor. "They already *are*, Aysha. I'm sorry to have to tell you."

She stared at Nick blankly. "What do you mean?"

"Your brothers. They've been rounded up by the security forces."

Aysha shook her head vigorously, as if her repudiation of Nick's words could render them untrue. "No, that's not possible."

"Your father said soldiers came to the house yesterday. They took Khaliq and Nabir. They told Naseem they were being held at a military jail, on suspicion of collaborating with the mujahideen. No one knows where, exactly."

Aysha teetered, as the news finally struck home. Dropping the child's arm, she staggered backward, falling into the chair behind her. She pressed her palms against her cheeks, her lips parted in disbelief.

"Aysha . . . ?" Nick said, before stopping himself short. He felt a compelling urge to reach out to her, as he had done only days ago. But he knew now that she would not accept him. He was not part of the world crumbling around her; he could share only that suffering of hers into which he was invited. He left her alone.

CHAPTER 49

Two weeks after the "glorious attack," as they came to call the massacre, Abdul met with Muzzafar and his retinue of lieutenants in their new safe house, an abandoned stone-walled *bahik* in the mountains northwest of the village.

Meeting in Abdul's basement was no longer feasible given the heavy presence of security forces in the village. Over the past week, the Indians had rounded up most of the local Muslim men and boys, including Abdul. While some were released, others, like Aysha's brothers, were not so lucky. Each day, distraught parents and wives gathered at the local army bases and police stations, demanding information about their children and husbands. The security forces ignored them. The result was more violence— rock throwing at the *jawan*s, attempts to storm police stations, and the like. The outbursts were subdued by batons, warning shots, and more arrests. But the rising outrage at the Indian authority, wholly new to Gilkamosh, exacerbated the already pervasive tension in the aftermath of the massacre, transforming the once quiet, remote outpost into a powder keg.

Abdul, however, was one of the lucky ones who escaped the eye of the authorities unscathed. Now in his early thirties, he was already considered older than the presumed age of most militants, fifteen to twenty-five years old, except for the *mehmaan* mujahideen, who could be any age but were easily identifiable by their foreign speech. After a few hours of questioning, the Indian counterinsurgency agents freed him. And although it was still conceivable that some other prisoner could point the finger under duress, the chance of such treachery was minimal. Everyone knew the severe consequences of doing such a thing. In neighboring villages, *mukhbirs* had been summarily executed, their throats slit in only the most humane of instances. Such reprisals tended to make people tight-lipped. However, it was also common knowledge that the security forces tortured suspects as well, and it was not unheard of for the same prisoner to be brutalized by the security forces into talking, and then murdered by the rebels for being a *mukhbir*. One had to choose a tormentor and fig-ure out a way to hedge one's bets.

Muzzafar had called the meeting to discuss the "tying up of loose ends." By this, Abdul hoped Muzzafar had made a decision regarding Abdul's possible assumption of command over Kazim, who had not been seen by anyone since the Gilkamosh massacre. However, Abdul, dim-witted as he was, had not deduced the full implications of Kazim's disap-pearance; indeed, he still expected Kazim to show up at the meeting.

Abdul's sluggish mind, though at times frustrating to Muzzafar, suited him just fine. He was sick and tired of being second-guessed by Kazim. What he needed now more than anything was a sheep, someone who would carry out his commands without deliberation, who would have no qualms about executing the bloody plans he had in store for tak-ing the insurgency to the next, necessary level.

The sober purpose of the meeting was easily masked behind the massacre's cause for praise. According to Muzzafar's worldview, one he shared with the great mullahs who orchestrated events in secrecy from hideaways in Afghanistan and Pakistan, the attack was a victory for the side of righteous-ness. His own orders were to move quickly to exploit the momentum from the attack, in order to rejuvenate the fading struggle for Kashmir, one of the crucial fronts in the global struggle to regain Islamic lands.

"We've witnessed a great victory for the jihad," Muzzafar sermonized to Abdul and the others. "We must seize the moment, drive home our advantage, if the Indian Goliath is to be crushed and evicted from our lands."

"Yes, Muzzafar," Abdul replied.

"If we are soft, if we lose our spine, the opportunity Allah has given us will slip through our fingers. The jihad needs leaders who can taste the victory, and will stop at nothing to achieve it," Muzzafar said.

Abdul tried his best to mimic Muzzafar's impassioned tone, but his response came out sounding obsequious and contrived. "Yes, Muzzafar, I can . . . I can taste it."

"The infidels will strike back hard," Muzzafar warned. "They've already jailed many of our brothers and sons."

"It will not keep us down, Muzzafar. Not us," Abdul chimed in excitedly.

"I have chosen *you* to command the cell now, Abdul. You respect the wrath of Allah as much as you do His compassion. I know I can trust you to do the right thing, inshallah."

"Oh, thank you! Thank you, Mullah! I am honored. I will not disappoint you, inshallah!"

"There are very many tasks. Difficult tasks that shall require a will of steel. I believe you are the right one to do it. Otherwise, I would not have chosen you."

"Anything, Muzzafar. Just tell me. Anything you say."

"You will start by ridding the insurgency of its traitors." Muzzafar leaned toward Abdul, staring intently into his eyes. "We have been betrayed, Abdul. All of us have. But especially you."

"*Betrayed?*" Abdul's incredulous expression did little to mask his mounting rage. "Me . . . ?"

"Yes, *you*," Muzzafar replied, repressing the urge to break into a smug smile.

"By whom, Muzzafar? Tell me, so I may eliminate the scourge, inshallah!"

"I cannot. You are too close to him. In jihad, we cannot allow ourselves to be motivated by spite and vengeance—only by His word."

"I understand, Mullah. But please. If I do not know the identity of the *muhkbir* how can I defend against his treachery?"

Muzzafar paused. "Very well. It is Kazim. He is the one who betrayed us."

Abdul struggled to digest Muzzafar's accusations. "But I am confused, Muzzafar. He *did* order the attack, did he not?"

"Brother, sometimes your wits are not equal to your resolve," Muzzafar said with a sigh. "But Allah has given each of us his own strengths and weaknesses. Kazim's men failed only because he murdered them."

Abdul blanched. "*Murdered?* Kazim?"

"Yes, Abdul. He disclosed the plans for the attack to the infidels. That is why his martyrs were shot to death before they had a chance to succeed. Your men were victorious only because we went to great lengths to keep the second prong of the attack—*your* attack, Abdul—secret from him. Why do you think he has fled?"

Abdul pulled on his red beard, trying to comprehend Muzzafar's words.

"I gave him a test, and he failed," Muzzafar added, watching Abdul struggle to understand. "It is as simple as that."

"A test?"

"Yes, Abdul, that is what I said," Muzzafar said, losing his patience. "I suspected he would betray us. He proved me right. You succeeded where he failed. You are pure, and he is a *mukhbir*."

Abdul shut his eyes and pressed his fingers against his temples. Abdul had known that Kazim was being tested and that he had reservations about ordering the attack, but he never imagined Kazim, his friend since childhood, would betray his own men. The thought of it made Abdul flush with anger, as much at his own stupidity in being fooled as from the act of betrayal itself.

Muzzafar noted the anguish written across Abdul's face and seized the opportunity to plunge his knife in to the hilt. He touched Abdul gingerly on the shoulder, then lifted his chin with his fingers, staring endearingly into Abdul's eyes.

"My Abdul. I know it hurts to be betrayed by one whom you trusted with your life. But deception is Shaitan's way. And Kazim, as clever as he was, has learned the artifice of evil. He is vain and ambitious. But he lacks faith and moral fortitude. He exploited your trust, and fed you lies in order to keep you subservient. He did this because he fears you, Abdul. Do you know why?"

"Why, Mullah?"

Muzzafar had never pretended to be a full-fledged mullah, but flattered by the title, he saw no reason to correct Abdul's mistake. "You are pure of heart. And the pure always triumph over the corrupt, no matter how clever they may be, because the heart is stronger than the mind. That is why I picked you to lead."

"Thank you, Mullah. Thank you."

"Good. Today—this day of celebration and victory for you and your warriors—is the start, Abdul."

"Start? What start is that, Mullah?"

"The start of the purification."

"*Purification?*"

"Yes, Abdul. The purification. You are crucial to this task. First, with Allah's help, we will rid Gilkamosh of *mukhbirs*. Then, one village at a time, we will slaughter all the infidels in Kashmir, inshallah. We will not stop, not for any reason, until we have driven them out, once and for all. Or they are all dead. This is the only way to win your freedom, Abdul. The only way India will let go of its greed."

CHAPTER 50

The morning after Nick broke the news of her brothers' abduction, Aysha woke up early to leave for the village, in order to ascertain as many details about their detainment as possible. Perhaps she hoped her status in the community would carry some weight and the security forces would be more forthcoming with her than they were her father. On the other hand, however, she could not help suspecting her brothers might have been targeted specifically *because* of her.

Dangerously complicating matters, Khaliq and Nabir in all likelihood knew which young men from the village were supporters of the insurgency and probably could identify the leaders. Indeed, the Gilkamosh Muslim community was closely knit, and the security forces' practice of questioning virtually all of the Muslim youth of fighting age was not entirely unreasonable, practically speaking, purely in terms of the size of the net to be cast. But the boys would not name any friends voluntarily, out of feelings of respect for their coreligionists, if not fear of retribution. Aysha knew that this stubborn reluctance increased the chance her brothers would be brutalized by their Indian interrogators. And the fact that a prominent Hindu such as Advani had not been able to secure the release of the twins was particularly worrying to the Fahads.

This time Aysha was reluctant to let Nick accompany her to Gilkamosh. The entire staff was needed at the hospital to man the ward, still stretched beyond capacity. It was, however, extremely unwise for an unaccompanied Muslim woman to be passing through military checkpoints. Rape of Muslim women by security forces was often reported in newspapers in the aftermath of attacks on Hindus, when Indian troops ran amok with the desire for vengeance. Aysha was not one to heed such risks. But Vilashni took the keys to the truck and would not turn them over until Aysha agreed to let a man accompany her, preferably Nick, since he was an outsider who was less likely to incur the soldiers' wrath.

*   *   *

Nick drove. They had passed through the shady pine thicket, the dark boughs sliding over the jeep road, barring their view of the clinic behind them. Shafts of sunlight penetrated the trees and lit the cloistered roadway.

Before starting the ascent of the mountain, they saw a man emerge from behind a cluster of pine trees. He looked feral, with a Kalashnikov strapped over his shoulder. Peering at the car, he walked into the middle of the road and stood about forty yards directly in front of their path.

Nick stomped on the brakes, causing the truck to skid to a halt. He slammed into reverse and stepped down on the accelerator, prepared to drive backward all the way back to the clinic.

"Stop," Aysha said, her eyes fixed on the man, who stood unmoving, making no effort either to communicate or to approach them.

Nick turned to Aysha, waiting for some explanation. She hesitated, wrestling with her thoughts. "It's okay," she said finally. "I know him."

"Are you sure?" Nick stared at the stolid figure with alarm.

"Yes." She nodded.

Nick waited a moment while the dust thrown up by the spinning wheels of the pickup settled. Then he did as she asked. He drove slowly forward, toward the stranger from the woods.

When they had approached close enough to see his face, Nick stopped. He recognized the man as the mujahideen commander who had shown him and Ghulam to the clinic over a year ago.

His hair was longer now, matted down by dust, his *shalwar kamiz* darkened by smoke stains and grime, as if he had been living in the mountains for weeks. His eyes fixed on Aysha, the man neither moved nor spoke. Aysha stared back at him intently. Nick's eyes shifted from Aysha to Kazim, then back to her.

Suddenly, Aysha shuddered with anger. She pushed open the door, climbed out of the truck, and charged at the man.

"Aysha!" Nick called. The next thing Nick knew she was upon him, pounding his chest and face. Kazim did nothing to resist. He took her blows without so much as turning a cheek, even when the flat of her balled fists hammered his jaw and the bridge of his nose. Tears streamed down Aysha's cheeks. A visceral cry burst from deep within her. It seemed to Nick that she was battering him with all of her being.

"Why!" she cried, inches from Kazim's face.

Not sure what to do, Nick climbed down from the truck and approached them. Cautiously, he stepped between Aysha and the mujahid, reaching to restrain her. But she continued to thrash blindly, without even realizing it was now Nick she was striking. Confused, Nick backed away.

"Damn you! Must you destroy *everything* that I've ever loved?" She fell to her knees.

Nick reached for her, trying to help her to her feet. But a firm grip on his shoulder stopped him. "Let her be," said Kazim. "I must speak to her. Alone."

Nick looked into Kazim's eyes. Though Nick did not know the man, and felt affronted by his tone, he had shown Aysha no hostility. And it was clear there was a history between them, something that needed to be played out. Nick retreated to the truck, still near enough to protect her if necessary.

Kazim knelt next to Aysha, who sat hunched on her knees in the road, rendered breathless by her flurry of violence. He placed a consoling hand on her shoulder, while Aysha shook her head, shielding her eyes. "How could you? How could you do it?"

Kazim bowed his head. "I tried to stop it, Aysha. I am sorry."

"*Sorry!* What does it matter what you *tried* to do today or yesterday or two weeks ago? You made the decision that led to this years ago. For *what*? Tell me, Kazim—is this your *azadi*?"

Kazim turned his face, as if slapped by Aysha's words. Aysha raised her eyes, frowning not out of disgust, but forlornness. "It's all over now," she said, tears streaming.

Kazim lowered his head, pressing his palms to his temples. "You are right," he said in frustration. "You have always been right. I should have listened to you, years ago, when we were just stupid children. Even then, you always knew better."

"Damnit, don't patronize me! I know nothing of right or wrong. You of all people know that. The only thing I've *ever* known, since you left me, is that this place is *all* that I am. Now you have destroyed it!"

Aysha held her face in her hands, shaking with muffled sobs. Kazim shut his eyes for a moment, struggling to stay composed.

"I came to tell you that you are in danger," he said, his voice deliberate. "I am not in control anymore. Abdul is doing their bidding now. You *know* how he is—he will do anything they ask of him. Aysha, you must close the clinic. Until I can get control of things again."

"No," Aysha replied.

"Aysha . . . they will come after you."

"I will go to the security forces for protection. Advani will see to it."

"He cannot protect you. Not anymore. Listen to me. If anyone knows, *I* do."

"So, let them come. I am sure I am not the only one. It was all a stupid fantasy anyway. That we could control a war, bottle it up like some evil djinn."

Kazim sighed in frustration. "Aysha, please. I do not have a lot of time. I know you do not owe me anything. But if not for yourself and your family, please . . . can you do it for the memory of what we once had?"

"What we once had, you took from me," she snapped.

He paused, then shook his head. "It was your *dream* to be a healer, Aysha."

"*You* were my dream."

He stared off into the woods for several moments, unable to face her. When he finally turned back, his face was grave. "Is that what this is about? To *punish* me? You don't understand me, Aysha. You never did. What I longed for, why I fought, it has always been meaningless to you . . ."

"I understand what you want. It is how you seek to achieve it—*that* I will never accept."

"*Please,* Aysha, I beg of you—just shut it down."

She shook her head. "I am fighting a war, too. My way. Now, leave me. Thanks to you, my brothers have been jailed. So you see, I, too, have no time for this. Not now, not ever."

"Your brothers . . . ?"

Aysha rose to her feet. "I never want to see you again, Kazim. Now, go," she said, before starting back to the truck.

Kazim stood, his face cast in utter dismay as Aysha walked away.

"Aysha, wait!" He ran toward her, crossing in front of her path. "Listen to me," he said, grabbing her arm. "Go to the security forces. Give them my name. In exchange for their release."

"What?"

"Believe me, I know the Indians. It's the only way they will let them go."

"They will hunt you down and kill you."

"I am hunted already."

Aysha stared at him a long moment. She pulled her arm from his grip. "Get out of my way, Kazim."

Kazim stood in the road and watched Aysha climb into the truck. Nick started to pull away. Kazim paused, then began to give chase, jogging alongside the passenger side as he pleaded with her.

"Aysha . . . do as I say . . ."

Aysha did not look at him. As the truck sped up and distanced from him, he called out again, "Trust me this *one* time, Aysha! It's the only option you have!"

CHAPTER 51

Advani's elderly security guard opened the compound gate and escorted them into the tearoom where they waited for Advani. Until then, Nick had not noticed how waiflike and diminutive the guard was. His obsolete Lee-Enfield seemed longer than he was tall, and though Nick had no doubt of its effectiveness, it rendered him in a rather comical, almost absurd, light.

"*Kitna nam hey*?" Nick inquired.

"Me, Sundip," he replied in his heavily accented English.

"Good to meet you, Sundip. I'm Nick."

Sundip nodded in acknowledgment and poured Nick and Aysha tea from a porcelain kettle that he placed on a tray in the middle of the floor. He seemed a sorry excuse for a security guard, far more amiable than he was intimidating, and when Advani arrived, instead of leaving them alone, Sundip stood by the doorway like a domestic servant. Despite his harmless appearance, Aysha was uncomfortable with his presence, preferring to talk only among people she knew. Advani noticed this and dismissed the old man, who waited out of earshot in the hallway.

After an initial exchange of pleasantries, Aysha delved into the real business at hand. "I have two things I must discuss with you. First, my family. Please tell me everything you know about my brothers."

Advani frowned. Though he was always discreet, this morning his voice was tainted with the helplessness of a man who, once influential, had just woken up to discover that his wings had been clipped.

"I have made inquiries with the high colonel of the Jammu and Kashmir police department *and* the regional captain of the Border Security Forces, both locally in the village and in Kargil and in Srinagar. The police know nothing; it is not in their hands. The commander of the security forces admits to having your brothers. His people tell me they are being interrogated at one of their 'centers'—they would not specify which one—along with dozens of other boys from our village. They are being held under suspicion of supporting terrorists."

317

Aysha looked overwrought, but before she could erupt, Advani held up his palm in petition to silence her.

"Please, Aysha. I told them it is complete nonsense, that your family—especially Naseem—has always been pro-union." Advani stopped speaking, as if he had nothing more to say.

"Well?" Aysha goaded him after a brief pause.

"That's all they would give me."

"No mention of how long they would be held?"

"Until the investigation is complete, they said. You and I both know that could mean anything, from a few days to years. They are pulling no punches on this investigation."

"What's the evidence against them? They have to have *some* evidence to hold them indefinitely."

Advani nervously patted the crown of his head. "Perhaps. There was no point in asking."

"You didn't ask them?" Aysha rejoined.

"Aysha, you *know* they can make up anything they want. Under the antiterror laws, all it takes is a fabricated rumor. They don't even have to disclose the source."

Aysha sighed. She knew he was right, but it made her even more frustrated to know that the Indians had such complete control over her brothers' lives.

"Perhaps your brothers were fingered by another man in custody," Advani ventured.

"That's impossible."

"It's *very* possible. Someone may have given your brothers' names precisely because they are *not* involved with the rebels. That way, the informant gets released by currying favor with the police while at the same time protecting himself from any repercussions from the militants."

"Or else they jailed my brothers to get to me," Aysha added.

Advani looked at her. "Do you know something that I do not?"

"Come on, Advani. It is obvious to them I can identify who it is they want. Just as you can."

Advani's eyes shifted to Nick.

"Its okay, Advani," Aysha assured him. "Nick can be trusted."

Advani hesitated, then he nodded. "Very well. Then listen to me," he replied in a stern voice. "Whatever you do, don't you dare think about striking a deal with them. These BSF officers, they are not like our local police. They answer only to the military authorities in Delhi. If you as much as hint we have information to share, they will have no compunction about throwing us both in jail. They do not make deals as a matter of policy, not with anyone. And they would love nothing more than to arrest a prominent doctor and a village politician suspected of harboring information, just in order to make an example."

Aysha eyed him skeptically. She nodded.

Advani sighed in relief. "Don't scare me like that."

"I'm sorry, Advani. You are right. I wouldn't think of offering to deal."

"Now, there is a rumor that someone is spreading disinformation to the security forces, either to harass those who are not supportive of the militants, or to befuddle the investigators," Advani said. "I believe this person—and not you—is the real source of your brothers' torment."

"Who?"

"Well, let me repeat that it's just a rumor. But word is that it's Abdul Mohammad. I heard through my sources he has taken on new responsibilities in the Gilkamosh cell. Despite this, when he was taken into custody, he was held only briefly before he was released."

"Have you talked to him?"

"I would like to say a thing or two to the little dimwit. But he has not been seen in the village for over a week. As I said, I am not sure he is the one framing your brothers. Even if Kazim is not calling the shots anymore, I don't think that Abdul would incriminate your family, as long as Kazim is still . . ." Advani caught himself.

"Still alive?" Aysha completed his sentence for him. "You can say it, Advani," she said defensively.

"But, of course. He must be alive. Unless you know something I do not?"

"No," she replied curtly. "I don't know anything about him."

Playing along with her lie, Nick fixed his eyes on the floor.

"So, what else can we do?" Aysha inquired.

"Besides the police and security forces," Advani explained, "I have talked to friends in Srinagar and Delhi, including Lakshmi Bhalla, my friend in the Parliament. I have not heard back from him. That is the full extent of my political connections, which seem not to carry much weight around here anymore. To be frank, it worries me, Aysha."

"I should speak with the BSF captain myself, at least to keep up the pressure."

"Don't do that, Aysha," he admonished. "You are a Muslim doctor who has treated wounded mujahideen. No matter what you say, it will be used against you, *and* your brothers. I am hoping this is just their way of teaching the villagers a lesson, and that your brothers will be returned to us shortly."

"I don't know," she replied. "So much Hindu blood has been spilled. I doubt a mere 'lesson' will satisfy them."

Advani rested his chin in his palm, deep in thought. "There is one other option I can think of," he said. "If you can get a lawyer involved. Have him file habeas corpus papers claiming illegal detention. It will not get them released, but it may intimidate the security forces a little, deter them from doing the boys any harm. Of course, lawyers are expensive."

"Father can't afford it. And you keep the books—so you know my salary is nonexistent."

Advani nodded. "I would pay for the lawyer myself. You know how dear your family has always been to me. But the way things have been lately with the business, I cannot."

"As always, I thank you for what you've done so far, Advani," Aysha responded after a pause.

"Do not thank me so fast, Aysha. You have not heard the worst of it yet."

"What do you mean?"

Advani hesitated. "You had *two* issues to discuss. I have a feeling what I have to say to you will be raised in due time."

A look of dread came over Aysha. "Okay," she said with hesitation. "Now that the security situation in the village has gone from bad to worse, I have concerns for the safety of my staff. As you know, we have always practiced the physician's code of medical neutrality. We treat everyone in need, no questions asked. That, unfortunately, is something that might not be tolerated any longer given the apparent change in leadership of the militants."

Advani held up his hand, cutting her short. "As I suspected, this leads me to say what I regret I must. I cannot guarantee the security of the clinic anymore. Gone are the days when the security forces will permit you to treat mujahideen. It is as simple as that.

"And even if you decided now to shut your doors to the militants, in effect becoming a progovernment hospital in the militants' eyes, the state will not spare any *jawans* to protect you. They would rather you pack up and leave the valley. This is what the commander of the BSF has told me, in so many words."

There was a moment of silence as Aysha struggled to grasp the ramifications of Advani's words.

"We need to shut down, Aysha," he said, to eliminate all doubt.

"That is absolutely *not* an option."

"It's the *only* option."

"What are you saying? You are withdrawing the funding?"

"Yes. There is no other way to safeguard you, your staff, or your patients. You know as well as I do, the rules of the game have changed. We have terrorism to thank for that."

"The clinic is the lifeblood of the village, Advani. It is what makes this place different—it holds us together. You cannot just give up on it after one bad attack."

"Aysha . . . it's not safe anymore."

"That's the damned point, Advani!" Aysha yelled, her voice filled with angry desperation. "Wars aren't supposed to be safe! We need to fight, too, damnit!"

Advani gaped at her, stunned by her sudden outburst. "I do not know what you are talking about. I am sorry." He shrugged.

"Don't be sorry—just listen to what I'm saying! Can't you see? We fight by saving lives—the lives that *they* try to take!"

As Advani's old security guard entered the room to see what the shouting was about, Nick put his hand on Aysha's shoulder, hoping to calm her. By the shocked look on Advani's face, it seemed he had never seen Aysha so agitated. In his eyes, she was always the precocious little girl who had captured the affection of the village by her compassion and capacity to heal. Now, for the first time, he saw her in an altogether different light—as a passionate, perhaps tragic advocate of a lost cause. Advani waited several long moments. Then he spoke, quietly, but with great clarity.

"Aysha, step back and look at what you are trying to do. You cannot keep the clinic open to make some kind of political statement. By doing so, you put your entire staff, and the very patients you are trying to save, in jeopardy."

"It is *not* a political statement, Advani. It's a *human* statement."

There was a dead silence, as Advani closed his eyes, lowering his head as if in meditation. When he finally spoke, his words were but a whisper.

"I've made my decision."

Aysha shut her eyes and lowered her head for a long moment. Then, slowly, she stood and walked out of the room.

Naseem's eyes were hollow with sleeplessness when he met Aysha and Nick at the door. His beard was unkempt, and his skin had turned a gray-yellow, as if the noxious inundation of his perpetual, nervous smoking had at last permanently tainted his complexion. Fatima looked no better for wear—pallid, with mottled eyes, and walled up in herself.

Aysha and Nick listened to Naseem vent his worry, reiterating the harrowing rumor of prisoners, unnamed boys from the village, beaten and tortured by the Indians, while Fatima covered her face and wept. Aysha tried her best to reassure her parents, telling them the rumors were just disinformation to rouse people's sympathy. Of course, no one could be sure, and Nick could tell from her downcast eyes that not even Aysha had any faith in her own reassurances.

Following Advani's suggestion, Aysha counseled her father to call upon the Fahad clan to pool money for a lawyer. Nick wished he could prepare the legal papers for them, but he could not draft documents in the local language, nor was he familiar with Indian law or permitted to file papers in the local courts. As expected, Naseem said he could not afford a lawyer, and being a prideful man, he was reluctant to reach out to his extended family and neighbors for the money.

"Baba, this is no time to let pride get in the way," Aysha scolded him. "We need to *do* something."

In the end, they reached a compromise, of sorts. Aysha volunteered to gather the extended family the following afternoon and raise the issue of collecting cash for a lawyer in the *presence* of Naseem, thereby giving it his sanction. This way, Naseem would save face, at least to some extent. But Naseem was not optimistic about the prospects of raising enough money—things were tight for everyone. Business had been bad for years now, with the tourist industry completely vanished, and the war otherwise depressing every aspect of the local economy, including the wool trade. Lately, he and his family had been reduced to subsistence farming for the first time since Naseem was a young man.

It was evening when they had finally resolved how to proceed. Since it would soon be dark, Naseem offered to permit Nick to spend the night at the house to avoid breaking curfew by driving at night. Omar was on duty at the clinic, and Aysha felt he could handle any emergencies. She phoned in to him from the village post to tell him that she and Nick would not be returning until the following day.

Aysha made no mention to her parents of the impending closure of the clinic, nor of Kazim's insistence that Aysha incriminate him in barter for her brothers' freedom. Nick could only guess she was loath to do anything that could cause him harm, even though he had begged her to give up his name. A vestige of the bond that once existed between them had withstood the effacement of time. Now, it seemed to haunt her with a terrible choice. This filled Nick with sadness. For Nick knew now, for the first time in his life, what it was like to feel another's affliction as his own.

CHAPTER 52

The meeting of the Fahad clan the following morning had not been fruitful. Scant savings were available, not nearly enough to hire a lawyer to prepare a habeas petition challenging the detention of Khaliq and Nabir. With nothing resolved, Aysha and Nick headed back to the clinic in the truck.

"What are you going to tell everyone?" Nick asked her on the drive over the mountain.

"The truth. That the funding has been cut off and I cannot afford them anymore."

"And then what?"

"I will continue working."

"Without any money?"

"If it is just me working, there will be no salaries to pay. I should be able to keep things running on the little bit of grant money I receive from the Muslim charities, at least for a while. I don't know how long supplies will last, but I'll scrape together what I can, for as long as I can."

"But what about your safety?"

"Whatever happens, so be it."

"Aysha, stop being so stubborn. Why don't you listen to Advani and close down for at least a while? In six months, a year, you can open again. If you get yourself killed, there will be no one to run the clinic at all. Ever."

"You don't understand—you aren't from here. If I give up now, then the *war* is lost. Not for me, but for the whole village."

"I thought you were supposed to be neutral," Nick said.

"Exactly. *My* war is the war against their war. I can't just roll over. Now that Advani has pulled out, it is all up to me. I cannot hold it against him. He has done far too much for me over the years. But I simply won't do the same."

"That's insane, Aysha. Think about your family. Think about . . ." Nick caught himself.

"Think about what?" she said, bewildered. "*You?* This war has nothing to do with you, Nick. Go home. Back to America."

"It's not that simple."

"Why not?"

While Aysha drove, Nick fixed his eyes on the sky thrust behind the mountains, mottled with cotton-ball clouds that were fading and reforming in a never-ending cycle. He felt the sudden urge to explain everything—about Yvette and Akhtar, his flight, his feelings for her. But he had lived the lie for too long. She would never understand, not now, he thought. Perhaps later, when her problems were laid to rest. Always later.

"I've been through so much here, I can't just up and leave."

"Forget it. I said before, it's not your war."

He paused. "Yes, it is—in a way."

She looked at him, perplexed. "I don't understand you. You're not easy to place."

"Can I take that as a compliment?" he said with diversionary humor.

She scrutinized him for a moment. "Yes," she replied sincerely. "I suppose a little mystery is complimentary. But another puzzle is not what I need right now."

Nick frowned. "I wish things were different, Aysha," he said, unable to mask the longing in his voice.

"I as well," she replied.

"Your friend—the mujahid—you're still in love with him, aren't you?"

She bristled at the question, as if some internal defense mechanism had been triggered. But then, to Nick's surprise, she softened.

"We were just children when we were engaged to be married," she said with resignation. "Then the war came, and everything changed. Now I cling to the boy Kazim used to be. Not the man he has become. . . . I do not know what love means anymore."

"Why won't you do what he asks? For your brothers?"

There was a long silence. Aysha trained her glazed, tired eyes on the winding road as they ascended the pass. When they turned a corner, a glint of sunlight struck her face, reflecting off the pale green of her irises.

"He asks me to betray a part of myself," she said finally. "The only part that has ever been my own."

* * *

When Aysha told the others the funding for the clinic had been rescinded and she could no longer pay their salaries, the response was not what she had anticipated. Each one of the staff—Aroon, Vilashni, Omar, and Ghulam (who, since the massacre, had been drawing a modest salary for his much-needed work)—nevertheless insisted on staying. They would cut back their hours, they said, in order to free time to do what was necessary to subsist, but would continue working for no salary.

"I will not let you," Aysha told them. "It is too dangerous. If anything happens to you, I will never forgive myself."

"Madam Doctor," Vilashni lectured her. "We are not your children. We know a danger when we see it. We do what we do by our own choosing."

"You do not understand. I do not *want* you here," Aysha insisted, trying her best not to show how touched she was.

"How can you run this place alone? It is not possible," Omar interjected.

"I will manage. Now, I won't hear any more of this."

"Madam Doctor, we *must* stay!" Ghulam interjected with zeal, his index finger wagging fervently. "We are not afraid of those terrible people. Charity is the work of Allah."

"Ghulam, I am not in the mood for a sermon. I am not talking about charity—I am talking about *reality*. And *you*, of all people, know it is high time for you to go home to your wives. Now, all of you, listen to me— I am the boss, and you are all fired. You are to be out of here by morning."

The next morning, when Aysha emerged to perform her rounds, she found everyone proceeding with business as usual.

"I fired you, damnit! *Leave!*" she yelled, stomping her feet, looking so much like a little girl throwing a tiff that it was all they could do to keep from laughing. When her antics did not work, she resorted to pleading. Still no one heeded her. Trying to conceal their grins, Omar, Aroon, Vilashni, Nick, and Ghulam all just kept working as Aysha continued to rant.

The same thing happened the following morning, and every morning thereafter, until Aysha eventually gave up trying to expel her staff altogether.

The days passed and the war continued, with sporadic skirmishes fought almost weekly following the massacre. More civilians were caught

in the crossfire and admitted for treatment. Even an occasional policeman or soldier was brought to the clinic—but no mujahideen. Despite
the lack of money to pay them, the staff became more devoted to their
work than ever.

When the villagers learned of the clinic's defiance in the face of
threats and evaporated funding, they did what they could to help. Volunteers brought food, helped to clean the ward and the grounds, and took
shifts nursing patients. Supplies were scarce, but they made do with what
they had, and some of the villagers even drove to Srinagar and begged the
hospitals there to donate blood, morphine, and other necessities.

In this small way, a people under siege, burdened by having so many
of their sons locked away by a government that claimed to be their own,
but that cared more about owning the dirt under their feet than securing
their loyalty, rediscovered their spirit. It was as if they knew in their
collective heart that only *they,* the people, could win the war, not the
national government and its reactionary security forces who eyed them
with suspicion, or the mujahideen and their dogma. A new trust had
rejuvenated them, built on empathy and not a little defiance, all of it rallied around Aysha and her clinic.

CHAPTER 53

Advani was tired of being cooped up. He had been secluded in his study all morning, going over his finances, which were a dismal sign of the times.

His textile business, which, contrary to popular belief, had been spiraling downward for years now, had taken even a steeper decline of late. The order he had expected from a factory in Bombay had not come in over the summer. When he phoned his customer, he was told demand was down due to the lapse in Indian textile exports to the European Union and the United States, whose protectionist politicians had slapped huge tariffs on cheap imports to satisfy their corporate supporters.

Advani had always lived well within his means and had kept his debts to a minimum. But now he was feeling the bite. What he had told Aysha had been true. He would not have been able to continue funding the clinic much longer, even if the danger to her and her staff in keeping it open were not a reality.

Still, when Aysha continued to operate the clinic despite all the risks, and the village rallied behind her, giving her what modest donations they could afford, their support made him look a bit like a tightwad. *But good for her,* he thought. Perhaps she was right to continue with the hospital, even though her resilience in the face of his capitulation had damaged his own reputation. When his cash flow augmented, as it would eventually, he resolved that he would step back in. But now, things were just too uncertain. Fortunately, he found a way to make up for some of the lost face he had suffered by coming to the aid of his longtime friend, Aysha's father, and thus, indirectly, Aysha as well.

Advani had been deeply troubled for weeks by the situation of Naseem's boys, and the five other teenagers from the village whom the security forces were still holding. It had been over two months since they had arrested the youths, and still the commander had given no word about a possible release. Advani used to visit Naseem every day; it was a small village, and it was easy to drop by. But since his sons' incarceration and Advani's inability to do anything about it, Advani had been unable to face his friend, or the other villagers with jailed children. Indeed, Advani was so mortified by his powerlessness he had felt ashamed even to walk down the street—in his *own* village.

When he heard rumors that village boys were being tortured in custody, it was too much to bear. Aysha had told him that the Fahad family had not raised enough money for a lawyer. Neither were the other families capable of doing so, most of them being victims of the depression in the wool business. So, in his typical fashion of addressing village problems, he decided to implement his favorite scheme—the community fund-raiser, the same method he had used years before for Aysha's medical training. If enough families in the village pitched in a little, he thought, he might lean on a lawyer he knew in Srinagar. Advani had guessed correctly that the lawyer would be inclined to cut his rate for future considerations from Advani on other work.

Advani's plan had worked even better than he had imagined. The villagers, already mobilized by Aysha's defiance in keeping the clinic functional, were full of spirit, confident they could do anything once they asserted their collective will. After initially giving Advani considerable flack for his ceasing to fund the clinic, the villagers raised enough money to pay the lawyer's reduced fee for a habeas corpus petition on behalf of all seven of the imprisoned Gilkamosh boys.

Just the day before, Advani had received a call from the lawyer informing him that the papers had been filed and personally served on Lieutenant Colonel Sunil Patel, the regional commander of the security forces in Srinagar. Although the lawyer had little faith the petition would be well received by the court, given the wide berth the antiterror laws gave to the security forces, the filing was good news indeed. Now, with a suit pending, the security forces knew that someone of influence was watching them, and they might think twice about mistreating the villagers' sons. Advani wished he could have seen Patel's face when the process server handed him the petition.

To heap on the pressure, the lawyer, at Advani's urging, also had called a newspaper reporter in Srinagar, and simultaneous with the filing a headline regarding the suit was run on the front page of the *Srinagar Times*—"Remote Village Sues Security Forces for Claimed Illegal Detention of Muslim Youth."

With the press on the story, the villagers were not just fighting back, they were taking the offensive. This would open a new era of tense relations between the village and the military authorities, something Advani had always gone to great lengths to avoid. Advani was a politician and a diplomat, not by any means an activist. But Advani had tried several times to resolve the situation privately with the commander, and had been inexplicably snubbed. In the end, he and the villagers had given them what they deserved.

Eager to spread the good news about the habeas petition in person, Advani Sharma decided to take a stroll through the village, first to Naseem's and then to the homes of the other families. It would be the first time he had ventured out on his own in quite a while, and this time, he would be walking proudly.

After telling his wife he was going out, Advani decided against asking Sundip to accompany him. He anticipated spending considerable time with Naseem and the others and would rather be alone. Furthermore, he was embarrassed to be seen walking around with a security guard. What kind of example would it set if people thought the mayor was too scared to take a stroll down the street without an armed guard?

Old Sundip transformed Advani into a laughingstock. Advani had hired him at the urging of his wife, Shanti, in the aftermath of the massacre. He thought the idea silly, but Shanti had been insisting on it for some time, and now that the violence had finally struck home, she got her way. Sundip was a retired policeman from Delhi who had moved to the Vale of Kashmir years ago, taking a job at the courthouse in Srinagar. He responded to Advani's advertisement for a home security worker almost immediately, as the idea of moving to a small mountain town suited him.

When Sundip showed up the first day of work with a curling white mustache and orange turban, wielding a baton and his antiquated Lee-Enfield for his only armament, Advani was more than a little skeptical. But Sundip was diligent enough, and had all kinds of entertaining "war stories" to tell about the old days on the police force in Delhi. After purchasing him a nine-millimeter pistol, Advani hired him. "Here, now you are a modern security guard," Advani said to him as he handed him the new gun.

Sundip was not impressed by the sidearm. "This gun no good," he claimed, patting his rifle affectionately. "'Mr. Enfield' can hit villains from 'very very' far. With pistol, they must be very close. *Too* close, sir."

After some haggling, they reached a compromise whereby Sundip carried both weapons, and when Advani went for walks, much to the amusement of the village, Sundip would march stiffly alongside him with his Enfield shouldered like some old-fashioned Rajput sepoy.

"Sundip, I'm going for a walk," Advani said to the old man dozing on his chair just inside the gate to the compound. Sundip snapped to alertness, embarrassed by his age-induced lassitude. "But I am coming, sir," he said, bolting to his feet.

"No, thank you, Sundip. I'm going to visit Naseem today, and I don't want to keep you away from Mrs. Sharma that long." These days, Shanti felt unsafe whenever Advani left her home alone for long periods.

"Are you sure, sir? You don't want me to call on Naseem to come here?"

"Quite sure, Sundip, thank you. I will be fine."

Sundip opened the gate for Advani, looking both ways out onto the street. He cupped his hand over his eyes and saw that the road was empty. Satisfied everything was quiet, he waved to Advani, who grinned, finding humor in Sundip's well-meant but superfluous precautions, before walking through the gate toward the center of town.

In a good mood for the first time in months, Advani sauntered past his neighbors' homes. Behind the homes were the wheat fields, and behind them, the river valley. Paths led down to the river, through the fields, where the women went to wash clothes, and he could see flashes of brilliant color through the lush trees where they had set their dyed fabrics out to dry on the riverbank. Harvest time was approaching, and the world smelled of ripened wheat, apples, and poppy blossoms. Birds chirped and fluttered among the lush trees, and the peaceful sound of the trickling irrigation channels made him wonder if the unspeakable violence that had occurred a few months ago had all been a terrible dream; for how could war and hatred raise its ugly head in such a sublime and blessed place?

His mind continued to meander, eventually focusing on Naseem's ordeal. It must be a terrible feeling of hopelessness, he thought, to have your own children whisked away from you without explanation, by your very own government. It is a wonder, he pondered, why even more people did not join the militants. For his India, a country forged in religious strife, had long treated its Muslims like half citizens, and then at the first sign of trouble, like the enemy. If India lost Kashmir, he thought, it would be India's own fault—not that of Pakistan or some international conspiracy of jihadis, as it was fashionable among the nation's intelligentsia to opine.

Distracted by these weighty musings, his eyes drawn to the surface of the river flickering with silver light under the midday sun, he did not notice two men approach from the junction of paths leading down to the riverbank. Had he not been so preoccupied by the pigheadedness of his own nation's leaders, he might have noticed one of the men reach down for the lip of his *pheran* and fling it up over his shoulder. For when Advani did finally look up, it was too late to see anything but the barrel of the Kalashnikov. Nothing else—no faces, no figures, no forms—just a tunnel vision leading from his eyes to the blued steel that suddenly came to life, bouncing in fleeting agitation, breathing hot gas onto his chest, an assassin's breath, before it stopped.

Time must have skipped a beat, for the next thing he knew he was lying on his back, unable to move, gazing at the cobalt blue Himalayan sky. One moment, he was locked in profound worry over the plight of a friend; the next, ebbing into oblivion. A shadow blotted out the light, replacing it with the face of the killer, all red beard and brutal simplicity, before it merged into the blackness.

CHAPTER 54

Aysha asked not a single question of the caller. She listened without a trace of emotion, her stolid demeanor causing Nick to wonder whether she had somehow intuited what the news would be. "Tell the others that Advani has been murdered," she told Nick without pause, before retreating into her office, locking the door behind her.

Advani's execution instantly squelched the elevated morale that had resulted from the villagers' rallying around the clinic in the aftermath of the massacre. With one pull of the trigger, the moral and financial wellspring of the village, and Aysha's lifelong benefactor, had been obliterated. There was a dreadful sense Advani had been there at the beginning, and he would be there at the end; thus, with his death, the end of Gilkamosh as they knew it was upon them.

The following morning Aysha called on Nick to drive with her into the village. She had made arrangements to meet with the commander of the security forces, who had come to Gilkamosh from Srinagar in person to investigate Advani's murder. One of the commander's underlings had told her he was staying for only two days, so Aysha needed to go immediately.

"What will you do when you meet with him?" Nick inquired with concern, while he negotiated the steep incline on the way to the village. It was only mid-October, but the leaves of the oaks drooped with an early frost. Aysha wore a thick wool sweater to ward off the crisp chill. Her hair was tucked behind her ears, but some strands rebelled in the wind, pattering her smooth cheekbones.

"The only thing I can think of to save my brothers."

Nick turned and studied her. "Aysha, remember what Advani said—there's no making any deals with them."

"And look what happened to him."

"What do you mean?"

"It seems odd that Advani was killed in broad daylight and there was no one around to stop it. Every time I have been in town since the massacre, it's been swarming with *jawans*."

Nick considered her words while he steered through the treacherous switchbacks. "That's what those people do—they wait until no one is around before they strike. They're good at it."

"Yes, they are. But these days one cannot even walk down the road without being watched. Unless whoever is supposed to be watching knows to look the other way."

Nick pulled over in front of the newly expanded Border Security Forces headquarters, a requisitioned schoolhouse near the center of the village. After the massacre, the BSF compound in Gilkamosh had expanded seemingly overnight. A fortified cinder-block wall lined with a large barbed-wire fence had been erected around the compound to deter potential bombers, and several bunkers with machine-gun nests were built into the corners of the complex. Dozens of officers had established temporary workplaces in the building, having been transferred in response to recent intelligence reports that the Gilkamosh region was becoming a new focus of the insurgency.

When they arrived at the facility, Aysha asked Nick to wait in the truck. Her "bargaining," she explained, was of the type to be done alone.

Lieutenant Colonel Sunil Patel was in his late fifties, a tall, dark-skinned Punjabi with square shoulders, pockmarked skin, and a neatly trimmed mustache that, despite the obvious care applied to its upkeep, appeared altogether inconsequential juxtaposed under the thick, black bushiness of his adjoining eyebrows. Career military, he had never quite gotten over being "promoted" to the Gilkamosh regional command two years before, a highly undesirable post because of its lack of action. He was convinced that his exile had been retribution for bad-mouthing a former superior to his current one, who, unbeknownst to the unfortunate Patel, was the former man's brother-in-law. A flatlander who loathed isolation, Patel preferred to spend most of his time in Srinagar, which was bustling in comparison to Gilkamosh, though he had been forced to come to Gilkamosh intermittently in the aftermath of the massacre to maintain the appearance of overseeing responsive operations. His present visit, which he hoped would last for no more than two days, was purportedly for the purpose of "looking into" the assassination of Advani Sharma, someone with whom he had frequent dealings in the past.

A son of Hindu refugees from a village now in present-day Pakistan, Patel had inherited an innate animosity toward Muslims from his father, who held them primarily responsible for the savagery that ensued following Partition. When Patel's eyes feasted on Aysha, however, he was willing to set aside his distaste and lend her an ear, at least for a moment.

Patel invited her into his office, then made her sit and wait while he addressed his retinue of lieutenants, who swarmed about him obsequiously, vying for his attention with a slew of logistical issues—troop rotations, supply shortages, preparations for early snowfall. Aysha watched quietly as Patel barked orders with an air of self-importance, which she gathered he was playing up to impress her. Finally, he dismissed his staff, and they were alone.

"Ah, Dr. Fahad," he cooed, sharply tugging the hair of his left brow between his thumb and forefinger. He walked around the front of his desk, perching himself on top of it. "I am sorry for boring you with these banal ministrations. People think that the work of an army officer is romantic. But ninety percent of the time it is rather mundane, especially when one is stuck in a low-intensity conflict, such as we find in Kashmir," he said, switching from Hindi to English in order to impress upon Aysha he was her equal in education. "It's a true pleasure to meet you."

"Thank you, Colonel," she replied, balking at his arrogance.

"Such a refined woman is a rarity in these remote hinterlands of our subcontinent."

"Thank you. Again." Despite his flattering tone, Aysha's voice and demeanor were grave.

"What can I do for you?" he replied, miffed at her unwillingness to engage in small talk.

"Well, as you might have guessed, I am here in part because of Advani Sharma's murder. He was a dear friend."

"A tragedy for us all. He was an excellent friend to me as well."

"Really. Well, of course."

Despite her efforts to conceal the fact, Aysha was nervous. Lieutenant Colonel Patel was a powerful man, despite his being shortshrifted in the bureaucratic infighting in the army ranks, and Aysha was about to assume a tack with him for which very few civilians would have the nerve.

"Advani was the primary benefactor of our medical clinic here in Gilkamosh, as you may know," she continued.

"We know most things that go on around here. It is the few things that we do not know about that concern us. You people are very tight-lipped."

Patel pulled his lips back in an attempt at a humorous smirk, only to expose his *paan*-stained teeth, and then he tugged impulsively on the hair of his eyebrow again. Aysha could not help but notice Patel's left brow—the one he kept pulling—appeared thinner than the right, even slightly patchy where he must have plucked the hair out completely. She wondered whether this habit was an unconscious tick, or whether he was *overly* conscious of his bushy unibrow, and he just could not keep himself from trying to give it a proper thinning.

"It's a small town," she replied. "I mention Advani's generosity, Colonel, to emphasize that I have a personal interest in bringing the murderers to justice."

"Of course. As do we all. These people are terrorists," he said. "And because you and Advani healed the victims of their terror, you became their target. That is clearly why they went after Advani."

"Precisely. Which makes me very reluctant to disclose what information I might be able to find out, about the identity of the militants operating in this region."

Patel paused, surprised by the turn of the conversation, as if he had expected a typical, boring venting of frustration with the lack of security leading to Advani's assassination, not an offer of information from a woman whom he had not even begun to bribe or to threaten. His interest kindled, he cleared his throat, leaning toward her. "Well, Madam Fahad. I understand your fear. But you can count on me to protect you. You have my personal word."

"Like you protected Advani?"

Patel fell silent. He increased the pace and vigor of the assault on his eyebrow. Aysha noted with inner satisfaction the little beads of sweat sprouting on his forehead, and his mustaches twitching with the grinding of his jaw.

"I'll be frank with you, Colonel," she said. "I think you know quite well, you have my brothers in the custody of your forces."

After a short silence, he tossed his head with indifference. "We've captured so many terrorists over the last year, I could not possibly remember all of them by name." He turned away from Aysha and looked out the window, stewing over the affront to his machismo caused by her perceived insolence.

"They are not terrorists. Their names, Colonel, are Khaliq and Nabir Fahad. You were personally served with the habeas corpus papers on their behalf just two days ago."

Patel shrugged, reluctant to give her the dignity of remembering her brothers' names. But he had to admit he recognized them, now that she had brought up the lawsuit. "Ah, yes, I think I remember something about that. From some windbag lawyer in Srinagar," he said with disdain.

"My family has heard nothing about my brothers for over a month. And I know for a fact they had nothing to do with the massacre or the militants. Nothing at all. As do you."

"Do I?" he said, tossing his head.

"Yes. You do," she replied, meeting his glare. "So here's my proposal. People in this village will never talk to you. To them, you are an occupying army and they would rather you leave. You obviously must know that by now, from your years of service in Kashmir. It is clear to everyone that you took our boys prisoner as a means of wringing information out of us—perhaps me, specifically."

"If you think I'm going to sit here while you—"

"Hear me out, Colonel," she cut him off, "and you'll see that I'm trying to help you."

Patel chortled, then gave a sarcastic toss of his hand. "I don't need your help. But, go on," he said, feigning boredom, "say what you must."

"The villagers won't tell you what you want to know, Colonel. Nor will the boys you have imprisoned, for they know too well what the militants would do to them if they did. Unless you torture them. And you'd better not do that now that there are lawyers and journalists watching you."

"Ha!" Patel scoffed.

Aysha was stretching the truth. She knew well that Patel's interrogators would torture the boys regardless of the lawsuit and any bad publicity. When push came to shove, the Indian judges would always be on the side of the security forces.

"But *I* am willing to get you the names that you want," she continued. "On condition that you release my brothers and the other boys."

She paused to let her offer sink in. Patel pretended to fume, tapping the back of his hand into the palm of the other. But she could tell he was intrigued by her offer.

"I should arrest you right now," he said. "You admit to me that you have information about the identity of terrorists, and yet you withhold it. That, *Doctor,* is a blatant violation of the antiterror ordinances." He picked up the phone, as if he was going to call someone to arrest her. Aysha did not flinch.

"I did not say I *had* the information. I said I could get it. But go ahead and arrest me," she challenged him. "Then you'll never get the information you want. Even if you torture me, I will not talk. About the terrorists, that is."

He placed the phone back on the receiver. "What is that supposed to mean?"

"I won't talk about the terrorists, though I may be inclined to say something about the payments that were accepted by certain members of the security forces, including yourself, in order to keep your forces out of the affairs of the village over the years. Not to mention the coincidence of Advani's murder just days after he helped arrange the lawsuit against your forces for wrongfully imprisoning our boys."

"I don't like where this conversation is going," Patel snapped.

"I don't blame you," Aysha replied, unflinching.

Patel glared at her. "After all we have done for you. I can see now it was a terrible mistake to let your clinic survive at Advani's insistence, even while you treated terrorists!"

"My clinic survived because Advani paid you to keep your security forces from shutting us down. It had nothing to do with *your* generosity. In fact, the entire village survived peacefully for as long as it did precisely because we paid you bribes *not* to do your job. Suddenly, now that you've involved yourself in our village, Advani is assassinated."

"This is absurd! Are you insinuating we had something to do with Advani's death? Is that what this is about?"

"I wouldn't put it past you. At a minimum, you looked the other way knowing he was on the hit list. With Advani out of the way, you were hoping all your dirty business was swept under the table."

"I overestimated you. I thought you were an intelligent woman. If my forces were taking *bribes* as you allege, why would we not just continue taking them?"

"Simple," Aysha replied. "Now, you are under pressure from your superiors to crack down on our village in retribution for the massacre of the *yatris*. There was no way you could keep your end of the bargain up anymore . . . and I wouldn't be surprised if Advani even threatened to go public with the bribery scheme, when you told him you were going to turn the screws on our village," she added. "Advani would have done anything to save his people—even at the expense of incriminating himself. When he was murdered, your risk of exposure was eliminated. It was a godsend for you. But far too convenient and well-timed to be dismissed as a mere fortuity."

"That is the brashest, most ignorantly misguided thing anyone has ever said to me," he sneered.

By the look in Patel's eyes, Aysha could tell she had tweaked a raw nerve in him. She swallowed nervously, aware of the recklessness of her words, and the jeopardy in which she had placed herself.

"If you don't accept my offer and release my brothers and the other boys," she said after a long, searching pause, "I'll go public with your acceptance of bribes from Advani. I know plenty of reporters who will be willing to print it. They are already watching you closely."

Aysha lied, for she had not spoken to any reporters. But with the article publicizing the habeas filing, her bluff appeared credible, even without any evidence. Patel got up and paced the room, his back to Aysha.

"Let me get this straight. You're offering to identify names of the terrorists in exchange for release of your brothers, who you claim are innocent. If I don't release your brothers then you will spread nasty, false rumors about me and my men."

"Rumors are not how it will be played in the Muslim press," Aysha replied. "Years of bribes, conspiracy in murder, is more like it. The government will be forced to investigate, the public outcry will require it."

"So you give me both the carrot *and* the stick."

Aysha considered this. "That is a fair characterization. The carrot—so you can claim victory to your superiors with some big arrests and justify the crackdown on the village. And the stick—to make sure you come through on your end of the bargain and don't steal the carrot."

He scoffed. "Are you not afraid of the same fate that befell your friend? You know as well as I do, the rebels won't spare you just because you are Muslim."

"Of course not," she said. "I would not put it past them. Or you."

Patel stared hard into Aysha's eyes. He shook his head. "You *are* a foolish woman. You'll have my answer in the morning."

CHAPTER 55

Aysha did not tell her parents about her meeting with the colonel; she did not want to worry them, or worse, get their hopes up for their sons' release. But she told Nick, and he worried enough for all concerned.

"Aysha, if they are capable of ridding themselves of Advani with all of his political clout—whether they did it themselves or stood back and watched while the militants shot him—they certainly can deal with you the same way."

"I told him I am ready to go public."

"But you're not. I mean, what's to stop them from arresting you tomorrow? They have plenty of grounds to do it, now that you've threatened them. Then you'll be locked in a cage who knows where, like the others."

"I know that is possible."

"No, Aysha, it's *likely*. Don't you see? By threatening to give the story to the press, you've just given them more incentive to arrest you now, before it's too late." Nick paused in thought. "Do you even *know* any reporters?"

"No. But there is the one whom Advani spoke to. It should not be hard to get his name from the newspaper, when it finally gets to Gilkamosh. We are usually a few days behind on Srinagar papers."

After some consideration, Nick came to a conclusion. "We have to write it all down in the form of a sworn statement. An affidavit, signed before witnesses. Right now. That way, if they arrest you, I can go to Srinagar and deliver the story to the reporter myself. It's not much, but at least if they arrest you tomorrow morning when you go back there, I'll be able to put your story in the public eye."

"Sworn statement? I don't have *time* to go to Srinagar to hire a lawyer, Nick."

That night, Nick, a fugitive vagabond, reached far into his past and became a lawyer once again. He prepared Aysha's statement, written in English and drafted in detail as a sworn affidavit, documenting her knowledge of Advani's payment of bribes to the security forces over the years, in exchange for their agreement not to shut down the clinic and to accept its neutrality. They also added the bit about Advani's efforts to negotiate for the release of the incarcerated village boys and his subsequent raising of money for the habeas petition. It was, of course, largely circumstantial in implicating the authorities in Advani's death, and sometimes stretched the truth, as effective affidavits tend to do. But it was juicy enough for the newspapers and would receive a whirlwind of attention in the event Aysha were to be arrested in the morning.

"I had no idea," Aysha said, impressed by the polished, very professional-looking document Nick had slid under her chin.

"About what?"

"Well . . . to be blunt, I didn't know you were educated at all, let alone a trained lawyer. I mean, I'm sorry, but let's face it—you don't look like a lawyer," she said, allowing herself a brief, wry moment despite the gravity of the circumstances. "You're far too hairy and unkempt. And that wardrobe."

"*Former* lawyer," Nick replied. "No apologies necessary. You don't know it, but what you said was kind of a compliment . . not the part about being hairy and all, but . . ."

Aysha signed the affidavit only after much hesitation, despite its necessity. "I cannot slight Advani's name," she said. "People will think he was corrupt."

"Paying money to save lives can never be corrupt. *You* told me that once," Nick reminded her. "This time one of those lives could be your own."

The following morning, Aysha returned to the colonel's office, expecting the worst—arrest, interrogation, and possibly torture. To her surprise, however, he greeted her amiably, this time immediately dismissing his inferior officers.

"I understand, Dr. Fahad, you have done many of our soldiers service at your clinic in years past."

His diplomacy threw Aysha off. She smelled a red herring in his praise, but sensed that it was best to play along.

"I don't know why you act surprised, Colonel. I am an Indian citizen like you. It is true I have treated many Indian soldiers, saving more than a few of their lives. Some of them from your very own command. This should not be news to you."

"Indeed. We are grateful for all you have done for the Indian security forces over the past few years, Doctor."

Aysha noted he was speaking loudly and formally, which struck her as odd.

"I have to tell you, however," he continued, "that you have been very reckless with respect to your safety and that of your staff. The terrorists will consider you a target for treating Indian soldiers. Though we have done all we can in the past, now the situation has changed, with the rise of terrorism in the region. We cannot protect you all of the time. Our forces are spread too thin."

"I know that. I have *always* known that I cannot count on your protection."

"Well . . . of course you can count on us to do everything within our means. But we cannot possibly be everywhere at once. Anyway, all this is to say that we recommend you cease your operation of the clinic immediately. We cannot force you to do anything against your will. I am just telling you, very precisely, that we cannot assure your safety and the safety of your patients and staff, despite our best efforts to do so. You are operating in a war zone and treating combatants. You do so at your own risk."

Aysha could barely restrain herself from wincing at his self-serving statements. It was then that she noticed the receiver of his desk phone was sitting off the hook. She put it together. Someone must be listening in on their conversation through the phone, perhaps taping it to create a record favorable to the security forces in case it was needed to counter Aysha's threat of a public relations disaster.

"In any event," Patel continued in his vigorous voice, "as a show of my gratitude for what you have done for my men and for the people of Gilkamosh, I have looked into the matter of your brothers and the other boys, and have been ensured that they will be released soon."

Aysha's face flushed with hope. Had her plan *worked*? It seemed as though Patel, a prideful man, was couching his accession to her demands in a favorable, face-saving manner. This suited Aysha fine, so long as she could have the assurance first.

"When?"

"Forthwith."

She paused. "That's not going to do it," she said. "Maybe for whoever is listening in through your phone right now, but not for me. You have got to be more specific than that. My brothers have already been held for over a month."

Patel scowled at her, and then reached to his desk and unabashedly hung up the receiver. What was coming next, he did not want to leave the room.

"They'll be released as soon as they are done being processed. Most likely by the end of the month," he said coolly.

"Okay, then we'll speak when they're released," Aysha replied, calling his bluff. She stood to leave.

"Stop!" Patel sprang to his feet and stepped toward her, so close she could smell his cheap cologne and the curry he had eaten for breakfast. "I'm leaving today for Srinagar. You will tell me what you know *now*."

"Surely, Colonel, you understand that I would not—"

"Silence!" Patel's hand swooped down and slapped her hard against the cheek. Stunned, Aysha flinched, her face recoiling with the blow. Her chest heaved as she quickly wiped her eyes with her sleeve, denying him the satisfaction of seeing any tears. Then she glared back at him with wrath in her eyes.

Patel was undeterred by her indignation. "Sit down!" he commanded, pushing her backward until she fell back into the chair. "Now you listen to me, you insolent Muslim bitch! I am going out on a limb to get your brothers released and I am not returning to Srinagar empty-handed. If you insist on trying to blackmail me, I shall have your hospital closed down in less than five minutes for rendering aid to the enemy, and then I'll have you thrown in prison for harboring a fugitive."

"A *fugitive*?" Aysha immediately thought of Kazim. They must know of his role in the militant cell, she thought, despite her own efforts to protect him.

"That's right. Wanted for *murder* in Pakistan."

Aysha cocked her head in confusion.

"His name is Sunder. The American. You know him quite well, from what I am told." Patel raised his eyebrows in insinuation. "Have a look."

Patel handed her a paper with a photocopied mug shot. It was Nick, his beard shorter, his face less weathered. There was a caption under the picture stating he was wanted for the murder of a Pakistani police officer, whom he had killed while fleeing the country under suspicion of murdering a French woman. The notice requested his arrest and extradition to Pakistan in the event he was found in India.

Aysha was dumbfounded. She struggled to keep her composure, but her hand shook and she dropped the paper. "He is an *aid worker*. I know nothing about this, even if it *is* true."

"Oh, it is true. Do you think us so stupid as to fabricate something that outrageous and so easy to check?"

Aysha did not respond. Patel raised his chin and folded his arms, a boastful, gloating posture. He knew he had her beaten.

"I would like to believe that you did not know about your friend's criminality," he continued. "Nonetheless, I find it hard, considering the closeness of your friendship with him. You have been seen together quite a bit about town. Some say you are . . . romantic."

Aysha longed to slap the smirk off his face. "Who I am romantic with is none of your concern," she demurred. "And in any event, he never told me *any* of this. He was looking to volunteer at the clinic in exchange for room and board. I obliged because I needed the help."

Patel shook his head. "Under normal circumstances, I might be inclined to believe you. But credibility is something you lack with me. Harboring a fugitive is a serious crime. And no one believes a criminal, let alone a woman of dubious morality with plenty of reason to lie. Not even people who read newspapers." He paused, peering at her with insinuating eyes. "You can, of course, always play your hand and watch where the cards may fall. From a jail cell."

Aysha was speechless.

"Let me make a suggestion," Patel said, relishing her dismay. "I am an accommodating man. Cooperation is the best way to regain my trust. I will be back in five minutes. When I return, you will tell me what I am sure you already know. Or you will go to jail.

"If you insist on making your allegations in the press—and I question how you can do that from behind bars without visitors—we know reporters, too. Believe me, we have enough on you right now to ruin your life forever."

He walked out of the office, leaving Aysha to her defeat. It took only a minute for her to realize she had lost all advantage. The tables had been turned against her, all because she had been betrayed by the person she trusted most.

"Abdul Mohammad Fazar is the leader of the Gilkamosh cell. He has been since the insurrection spread to this area. He received his schooling at the madrassa under tutelage of Yusuf, the traveling mullah who used to teach here until four years ago. Mullah Yusuf was a recruiter for Pakistani intelligence. I am told he is now teaching somewhere in Doda. I am sure you know how to find him.

"Abdul received his training in Pakistan, under the leadership of a Pashtun named Muzzafar Khan. Muzzafar commands the local cell of mujahideen from across the Line of Control and comes into Gilkamosh about two or three times a year to coordinate attacks. He was the mastermind of the August 30 massacre of the *yatris*. He used Abdul to carry it out, as well as the local boys who were killed by your men. Those are your culprits—Khan, Abdul, and Yusuf.

"I heard a rumor that Muzzafar was as recently as two days ago in the region of Passtu—staying in a shepherd's hut in one of the pastures above Kurgan that they use as a safe house. If you hurry, you may be able to capture him. That is it. That is all I know."

"How do you know all of this?"

She paused, trying not to appear evasive as she considered her response. "I have known Abdul Mohammad all of my life," she replied. "Since we were children. I treated him recently when he came into the hospital with wounds. He told me."

"You will testify when we capture him."

"I will not testify unless I may do so anonymously. My clinic—but more important the lives of my family and my staff—are at risk. I will identify him, if necessary. That should be sufficient."

Patel considered this silently. What she had told him was more than acceptable, and Aysha knew it.

"My lieutenant will have more questions. I will be leaving for Srinagar this afternoon."

"What will become of Nicholas Sunder?" she asked, without thinking of the ramifications of her question.

"I have not yet decided."

"I don't think he is capable of . . . murder."

"I have learned never to trust anything the Pakistanis say. In the face of everything, they still deny they support the insurrection, which is beyond absurd. Yet, the fact remains, he is a fugitive."

"When will you decide?"

Patel stood, walked to the door of his chamber, and opened it. "I've told you all you need to know."

CHAPTER 56

In an effort to divert his mind from worrying about Aysha, Nick volunteered to help Naseem cull the wheat field behind the Fahad home. It was a clear autumn morning, the sun showering the stalks of wheat as tall as Nick's chest. A cool breeze swept through the ripened ears, causing them to hiss and rattle. The two men swung their sickles rhythmically, the blades glinting in the sunlight, each cut releasing the sweet odor of the freshly cut grain. By midmorning, the burn of his fatigued muscles, coupled with the splendor of the harvest, infused Nick with an elation that only working the earth with one's hands can produce. He could get used to such work, Nick thought to himself.

The two men toiled until their bodies demanded rest, then sat on a berth overlooking the river valley, drinking sweet goat's milk tea Naseem had boiled over a kerosene camping stove. They breathed in the aura of the valley, the jagged mountains, and the cloudless sky. The distant roar of the river in the valley below was serene, the smell of the wheat chaff pleasing, but still Nick was distracted with melancholy. It seemed to him that all the elements of nature portended one thing—the end. The end of the growing season and the warmth of the sun, and at that moment, the end of his time in Gilkamosh.

"You go home 'Amrika' soon?" Naseem inquired of Nick, as if reading his thoughts.

"I don't think I want to."

"Ahhh, you like my country?"

Nick nodded. "Yes."

Naseem held out his palms wide, as if trying to encapsulate the entire valley in them, before giving a thumbs-up sign, something he no doubt had learned from English tourists over the years.

"Yes, it's very beautiful," Nick agreed, responding to Naseem's unspoken comment.

"Aysha better," Naseem remarked.

"Maybe a little," Nick replied, feeling inwardly guilty that Naseem was entirely unaware that his daughter, at that very moment, was placing herself in a position of dire jeopardy. "She is very worried about her brothers."

"Yes," he observed somberly. "But I think she better. You good friend for her. *Shukria.*"

"I didn't do anything," Nick said.

"Yes. You do very much." Naseem pointed at Nick, then back at himself. "Me . . . you . . . *Dost.*"

"Yes, Naseem. Friends." When he looked at him, the sincerity of Naseem's eyes dispelled any awkwardness the moment might have engendered, and there was a brief understanding between them, a moment of silence that spoke volumes, before the two men resumed drinking their tea in silence.

Later, Aysha arrived unharmed. They bade farewell to Naseem, and without exchanging a word, started the drive back to the clinic. Her expression was dour but resigned, and Nick could tell that whatever had happened at the meeting, Aysha did not want to talk about it. He waited until they cleared the outskirts of town before he finally asked.

"Is Patel going to let your brothers go?"

"I do not know."

Nick was addled. "You mean he turned away information?"

"No. I told him," she said abruptly.

Nick was incredulous. "But why, Aysha? You were supposed to wait until they were released. Now you've lost your leverage."

"Yes. I did! *All* of it!"

There was a long span of silence, in which Nick grappled for the possible reasons for her grave misstep, before she spoke again.

"Exactly what kind of life did you lead before you came to my clinic, Nick?"

Her tone was insinuating, but its anger was deflated by an underlying sense of profound disappointment. She had the right to question him, Nick thought. And although he had always believed that lying in response to some questions was a necessary part of living, Aysha was one person to whom he wished he did not feel the need to be untruthful.

"Restless," he replied. "Like I wanted everything and nothing at the same time, and envied everyone who had something I didn't, without knowing why. . . . But since I've been here, all the wanting, it's not so important anymore. I can't put my finger on it. Ghulam told me a while ago I've been given some kind of gift. Maybe he's right."

"A gift," she muttered, shaking her head in disbelief.

Nick looked at her. A sadness overcame him. Each time that he felt as if he were drifting close enough to touch her, he seemed destined to push her away. "Do you believe people can change, Aysha? I mean *really* change?"

Aysha did not reply, her eyes fixed on the valley floor ahead of them.

"I'm beginning to think, at some point, we all make decisions, do things, that change the course of our lives forever," Nick said, "whether we're proud of what we've done or not. People talk about the power to forgive others—but the power to forgive oneself, it seems to me, is the key to surviving. Because if we can't forgive ourselves, how can we expect others to do it? How can we ever change?"

Aysha shook her head, peering at Nick impassively. But behind her inscrutable eyes, she understood, at least partly, his meaning. For her adult life in its entirety had been inexorably molded by her decision that one day in the rain, along the riverbank with Kazim. Undeterred by her silence, Nick continued, letting his thoughts roll off his tongue.

"But clearly there are things that are *un*forgivable. Like the massacre of the pilgrims. What do you do in that circumstance, if you are responsible for something like that? Some say you should never forget the unforgivable, so that terrible things won't repeat themselves. That, I guess, is the essence of repentance—atoning for the past. But Ghulam also said that forgetting—completely, utterly—is the *only* way for people to really change. Otherwise, we are destined to keep reliving our mistakes."

Aysha angled her head reflectively—something Nick said in his rant having set her mind adrift. "*Kazim* changed," she said. "He must have. How else could a boy who had such a pure heart, who I thought could do only good, turn out to do so much bad?"

"Are people nothing more than the sum of their deeds? . . . Maybe some of the boy still survives inside him."

Aysha shrugged. "I used to think people were good or bad, right or wrong, in their essence," she added. "I still *want* to believe that. But I know now that is not true. There is a sharp and blunt edge to every sword. But it does not *matter* whether there is goodness or badness in people apart from what they have done. In the end, we *are* judged only by our deeds."

Aysha paused, looking Nick in the eyes. "To me, lying—deception—

I cannot forgive. Kazim, I truly believe, never lied to me. Even when the truth was painful to tell."

Nick fell silent, realizing that her words were a condemnation of him. He averted his eyes, fixing them on the road as he drove.

"Perhaps yours is a problem with truth," she continued, "and not with forgiveness."

There was a long pause. Nick turned to her. "What happened back there, Aysha?"

"You *betrayed* me—that's what happened."

Nick slammed on the brakes. In a cloud of dust, the truck skidded to a violent stop.

"What are you doing?" Aysha blurted out in a panic.

Nick grabbed both her forearms firmly in his hands. "Tell me what he said."

"Don't touch me!" She tried to pull away, to run from the truck, but Nick held her fast. Fear flashed in Aysha's eyes. Nick was ridden by guilt for inflicting it, but at the same time he felt compelled to do so.

"Tell me!" Nick insisted, shaking her arms forcefully.

"Let go of me, damn you! You already know!"

Nick stopped. She was right. He *did* know.

"And you're lying to me again by pretending you do not."

He let go of her wrists. Pressing his palms against his temples, he clenched his eyes shut, shouldering the immensity of his lies. "I wanted to tell you, Aysha. I really did, but . . ."

"But you did not."

"You wouldn't have given me a chance if I had."

"So instead you lied," she said calmly. "And used me and the clinic as your hideout, putting all of my people at risk."

"It was supposed to be for only a few weeks. But then things changed. I was . . . drawn in. By what you were doing. By *you*."

Nick looked at her, desperate for some indication she believed in him. But her eyes were fixed on the mountains.

"They are going to arrest you, Nick," she said without turning.

He pondered silently. Then, "What do you think they will do to your brothers? And to you?"

"I don't know what will become of Khaliq and Nabir. And me? They threatened to jail me for harboring a fugitive. But I don't think they will, unless I start making noise again."

"You didn't *know* about me, Aysha. They can't hold you on a fugitive charge."

She scoffed. "They've got plenty to hold against me."

They sat in silence, their heads hung low. Nick was consumed by an overwhelming sense of hopelessness. It seemed clear to him now that he could *never* forge ahead. Every time he tried to, *she* caught up to him, dragging him back into the icy water of the sinkhole from which he only thought he had escaped, down under the glacier where the ancient ice did not give rise to new beginnings, but merely preserved the past. He had tried to do what Ghulam had told him—write the future across a blank slate—but every new chapter lead him back to what was written before. *Yvette.*

"You must go, Nick," Aysha said finally.

"No. If I run now, they'll think you tipped me off."

"I *did* tip you off. But it won't make a difference. They've got me where they want me, regardless."

"I'll turn myself in. I'll tell them you didn't know anything," he said decidedly.

"They won't believe you. Just forget it. Forget everything—the clinic, this war, everything. What is the matter with you, for God's sake? Go back home to America, where it is safe! There's nothing here for you but ruin—or death!"

"I don't want to."

"Do it!"

"You don't understand, Aysha. I love you."

She fell silent, plunging her head into her hands. When she finally looked up, Nick caught a glint of green from her eyes. Her lower lip trembled once, as though Nick had heaped on yet another injustice. Then she turned toward the sun, now descending behind the jagged mountains, stone sentries that had failed her in the end.

"Whatever you think might have passed between us in the wood behind Rasheed's hut that day . . . it didn't. You are leaving here tomorrow. Or I will request the security forces to come and take you away."

CHAPTER 57

That night Nick told the staff he would be leaving in the morning. "It's time," was all Nick offered by way of explanation.

The others had expected all along that Nick would eventually leave. Nevertheless, in the aftermath of the massacre they had become as close as a family, and upon Nick's announcement, a pall descended over the group.

"So soon?" said Omar, wondering why Nick had not said anything before.

"I'm sorry for not telling you in advance. I just made the decision myself," Nick said evasively.

"When are you coming back? A few weeks?" said Aroon, obviously not grasping the vast distance separating Kashmir and America.

Vilashni broke down in tears, her sorrow only exacerbated when Ghulam decided to leave at the same time as well. Ghulam had brightened Vilashni's life the past few months, and he had become part of their circle. But he had been away from his family too long. And with Nick's announced departure, Nick's friendship was no longer an incentive to stay.

Ghulam offered to accompany Nick as far as his village, Kurgan, which was on the way to Leh, where Nick had decided to go. Nick figured Leh would be his best option. It was heavily visited by Westerners and generally untouched by the violence. He calculated he could bide his time there in comparative anonymity while he figured out what to do next— something he had not worked out despite his nearly two-year stay at Aysha's clinic. Things had gained their own momentum and time had passed quickly. He had been swept up not only in his work and his feelings for Aysha, but the whole village, its tranquility and its plight. The security forces' discovery of his past made him painfully aware that his time in Gilkamosh had been in essence a diversion. In the end, he had only succeeded in delaying the inevitable.

*   *   *

That night, Nick packed his things in a canvas backpack Omar had given him as a going-away gift, stuffing the main compartment with a sweater and provisions prepared by Vilashni—a dozen loaves of naan, some curried vegetables, dried apricots, and cashew nuts—slipping in some of Aroon's hand-rolled bidis to smoke on the journey. He still had no identification whatsoever—no official proof that he and Nicholas Sunder were one and the same—having lost it all during his ordeal in Pakistan. Now, however, for some reason he could not define, this no longer made him feel quite so insecure.

Nonetheless, packing dredged up dreadful memories: the knock on his hotel-room door, the two Pakistani policemen barging into the room, interrogation and torture, and most painful of all, Yvette's perfect, blue-lipped corpse. He shuddered, her death still vivid in his mind. He remembered the times, soon after his arrival in Gilkamosh, when he would stand on the cliffs overlooking the clinic and think about ending his life. Now that he was leaving, he feared that the burden of Yvette's death would once again push him to the brink.

Omar offered to drive Nick and Ghulam in the morning to the turnoff between Gilkamosh and Kargil, about four hours' drive on the jeep road. From there, it was a full day-and-a-half walk to Kargil, or a much faster drive if Nick could find a jeep to hitch a ride on. Once in Kargil, Nick could easily hitch or walk along the Indus River in the direction of Leh. Before he arrived in Kargil, Ghulam would leave Nick for remote Kurgan, which was only accessible by footpath.

As Nick prepared for his departure, Aysha shut herself in her office, choosing not to come out while he was present in the ward. Nick did not know what more he might have said to her. Nonetheless, he longed to see her one last time, perhaps hoping to detect some indication, some glimmer of a possibility that she harbored genuine feelings for him. Could not her sudden denial that anything meaningful had happened that day in the forest behind Rasheed's hut—after having refused for so long to acknowledge the incident at all—be an implicit admission that some real emotion indeed had transpired? Or perhaps he was delusional, he thought, and this was his real torment.

*   *   *

The following morning, when it was time to leave, Nick was granted his wish. No word crossed either of their lips. But it gave him one last vision to file away forever, something he could use to reflect on, a sign of what could have been had he chosen a different way. Regret, he felt, was better company than uncertainty.

She appeared at the doorway to the ward as Nick carried his bag to the truck. Her eyes the color of jade, silken hair flowing down her nape, she wore a woolen sweater pulled tightly over a man's *shalwar*. As she leaned against the doorframe, her slender body angled toward him. Nick could tell from even that distance that she was saddened. He wanted to go to her, and without thinking, he started to. But with a subtle lift of her palm, she stopped him in his tracks. Then, turning her head ever so slightly, she sent him away.

Minutes later Omar steered the truck along the bumpy road to Gilkamosh. Nick sat behind Ghulam in the passenger seat, staring at the clinic receding behind him. He felt a dreadful sinking in his chest, as though he were leaving the one place for which he had longed his whole life, but only now knew it. And that place was not just Gilkamosh or the person he felt he could become there. It was Aysha.

As the truck spun around the first hairpin turn up the mountain, kicking up a cloud of dust that blotted out his vision of the clinic, his mind recalled the last time he had felt such a profound sense of loss. The time from which he was running still.

The man who had called himself "Prince" had just pulled up in front of the Rose Hotel in Peshawar in a faded green 1976 Fiat driven by a youth named Babar, a teenager with straight, dark hair that flopped over his equally dark brow and round, boyish face.

Yvette had told Prince that Simon, who had arranged the trip, was sick with a stomach complaint. After politely expressing his regrets, Prince had seemed not to care, so long as he was taking some paying customer. So Nick and Yvette had climbed in, and they drove through the urban sprawl of Peshawar in the direction of Afghanistan.

Yvette sat in the backseat with her knees pulled up to her chest, staring out the window. Her eyes were hidden behind modish sunglasses. She wore a bright red scarf, which failed to cover the unruly blond strands that jutted out from underneath. Opposite her Nick stewed in silent agitation over his discovery that Yvette had spent the night in Simon's hotel room. His mind raced with angry questions he needed her to answer, but which pride repressed him from asking. Maybe he should have stayed in Peshawar, he thought, as she had insisted he do. But he felt an irrepressible compulsion to go, and not just because he did not trust Prince alone with her.

Perhaps Prince had detected the tension between his two guests, because after a good twenty minutes, he abandoned his efforts at cordial conversation. Pulling a wooden block flute from under his *kamiz*, he began piping out notes to fill the awkward silence. The sound of the instrument was shrill and grating.

"I am musician, you know?" he stated proudly. "You like?"

"Very nice," Nick replied, trying to disguise his irritation with the flute, as well as Babar's erratic driving. The youth kept stealing glances at Yvette in the rearview mirror, and more than once he narrowly avoided hitting random goats and wobbly mopeds overloaded with multiple passengers.

They finally steered off the Grand Trunk Highway. When they reached the checkpoint of the Tribal Areas, a Kalashnikov-bearing tribesman in a dark green *shalwar kamiz*—the uniform of the Frontier Guard—strode up to the car. Prince rolled down the smudged glass. In convivial Pashto, the two men greeted each other as old friends. The guard peered at Nick and Yvette sitting in the backseat.

"What country?" he asked.

"They are from Canada," Prince answered before they could respond, handing the guard a folded newspaper. The guard casually looked inside the folds, then peered into the backseat, his eyes shifting between Yvette and Nick.

"Canada okay," he said, giving Nick and Yvette a thumbs-up before waving them past the guard post.

When they were a safe distance away, Prince turned. "From here on, better you are Canadian. Understand?"

"They hate us that much?" Nick asked nonchalantly, not really expecting or wanting an answer.

"America dropped bombs not far from here. Women, children die. It is better not to risk it."

"There is only one American in this car," Yvette retorted.

"Yes, madam. But if anyone asks, please, you are *both* from Canada. Otherwise, they will suspect you are not married," he cautioned.

"We are not."

"Yes. But where we are going, a single woman in the bazaar, one so beautiful . . . they will not understand. Better you pretend."

"Why does everyone have to tell me what to do!" she snapped, her tiny nostrils flaring. "I am so sick of it."

Prince's face turned grim. He twisted in his seat to face her, forcing a smile to hide the insult. "As you wish, madam."

Nick poked Yvette's thigh, admonishing her with a steely glance.

"That goes for you, Nicholas," she rebuked. "I told you not to come."

Nick was about to lash back, but thinking it best not to provoke her into an even bigger outburst, he bit his tongue.

The road passed by desiccated fields and occasional flat-roofed dwellings of mud brick, then meandered through miles of rocky hills, some of them crowned with fortified block-walled redoubts. After nearly two hours of driving, they finally pulled into a gravelly parking lot. They stepped out of the Fiat, leaving Babar with the car. "Better the boy stay," Prince explained, "or we might lose petrol and tires."

Prince led them down a long row of prefab stalls displaying an array of smuggled electronic goods—TVs, radios, computers. Chinese and Indian pop music blared from multiple speakers, the many strains of music melding into a screeching noise. Long wooden tables were stacked with cartons of smuggled Marlboros and Dunhills. They passed through an automotive section, where tires, wheels, and random motor parts were splayed out on the ground, haggling men foraging through them. There was even a whole Mercedes-Benz for sale—a C Class, top-of-the-line black sedan with tinted windows.

At the end of the row of covered stalls, they came to a cinder-block wall. A small corrugated aluminum gate, not large enough for vehicles, led to a narrow walkway. Standing in front of the gate was a turbaned guard armed with an automatic pistol. Recognizing Prince, he greeted them in Pashto and stepped aside.

After a short walk down the alley, Nick gathered from the goods on sale they had reached the innermost section of the bazaar. Here, the shops were stocked with weapons, many of them carbon copies made in the makeshift gun factories of Darra and other tribal villages. Still others appeared to be brand-new—AK-47s and rocket-propelled grenade launchers, displayed in their factory crates labeled with Chinese and Russian writing.

After passing through the gun markets, they could smell the hashish before they saw it—the sweet, earthy aroma permeating the air. Bricks of deep green were stacked high on long wooden tables, along with sacks filled with dark opium resin. No effort at all was made to hide the stock.

As they browsed wide-eyed through the drug bazaar, tribesmen and young boys turned their heads, fixing their eyes on Yvette. Several of them stood, calling their friends over, until a whole crowd followed behind her. After over a month in Pakistan, Nick had thought he had gotten used to men ogling her. But this felt different—as though he had carried a wounded rabbit into a hyena's den. When he looked over his shoulder, they backed off. But as soon as he turned back around, he could sense them stalking closely behind. Had any one of them jeered, whistled, or made some other ribald sound, he might not have been so rankled. But their silence, their calculated leering, unnerved him most of all.

"Let's do this quick and get of here," said Nick. "These guys act like they've never seen a woman before."

"What do I care if they are staring at me?" Yvette scoffed. "The problem is yours—not mine."

Prince, who had said nothing of the crowd, turned into one of the hashish shops—a tin-roofed stall open to the walkway. A few of the crowd tried to shuffle in behind them, but the shopkeeper barked at them in Pashto and they stopped just outside, where they continued their gawking from afar. Inside, behind a bench stacked with bars of hashish, sat a grinning boy in a white skullcap, a tinge of fuzz ringing his chin. He was handsome, with jet-black hair, striking blue eyes, and a pleasing thinness about his face. The boy's face lit up at the sight of Yvette. Foreigners were a rarity, but like the tribesmen watching outside, he had never seen anyone like Yvette, with her waiflike thinness and exotic blond hair.

Smiling, the boy took the shopkeeper's cue and loaded a pebble-sized chunk of hashish into a wooden pipe. He handed the pipe to Prince, who held it out for Yvette. "This will be good for Mr. Simon's stomach, madam," said Prince.

Yvette took the pipe in both hands, encircling it with her lips. The boy produced a long wooden matchstick, struck it on the table, and lit the bowl. She sucked deeply, her pupils contracting slightly as she held the smoke deep in her lungs. When she exhaled, a rich white plume curled from her nose and mouth.

"Good?" Prince asked. Yvette nodded, then without asking, took another match from a brass cup on the table. She lit the pipe again.

"Slowly, madam," Prince warned. When she finished, Prince took the pipe from her, filling it with a fresh piece. He handed it to Nick. "Sir?"

Nick hesitated. He felt vulnerable, too paranoid to smoke it in the open, with so many onlookers packed in the walkway. But not wanting to be rude, he accepted. The hashish was smooth and he felt no urge to cough. It took only a few moments for the details around him to vivify almost surrealistically—the expressions of the staring men, the sounds of their murmuring, even his own suspiration. His head started to spin, and he felt as though his lungs were not taking their fill. He grabbed the table for balance.

When everything was still again, Prince and the boy were peering at him with amused expressions. "What do you think, sir?" Prince asked.

"Think?" Nick replied. "Yeah . . . it's good."

Prince and the boy smirked knowingly. "How much you want?" Prince asked.

"A little of this will go a long way. I'd say an ounce—or twenty-eight grams—will be plenty." Nick glanced at Yvette to see if she would object. "How much is it?" he asked, as an afterthought.

Prince talked to the boy briefly in Pashto, until an accord was reached. "Eighty-five American dollars."

"Okay," Nick replied, laughing inwardly at the dirt-cheap price.

Prince winked at the boy, who measured a chunk with his fingers and then sawed it off with a long bone-handled knife. He weighed the piece on an antique metal balance, added a couple of smaller fragments to get the amount just right, then wrapped it all in newspaper. Nick dug into his money belt, handing the boy a wad of bills, soggy from the sweat that had seeped through his pants. As soon as he paid, Yvette chimed in.

"Tell them I want to see the heroin," she said to Prince.

"Excuse me, madam?"

"Heroin. I want to buy some heroin." Her tone was almost argumentative.

Prince paused a moment. "Of course, madam."

"Yvette," Nick interjected, still feeling wobbly from the potent hashish.

"Stay out of it." Yvette scowled.

Prince's eyes darted between them. "Madam," he said. "Perhaps sir is correct. Maybe it is not a good idea." His tone was too obsequious to be sincere.

"To hell with you both!" Her face turned red with frustration. "I'm not leaving until I get what I came for."

Prince's eyes darted anxiously toward the crowd. "Please, madam. These words, they are not good." He turned to Nick.

Nick stared at Yvette, perplexed. "Since when do you shoot smack?"

"Just shut up, Nicholas! What do you know about me? I need to do it, okay?"

Nick shook his head in disgust. "Oh, I see. First you fuck him, now this? . . . You know what? Go ahead. Be his junkie whore if you want. But I'm not paying for it."

The thin muscles at Yvette's temples rippled with tension. Perhaps the drug delayed her response. But when she finally replied, her voice was penetrating.

"You selfish asshole! Does everything have to be about you? I don't need your goddamn money!"

Nick snatched her by the elbow. He hauled her out of the stall, parting the murmuring crowd of onlookers. Startled by his forcefulness, Yvette huffed and writhed, her eyes seething. "Let me go!" she cried.

Out in the alleyway, the glow of the sun, diffused by the dust kicked up in their struggle, cast the figures of the tribesmen in a russet haze. There, in front of the turbaned shadows huddled around them, she came at him, pounding him with fists and feet. "Get away from me!"

Not until Nick finally caught hold of her wrists did he notice the crowd was shuffling to encircle them. On their faces was an expression of outrage mingled with lust.

"Yvette!" said Nick in a hushed tone. He pulled her body firmly into his chest, his eyes fixed on the agitated mob.

She bit him. Startled, Nick cried out. She jarred herself free. "I said don't touch me!" she snapped, backing away.

Nick rushed toward her. She backpedaled again.

"Yes, I fucked Simon last night!" she cried. "Okay?"

Nick froze in his tracks, stunned, as if her words alone were proof of his worthlessness. He saw her then, for the first time, unattainable even in her squalor.

"Now . . . leave me alone and let me do this thing."

The movement of the tribesmen around them pulled Nick's eyes away from her. He turned. The throng, now grown to the size of a mob, had closed in, so close he could smell the stench of their breaths. He searched the dark, angry faces glowering from behind their thorny beards and disheveled turbans. He heard a faint thud, like someone beating a carpet, followed by a truncated gasp.

When Nick looked back at Yvette, she was staring at a greasy smudge on her breast. At her foot, a fat glob of shit. "What . . . who . . . ?" she stuttered, fumbling for words. "You . . . you *pigs!*"

Another piece of dung hit her, sticking fast to her blond tousle of hair. She spun around, sweeping it off with disgust.

"What the hell?" Nick scanned the crowd for some evidence of who had thrown it. The tribesmen peered back at him. Not one of them laughed or even chuckled.

Just then, a voice sounded from behind him. "Beat her," it said, almost pleadingly. Confused, Nick turned. It was Prince.

In that instant, a cry of rage pierced the silence. Scowling with hatred, Yvette charged one of the tribesmen clutching something in his hand. She slapped and clawed at him, but a wall of men shoved her backward onto her buttocks. Another object flew at her, hitting her in the back. "*Merde!*" she cried, this time painfully.

Nick searched the ground and saw that it was a stone. "Hey!" he hollered. His fists clenched, he ran toward its source. But the voice of Prince stopped him again.

"No, no, sir, don't do it!" he beseeched. "Please. You *must* beat her! It's the only way to restore their honor."

Nick looked at Prince, then toward Yvette, where she knelt now, her hair smeared with manure, her breasts heaving anxiously against the tight fabric of her T-shirt.

"Do it now! To claim her, you must beat her!"

Nick's eyes searched for hers. Though he looked into them, he did not see her. Instead, he saw only a fleeting glimpse of himself, juxtaposed against the reddish mist reflected in her pupils. As he stood, transfixed by the eyes of the aggrieved, the narcotic trance in which he had immersed himself did nothing to ease the choice of a man suspended at the collision of conflicting worlds.

Moments later, as he made his way through the onslaught of rushing tribesmen, he knew he could no longer belong to either.

CHAPTER 58

He could feel his blood pulse through the back of his head and up through his temples. His legs, burning with fatigue, pushed against the loose scree, sending slides of rocks down below him as he climbed. Every few steps he would slip, his bloodied hands thrusting palm-first into the rocks. But still he continued, clambering hand over foot toward the top of the ridge, his Kalashnikov swinging on its sling behind him.

When he reached the crest, his lungs heaving in the thin mountain air, he fell to his knees in exhaustion. Struggling to catch his breath, he lifted his hand to his forehead, shielding his eyes from the blinding sun. He scanned the valley below. "They must be down there," he thought.

At dawn he had been only a couple of hours behind them, judging by the smoldering embers they had left in the *bahik*. They had been sloppy. He would have never left a campsite like that, so easy for patrols to read. But their stupidity was his blessing. For now he was on their trail, and with his speed, it should only be a matter of hours before he caught up with them.

He had been trailing them for days, even while they thought they were hunting *him*. After the murder of Advani, he had searched all the places they should have been, hoping to intercept them before they got to this valley—where he knew they would end up. But he had caught their trail late. Now he was desperate and exhausted. And ever since he had endured his initial brush with death almost ten years ago, he had never been more afraid.

There! One . . . two . . . three of them, walking briskly in single file, like marching ants in the valley below. He looked to the sun behind him, then back at the men, then to his watch.

They were still more than an hour ahead, even if he had the strength to continue to run double time. Too far. *Allah give me wings!* he prayed to himself in silence.

CHAPTER 59

"Mr. Nick, why do you leave Madam Doctor?" said Ghulam, trying one last time to make Nick change his mind. "There is still time to go back. You two are fitting very good together."

"I don't think she'd agree, Ghulam," Nick replied, as the truck bounced along the road, away from the clinic.

Ghulam scratched his head. "Ghulam does not understand. Mr. Nick, you are good man. When I first met you in desert—I think not so good. But now—good," he said, thrusting his lower lip with certitude.

Nick couldn't help smiling, despite his sorrow. "You may be the only one who thinks so, so I guess I better take it. Thank you, Ghulam."

"Ghulam does not think. Ghulam knows."

Omar veered the truck up the steep switchbacks, climbing the pass toward the Gilkamosh Valley. A falcon darted and shrieked, greeting the tired autumn sun as it labored to rise above the icy peaks. Two months ago the sun had been potent, incubating the dirt until golden fields sprouted from it, only to be reaped by the same sun-browned arms that had sown the seeds months before. But now, the sun lacked the strength to dispel the cold breath of winter that chilled their bones as they hunkered under woolen blankets. The earth had shed its greenery and turned to a mottled brown. The season for war would soon be reprieved by winter, when God, as if ashamed by His own creation, would cast down veils of snow to bury the fresh headstones of the latest casualties of His greatest folly—man.

Nick looked at Ghulam, his friend who had trusted him consistently over the past year and a half, a trust that Nick did not deserve and thus had taken as blind, but which he now knew was by design. He was still the same monklike Ghulam, childlike but wise, peaceful yet ever thirsting for life. Nick had come to hold in great reverence his quick, far-seeing eyes, ever moving, watching out for all the wonders about him. He was a man who had an inexplicable ability to see things for what they were—not as they appeared through the contorting prism of perception, deliberation, and mutating thoughts. Devout, yet blessed with the lightheartedness of a man at peace with his fate, Ghulam was infinitely contented, even while struggling to survive in a land as filled with hardship and pain as it was beautiful.

Watching the valley recede below, Nick's eyes settled on the now tiny clinic, the place that housed the soul he had come to love, until it vanished behind the proud uprights of tall poplars and pines that aspired to breach the impossibly blue sky.

The long spiral of smoke barely moved in the still morning air, like a static twister rising above the grove of trees where the clinic was situated. Had it risen from the earth one second later, the truck would have reached the crest and begun to descend, blinding them to the calamity unfurling below.

"Stop!" Nick pointed to the rising smoke from the top of the ridge.

Omar looked over his shoulder from behind the wheel, nearly missing a turn and careening off the road.

"Stop the truck, Omar!" Nick commanded again. They skidded to a halt at the very top of the ascent.

Nick looked at Omar, and he at Nick, then they both turned to Ghulam. Without a word, Omar wheeled a five-point turn, nearly burning through the clutch, before they descended recklessly back toward the clinic.

During the entire ten minutes it took to race back down the mountain, Nick was so fixated on the ominous pillar of smoke, he was oblivious to the truck's catapulting over potholes and boulders, swerving dangerously close to the edge of the cliff. The smoke thickened as they neared the clinic, throwing black soot high into the air.

They reached the base of the mountain, speeding across the flat, forested valley floor. The smell of burned fuel permeated the air. When they pulled through the last stand of pines, they saw the ward. Orange tongues of fire, roaring like a blast furnace, leaped up from the base of the walls and lashed at the roof. The sky was black.

Nick spotted two men wearing ski masks with Kalashnikovs strapped across their backs dousing the office and supply room to the left of the ward with gasoline they poured from jerry cans. A third man poured gas onto a rag, lit it, and then threw the burning cloth onto the wood-planked roof, igniting a conflagration that spread like wildfire.

Omar braked to an abrupt stop. Ghulam and Nick leaped out of the truck, unthinking of the ramifications from either the fire or the arsonists. The attackers had circled to the back of the building. Perhaps they had spooked them, or they did not detect the truck's arrival—the roaring flames drowning out all sound as Nick and Ghulam ran toward the burning structure, obscured by smoke. They could not see a single worker or patient anywhere.

Not until Nick ran up to the double doors to the ward did he realize the reason for the absence of people. The metal doors had been locked shut by a steel crowbar jammed through the handles. The ward lacked windows. The arsonists' intention was clear—to incinerate everyone inside.

Nick grabbed the bar, only to leap back in pain when the superhot metal scorched his hands. Unable to touch it, he kicked at the bar with his boot-covered foot. Suddenly, Ghulam was beside him, kicking at it, too, but the handles were too high for either of them to strike a square blow with their feet. It would not dislodge. Muffled cries for help emanated from inside. The door shuddered from the futile pounding of those trapped within.

All Nick could think of was Aysha. With bare hands, he grasped for the white-hot steel and held it fast, pulling at it with all his strength, undeterred by the intense pain that shot through his arms like voltage. The bar slid from its mooring.

Nick dropped the hot metal in agony and fell down in the dirt beside it. His hands were seared through to the muscle. He smelled of burnt flesh.

The doors burst open. People flooded out, stumbling over one another, choking on the thick, noxious smoke that billowed through the entryway. When the stampede cleared, Nick rose to his feet. Without pausing to consider his blistered hands, he bolted into the thick smoke, Ghulam and Omar at his heels.

The interior was a hell of heat and flames. Fire had ripped through the roof and walls. Smoke stung Nick's eyes, blinding him so that he was forced to home in on the sounds of choking people to locate the patients unable to escape on their own. With them, he knew that he would find her.

"Aysha!" he cried above the din of combustion.

"Here . . . !"

Nick stopped at the sound of her voice, peering into the thick smoke around him.

"Help me with these patients!"

Nick turned to where he had heard the voice and ran through a maelstrom of careening roof timbers and igniting bedsheets. He nearly collided with her as she and Vilashni stood next to each other. Bent at the waist, they struggled to lift an amputee, but the man was too heavy. Nick grabbed the man under his arms, dragging his full weight. "Get out!" he hollered. "The roof's going to cave!"

"No, there're more!" Aysha insisted. She moved deeper into the flames.

Nick heaved the unconscious patient across the ward, the intravenous line still attached to the man's arm dragging across the ashbedecked floor. He passed by Ghulam and Omar. "Aysha and Vilashni are inside!" Nick yelled. "Go!" As Nick hauled the man toward the door, chunks of burning roof started to fall, pelting Nick and his human freight, the smoke getting thicker by the second.

Finally, Nick made it outside. Aroon helped him carry the patient a safe distance from the burning hulk. Nick went right back into the inferno, passing Omar dragging an unconscious Hindu woman by her feet. Then came Aysha and Vilashni, towing another patient, just as a huge beam from the roof crashed down, sending a plume of sparks through the air. Aysha stopped. "Ghulam!"

The ward was now a furnace, fire raging from all four walls, tearing through the roof. "Ghulam's still inside!" Aysha cried as she and Vilashni labored to pull the man to safety. "He's got the last patient!" Nick ran through the flames, shielding his head with his forearms. He clambered over flaming debris and between burning gurneys to where he thought the last patient would be.

He found Ghulam struggling in vain to move the man, who had been ignited by a falling chunk of roof. The patient's hair, clothes, even his skin was on fire. Nick snatched one of the man's legs from Ghulam. They heaved, both of them crying out in pain as they dragged the man through a wall of flames.

When they passed through what was left of the doorframe, Ghulam and Nick were both on fire. They fell to the ground, rolling in the dirt, trying to squelch the flames from their clothes. Nick could not even open his eyes for fear of having them burned. It was not until a splash of cool liquid had doused him, followed by another, then another, that he opened them to find Aroon, Omar, and the others clutching empty buckets.

Immediately, he looked around for Aysha. He spotted her huddled over the burn victim he and Ghulam had pulled out of the fire. The man's clothes had been scorched off his body, his reddened skin blistered. "Your shirt!" Aysha said to Omar. Omar took off his *kamiz*, dunked it in a bucket of water, and handed it to her. She began wrapping the patient's body with the wet garment.

Relieved to see Aysha alive and unscathed, Nick lay back on the ground, fighting for breath. Ghulam lay prone to Nick's right, staring in bewilderment at the burning clinic, shaken but not badly burned. Dazed patients were scattered about the grounds, bleary-eyed, suffering from burns and smoke inhalation.

Suddenly, a large boom reverberated over the valley. The hospital imploded in a furious ball of fire, its roof and walls falling in on themselves in a tornado of embers and sparks.

Nick and the others were so preoccupied by the destruction, they did not see the three men in the black ski masks approach until they were upon them.

The two on either flank trained their Kalashnikovs on the group, ready to cut down the lot. The man in the middle, the shorter one, stood with his arms by his sides, his gun slung across his back. His hands were gloved, fists clenched, as if holding something. He moved toward the middle of the group, where Aysha knelt on the ground with her back toward them, bandaging the burned man with the torn strips of Omar's wet shirt. The men had come so quickly, and everyone was so overwhelmed, no one even thought to cry out in warning. The patients and staff were unarmed, and unable to defend themselves in any event. The three intruders were either going to kill them or not. Death had lost all novelty; they were tired of running from it.

The man walked right up behind Aysha as she continued working. He paused for a suspended moment, as if perplexed by the group's failure to react to him.

"Whore!" Nick heard the man say under his breath. He snatched a handful of Aysha's long mane and wrenched her neck back so violently that her body toppled, her feet thrusting forward from under her. The man's free arm passed over her face and neck, once, twice, three times, as if he were a priest anointing her with holy water. It happened so quickly she was too startled to scream. There was no fire, just smoke steaming fiercely from her skin, and an acrid aroma. When the scream finally did come, Nick was unconvinced it was she. Someone as beautiful as Aysha could not have made such a sound, so purely animal. She had no right, Nick thought, to scream that way.

But it *was* she.

Nick saw something gleam in the man's gloved hand. And the next thing he knew he was on top of him, pounding with his burned hands so numbed with pain he could not feel the bones and teeth crushing under the mask. Then there was a hard jolt on the back of his head. He fell into the dirt, his face rolling toward the sky. He heard the flurry of gunshots and the cries of men.

CHAPTER 60

Kazim spotted the smoke from midway down the ridge. He fell to his knees in despair. He was still a good fifteen minutes from the hospital, and judging from the thickness of the smoke, he was too late.

He pushed himself to his feet with the butt of his rifle and scrambled down the ridge. He reached the basin of the valley at a full run, hanging on to a prayer that perhaps for some reason, by some stroke of fortune, she was not inside. Maybe she was staying in the village with her parents? Or she was out walking alone along the river valley as she often liked to do in her youth?

Using every last bit of his energy, he dashed through the trees, leaping over rocks and splashing through streams, across the valley toward the column of smoke rising almost perfectly straight into the air, unwavering, like an arrow shot from the hell of earth.

When he finally reached the edge of the clearing where the compound stood, he stopped. Huge tongues of fire burst through the roof of the clinic, the roar of combustion echoing in his ears. He clutched his head in dismay. No person could survive that.

But then, a spark of hope—a cluster of people, faces blackened with soot, lying on a patch of earth away from the roiling inferno. Racing with anticipation, he ran toward them, his head hunched low under cover of the tree line.

When he was just a few hundred yards away from the survivors, he saw her. "*Allah-o-Akbar!*" Kazim uttered aloud, praising God for sparing her. *She is alive!*

She knelt over a man, his body burned red and black, wrapping his scorched flesh in pieces of clothing she tore apart with her hands. Kazim watched her from the distance, elated.

But as quickly as jubilation had swept over him, the others, the ones he had been pursuing, emerged from the trees wearing masks. They approached rapidly, almost at a jog, guns at the ready. The suvivors seemed not even to notice. Kazim took off at a sprint.

As he ran, he saw one of the men, now nearly on top of Aysha, yank her backward by the hair. She screamed as he held her fast, her face to the sky. It was a chilling scream—*inhuman.*

Another man, the American whom he had brought to Aysha's clinic nearly two years ago, leaped up and tackled her assailant, beating him with fists of rage, until one of the gunmen smashed him on the head with the butt of his gun.

There was no time. Kazim fell down to his knees, bracing his rifle against them. He faltered, shaking, too breathless to hold steady. He inhaled deeply, holding his breath to keep still. He fired.

Stunned by the bullet, the gunman dropped his weapon. Raising his hands as if surrendering to the sky, he crumpled to the ground. The masked man on the right, the one who had struck the American, vanished behind the huddled backs of the others. His gun discharged wildly into the air as they tackled him, struggling to break free, and beat him until he was unconscious.

Kazim jumped to his feet and ran toward her. He could see her clawing at her face and head. Her cry was like none he had ever heard before during any of his battles, worse than the cries of the dying and the maimed, for it was coming from the only one he had ever loved.

When he finally came upon her, he pulled her hands from her face to get at the source of her agony, trying to snuff it out. But under her hands, behind the acrid smoke, there was burning and pain, but no fire. Her flesh was being eaten away by *nothing.* Confused, he tried to hold her still. But she writhed and clawed at her own face, trying to rip off the layers of blistering skin. When his own hands started to burn, too, he realized what it was.

"Water!" he yelled. "Somebody get water!"

It seemed forever before someone poured a bucket over her head. Kazim rubbed the water into her face and neck, the pungent stench of scorched flesh and chemicals watering his eyes. Others joined, too, dousing her face and scalp with cupped hands, each trying to save the beauty that had once belonged to Kazim—to all of them—now liquefying before their eyes.

When it was all over, and the acid had burned out, they wrapped Aysha's head in wet strips of someone's garment, while Kazim knelt, staring with empty eyes at clumps of burned hair he clutched in his hands, all that remained of her once-silken mane that had spellbound him as a youth. He wept. No one noticed. But that was what he did.

Afterward, he picked up his weapon and walked to Abdul, who was propped up on his elbows, dazed, holding his shattered jaw. Without a word, he shot his friend in the head. Then he walked off into the woods, watched by the others.

Minutes later, another shot rang out, solitary and distant.

EPILOGUE

A year and six months had passed since the day the clinic burned down, and Nicholas Sunder was still in Gilkamosh. He had no plans to leave. Even if he had wanted to, he had no place else to go.

Three weeks after the fire, one of Colonel Patel's lieutenants paid Nick a visit in the hospital in Leh, where Nick had been brought for treatment for severe concussion and burns. Nick was told "off the record" that India would pretend he had never walked across the Line of Control. Thus, "officially," Nick was not known to be in India at all; if Pakistan's or any other country's authorities ever asked, the Indian government would know nothing of any Nicholas Sunder. This did not preclude Nick from staying there, the lieutenant hinted in so many words. For it is possible for anyone to "disappear" among the millions who come and go across India's porous borders, or are born and die each year without the government's ever knowing they existed—the inevitable anonymity of a nation swarming with over a billion souls.

As for America, returning was not an option for Nick, at least for the foreseeable future. Soon after his release from the hospital, Nick made inquiries to the embassy through a lawyer in New Delhi. He was told that the United States would likely be inclined to extradite him to stand trial for the murder of Akhtar, if Pakistan requested it. Accordingly, a sympathetic embassy employee was kind enough to advise him, off the record, not to apply for a replacement passport. The less that was officially known about him, the better off he would be. Nick suspected the reason, though not expressed in so many words, had more to do with politics than "justice." The United States needed Pakistan in order to hunt the terrorists of its choosing within Pakistan's borders, and could ill afford to violate its extradition treaty with the nation America was calling its most crucial partner in its War on Terror. Nick's predicament, after all, came when Muslim South and Central Asia, so long ignored as insignificant backwaters, had become the origin of events that changed history, center stage in what some liked to call the "clash of civilizations" between the West and Islam. Understandably, there were interests to be served having clear precedence over those of one insignificant expatriate. It took a long, difficult time before Nick finally came to terms with the reality of his country's abandonment. But his life was in Gilkamosh now. And though the village could no longer lay claim to being Paradise on earth, it was *there* that he belonged.

For nearly two months, Nick was bedridden in the military hospital in Leh. Brief respite came in the form of visits from his friends—Ghulam, Omar, and Aroon—the latter two making the long journey together by combination of jeep, bus, and foot to visit him. But not Aysha. Although Nick longed to see her, he understood. A whole new array of emotions had entered into her repertoire—fear, lament, self-hatred.

When Nick's strength recovered enough for him to make the trip back to Gilkamosh, Naseem told him that Aysha had not left the house since the fire. She had become a hermit. "Please," Nick said. "I just want to speak with her. I don't care about anything else." But Aysha refused to talk to him, not even through the closed door of the bedroom in which she was spending almost all of her time.

Nick, however, was persistent. "Please tell her I'm coming again tomorrow," he asked Naseem, who could intuit the meaning of Nick's words from the determination in his voice. "I'm going to come every day until she agrees to see me. I don't care how long it takes."

And so, day after day Nick went to the Fahad home. Neither Naseem nor Fatima discouraged him, because they themselves were at a loss about what to do, and perhaps figured that permitting this persistent foreigner access to their daughter could not make her condition any worse. Each day, they would announce Nick's presence through the closed door, only to send him away with a grim look. Then, after several weeks, when everyone thought it was hopeless, Nick had finally worn her down. "She say, okay," said a surprised Naseem. "But . . . she not let even Fatima see her face," he warned Nick, as he let him into her room.

She sat cross-legged on the floor facing the window, covered from head to toe in a black burqa. The room was unlit except for a single cone of sunlight that reflected off her draped shoulders and head, making her appear like a wraith of the woman he once knew. As Nick entered, she did not turn to look at him.

"Aysha," Nick said, standing some distance behind her. She remained silent, completely inert. She could have been made of stone for all he knew. Then, when he stepped around to face her, she lowered her veiled head.

"Aysha . . . ?" he pleaded again. As he stood before her, the utter silence was stifling. Only the faint ticking of a clock served as a reminder that the world was still spinning through time. "I can't see you. Just . . . *please*, look up at me."

Finally, she lifted her head. Nick's eye caught just a glint of green through the bare slit of her burqa, the only evidence that the woman before him was she.

He leaned toward her, as if searching for the final proof. And when he finally locked on to her eyes, like pure jade set against the deep black fabric of her burqa, he felt the air rush from his lungs. He dropped to his knees before her. Her hooded form began to shudder. He heard the gasp of her sobs.

Nick wanted badly to pull her into his arms, tear the veil from her face, and press his lips to every inch of her, even her scars. But he knew that if he did that, she would send him away forever. The acid had burned just her skin, but her wounds had run through her, emptying her of all but the pain. She did not want to know how much he desired her still. She *could* not know that. Not now.

Slowly, with gentle caution, he lifted his hand to her cheek. He left it there, pressed against the fabric of her veil, until she stopped shaking. Then, fighting back her fear, she finally took his fingers into her own.

Nick could not fathom the feeling of degradation Aysha had suffered. Her beauty had been a part of her identity since she was a child, as much as her courage and compassion, and her feeling now that it had been marred forever had dismantled her whole concept of self-worth. It took days before she was able even to talk about her injury.

When she was finally willing to do so, Nick could not help but tell her his sincere feeling that her retreat behind the veil, after a lifetime of refusing to do so in the face of the edicts and threats from Yusuf, Abdul, and others, had handed her assailants their victory.

"That's exactly what they wanted—to force you into submission to their will."

"It was just Abdul's doing. He always hated me. Ever since we were children and I chose Kazim instead of him." Her tone was dismissive.

"You *know* there's more to it than that," Nick rejoined. "You were the backbone of the village. To destroy Gilkamosh, break its spirit, they needed to defeat you. Killing you would have made you a martyr. Your defiance would have rallied people even in your death. When you survived the fire, he decided to mar you, hoping that you would react just as you are doing now. . . . Can't you see, Aysha? By hiding yourself here, you do their bidding."

"What do you suggest, Nick? Let them see how grotesque I have become, so they all *share* in my disgrace?" Her voice was choked with emotion.

"You're looking at it wrong, Aysha. Show them your spirit again. After the massacre, they rallied around *you*. Not because of how you looked, but because of what you represented."

"I represented nothing but arrogance. I knew it was dangerous to keep the clinic running. Even before Advani and Kazim warned me," she admitted, wiping a tear of remorse from her eye. "Yet I continued with it. I even pushed Advani to bribe the security forces, just so I could prove how righteous I was. Now he's dead. And this"—she pointed to the hood covering her disfigured face—"is my punishment."

"Your fight, Aysha, was the whole village's fight—one and the same— you once said so yourself. *You* had the courage to wage it. The others followed. Advani did, too. He paid for that, as did you. But you didn't kill him. What you did, you did for everyone."

"No! What I did, I did to defy *him*. Kazim."

Humiliation had cut Aysha so deeply that even the efforts of the villagers, who had inspired her in the face of adversity since she was a girl, could not convince her to break out of her shell. Once the word spread that she had received a visitor, if only Nick, scores of villagers started to come, too, in an attempt to lift her spirits, to reclaim the Emerald of Gilkamosh who once had been theirs. But the outpouring of sympathy only made her worse. For days on end, she remained in self-induced isolation, depressed and barely eating. And despite Nick's efforts to bolster her courage, still she let no one see her face. Eventually, the villagers stopped dropping by the Fahad household altogether, thinking better of it.

Until, one day, without explanation, she decided she'd had enough. "I am taking this off," she announced to Nick succinctly, before lifting the hood of the burqa from her head.

The acid had burned her entire face, eating into her hairline and down the front to her neck. The skin under her cheeks was badly wrinkled, blistery and colorless, the rich dark pigment with which she once had been blessed burned away in blotches. But her eyes remained pristine, and by fixating on their beauty, Nick could attenuate the shock he felt viewing her extensive wounds for the first time.

Aysha revealed her scars first to Nick, then to her family. And then, on the following day, to the entire village.

Initially, the people stared brazenly at the sallow and withered scar tissue masking the mythical beauty that had once been the pride of the village. But with time, she came to realize they did so not out of pity or abhorrence, but rather, because her scars were to be borne by all of them. Her scars were their own.

Muzzafar Khan was killed within days of the fire in a cordon and sweep operation in the mountains above Passtu. Afterward, there was a lull in the fighting. Perhaps the security forces felt they had exacted sufficient retribution on the village, or that Aysha had made satisfactory amends by providing the information that led to what the Indians touted as a major victory against terror. In any event, a couple of weeks later, the security forces emptied their jails, releasing the men and boys they had held hostage for so long, including Khaliq and Nabir.

With the return of Aysha's brothers, the Fahad family was restored in size, even if, with Aysha's slow recovery, it took some time to rejuvenate in spirit. They built Aysha her own dwelling, a few plots from Naseem and the rest of the family. A modest home, built in the traditional style of mud brick and flat roof, its back door opened onto the fields of the Gilka-mosh Valley and the river below. In the morning, the sun shone on the arcade where, during warmer months, the Fahads would gather to drink their tea, and from which the snowy peaks could be viewed to the east. During September, when the air was fragrant with ripening apples and winnowed grain, great skeins of migratory birds would float like arrows across the cloudless sky as they made their way from the Tibetan plateau to the lakes nestled in the Vale of Kashmir.

Nick helped Naseem in the fields when he was not working in the new clinic, which they erected this time in the center of the village. There, they hoped, it would be safer, and both the security forces and the mujahideen would spare the clinic their wrath, even if it happened to treat a soldier or insurgent every now and again. The tragedy that befell the original clinic created a stir among the medical community in northern India. As a result of the publicity, they were inundated with contributions of supplies and even grants. This had permitted them to rebuild and expand, and finally purchase much-needed equipment. Nevertheless, in a land of scant resources, they held no illusion that the outpouring of benevolence would continue, and knew they would ultimately be left to fend for themselves.

Ghulam came to visit almost monthly from Kurgan. He would journey to Gilkamosh with his daughters for "medical attention," using the trip as an excuse to socialize away from his wives; suspiciously, his daughters rarely had ailments requiring any treatment. Sometimes he would hop around the ward on crutches with a mischievous grin, harassing Vilashni for old times' sake. Occasionally, he would stay the night, while he and Nick laughed, drank tea, and talked until early morning. Inevitably the conversation would wander to weightier issues, as was his custom; for if Ghulam had taught Nick one thing, it was to ponder life's mysteries each day anew. And the mystery of Fidali, Nick's unsolicited savior, never ceased to be fodder for Nick's turbid mind.

"I'm still puzzled by what Fidali did," Nick confessed to Ghulam one spring night when the birds, hoodwinked by the bright moonlight, sang among the apricot trees lining the homestead as if it were morning. "Just when I feel I've got a grasp, it still eludes me."

"The meaning of what Fidali did is like clouds as they drift across the mountain peaks. Some people see evil djinn in the changing shapes, others see the Merciful One. All of life—what we see and smell and taste, everything—is only illusion. It is different for each man who views it," he replied in a placating voice. "Good meat should be chewed only once, Mr. Nick. Enjoy it, then swallow it whole."

"But that's just it—I can't swallow it. I don't know *how*," Nick replied. "Remember, long ago, you got angry with me for saying that Fidali sacrificed his life in order to redeem himself for the bad things he had done?

Well, if that wasn't the reason for it, then why? Certainly, he made a *conscious* choice to do what he did—he had enough time to think what he was doing before pushing me off the mine."

Ghulam pulled on his scraggly beard, then shook his head, settling his thoughts into place. "Maybe he decided *without* thinking," Ghulam said finally.

"Making a decision, by its very nature, requires *some* thought, Ghulam," Nick rejoined. "If only to realize that one has alternatives."

"Ghulam does not believe what you say," he objected. "By surrendering all thoughts, man can decide with *qalb*—the heart. The only *pure* decision—the only true choice, unpolluted by the mind—is made with *qalb* alone."

Ghulam pulled his legs up to his chest, squatting compactly. It seemed to Nick that Ghulam, out of infinite modesty, was striving to condense his body to the smallest possible volume, so as not to impose his being on the world any more than necessary.

"So maybe the heart of Fidali told him to do what the mind can never command," Ghulam continued. "To surrender the self. It took much pain for Fidali to learn this way. But he did not let Allah's challenge go wasted in the end, Ghulam think."

The two men sat in silence, absorbed in their thoughts. The nocturnal air, the branches of the fruit trees, the lambent stars, everything was still. Yet Nick's mind still brooded.

"I don't accept that, Ghulam," Nick said, shaking his head. "If there was no thought—no analytical choice at all—then you're saying he had a mindless reaction. I *need* to believe that Fidali's choice was premeditated. That he exercised free choice. Otherwise . . . it cheapens what he did."

"No, Mr. Nick. It makes it more noble. You must *not* think of Fidali trading one life for another—his for yours," he said.

"Why not? That's exactly what he did."

"Because Fidali did not think that way."

Nick paused. "Well, *I* thought that way—when I held on to you over the sinkhole on the glacier that morning. I kept thinking that we both would die if I didn't let go. And I think I might have, to save myself," Nick confessed, his voice filled with shame. "If Fidali had thrown the rope a second later, you could be dead now."

Ghulam shrugged his shoulders. "A man must bear witness alone, inshallah."

"But it only makes it worse," Nick said, "to know that Fidali did what I would not."

Ghulam was unfazed by Nick's confession; even if he had suspected Nick's vacillation that day on the glacier, it was not in his nature to care about matters of fate. He was concerned more with Nick's own moiled expression. "Ghulam can see Mr. Nick very troubled. Let me see if Ghulam can explain what he thinks. Then Mr. Nick can decide on his own what Fidali did."

Ghulam gazed at the mountains, illuminated with yellow moonlight, as he conjured his thoughts. After some time, he spoke. "Fidali did not *exist* the way Mr. Nick thinks. Yes, he was flesh and blood and bone. But what you saw of him was only your own thoughts of who Fidali was. To Fidali *himself*—after he suffered the murder of his family, and then, in vengeance, he massacred all those innocent people, those families on the bus—Fidali was not 'Fidali' anymore. He lived, of course. But he had destroyed all thought of his self."

"I understand he acted selflessly. It doesn't mean he didn't make a choice."

Ghulam shook his head, "No, no, Mr. Nick still does not understand what Ghulam say. 'Die before you die,' said the Prophet, blessed be his name. You see, a man's understanding of who he is—it is nothing but thoughts, of our past, our future. It is all up here." He tapped his head. "If we put our hopes in these things in our head, they will destroy us.

"Fidali made the mistake of man—he fought and killed—for what? Country, race, freedom—all just *ideas* made up by man, false idols he worships in hope to give meaning to life that will *always* be mystery. To pursue these things, to devote yourself to them, is the path of the mind, and it *always* leads to suffering. In the end, Fidali learned the only true way to resist these sins of the mind—to destroy the source of them. *He died before he died*. In doing this, he found his true path—his *tariqah*."

"Still, even the practice of self-denial implies *thought* about yourself, doesn't it?" Nick said, unable to conceal his nagging doubt. "If for nothing else, simply to resist self-indulgence."

Ghulam stopped and turned, peering at Nick with his round, dark eyes. "'To ask good questions is half of learning,' said the Prophet. You see, Mr. Nick, you ask Ghulam bad question. Fidali no longer had any 'self' to deny. He was part of the *One*," he said, holding his palms up toward the sky.

"And when you say 'practice,' you mean that Fidali followed some code about how to act. This, my friend, disrespects what he did—more than saying he acted with no thought at all, which is why it is righteous. It is the difference between duty and love. *Duty* is a false path created by man. To follow it is the way of the Self.

"But to act out of love, *that* is Divine. And love, Mr. Nick—real *Love*, untouched by thought—is never a sacrifice. It is bliss."

Another evening, a few months later, Ghulam told Nick a story that he attributed to a Sufi teacher plucked from Kashmir's ancient past:

"A man was chased off a cliff by a tiger. He fell, and just managed to hold on to a branch. Two meters above him stood the tiger, snarling, its jaws dripping with saliva. Hundreds of meters below, a violent sea lashed at fierce rocks. Then to his horror, he noticed that the branch he was clutching was being gnawed at its roots by two rats. Seeing he was doomed, he cried out, 'Allah, please save me!'

"The man heard a voice reply, 'Of course I will save you. But first, *let go of the branch.*'"

It was the choice Nick could not make on the glacier that day, holding Ghulam over the icy sinkhole. For he had learned neither to accept nor to forget the self that had so disappointed him—that was fated to fail him and had masqueraded in the form of longing for Yvette, but to which he still clung like a broken branch. Perhaps he could only hope that he had learned from Fidali's lesson, his gift to Nick, to trust not in *himself,* but in the heart.

Nearly two years after the fateful fire, the unexpected happened. Nick was alone on the ward one late summer afternoon, giving a shot of antibiotics to a shepherd who had cut off some toes with an ax and let the wound fester before coming down from the mountains to treat it. The foot was gangrenous, and the man would have lost it had he not come in when he did. Nick had just finished dressing the wound and had stepped outside to scrub some instruments in the outdoor sink when a vaguely familiar voice echoed from across the dirt road.

"Well, aren't *you* an inspiration." The voice was facetious, cockneyed.

Nick peered up at the intruder. Clean-shaven, long-haired, he wore a ragged backpack and unwashed clothes. At first, Nick was not quite able to place the face, which looked so different, so much fresher despite the ragged clothing, since the last time he had seen it in the filthy jail cell in Peshawar.

"Simon?" Nick approached, stopping at a distance of several meters and stared incredulously. "You're alive."

"Typical American—master of the obvious."

There was a long pause as they studied each other, Nick feeling overcome with relief, but at the same time expecting Simon to be infuriated with him, even bent on doing him harm. Simon, for his part, watched Nick with sharp eyes, and was not at all inclined to ease Nick's unsettled mind.

"How did you find me?" Nick said.

"That rookie inspector, Shiraz, told me he suspected you fled through the mountains into Kashmir, and that you hadn't been caught—at least not by the Pakistanis. He gave you a pretty bleak chance of having made it across the Line of Control without falling into a crevasse or getting captured or shot by the Indians. But it was enough to make me wonder."

"Shiraz?" Nick remembered the Pakistani's thin, intellectual face, the hours of interrogation and the torture, as if it were all just yesterday.

"You know I was convicted of murdering Yvette?" Simon said, his voiced filled with hostility.

Nick looked at Simon with a blank expression. He shook his head no. "I read that you were charged, but I never learned how the trial turned out. They made me agree to testify against you as a condition to releasing me from jail. But as soon as I got out, I ran."

Simon scoffed. "You expect me to thank you for that? You had another choice. You could have told them the truth—that I wasn't anywhere near the Tribal Areas when Yvette was murdered."

"You're right," Nick said, after some hesitation. "I was thinking only of myself. Defending you meant I was taking the fall—if not for murder, then for the drugs, an equally bad fate."

"You son of a bitch," Simon fumed, stepping toward Nick. "They were going to execute me!"

Nick held his ground but stood passively, now certain that Simon had come for payback. Somehow, after all Nick had been through, he was resigned to whatever retribution Simon might inflict. After a moment, however, Simon's eyes softened.

"When I found out you were going to testify against me," Simon continued, "I hated you. I mean . . . I really wished you dead. Then, after you fled Peshawar and shot Akhtar—you looked like the guilty one. Guilty as all hell. . . . Shiraz got my execution stayed. Convinced the judges to let him take another look at the case before they strung me up. That guide, Prince, was long gone. But Shiraz was able to track down a guard at the crossing into the Tribal Areas—one of the guys Prince had paid off to let you and Evvie through the day she was murdered. Shiraz showed him your mug shot and got him to talk. He identified *you* as being the white guy in the car with Yvette.

"So there you have it. It took almost three years, but I was cleared. You see, in the end, it was *your* decision to run—along with Shiraz having enough integrity to give a shit—that saved my life."

Nick paused, relieved that Simon had been exculpated, but at the same time, tasting the guilt well up inside him. "I'm sorry, Simon. I really am. And I thank God that you're alive. I wish . . . there was something I could say, *anything* that could explain, or even begin to make up for what I did. But in all honesty, whatever I could say—it would only make you angrier."

There was a long silence before Simon spoke. "In prison, I had a lot of time to think. In the end, I can't say with certainty I wouldn't have made a run for it, too. If I had the chance. Doesn't mean you're forgiven, you selfish son of a bitch," he added.

Nick acknowledged Simon's words, then wiped his wet hands with a towel. "Sounds like I'm still the main suspect in Yvette's murder, then."

"I wouldn't go back to Pakistan any time soon," he replied. "If it's any consolation, though, Shiraz isn't convinced you killed her. He said he didn't think you were capable of . . . murdering her in that way. With that kind of brutality."

In his mind's eye, Nick remembered the horrible sight of Yvette's corpse—the near decapitation, the bruising, the unspeakable waste of life. He fixed his eyes on the distance, struggling to hold his composure. "How did you find me, here of all places?"

"I ran into a rather diminutive hunter in a village near the Siachen who told me he had an American friend who he visits every month. He was short, sort of Tibetan looking."

"Ghulam Muhammad."

"That's him. Funny little bloke. He was sort of protective of you. I said I was a friend, but he wasn't inclined to tell me your whereabouts. Then, when I told him my name, he seemed to reconsider. I found that odd. But I didn't press him on it. Anyway, he relented and told me to find you here."

"Maybe he recognized your name from the article," Nick said, explaining the time Ghulam had confronted Nick with the newspaper article about them during their trek through the Karakoram. "It figures he'd sell me out. Ghulam is a firm believer in the value of a man facing up to his past."

Nick led Simon to the green lawn behind the clinic overlooking the barley fields and the river below. There, they sat at a wooden tea table where the staff took their midday meals. Nick noticed that Simon had lost even more weight since the last time he saw him years ago. But even so, his face had color and there was a clarity about him. Nick could tell in an instant that he was no longer using. "Why did you go to the trouble?" said Nick, although the answer was becoming increasingly obvious to him—Simon's suspicion was still not erased. "I mean, it's not like we parted on good terms."

"Really? A chipped tooth and a bruised jaw are a lovely adieu." Simon's brief humor gave way to gloom. He took a long drag of his cigarette. Then he stared into Nick's eyes.

"I swear to you—I'm not going to tell anyone. Especially not the authorities. God knows, my own hands are far from clean. I just need to know what happened, Nick. I can't go on without knowing. You were *with* her—you know *something*."

Nick paused in reflection. He had in fact confessed—first to Fidali, later to Aysha, Ghulam, himself—but perhaps not to the one person who needed to hear it most. He breathed deeply, then finally, he spoke. "We got into a fight."

"A fight?" said Simon after a pause.

"She wanted to buy heroin. I wouldn't let her. We argued, things spiraled out of control. A mob of tribesman rushed her—attacked her with stones."

Simon's mouth fell open. "The bruises," he said, covering his face in his hands. "Oh, God . . . it's my fault. Since I left Rangoon, I'd been trying to get clean. Evvie stayed by my side that last night, pleading with me to fight it . . .

"In the morning, I was too weak to move," he continued, choking on his words. "I begged her to go do it. Just enough to hold me over until I got out of Pakistan. I promised her, after that, I'd go someplace where I could get help."

Nick closed his eyes, his face turning the color of ash. As the impact of Simon's words found their mark, he felt as though the devastating brunt of his own blind selfishness had stabbed him in the chest. "She was . . . trying to *help* you?" Nick muttered.

Both men sat for several minutes in silence, their heads buried in their arms, though there was no one to hide from but themselves.

"I sent her to her death, Nick," said Simon at last. "I sent her to her *death*."

"No, Simon—*I'm* to blame!"

Simon looked up. "What do you mean?"

"I *knew* she was in danger," Nick replied. "I left her there anyway. . . . You see, I didn't do the cutting. But I killed her just the same."

Horrified, Simon peered into Nick's eyes, and saw that it was true. He shook his head in his hands, violently, until he let it fall against his chest. "We *both* did."

For a long time, the former friends and rivals sat in the brutal silence of two men bonded by the same profound guilt, knowing that despite anything they could say or do, they would never again feel worthy or complete. Finally, Nick spoke.

"A Kashmiri friend said something to me. 'Whatever you have in your mind—forget it; whatever you have in your hand—give it; whatever is to be your fate—face it.' The things we do stick with us—*forever*."

After a pause, Simon nodded. "Forever."

Simon spent that night in Gilkamosh. The following morning he packed his bags for the long journey to Delhi.

Before his departure, they hiked to the top of the highest ridge overlooking the whole of the Valley of Gilkamosh, which from that height appeared like a giant brushstroke of brilliant green sweeping through the massive amphitheater of cathedral spires. Between the interstices of the peaks, one could see toward the west, where Yvette had died, across the vast saw-toothed mountains of ice and rock stretching all the way into Pakistan. On top of the ridge was a meadow, too small to be used as a pasture.

There, Nick and Simon dug a hole, and at the bottom of the hole they placed a snapshot that Simon had been carrying. The photo was of the three of them—Nick, Simon, and Yvette—when they had first met in Pushkar years ago, their arms locked in new friendship. In the hole, covering the photo, they planted a juniper sapling, with the hope that knotty roots of life would take hold in the shallow soil, and that the chance for a new beginning would spring from the inextricable bond of their fates.

"What's your plan now?" Nick asked later, as they wiped the dirt from their hands.

"It's been seven years since I've been back to England. For now, I just want to stay clean for a while. Grab some respect. I may head to France, try to track down Evvie's mother in Lyon. They didn't talk. But you never know. She might want to know what happened. I would. After that, who knows. Eventually, I'm sure I'll hit the road again. Can't stop thinking there's something around the next bend that will make sense of it all. I guess it will always be that way."

The two men pivoted their heads about, not sure how to express the thoughts they felt compelled to convey.

"You know, I was . . . envious of you, Simon," said Nick at last. "For a lot of reasons. But mostly because of Yvette. I never understood why you left her. I mean, I really couldn't. And then, when you came back . . . I figured, well, maybe you really *did* love her. . . . Now I know the answer. And it only makes it harder."

"Aye," Simon replied.

"I thought I loved her, too," Nick continued. "I know now that I did not. In some ways, that's the hardest part. All the madness I mistook as love—it was only because she had chosen you."

After a moment of silence, Simon shook his head. "No, Nick. I'll tell you the hardest part. You had it wrong. She told me the night before she died. She was going to stay with you. It was *you* she loved."

The war raged on, and the massacre of Gilkamosh was eclipsed by new acts of violence committed by security forces and rebels alike. The mujahideen continued to creep across the Line of Control, while Pakistan persisted in its denial of the proxy war that it had fought against India since its birth. There were lulls in the fighting, particularly whenever all-out war was threatened by one side or the other. In the end, however, so long as the influential nations of the world failed to find the will to intervene with sufficient persuasion, the savagery for the people of Kashmir would endure.

Yet within this turbulent microcosm of a larger conflict sweeping the globe, Aysha and Nick found in each other the strength to continue their struggle to save the lives that the men of ideas tried to extinguish. Theirs was a union reaffirmed after Nick had said the last words that passed Fidali's lips the moment he had granted Nick a second life—*la ilaha illa Allah.*

Spoken before two witnesses, Ghulam Muhammad and Aysha. Two people who had come to know a man completely—the evil he had done and the good of which he was capable—and instead of judging, they trusted, even before he trusted himself. Words that he uttered, as he stared beyond the scars of his beloved, through the windows of her emerald eyes.

ACKNOWLEDGMENTS

I wish to thank my editor, Colin Harrison, for his extraordinary attention to the manuscript and inspiring advice; my agent, Sloan Harris, for his constant commitment to the work and thoughtful consideration of its many drafts; and Alan Rautbort, for his enthusiasm and much appreciated support.

I also wish to thank my wife, Hope, for her input and unwavering patience throughout the writing of this novel, as well as her companionship and courage during our fantastic but often difficult travels to the remote regions that inspired these pages. I am also very grateful for the encouragement of my lifelong friend, fellow vagabond, and kindred spirit, Ming-Tai Kuo; my sister and brother-in-law Maria and André Jacquemetton; and the rest of the Mastras clan, including my brother, parents, and, of course, my two beloved daughters. Thanks also to the Toffel family for their many hours of babysitting while I toiled over the manuscript.

Lastly, I want to express my gratitude to those friends and acquaintances, too numerous to name, in Pakistan, India, and Kashmir, many of whom invited me into their homes and introduced me to the beauty of their culture during my trips to the region. I will always remember you and the astounding places you have shown me. The initial draft of this novel was written on the Greek islands of Santorini and Folegandros, and the Indonesian islands of Lombok and Bali. The staff at the various guesthouses and beach bungalows where I worked showed me great hospitality, without which the task of completing this novel would have been more difficult.

The town of Gilkamosh is fictional, albeit inspired by several towns and valleys on both sides of the Line of Control.

For background on the Kashmir conflict, I consulted a number of works, including: *Pakistan: Eye of the Storm* by Owen Bennet Jones (Yale University Press, 2002); *War on Top of the World: The Struggle for Afghan-*

istan, Kashmir, and Tibet by Eric S. Margolis (Routledge, 2002); *Lost Rebellion: Kashmir in the Nineties* by Manoj Joshi (Penguin, 1999); *Islamic Groups and Pakistan's Foreign Policy—Lashkar-e-Toiba and Jaish Mohammad* by Samina Yasmeen, printed in *Islam and the West: Reflections from Australia* (USNW Press, 2005); and *Terrorists' Modus Operandi in Jammu and Kashmir* by N. S. Jamwal, printed in *Strategic Analysis,* Vol. 27, No. 3, July–September 2003 (Routledge, in association with Institute for Defense Studies Analysis, 2003). I also consulted the following sources with regard to cultural history, geography, flora, and fauna of the region: *Kashmir as It Was* by Francis Younghusband (1908, reprinted by Rupa & Co., 2000); *Among the Mountains: Travels through Asia* by Wilfred Thesiger (Flamingo, 2000); *The Himalayas* by Alain Chenevière (Konecky & Konecky, 1998); *Karakoram Highway: The High Road to China* by John King (Lonely Planet Publications, 1998); *Islamic Sufism: The Science of Flight in God* by Wahid Baksh Rabbanni (A.S. Noordeen, 1990); and *What Is Sufism?* by Martin Lings (Premier Publishing, 2000). The Sufi parable cited in the Epilogue appears in the published anthology entitled *Perfume of the Desert: Inspirations from Sufi Wisdom* by Andrew Harvey and Eryk Hanut (Theosophical Publishing House, 1999), as well as numerous online collections. Neither the published nor online version identifies an author.

ABOUT THE AUTHOR

George Mastras has worked as a criminal investigator for the public defender service, a counselor at a juvenile correctional facility, and a litigator with both New York and Los Angeles firms. After ten years of practicing law, he quit his job, sold his belongings, and spent several years backpacking around the globe and trekking in the Himalayas, Karakorams, and Hindu Kush. Since returning to the United States, he has written for several television series, including most recently the Emmy Award–winning drama *Breaking Bad* on AMC. From Boston, he is a graduate of Yale, UCLA Law School, and Outward Bound. He was awarded the Walt Disney-ABC Creative Writing Fellowship in Drama in 2005. *Fidali's Way* is his first novel.